# THE
# MOMENT
# BETWEEN

## A NOVEL

# THE
# MOMENT
# BETWEEN

## A NOVEL

BY

## GARETH FRANK

Three Women Press
www.threewomenpress.com

For information or discounts for bulk purchases, please contact: Three Women Press, P.O. Box 208, Allamuchy, NJ, 07820 or publicity@threewomenpress.com.

Interior Design: Booknook.biz

Editors: John Payne, John Rickards, Jack Buckley

Publisher's Cataloging-in-publication data
Name: Frank, Gareth, author
Title: The Moment Between / by Gareth Frank
Description: Allamuchy, NJ : Three Women Press, 2019
Identifiers:  ISBN: 978-1-7322942-0-2 (print) | 978-1-7322942-1-9 (ebook)
Library of Congress Control Number: 2018910102

Printed in USA

# Dedication

For family and friends who enriched my life in immeasurable ways and for whom *The Moment Between* is no longer a theoretical or literary conjecture. I miss them dearly.

Mom

Sophie Pechenik Frank

Daniel Ivkovich

Ella Gotz

Michael Lescault

Paul Booth

Debbie Miller Kling

Candy Johnson Erickson

John Gardner

Tom Breen

# BEFORE

The walls around him were white and scuffed, the linoleum floor cracked and scarred. James sat with his thirteen-year-old son on chairs that looked like they had survived decades of abuse. Even the air smelled as if it was left over from a previous generation. It was the kind of health clinic James had been to countless times before, in countless neighborhoods. The boy had improved, but would never be cured.

James felt the familiar anchor of guilt pulling him down into deep water. His remorse had driven him to quit drinking, but it hadn't completely changed who he was. He still moved from job to job, each time sure that this one would deliver him, pay for the doctors and medicine, give his wife all the fine things that she demanded. It was a kind delusion, but reality was cruel.

A harsh voice interrupted James' thoughts. "Aaron Pierce," the receptionist called, her grimacing face fixed downward. James looked at the woman, imagined her life, a decent job, healthy kids, good marriage. He wondered what made people like her sound so unhappy. With her life, with Aaron healthy, he could easily be content. He held Aaron's hand and stood, feeling a touch of resistance, knowing that the boy was getting a little old for such a public display of affection. James did not let go. It was as if his grip could hold back Aaron's adolescence.

It was their first visit to this clinic. James knew the routine and talked for ten minutes straight, providing a detailed history of Aaron's condition, along with a list of previous medications, failing to mention all those times that Aaron had run out of his pills. The doctor listened, interrupting now and then to ask questions. When James finished, the doctor put pen to paper and wrote a prescription, then slid it across the table.

James read the scribble, saw the familiar medication, and paused. He looked silently at the doctor for a few seconds. Made sure that his face was appropriately deferential and a touch embarrassed. Finally, he spoke.

"Listen, Doc, I scraped together the twenty-dollar clinic charge, but I can't afford the meds right now. I'm unemployed."

As James had hoped, the doctor rose from his seat, went to the cabinet and fished around for samples.

"Here's a week's supply," the doctor said as he handed James a thin cardboard box.

"Please, Doc, if you could spare two weeks, that'd really help."

On the walk home from the clinic Aaron bounced along, not a care in his step. James would have preferred for him to slow down, to walk as he used to, right at James' side, or within his embrace, or even to ride atop his shoulders. As these longings tugged at him, he saw Aaron slow to a stop and stare up into the sky, a vacant look blossoming across his pubescent face. James' heart froze. He had seen auras take hold of his son numerous times before, watched as the demons captured his will and drew his attention skyward. Frozen in place, Aaron would stare as if captivated by something no one else could see or perhaps even imagine. Seconds later the epilepsy would take control of his body and he would momentarily go limp like a rag doll, before the thrashing started. Fear gripped James. He ran to his son, grabbed hold of him, and pulled him into a protective embrace. But Aaron did not collapse. His arms jerked in resistance.

"Jesus, Dad. What are you doing? I'm fine."

Aaron pulled back, stepping away from his father, his head swiveling, his eyes scanning left and right, embarrassment making him cower for an instant before it was replaced with anger.

"You were going to have a seizure. I saw the aura taking over."

"I was just looking at that plane." Aaron pointed upward. "It's flying so low."

A few blocks later, Aaron was once again the happy-go-lucky thirteen-year-old. He sprinted forward, jumped an upended trashcan, grabbed a metal railing and slid down the few steps to their basement apartment.

"Want to play Madden?" he asked as he shoved his key into the door.

James smiled. "Okey dokey, dominokey."

He followed his boy into the small living room and threw the bag with the meds onto the chipped and dented Formica-topped kitchen table. They had abandoned their old furniture when they ran out on the overdue rent in Miami, and bought the table for a few bucks at the Salvation Army when they got to Washington, DC.

James had been twenty-two when he met Sarah. At seventeen she had been beautiful, irresistible and vulnerable. She talked little of her father and mother, other than to say she hated them and wanted something better. With his promise to give her that, they took off. The next five years were carefree and exciting. They moved from town to town, city to city, spitting out jobs and friends like they were stale wads of chewing gum. Then came Aaron. Only slowly did responsibility lift itself above self-gratification. When Aaron was five, the seizures began.

James toggled the video game controller left and right, released the pass, and watched it sail across the television screen. His man caught it, and James broke loose with a triumphant cheer. He was on the six-yard line, determined to score. He watched his players line up, then his quarterback dropped back. The front door opened, and his wife walked in.

"I don't know which one of you is the child. Did you even look for a job today?" Sarah asked.

James' pass was intercepted. Aaron screamed with excitement, jumped to his feet and raised his fist in the air. "Gotcha, Dad," he howled at the same time James answered his wife.

"Had to take Aaron to the doctor. Remember? We got enough samples for two weeks."

Sarah's eyes bore down on him. He waited for her verbal assault, but she just shook her head and walked past them both, saying nothing. James hardly noticed her beauty anymore. She had worn no makeup at seventeen. Now her eyeliner, blush and mascara were expertly applied. James liked Sarah's younger self better, the girl who had looked up to her older, more worldly boyfriend. A blur of gold and black came into focus just before her perfectly-rounded backside disappeared into the bedroom. He didn't recognize the dress. Had she bought another one? The thought angered him, even though he knew that her ass and her fine clothes were probably responsible for securing the secretarial job she had gotten immediately after they had arrived in Washington.

Minutes later, Sarah reemerged. She wore designer blue jeans that made her legs appear as if she had been dipped into a vat of denim-colored chocolate. As she moved, silver thread sparkled in the red sweater that clung to her breasts. James knew from experience that she had refreshed her makeup.

"I'm going out," she said.

He didn't even ask where.

~

In the early morning, James awoke with a start. He felt a sting in his ass like some sort of insect had bitten him. He reached back with his hand, and his body rolled over reflexively. Sarah was kneeling next to him on the bed.

"What was that?"

"Go back to sleep," she told him.

James looked at her. He rubbed his ass, couldn't tell if anything had really stung him. Had he been dreaming? He noticed Sarah's arm bent behind her back. "What are you hiding?"

"Nothing. Go back to sleep." He heard anger in her voice, the anger he had grown accustomed to, but there was something else, something that wasn't right. Sarah was moving now, backing out of bed. He grabbed her arm.

"Let go of me, you stupid bastard."

She tried to twist away, and her hand slipped from behind her back. In it, she cradled a syringe, the hypodermic needle pointing at him.

"What the fuck is that?" he said.

James reached for her hand with his other arm, and felt the force of her slap across his face. It was surprisingly fierce. His hand released. She jumped backward.

"You're pitiful," she said. Her voice held a cold rage.

James looked at her. The dull light of a breaking dawn barely illuminated his bedroom, a soft, momentarily comforting glow. He reached back and rubbed his ass. There was a tiny point of soreness. Without meaning to move, he felt his body settle back into bed. His eyes found hers once more. He saw emotion, but could not read it. He wondered, when had been the last time they'd made love, or the last time they'd had a conversation that wasn't an argument? His eyelids felt heavy.

"What?" His word was barely a whisper. *What did you give me?*

He struggled to hold his eyes open. It was no use. Sarah's face disappeared behind thin lids of skin, like a slow sunset on a distant horizon. *What in the hell is happening?*

The room was silent. He wanted to speak, to get out of bed. Nothing moved. He felt Sarah's hand on his shoulder shoving him roughly. She said nothing. He felt her slap his face, an oddly dull force, accompanied by a crisp crack in his ear.

The panic came. He screamed without voice.

"Die," he heard her say, her voice soft, her emotion heavy.

He felt, but did not see her standing above him. He could hear his own breath, shallow and labored. He could sense hers strong and excited.

*No*, he wanted to scream. *I don't want to die.* He heard Sarah's feet on the carpet. *Don't leave me.*

She was murdering him, yet he could not bear the thought of being alone. If she stayed, there was still a chance that she could change her mind, call an ambulance. He knew that she no longer loved him; that had been clear for some time. In truth, they had both lost what they once had, but he could not believe she would let him die. He heard the door close. He prayed that Aaron had heard the commotion, but Aaron was not home. He had met a new friend and stayed overnight.

James remembered Aaron as a baby. He pictured his small, happy face babbling nonsense, felt his own overwhelming love reflected back in Aaron's beautiful blue eyes, the color of James' own mother's eyes. The thought calmed him just a little. It allowed him to think. He was still alive. He tried to assess the situation. He had no idea what Sarah had injected into him. His first guess was heroin, or something like it, but he was not high. His mind had never felt so clear. He concentrated, tried to move his hands, his feet, his arms, his legs. Nothing. He tried to open his eyes. He concentrated on his mouth, felt it slack and open. He could even feel drool rolling down his cheek. It made no sense.

And then, he realized something else, something so much more frightening than he had imagined just two or three seconds earlier. *I can't breathe.*

He felt hot, like he was roasting under the Miami sun. He pleaded without words for his wife Sarah, for Aaron. *Help!* The word screamed with unrealized volume. He told his chest to expand, to draw air in through his nose. Nothing.

His fear was overwhelming. Time ticked on. He shouted at himself to wake up, but he was awake. He shouted at God to save him, but God did not act. Just when he thought the panic could get no worse, he felt an instance of muted pain in his chest. Somehow, he knew it was a heart attack. The dull pressure spread into his shoulder, down his arm. He was frightened beyond the terror of his worst nightmare.

It was unbearable, and then it was gone. In that moment, he felt lighter than air. Without trying, he rose up from bed, feeling neither an ounce of effort nor a milligram of physical sensation. He was sitting, and then he was nearly upright, floating in the air. It felt wonderful.

*Am I dead?* he wondered.

James floated up toward the ceiling. *Yes,* he knew beyond doubt that he was dead — what a wonderful feeling. He felt endless energy within him, through him and around him. A cool bluish light filled the room, and a yellowish glow appeared in the air in his place. A feeling of complete peace like he had never known enveloped him. Nothing from his life seemed important anymore. No troubles mattered. James Aaron Pierce saw his body on the bed below him and knew that it was no longer who he was. He floated through the wall of his apartment building. The colors of the outside world were as brilliant as the most fantastic sunrise ever painted. Everything, sky, trees, leaves, even the road shimmered. Shades of vibrant blue — indigo, oxford, turquoise and cobalt. Red — crimson, rose, burgundy and fuschia. Green — emerald, teal, malachite and chartreuse. Each color was incredibly vivid. It reminded him of dropping acid in his youth, but it had a clarity and reality that LSD could never match.

In the distance, a magnificent light grew out of a single point smaller than the tip of a pin. He was surrounded by everything and nothing, a great emptiness that was at the same time filled with vibrant emotion. He understood that he was and had always been part of this great fabric of effervescent thought. It was everything, and he was everything. He heard the voices of his grandparents, of his brother who had died as a teenager in a car wreck. He heard other unfamiliar voices, a multitude so vast as to be uncountable and previously unimaginable. He marveled at the sound, not chatter, every voice clear, every thought understandable. He and everything that ever existed were one. Death was not what he had expected.

# Chapter 1

Dr. Hackett Metzger handed the compact disk to Yu Lai Wang, his chief resident. He listened as the box chugged and churned, digesting the data in bits and bytes. Yu Lai Wang's delicate fingers moved over the keyboard, clicking and clacking. She was thirty and petite with oversized black-rimmed glasses which magnified her eyes into big glassy orbs. As she worked, her black hair hung like silk over her clean white jacket.

Hackett stared silently as she skimmed through cross sections of the brain, waiting for her to arrive at the one that mattered, the area they had discussed. "Here it is," she announced and magnified what looked like a tangle of worms swimming around a pregnant belly. "That's a big one, isn't it?"

Yu Lai's hand came to rest on top of Hackett's, and he felt a subtle, brief squeeze of his flesh. It made his heart jump, like someone had placed paddles on his chest and sent electricity coursing through his body.

Her hand no longer touching his, she stood, offering him the seat, urging him to take a closer look. He barely focused on the screen, having already seen enough to know she was right. Instead, his thoughts drifted from Yu Lai to his dead wife, Jean, whose memory melted over him like hot, humid air keeping him awake on a summer's night. He remembered how they lay next to each other in bed, Jean's back toward him, her body enveloped in his arms, his hand always on the soft flesh of her breast. It was the same position each night, for him a comfort and a reassurance that all the troubles of the day could not reach him. No matter what happened at the hospital or in his office, no matter what tragedy he dealt with at work, he could always find refuge in Jean. Now she was gone.

He broke free of his memories, forced himself to focus on the MRI, and after a few seconds he gave Yu Lai the verbal confirmation she awaited.

"Too big. We have to take it immediately."

Hackett called Surgery and then back up to Neurology, telling both to get ready. When he hung up, he felt Yu Lai's hand alight on his shoulder, a butterfly — there and gone before he could react. He had dreamt about asking her out to dinner, but each time he tried his nerve failed.

"Let's go get a cup of coffee," he said. "We have time — Starbucks, not the normal hospital crap."

In the elevator, his wife's memory still surrounded him, touching him with guilt. He breathed in. Her smell filled him, not the manufactured aroma of her favorite perfume, cold and hanging in the air like ether, the scent of her lying next to him at night, her essence musty and feral. Alongside his wife, he felt Yu Lai's irresistible presence. He told himself not to stare. Instead he looked ahead into his own reflection in the elevator door, so aware of his nervousness that he glanced away from his own eyes.

Yu Lai's voice was light, her speech effortless. She smiled and laughed, talked about nothing, and made it sound easy. Hackett added a word here and there, smiled back, forced a responsive laugh. When the elevator door opened, they walked out, crossed the lobby and exited into sunlight and car exhaust. The coffee shop was just around the corner. They waited in line, finally got their drinks. She added sugar and stirred. He sipped it black, careful not to burn his mouth. Silence hung in the air.

Hackett's eyes locked onto Yu Lai as she sucked in a stream of air along with a tiny sip of coffee. Even in that she was beautiful. Hackett wanted to talk. As usual, his question was caged behind his teeth. They left and walked back to the hospital to prep for surgery.

~

Flayed scalp was bent back around the surgical opening at the base of the young mother's skull, held in place by scalp clips. Other small strips of metal held the tunnel-like pathway open as Hackett probed through a jumble of white, pink and red sinuous matter, dissecting strands with tiny scissors, cutting here and there with the even tinier scalpel to clear the way. With light focused on the surgical opening, and the room dimmed around him, Hackett worked slowly as Yu Lai suctioned fluids.

"Where are we?" he asked, falling into the comfortable role of teacher, unable to resist looking at Yu Lai's eyes, even though the rest of her face was covered with a mask.

"The Lilliequist membrane," she answered.

Hackett cut through into the posterior fossa. He lifted his instruments from the patient's brain and paused. The light noise of suction continued. "Do you see the basilar artery?" he asked.

"Where?" she responded, but then matter moved and blood pulsed. "I can't really see it, but it's under here." She pointed with the tip of the suction tube slightly to the right. Hackett slid a clamp down into the tunnel, pulled on a stringy membrane, cut it with his scalpel, then scraped at other gelatinous matter. The pale wall of the artery came into view. Below it lay the larger purplish mass of the aneurysm. His instruments hovered in place. He did not proceed. Instead, Hackett's head turned again. He watched Yu Lai as she stared into the hole in their patient's skull. He smiled underneath his mask, felt warm desire, then his brain registered a silent warning. Hackett's eyes refocused on the artery. His scalpel lay pressed against it. A slip of his hand, or even a deep breath, could have spelled disaster. Carefully, he lifted his hands up and away from the patient.

"Is something wrong?" Yu Lai asked.

"No," Hackett answered. That was true, but Hackett's stomach turned nonetheless. He had been distracted by her and almost made a rookie mistake. With such delicate surgery, his carelessness could have been fatal. *Never take your eyes off of the surgical site, until your hands and instruments are free*, a long ago voice from his residency admonished him. Hackett shivered as he remembered the story of a doctor who sneezed during brain surgery and erased large chunks of the patient's memories. He took a moment to gather himself before proceeding. As Yu Lai watched, he moved the artery aside, continuing to clip and cut until the aneurysm was fully exposed. He concentrated, tried to calm himself, to stop his fluttering heart. He glanced at Yu Lai, then glanced back. He examined the aneurysm, saw where the artery had weakened and blood had created a balloon in the wall. He saw blood seeping slowly through the now-thin covering of the balloon. Yu Lai suctioned it away. He moved his clamp forward. Rested it on the outside of the base of the aneurysm and squeezed the bulb closed. Once again, Hackett lifted his hands up and away from the patient.

"How does it look?"

Yu Lai cleared the area of blood and fluids. Hackett watched her fingers as she prodded and examined. His momentary panic had subsided.

"Good," she said, but it wasn't quite right. Both of them should have seen that the clip had not fully sealed the aneurysm from the artery. For a split second, everything was fine, then the aneurysm ruptured. At first blood simply pooled in the cavity. A second later a stream of crimson arced into the air. "Suction," he announced with alarm, but Yu Lai needed no prompting. Hackett worked quickly, calling for a second clamp and sliding it in close behind the first, completely closing it this time and sighing in relief when the miniature geyser disappeared.

~

Two days passed without the warm touch of sunlight on skin to lift Hackett's spirits. The soft rubber soles of his shoes squeaked as they separated from the shiny clean hospital floor, creating an annoying off-tune symphony. Another day had dawned inside the hospital. He stopped for an instant, his hand slapping the circular metal disk on the wall. He felt its familiar recoil and was moving again even before the heavy metal doors began to open. As he entered the neurology ward, his eyes involuntarily looked down the hall to his left. He imagined mechanical beeps and clicks punctuated by a rhythmic whooshing of air, the young mother's chest expanding with the help of a ventilator.

*I should have saved her*, he chastised himself. Hackett breathed deeply, in time with the rhythm of his feet, seeking comfort in the repetition.

Four years earlier, after his wife's death, a counselor had recommended meditation. Desperate to be rid of the constant chatter and self-accusations in his brain, he had worked at it day after day. On a few occasions he would feel a small measure of peace, but it never really did the trick. He didn't understand why he had to work so hard for peace of mind. He took another breath, then continued down the hallway, thoughts of Jean and the sound of the ventilator squeaking in harmony with his shoes.

"Is Doctor Wang here?" he asked when he reached the nurses' station.

"Room 3831," Ella Mae Pulaski, a compact and forceful-looking charge nurse said. As she talked, an unfamiliar new nurse walked past the station. Ella Mae's attention was immediately redirected. "Do you hear something, Nurse Gortag?" Her voice was hard and challenging.

Fright registered on the young nurse's face. She looked as if she expected a physical assault to follow the question. When she shrugged and did not respond, Ella Mae spoke once again. "That IV pump is still beeping in 3812. When are you going to change the IV bag?"

*Oh, stop bullying her. You get more flies with honey.* An echo of his wife's voice played in Hackett's mind, chiding Ella Mae just like Jean had five years earlier when they had gone on vacation together.

When Ella Mae turned her face, she was inches from Hackett. "And what are you grinning at, Doctor?" she asked sternly.

"I was just remembering how Jean was always telling you to calm down and let your inner teddy bear out."

Ella Mae's face softened at the sound of her best friend's name. She turned her head back in Nurse Gortag's direction and yelled, "Please," before once again addressing Hackett. "Happy now?"

"Better. What room was that?"

"3831. Doctor Wang beat you, by about five minutes," Ella Mae said. "Are you following her around again?"

Hackett cringed. "Absolutely not."

"Don't worry, Hack, I'm just teasing."

Hackett arrived at the room just as Yu Lai exited. He saw her eyes turn to him and widen with discomfort.

"Time for Mrs. Carrollton?" she asked.

Hackett nodded. "Let's get it over with."

Hackett remembered his patient as she had been before surgery, brimming with life. He told himself it was not his fault. He could not have saved her. Doris Carrollton, a thirty-five-year-old mother, had arrived at the hospital presenting severe headaches, dizziness and vomiting. Hackett had also seen a slight slackening of the skin on the left side of her face, and noticed that her articulation was affected. The MRI confirmed she had a very large basal artery aneurysm. Hackett and Yu Lai had found it in time. Surgery had been a success. A day later it all went to hell. The patient again complained of a headache. She dropped in and out of consciousness. He had arrived at her room to find nurses and doctors swarming, trying to stabilize her so she could be rushed into surgery once again.

It turned out that she'd had an exceedingly rare reaction to the first surgery, or maybe it wasn't even the surgery at all. Maybe it was just nature's inevitable cruelty, taking life as it always did. As soon as they reopened her skull, there was an audible rush of air. The technical name for her condition was prepontine tension pneumocephalus, a buildup of air pressure in the anterior part of the brain, but at that point, those big words no longer needed a definition. They were just a bunch of letters that added up to never regaining consciousness.

Mrs. Carrollton was placed on life support. Hackett's initial success had turned into failure. He talked to her husband, who confirmed Doris' wish to be an organ donor. All that remained for this visit was to officially pronounce death and turn over the body to Doctor Elliot, the transplant prep surgeon. Hackett thought about Yu Lai's moniker for him. The Reaper was an image of death that had seemed like a silly cartoon before Jean died, but now the dark visage felt ominous and real. He no longer imagined the silhouette with an oversized sickle in his hand. Instead, the reaper was a black, vaporous evil that hung over the sick and dying, waiting to suck the last life out of their bodies.

Hackett and Yu Lai approached the doorway and did an awkward shuffle that was ingrained in their habits. A couple of feet before the door Yu Lai hesitated to let the senior doctor enter first. Seeing her hesitation, Hackett's feet involuntarily stopped moving and his arm swept chivalrously in front of him. After issuing an awkward smile, Yu Lai moved forward into the room then stepped aside so that Hackett reached the bed first. The respiratory therapist and nurse were already at the bedside. "Ready?" Hackett said.

"I guess so," Yu Lai replied.

Hackett verbally walked through the checklist of prerequisites before asking the nurse to dim the room lights and flashed his pen light into one eye, then the other. After that, he dragged a small piece of wet gauze across the cornea. After each test, Yu Lai confirmed that she, too, saw no response. Hackett took a syringe and squirted ice water into the left ear canal. Yu Lai nodded. He repeated the test in the right ear. Yu Lai nodded again. Through each step of the test, Hackett's actions were practiced and routine, but as the final respiratory test approached, Hackett's apprehension grew. He knew that respiratory tests were extreme. If a patient on a respirator was not yet dead, the test, in and of itself, could kill her.

Hackett dismissed his emotions and reached over to the patient, placing his hand on the ventilator tube and moving it back and forth within her throat. No living person, conscious or unconscious could avoid responding to such a noxious stimulus. He watched as Yu Lai oxygenated the patient in preparation for disconnecting the hose. By filling the patient with oxygen, Yu Lai was giving them a larger window to restart the ventilator if they noticed any sign of life.

When she was done, he pulled the connecting tube free and she attached the breathing bag. They waited. At that moment the nurse tripped and rammed the bed. The patient's head recoiled from the impact and still active nerves in her spinal column reacted. Doris Carrollton's arms lifted up off the bed, rising from her sides and drawing slightly back toward her head. Hackett remembered the first time he had seen the Lazarus reflex in a dead man. *He's alive,* Hackett had thought even though textbooks had prepared him for the sight. Hackett now watched Doris Carrollton's arms fall. He knew the entire movement was an involuntary reflex and indicated nothing. He watched for signs of breath. There were none.

As soon as Hackett signed the death certificate, Doctor Elliot walked in. Hackett thought about life vacating his patient's body, comparing it to a train leaving the station, Doris Carrollton running behind like a dog chasing the fast-moving wheels of the locomotive. He felt the weight of sagging skin pulling his jowls into a frown. When he looked at Yu Lai, he saw the same shadow of grief haunting her face.

"Are you alright?" he asked.

"Yeah, sure," she said and returned to silence.

They left Doctor Elliot to his work. As they walked down the hall, Hackett tried to clear his head.

"Doesn't he bother you?" Yu Lai said.

"Doesn't who bother me?"

"Doctor Elliot, how he hovers outside waiting for them to die. How he looks all too happy to pounce on their remains?"

"Mrs. Carrollton was already dead. Doctor Elliot was just waiting for us to make it official."

"I know that's what we are taught, and I know that it makes all the sense in the world, but I'm not just a doctor, I'm a person. I can't dismiss my emotions. Can you?"

"No, I just try to hide them when they get in the way."

Hackett had long since dealt with the same dilemma. Doctors naturally formed attachments to their patients. It was hard to watch them die, and when they did, it was difficult to separate the living patient from the dead donor. Transplant teams saw the world in reverse, they had another living patient to save, the donor was always dead, a receptacle holding the gift of life. They had sympathy for the other family, but their empathy for the dead was overwhelmed by hope for the living. Hackett had always understood their perspective, but like Yu Lai, it had taken him awhile to be comfortable with it.

Yu Lai's eyes radiated sadness, and there was a slight tremble in her lips. Hackett could see her trying to flush out her emotions before speaking.

"Nobody really knows what death is, when it starts or when it is complete," she said. You and I both know the body dies gradually. Under the right circumstances, someone whose brain stops functioning and whose heart stops beating can be brought back to life an hour later, even more. The cells of the brain don't just die the second blood flow is cut off."

"What are you saying, Doctor? Are you advocating that we outlaw transplants?"

"No. You know I'm not. I guess I was just spooked by the way her arms lifted up. It was clear that Mrs. Carrollton wasn't coming back, but I don't know if she was truly and totally gone."

Hackett wanted to yell, wanted to shut her up. Death was death. When the brain died, the conscious mind went with it. Hackett had learned the hard way that it was better to face that fact.

"The spark of consciousness?" Hackett bellowed. "It sounds like that study of near-death experiences you were pestering me to allow in the hospital. Are you raising a metaphysical question instead of a medical one?"

"Maybe I am. No one knows where the physical stops and the metaphysical begins."

"Or if there even is a metaphysical answer. I am more concerned about what we do know, and what has been proven." Hackett's face reddened. "Our patient had no brain activity whatsoever. She could not breathe on her own. She could not see, hear or feel. There was no consciousness left in her that we could measure. Sure, there was still some life left in her body. Her hair cells were still growing. Perhaps some of her brain cells were capable of firing, if there had been blood flow to allow stimulation, but that's not life as we know it. That is the process of death. Our patient was already dead. All we did was make it legal. She and her family had the good sense to give her organs to people in need. We can at least celebrate that."

Yu Lai was quiet. Hackett looked away. Conversation evaporated. Memories washed over him once again. He saw his wife Jean in death, remembered his initial panic, felt that panic change into a warm shiver of hope, and then his sense of hope morph into something entirely different, a feeling that Jean was talking to him, consoling him, even if he could not hear her or recognize her words. It had been a bitter illusion, leaving him unmoored from reality.

They stepped into the elevator still drowning in silence, each quickly doing an about-face to reorient themselves to the elevator doors. Hackett caught Yu Lai's silvery reflection looking at him, deep concern etched on her face. He smiled, as if to offer her reassurance. She smiled back, and he felt her warmth.

When they stepped out Yu Lai finally spoke. "I'm sorry. I was out of line. We need to concentrate on the people that will benefit from her organs."

Hackett again felt her warmth, and apologized for his own anger, though not the substance of his words. They talked about Mrs. Carrollton's second surgery instead, agreeing that her condition had been unforeseeable and her life unsavable. A purging relief washed over him. He looked at Yu Lai's bright eyes. Hope replaced anxiety. Words formed in his mouth.

"Would you consider going to dinner with me?" His voice cracked midway through the sentence. He looked at Yu Lai, sanguine with anticipation. But then he saw an awkward expression form on her face.

"Do you mean dinner like a date?" It looked painful for her to talk.

"Never mind," he said. "I shouldn't have asked."

"I'm sorry, Doctor Metzger. You are a wonderful man, and an incredible doctor. I really admire you, and I am flattered, but I don't think it would be appropriate for us to date. You're my supervisor."

What was left of the color in Hackett's pale skin drained

away. "I'm so sorry. Please forget that I ever mentioned it." They both looked away.

# Chapter 2

A familiar antiseptic aroma hung in the air. The same old waiting room magazines were stacked on end tables and cheap art hung from the walls. Still, this doctor's office maintained an aura of wealth. Sarah Filicidees ignored the familiarity of it all, and instead sat with her own entertainment to pass the time while she waited for her seventeen-year-old son who was with the doctor. Her cross stitch was a geometric pattern that somehow reminded her of both flowers and snowflakes. It was neither. She intently threaded the needle down through one hole and then up through the next — the thin line of embroidery floss filling each hole in the tan fabric matrix with color. Time stood still for her as she meticulously wove the needle in and out. She was in no rush, felt no need to finish or even make much progress. Her pleasure was all in the slow, calming monotony. The needle and floss constituted her only retreat from this world.

A young boy near Sarah jumped off his mother's lap and pushed a small toy car on the top of an end table. His mouth sputtered like a motor. Sarah slid the needle through the fabric once more, a slight grimace appearing on her face. The boy turned his car up onto the wall and outlined the chair his mother sat in, crawling on her lap as he went. Sarah completed another stitch and reached for a skein of orange floss. The boy slid away, chair by chair until he no longer intruded on her world.

Over the years, Sarah Felicidees had learned to act before others took advantage. Her mother died when she was eight, and her father, a hot-tempered abusive drunk, remarried a cruel and controlling woman who resented Sarah. As a young woman,

Sarah took the first opportunity to escape, leaving home at seventeen and getting married before she turned nineteen. She eventually discovered she had traded one prison for another, the first cold and dark, the second just cold. At least the early years of her marriage had been exciting, the young often needing little to create a lot. They moved from city to city, taking jobs as they found them and adventure as it came. When James lost his job, as he eventually always did, they'd move again. The adventure lasted through California, Alaska, Colorado and Montana, each step driven by Sarah's need to escape from childhood and family. Along the way, Sarah had gotten pregnant. She cared for their new baby while James worked construction. A year later, she was pregnant again. This time, she had an abortion without telling him. As far as she was concerned, it was none of his business. They kept moving: Chicago, New Orleans, New York and Miami.

The needle flowed in and out of holes so tiny they were close to invisible. Her movements were smooth, appearing to require no conscious effort. It was as if Sarah's fingers themselves could see. The boy was now on the other side of the room.

The first seizure came the day after her son's fifth birthday. They were in the supermarket, Sarah picking out bargain brand cereal as Aaron ran down the aisle toward her. Suddenly, he stopped running. His eyes aimlessly scanned the cartons and cans all around him. He looked confused. She spoke his name and his mouth opened as if he was going to answer, but nothing came out. She remembered thinking how funny he looked. When he plopped awkwardly to the floor, she yelled at him to get up. When he started thrashing, she started screaming. Over the next year, the seizures became common, and she grew accustomed to them, another weight in her heavy life. The burden of an epileptic child and a useless husband suffocated her. As she had as a child, Sarah turned to her dreams for comfort. She saw a future of wealth and happiness, a life in which she no longer loathed her own pitiful husband, a life in which she was not held back by his lack of passion, intelligence and industry. A new future, it was what she deserved and would one day have.

Slowly the boy moved closer, his car engine going from a soft sputter to an incessant thrum. Sarah maintained her concentration. Her needle hummed its own tune.

When James died, Sarah's opportunity finally came. On that morning in 2005, after she dialed 9-1-1 and the dispatcher answered, Sarah calmly said that her husband might have had a heart attack. Curiously, she thought of her stepmother as she talked. Sarah remembered the false sweetness in the woman's voice, proclaiming her love for Sarah while Sarah sat locked in her bedroom closet. She now saw James' profession of love in much the same light, a false love without benefit of service. She compared her own strength to that of her husband. She had endured much harder tests than he. She was a survivor. He was a loser and she was better off without him. Without him, there was the life insurance policy — five hundred thousand dollars. She deserved it. The money did indeed pave the way to a better life. She no longer bounced from doctor to doctor. Through new medication, her son became almost completely seizure free. She even had enough money to buy a car and a small townhouse near her new job as a secretary at Catholic University, but it did not turn her dreams into reality. It just bought her time.

The boy sat back down next to Sarah's neighbor. The volume of his engine rose with his proximity. He carefully laid out magazines for a race course and jump. He gleefully ran his car down the jump, watched it fly into the air. The car soared. The boy jumped out of his chair and caught it in mid-air. Sarah's eyes followed him as her fingers continued to pull floss in and out. The boy sat back down, held his car high in the air sputtering and spitting as he went. He lifted it up onto the pile of magazines. He let go and shrieked. The small metal car, nicked and battered, launched into the air then crashed at Sarah's feet. The boy scurried after it, reaching the spiky stem of Sarah's high heels, just as she bent forward and snatched the toy from the carpet, holding it close, but facing it toward the boy in apparent offering. He stopped, looked into Sarah's eyes and fell silent.

Her head inches from the boy's, her gaze locked, she whispered, "If you don't sit down and be quiet, I'll stick this needle right into your eye."

Five hundred thousand dollars. For a while it had seemed a fortune.

~

Dr. Hackett Metzger stood in the windowless examining room of his office on 19th Street NW, and felt a clammy dew of sweat across his near hairless scalp. He looked up at the banks of fluorescent light above, wondering about vitamin D deficiency and the subterranean life he led as he moved from room to room, building to building, hardly exposing himself to the effects of the sun. *Get outside, get some exercise,* he reprimanded himself. He was over fifty, his bones ached, his head sweated and his mood was in the shitter as usual — all symptoms of a vitamin D deficiency. The depression was all he really cared about; he could live with the rest. Would more sun bring back his happiness? What a ludicrous question. Sunlight would not bring back his wife. Sunlight would not return his old interest in his work.

He focused on his patient. Aaron, a thin young man of seventeen with purple streaks in his hair and a wry, vibrant smile on his lips, sat on the examining table rubbing his right hand on his pant leg.

"How many seizures have you experienced over the last two weeks?" Hackett asked.

"Three."

"And before that?"

"A couple more over the last month. Before that, none since you changed the meds last year."

"How are things going in general? Are you doing alright in school, any problems causing extra stress at the moment?"

Hackett's voice was calm and encouraging. He knew that Aaron heard the reassuring timbre in it, felt the ataractic effect of his fatherly, non-threatening appearance. He had grown used to the reaction of his patients, even if he was still surprised by the face that stared back at him from the mirror each morning. He was not a handsome man, nor even overly intelligent-looking. His eyes were round, his flesh soft and pulpy, his hair sparse. Just the sight of him could lull you to sleep. He remembered telling his wife that he felt like some sort of troll under a bridge, ugly but entrancing. She rebuked him by saying that trolls were not entrancing. Then she had laughed, knowing exactly what she had left out.

Of course, Hackett was a doctor and he talked with a doctor's surety, but that did not lessen his illusion of commonness. In point of fact, Hackett was an everyday soul inhabiting a superlative mind, even when it was shackled by melancholia. He was a great physician with a phenomenal memory, had a sympathetic bedside manner, and could solve difficult math problems without aid of pen and paper, let alone that abomination of the modern age, a calculator.

*Focus on your patient*, he could almost hear his wife Jean's words. The voice wasn't real, he knew that. It wasn't a ghost; it wasn't even a hallucination. The voice was just his longing for Jean, his desire to see her battling with the reality of her death, trying to stop her from fading out of his life entirely. The words he heard were nothing more than his own self-castigation. She had not been like that in life. Sure, she had told him off when he needed it, argued when she got angry, but more times than not their conversations were full of everyday phrases like "pass the salt" and "looks like rain today." Now that Hackett controlled her words, she had become a bit of a harpy.

Hackett listened as Aaron spoke. He sounded like a far more typical high school senior than Hackett had been. He was worried about his grades, about getting accepted into his first choice for college, about friends and about girls — nothing unusual, but Hackett knew those everyday things could be incredibly stressful for a teenager, especially one who had suffered through his youth under the cloud of epilepsy. Still, he doubted that the return of seizures was stress related. Hackett thought back to meeting Aaron four years before, a thirteen-year-old in mourning for his Dad who had died unexpectedly. It was sad to think about it, but by dying his father had done him a favor. He had left a life insurance policy. Previously, the boy had bounced from clinic to clinic, hospital to hospital, and had been shuffled from medication to medication. It hadn't alleviated the seizures, and as far as Hackett could tell, the process hadn't been adequately monitored or tested. Aaron had suffered without reason. With the insurance money, Aaron's mom had sought out a new doctor, and found Hackett.

Hackett had a special empathy for the suffering of ostracized children. He had been one. His mind had not worked like other kids'. He had inhabited a world of distractions, personal relationships were difficult, and he was more comfortable alone with his thoughts. Nowadays, a child like him might be diagnosed with mild autism. Back then, he was just considered odd. He had lived his early life apart from others, so much so that his parents had sought treatment. They had told the psychiatrist that he was a lonely and frightened child, scared to interact with other children and closed off in a world of his own making. It took him years to peel away their opinions, and see the world as he himself had experienced it. He wasn't so much frightened as he was uninterested. People demanded that he interact, and he did not even want to. He had preferred solitude, not because the outside world scared him, but because the inside world embraced him. Perhaps his isolation had a different cause than Aaron's, but he imagined it had a similar outcome. It wasn't until college that his intellect rose above his awkwardness.

Hackett hoped that Aaron could forget his own childhood pain, and he was impressed with the change from the awkward, sad thirteen-year-old he had first met. He remembered how withdrawn Aaron had been. Many people don't understand the psychological toll epilepsy can have on someone, especially a child. Hackett imagined Aaron as a young boy, playing baseball, sitting in class, eating at McDonald's, feeling the aura of an approaching tonic-clonic seizure, knowing that he was about to lose control. Aaron would have been feeling fear deep down into his bones — not just the fear of physical injury and death, but also a far deeper fear of his own vulnerability and his difference from other children.

"Do these seizures feel any different than your previous

ones?" Hackett asked, knowing that epileptics could suffer psychosomatic seizures. It was a cruel twist of fate; the mind tricked itself into mimicking the very illness from which it sought freedom. Psychogenic Nonepileptic Seizures (P-NES) could appear very similar to the real thing.

"No."

"Did you lose bladder control at all?"

"Yes, once."

Some P-NES patients reported loss of bladder control, but in Hackett's opinion, it was a strong indicator that these were real epileptic seizures.

"Let's do an EEG."

Hackett opened a drawer and handed Aaron the EEG cap, a soft black cloth helmet. The teenager took hold of it and slipped it on quickly, adjusting the chin strap with acquired efficiency. It fit tight to the scalp. On the outside, thin multi-colored wires were formed into bundles in neat lines like the inside of a commercial telephone cabinet, but less crammed and confused.

"Wired up and ready to travel the universe," Aaron said, a slight smile creasing his lips.

As Hackett expected, the EEG results were normal, as was true for many patients in between seizures. That fit with Aaron's history.

"We may need to change your medications again," Hackett said, but as he talked he noticed a flicker in Aaron's eyelid.

Has that been happening often?" he asked.

"Has what been happening?"

"Has your eye been twitching?"

"Yeah, I guess so. I've noticed it lately."

"Do you remember me telling you about the side effects and interactions of your medication, the things you couldn't eat or drink?"

"Yeah, I can't have grapefruit and I haven't."

"What about drinking alcohol?" Hackett expected the boy to lie, so he watched his face carefully for telltale signs.

Surprisingly, Aaron smiled and answered directly. "They

always say don't drink when you take medicine, even cold medicine. It's a bunch of crap; a couple of beers ain't gonna hurt."

"Well, in this case it isn't crap at all. Two of the potential reactions from mixing alcohol and Dilantin are tremors in your eyelids and a compromised effectiveness of the drug. I'd say you hit the jackpot on both counts."

"Shit, man, do you have to tell my mom? She'll flip like usual."

It was Hackett's turn to smile. "That depends. You're a minor and I have a duty to tell her if I think you will continue drinking and it will affect your health."

"Come on, Doc, you think that I would want to drink a few beers knowing that I was going to have seizures? That's plain nuts."

"Come on, Aaron," Hackett parroted and paused to make sure Aaron saw his smile. "You already did."

"Not no more, Doc. I may be dumb, but I ain't a freakin' idiot." They talked a little more, until Hackett was satisfied.

Just before they went back out to talk to Aaron's mother, the boy cleared his throat. "Doc, one more question just between us two. Okay?"

"Shoot."

"What about weed?"

"Do you mean marijuana?"

"Yeah, mar-ee-juan-ahh," Aaron said with a laugh. "This is confidential, no telling Mom."

"Well, professionally, I have to advise you against illegal drug use of any kind, and I do not know of any studies that have specifically looked at the interaction of Dilantin and marijuana, but the bottom line is I doubt that marijuana will have negative consequences." Drugs were as far away from Hackett's experience as playing in the World Cricket Championship, but he didn't judge. He just didn't tell Aaron that the Epilepsy Foundation had recently called for the medical use of cannabis oil. That would be going a little too far. After all, pot was illegal, and Aaron was a minor.

They walked back out into the waiting room where Aaron's mother sat working on her cross stitch. Hackett invited them into his office and made small talk as they moved down the hallway, discussing the weather and the coming holiday. He had honed his skills for conversation through years of practice, studying others, reading psychology texts and popular psychology articles, until he put his youthful awkwardness behind him. *Sometimes you sound like you have been programmed by a computer.* It was his own insecurity talking again.

Aaron's mother wore a snug black and white checked dress. Hackett stopped at the doorway to his office and let her pass, noticing the soft curves of her body as she walked into the room, imagining her breasts, wanting to touch her ass.

"You look very nice today, Ms. Felicidees." He wanted to retract the words as soon as he said them, but she simply said "thank you" and smiled.

Hackett felt both embarrassment and grief slipping into his consciousness, replacing his lust. He silently begged Jean's forgiveness, then looked at Aaron's mother with a more impartial eye. Sarah was perhaps forty, more than ten years younger than Hackett. She was pretty, but Hackett didn't like heavy makeup or platinum hair. It made him feel less guilty to downplay her beauty.

His eyes were still focused on Sarah, and he realized that she was looking back at him. His face turned red. He looked away. There upon his desk was a photo of Jean taken years ago on vacation in Papua New Guinea. The glow of her skin warmed him, even now. Jean had been thirty-six, a little plump, and not as pale as normal in the golden sunlight. Nobody would have characterized her as sexy, or even pretty, but to Hackett, she was absolutely beautiful. That trip had meant so much to both of them. Without it, their young marriage might never have survived.

Hackett looked back at the pretty woman in front of him, so different from Jean. He lowered himself into his seat and let a professional smile form on his face. "I think that the recent seizure activity is due to a food interaction with Aaron's medication. It could also be related to stress, but Aaron seems to be handling stress pretty well. I've asked him to start a log and record his food intake and sleep patterns, as well as feelings of stress or anxiety. If he has any more seizures, please call me immediately. We may have to change medications again."

Hackett watched discomfort grow on Sarah's face. He felt something cold in her. It was an odd subjective feeling on his part, unsupported by knowledge or fact.

"Food?" she said. "It's more likely to be alcohol. His father was an alcoholic. My father was an alcoholic. So far, Aaron's just an idiot, but I've seen how idiots turn into drunks. He should know better."

Hackett felt his gut tightening. With effort, he masked his surprise. "We did talk about alcohol. I advised Aaron that alcohol and Dilantin don't mix. I think he understands and won't risk seizures for a few beers."

"Sure." She turned toward Aaron and stared angrily at him. Hackett followed her eyes and watched as Aaron turned his face to the wall. She continued, "What about the drugs, Aaron? Tell Doctor Metzger about the drugs."

"I already told him." Aaron continued to stare at the wall. "A little weed isn't going to hurt me."

"God knows what else you are taking." She was practically screaming at him.

Hackett had spent his medical life looking for the truth behind people's words. A good neurologist needed to crack the eggshell and reveal the yolk hidden within to make a good diagnosis. Had he failed to see something in this boy? It was an argument that Hackett had had with himself far too often in recent years. He longed for the days when he approached every case with the certainty that he could solve it, and the confidence that any small mistakes he might make were greatly outdistanced by his abilities.

Aaron returned his mom's angry stare with one of his own. "I'm not taking any other drugs. Sometimes you act so damn crazy."

"Listen, Aaron." Hackett jumped into the conversation. "I don't know if you are taking drugs or not, but I have to warn you in the most serious terms not to. You should know that drug use, whether it is cocaine, meth, amphetamines or any other hard drug, could have dire consequences for you."

"Jesus Christ, Doc, don't listen to her. She's nuts."

Hackett obliged. He was too busy watching Sarah's backside as she stood and left the room.

# Chapter 3

It was too late to cook, too late to even change out of her scrubs. Once again Ella Mae would be alone for dinner, no one waiting at home in her apartment, not even a cat. She had no reason or desire to cook, so she drove directly to the small neighborhood restaurant a few blocks from her apartment in Silver Spring, Maryland. When she opened the door, a cacophony of voices assaulted her along with the metallic clatter of a busy kitchen. She had never seen the place so crowded on a Monday night. Humanity closed around her. She felt exhausted, wanted peace. Too hungry to leave, she searched for an open table. Seeing none, she turned to the bar and eyed a single vacant stool. In slow measured steps she moved between tables, avoiding chairs and elbows.

"Is anyone sitting here?" she asked the gray-haired man seated at the bar.

"Nobody. It's all yours," he said, hardly lifting his eyes from the pages of his book.

Ella Mae ordered a glass of pinot grigio and sipped as she perused the menu. On her left a young couple huddled together in intimate conversation, the man's right hand folded in front of his body and wrapped around her fingers, their eyes locked, his lips almost touching her ear as he talked. Ella Mae shut it out. In the mirror behind the bar, she could see the man next to her. He wore a white-gray beard and a charcoal suit. A blue shirt was unbuttoned at his neck. His wedding finger lay naked against his book, curled against the image of a muscled man, his arms wrapped around a beautiful girl whose hair was blowing wild above a windswept coastline. Ella Mae lost momentary control and laughed out a short, odd snort. He glanced up at her reflection, then turned his eyes back to his book.

She gave him a good hard look, trying to divine the whole of the man from what was visible: a neat but not finely tailored suit, recently trimmed hair, thin wrists and sinuous tendons, long fingers, only a slight paunch in his midsection, lines on his forehead and wrinkles like her own radiating from his eyes. She thought about the last man she had been with, tried to estimate the time that had passed — five years, maybe six. She decided he'd do despite the age, even if it was just a dinner fantasy.

The man looked up into the mirror, his eyes grabbing hers for an instant, and he smiled brightly. She looked away. By the time she had the nerve to look again, he was reading. Ella Mae took a long slurp of wine, let it settle and take the edge off her day. When her mouth ran dry, she took another.

"Is the book any good?" she asked.

He looked up into the mirror again, then turned to face her directly. "Kind of." He paused ever so briefly. "To tell the truth, it's pretty bad, but I am a little addicted to this trash." He tilted the cover in her direction, acknowledging what she already knew. "I read them all the time, takes my mind off work."

"I've never met a man who reads romance novels, or at least one who admits it."

"We exist, and some of us aren't even gay." The man's smile was wide, and gentle.

"Well," Ella Mae said, and leaned towards him conspiratorially. "I confess to an appetite for Nora Roberts; never can get enough of that particular kind of trash. You know, she went to high school right down the street at Blair."

"She's too highbrow for me," he said, and his smile warmed Ella Mae. "I like my trash a little more raunchy. Who cares about characterization and setting."

When Ella Mae laughed, he bellowed out a deep hearty chortle of his own. "George," he said holding out his hand.

They talked about romance novels through two glasses of wine. Just when Ella Mae felt the subject was wearing thin, he asked her if she was a doctor or a nurse. She liked him even more. People seldom asked, just assumed that women were nurses. She told him about work, and he seemed to hang on every word.

"Who is Hackett?" he asked interrupting one of her stories.

"Oh, that's Doctor Metzger. He's Chief of Neurology and an old friend."

"Hackett Metzger? Funny name, sounds like a serial killer to me. Hannibal Lecter, Hackett Metzger, could be interchangeable. I'd watch out for him if I were you."

"A serial killer? More like the opposite." Ella Mae's voice turned serious. "Hackett has saved more lives than I can count."

"No offense meant, just kidding."

Ella Mae accepted his apology, and as they talked, she found herself comparing George to Hackett. George was more attractive, but he was also older and he had just told her he was a furniture salesman, for heaven's sake. He could not match Hackett's intellect and stature in the medical community. Her mind drifted back to the day Jean died. Ella Mae had rushed to Hackett, thrown her arms around him and cried with him. In his arms, she grieved for her best friend, but she harbored a feeling that she did not want to admit to herself. At that moment as Ella Mae felt Hackett falling apart, her heart told her that he was now available to her. Four years later, it had not turned out that way. Hackett mourned and Ella Mae comforted, but Hackett could not give up the ghost that he held in his heart. She had watched as he descended into despair. She became the shoulder he cried on, the person with whom he remembered. Slowly he marched up the steep hill of recovery. Slowly she saw her own dream fade.

"Is something the matter?" George asked and Ella Mae told him she had been thinking about Jean.

"She was my best friend. I really miss her."

They conversed about God, and about heaven and hell. He told her that he was a lapsed Catholic who still believed, just wasn't dogmatic.

"I don't go to church anymore either," she responded. "But God is real, and I know that Jean is with him."

George cocked his head and looked at her questioningly. "You sound so sincere, but you can't really be sure."

"I am absolutely positive." George said nothing, but she felt the question he was holding back. "Death is not an ending, it is just another stage of life," she answered.

His silence felt heavy, but not oppressive. There was a sympathetic curiosity in it, and so she opened up. "I know, because I died." And then she told him her story. It was so much easier to confide in strangers.

On her twenty-sixth birthday, in 1982, Ella Mae sat in a plane on the runway of National Airport looking at the snow and slush covering the wing outside her window. She was scared of flying and the weather made her all the more fearful. As the plane lifted off the runway, the aircraft shook violently and then pitched to the side. Her fear turned to panic. Ella Mae's blood-curdling scream was merely one voice in a sea of hysteria. In the next few seconds, most of those around her would die and she had no reason to see herself as an exception.

The world slowed. She heard a different, non-human cry. It was the sound of tearing and grinding metal, as a wing tip hit the bridge and sliced through cars. She felt a clarity that she couldn't explain. It was as if she could sense life slipping away on the bridge below. At the same time, she had a premonition of bodies being torn apart around her. She never did see or feel the full impact. She simply lost consciousness.

She awoke in the frigid waters of the Potomac River, not knowing how long she had been out. There were but a few voices around her, and not a single scream. She heard a lonely whimpering cry and then a single woman's voice calling out for her husband and baby. Ella Mae didn't remember moving her arms and legs. She was just floating in the ice-filled water. Ahead of her, she saw the tail of the airplane and the Air Florida logo, a small "a" next to a capital "F." A man's voice caught her attention. She turned to the noise just in time to see him jump from the shoreline into the water. She thought he was coming to save her, but he swam toward another person much closer to shore. As she watched, the effects of hypothermia took hold and she slipped under the cold dark water. Five minutes later, her lifeless body was pulled from the river.

"When I woke up in the hospital, I told the doctor that I had died and gone over to the other side. He laughed and asked if angels had wings and if God had a white beard."

"Did you really see God?" George asked, his eyes full of curiosity, his face telling her that he believed everything she said.

"In a way. It felt like I was part of a universe of pure energy. Everything around me hummed with a kind of electricity, creating the most beautiful music, like chanting monks. It was beautiful and so peaceful. No one talked, but I heard their thoughts just the same." She continued talking in rapid fire. "I knew that they all loved me, everyone in the universe. I knew I had died, and thought I was going to heaven, but a voice told me that it wasn't my time, and they sent me back. When I woke up, the doctor told me it was all a hallucination. He acted like I had gone crazy."

Ella Mae still remembered the doctor's dismissive rumbling laugh. She hated him for it. She hadn't even told him of the colors, so vibrant and real beyond what she had seen in life, or the shapes — butterflies, birds and flowers floating everywhere, such a wondrous menagerie. Everything in life paled next to it.

"I never again told anybody in the medical profession, for fear that it would hurt my career. Doctors can be so condescending."

They talked right through dinner. "Dessert menus?" the bartender asked. Ella Mae waved him away, and then immediately regretted it. She looked at George, hoping he would order and she would have a chance to linger with him.

"I'm quite full, plus I really have to get home. I have an early flight."

Ella Mae watched his reflection, as he lifted his wine glass and drank the last drops. She wondered if that was it. Would he just walk out the door, a missed opportunity? The wait for the check lasted forever. Neither of them had much more to say now that the awkwardness of leaving had arrived. She adjusted her dress and wiggled her ass seeking comfort on the hard wooden stool that to this point she had hardly noticed. She thought he might offer to pay, but his chance passed and each signed their own credit card receipt. George stood up.

Ella Mae felt a ripple of nervous regret running through her mind. She watched as his hands adjusted his belt and tucked in his shirt. She looked at his face and noticed how he had somehow transformed into a much more handsome man over the course of dinner. His face now seemed ruggedly strong, the wrinkles adding to his allure instead of advertising his age. He smiled and told her how nice it had been to talk to her, then he turned to leave. Ella Mae looked back into the mirror at her own reflection. Sitting on the counter was the pen she had used to sign the credit card receipt.

"Fuck it," Ella Mae said aloud, arresting George's forward motion. He looked back into the mirror with the same curious grin that had been pasted on his face when she told him about her own death. Briefly, their eyes met. She turned her gaze back to the counter, picked up the pen, flipped over the receipt and wrote her phone number on the back.

"Call me," she said and handed it to him.

# Chapter 4

The sun sat high in the late afternoon sky, a beacon calling Sarah to get her bike and go for a ride, to pedal hard and release her pent-up demons. She turned down the alley and pulled into the parking place that took up nearly half of her backyard. By habit, she yanked up on her emergency brake and stepped out of the well-polished BMW Z4. The yard was tidy and well kept, except for a bag of garbage that had apparently been pulled apart by a neighborhood dog or raccoon.

"Goddamn it, Aaron," Sarah said aloud to the empty yard. *Why can't he take the time to put the trash inside the garbage can*, she added silently. *I work myself to the bone.* She felt like she was a character in an old movie speaking someone else's words. Even before James had died, Sarah had been planning a better life for herself, and it had gotten better, just not as good as she deserved. Aaron was getting more and more like his father, and that wouldn't do. Plus, she had quickly learned that five hundred thousand was no fortune, not even close. She left the trash, telling herself that Aaron could damn well clean it up himself.

Inside the house, Sarah sat on one of the kitchen chairs she had bought at IKEA. She hated them, along with the cheap table in front of her. Before her sat a prescription bag from CVS, Aaron's name printed on the receipt. She reached out, brought it closer and stared. After a minute she ripped the bag open and poured the contents of the plastic bottle into her own hand. Slowly, one by one she dropped them back into their container. *Twenty bucks a pill*, she thought. These pills, this teenage boy, this disease, it was all the same thing, a snapping dog inside her head, taunting and mocking her. *Screw it all*, she announced silently, spitting the words at the imaginary mongrel. She would triumph.

She pulled another plastic bottle out of her purse, upended a few pills into her hand. They looked alike, same size and shape, the letters printed on each were only slightly different. She counted out ten pills from Aaron's prescription, laid them out on the table and replaced them with ten from her bottle, closed each bottle and scooped the discarded pills into a ziplock bag.

When she was finished, Sarah walked to the front door, opened it and retrieved the mail, leafing through it as she stood on the concrete floor of the porch. Comcast $109, she knew without opening. PEPCO probably $150, because of the air conditioning. Bank of America Visa, she didn't want to guess. She opened a small wooden box on the desk in the living room and as she threw the envelopes in, her cell phone rang.

Sarah walked back to the kitchen table and lifted her purse without urgency. She found the phone, flipped it open, saw her boyfriend Eric's familiar number and waited for it to roll over to voicemail. She was sick of him. He couldn't give her what she needed and he wouldn't let go. She knew from experience that he would stop calling eventually, but she hated him for his persistence. Hadn't she made it amply clear? They were done.

When James died, Sarah had been in the blush of new wealth. She swore she would never marry again. She would enjoy men on her own terms, and she had done exactly that, picking them up and tossing them aside. A few like Eric had lasted longer, but most were typical men who failed to capture her interest. Eric had proven different for a while. He was athletic, adventurous and fun, but he had little money, and hers was running out. He had to go.

The back door opened with a creak, and then the storm door slammed with a clamorous rattle of metal and glass. Sarah turned to watch her son drop his backpack on the floor, and swing open the refrigerator door. Aaron lifted a half gallon of milk, removed the cap and took a long gulping slug directly from the carton.

"I'm standing right here," she said in a loud commanding voice.

"I know. I can see."

"Yet you put your filthy lips on that carton when you know how much it disgusts me."

"Jesus Christ, Mom. I wish you would lighten up sometimes. You don't even drink milk, and nobody else lives here."

A tense feeling crawled up Sarah's neck and buried itself in the back of her head, forming a picture of her dead husband slobbering on a beer can. She walked towards Aaron. He stood motionless, still holding the milk carton at shoulder height. Sarah's hand darted out and grabbed it from him. A splash of milk wetted his shirt and splattered the floor. She turned abruptly and stepped over to the counter, then she upended the carton, and watched as the white liquid splattered across the stainless steel sink.

"And that is the last carton of milk that I will buy. Get outside this instant and clean up the trash strewn across our yard."

Sarah watched him turn slowly, observing his head as it shook back and forth disrespectfully.

*He doesn't know how lucky he is,* she told herself. *Just like his father.*

Ten minutes later, she rolled her bicycle out the back door and rigged her bike rack to the BMW.

~

As Hackett walked into the patient's room, Yu Lai's head briefly turned in his direction before returning to the patient's chart. The sight of her caused a pleasant but embarrassing sensation in his groin. He tried not to be obvious while he tugged at his pants and underpants, seeking relief. She stood next to the bed, her head tilted upward, her feet set wide, one hand resting comfortably on her hip, and the other stretching toward him with the chart. Hackett recognized the dominance in her posture, so contrary to her slight diminutive figure. Observing body language was something that he did out of habit. He had started as a young doctor, determined to overcome his childhood social awkwardness and hone the perfect bedside manner.

"Hello, Doctor Wang," he said for the benefit of the young patient and especially the mother and father standing nervously at the bedside. Before he realized what he was doing, he rested his hand on her shoulder. His fingers contracted ever so lightly.

Yu Lai smiled. "Sudden loss of vision, no traumatic event known." There was no sense of embarrassment in her voice, which Hackett appreciated. In fact, nothing about the way she treated him had changed since he had asked her out.

She handed him the chart. He accepted it with his left hand as he reached out his right to the man beside the bed. "I'm Doctor Metzger. I assume that you have met Doctor Wang."

"Billy Reynolds," the man answered in a gruff voice. "I'm not the father."

"Delia Shepard," the woman next to him said, scowling and extending her hand at the same time. "I'm Jessica's mother."

"Pleased to meet you both. We need to ask Jessica a few questions and then we'll administer a quick neurological exam." Hackett stepped past the mother and bent closer to the girl on the bed. Her chart said she was fifteen years old. "How do you feel, Jessica?"

"Terrible. I'm blind."

Two stuffed animals lay next to the girl, tucked into the bed sheets on either side of her. Hackett discreetly motioned toward them and Yu Lai nodded her head in understanding. It was one of the early lessons Hackett had taught his students about young women presenting unsupported neurological ailments. "Always look for age-inappropriate stuffed animals," he would say during rounds. "They are half the diagnosis." He had always stressed that diagnosis was an art that required much more than lab tests. A good neurologist asked the right questions and keenly observed the patient's behavior.

"Can you tell me how this happened?"

Before the girl could answer, her mother jumped into the conversation. "Jessica has serious medical concerns. She has migraines and fainting spells. She is extremely light sensitive and that is one of the things that triggers her headaches. I think that she might have some kind of epilepsy or maybe even an aneurysm, but the damn doctors never seem to identify the cause."

Hackett turned back to the girl. "Can you tell me when it was exactly that you lost your vision?"

"I told you," the mother cut in again.

"Mrs. Shepard, please just give me a second here. I need to ask your daughter a few questions and it is important that I get her answers. Even if you already know what has happened, it is best that I hear the details from her." He used his most patient voice. "Is that okay?"

The woman said okay, but her face told another story.

"Jessica, can you tell me what happened when you lost your sight?"

"I just woke up this way." The girl's voice was timid.

"It is important for you to describe any pain that you may have had."

"I don't remember." This time, there was a flash of anger in the girl's voice.

"Think back. Can you remember what you were thinking?"

"I was scared because everything went black." Again, Hackett heard anger.

"Did it go black after you opened your eyes?"

"It was just black."

"Goddamn it!" The mother's voice was like fingernails on a chalkboard. "It's always the same with you doctors, a hundred stupid questions and no answers. Can't you examine her or something? Find out what's wrong!"

Hackett couldn't stop the scowl that spread across his face as he reached into his pocket and pulled out a pen flashlight. He leaned down, stretched one of the girl's eyelids wide open and flashed the light directly into her pupil. Then he did the same with the other eye. After that, he reached into his pocket and pulled out a small spiral notepad, flipped through the pages until he came to a photograph, carefully raised the pad up to the left side of her face, making sure that only she could see the picture.

He slowly moved the picture across her field of vision. Her eyes followed.

He paused before talking once more. "Mrs. Shepard, if you don't mind, we need to conduct another test. Could you both, please, step out for just a few minutes." Hackett wanted to talk to the girl without her mother interpreting his words and poisoning their effect.

"If you think I trust you, you have another thing coming. I'm staying right here."

Yu Lai turned to the mother, and Hackett knew that the woman didn't stand a chance. "I'll be here, too, Mrs. Shepard. I can assure you that your daughter will be in good hands. Doctor Metzger is the best neurologist in the metro area." Yu Lai's voice was soothing, even musical. She had the best bedside manner of any student Hackett had worked with in the last twenty years. As Hackett had seen so many times before, Yu Lai raised her hand slowly and brought it up to the woman's shoulder, touching her so lightly that the weight of her fingers must have been barely perceptible.

A moment later, Yu Lai was back in the room. Hackett turned back to the girl.

"Jessica, you're going to be alright. There is nothing medically wrong with your eyes. Sometimes, the brain just shuts down certain senses. We call it conversion disorder. In these cases, sight usually returns fairly quickly." Hackett was careful not to use the terms hysterical blindness or psychosomatic. He knew that patients translated that as "crazy" and often reacted adversely.

"Oh," the girl said and paused. "Are you sure?"

"Yes, but I think there is something else that you aren't telling us."

The girl said nothing.

"Has something happened recently to upset you, before you lost your vision?" The girl was immobile on the hospital bed, but Hackett noticed a tear in her eye. "I tell you what, we have some additional tests that we can do and perhaps some medication that can help bring back your sight more quickly. We'll be back."

Hackett walked into the hallway, with Yu Lai at his side. She shut the door as they left. The mother stood before him scowling, waiting for an answer that she obviously thought she wouldn't like.

"I think we have good news, Mrs. Shepard. From every indication, Jessica is going to be fine. I think her vision should come back all by itself. It's best that she get some rest overnight and try to relax as much as possible. You can go in, but you may want to try to let her rest peacefully without too much talking." The woman argued with Hackett, wanted more detail, wanted a second opinion, apparently only wanted to finally hear the horrible truth that all of the doctors had concealed, but eventually she accepted his words.

As they walked out of earshot, Yu Lai leaned towards Hackett and whispered into his ear so close that her breath was like a feather tickling him. "Do you think they'll let her rest?"

"Probably not."

He wanted to stay close like that, to feel her near. Instead, he stepped back and focused on his own annoyance at the patient. "I hate this crap," Hackett finally continued. "It is a waste of our bed space and our time. She should be in a psychiatrist's office, not in the neurology ward."

Even as he said the words, Hackett regretted them. Life had proven that everyone, including he, himself, was blinded by their own hubris to some extent. Yu Lai's giggle filtered through the haze around him. She looped her arm through his. Her voice was bright and conspiratorial.

"Which picture did you use?" she asked.

"The penis."

Hackett always carried a few pictures on his rounds, just for cases like this. Hysterical reactions such as these weren't as unusual as most people think. He knew that someone who was not really blind couldn't stop their eyes from following an object that was innately stimulating. It was an uncontrollable reaction. He often used the penis photo on women. With men he was more likely to just use one printed word — "asshole."

"How appropriate," Yu Lai said and Hackett again heard her

soft high giggle. "It's just a hunch, but I think we might want to order a pregnancy test."

"Really?" Hackett couldn't hide the surprise in his voice. "What makes you think so?"

"Well, the girl looked so uncomfortable when the mom was in the room, and she didn't really seem that concerned about her vision, but then there is the other thing." She paused for effect. "Don't you think she is a little thin to have that tummy bump?"

Hackett prided himself on picking up the clues that others missed, and he quietly played back the exam in his mind, this time seeing what Yu Lai saw. In the months after Jean's death, Hackett's mind had lost focus, drifting from the present to Jean and the past at every opportunity. Slowly, he had forced his way through the fog and retrained himself to maintain clarity, but try as he might, he was no longer the same man, especially on days when the stress of failure bore down on him. Where every day as a doctor had once been a rewarding and fascinating affair, it had become a fretful and challenging struggle.

"Well, Doctor," he said. "Find a way to get the patient's consent and run the test."

Hackett's eyes remained fixed on Yu Lai for a long, uncomfortable moment. There she stood, smiling, beautiful and young. Her hair was long and silky, a thin ribbon of it tucked beautifully behind her ear. His head was bald, covered in a patchwork of short wispy gray hairs and scaly skin. Her cheeks held high on her face, parted by smiling red lips. His jowls hung loose. When Hackett smiled, it was lopsided and awkward. She was young and pretty. He was aging without the benefit of handsomeness.

He shook free of the last of his fantasy, sad, but determined to let it go. He was a lonely, chubby, horny old man and it hurt.

~

Cafeteria trays sat before Hackett and Yu Lai, his filled with a plain hamburger on a plain bun slathered in catsup and an order of wilted French fries in their own thick red puddle, hers filled with a salad of limp translucent lettuce, cucumber and tomato. The smell of hospital cafeteria hung thick in the air. Hackett had been in countless hospitals. He had listened to hospital executives preach about how important it was to improve the cafeteria fare, make meals enjoyable, but nothing ever changed — add a new deli counter, put in a frozen yogurt machine, contract with Pizza Hut. They changed everything, yet they changed nothing. The food adopted the hospital's nature, not vice versa. He breathed through his mouth.

Hackett read from the paper in front of him as he bit into a cold French fry. It was mush between his teeth.

"Have you looked over the material I gave you about the near-death study?" Yu Lai asked between bites of her salad.

"I am not interested," Hackett told her, his voice a little shorter than he meant it to be. What he didn't want to tell her was that when he had read the material, he couldn't stop thinking about Jean. He remembered her face, hollow and vacant, and later his face in the mirror after the ambulance had taken her away, appearing just as dead as hers. *Life after death, what a goddamn sham*, he told himself.

Another memory crowded him, this one from childhood. He felt his mother's hand on his back pushing him forward, her voice coaxing, then demanding that he go to the casket. His grandmother had cared for him as a baby while his mother worked. She was the only person who accepted and understood his odd, lonely behavior.

"Go on Hackett," his mother insisted. "You have to pay your respects. Grandma would be disappointed if you didn't say goodbye."

Eventually his mother grabbed him by the hand and pulled him up the church aisle. She lifted him by the shoulders and deposited him on a little step stool next to the coffin. As he sobbed, she bent down and whispered, "Tell Grandma how much you're going to miss her."

He had been told there was nothing to fear, that death was not the end of life, that Grandma was still there, but what he saw wasn't Grandma, it was some kind of withered white ghost. His eyes peered over the rim of the casket. Her papery, translucent skin hung slack. Underneath, her once purple veins were now nearly black. He thought of the strange stories he had heard about worms eating our bodies when we die. Had they eaten Grandma and left this thing in her place? Tears ran down his cheeks.

"Gamma," he sputtered, and then her finger moved. Hackett fell backward off the stool, unconscious.

Years later, he asked his mother about what he had seen that day. "You were a pretty sensitive kid. You just dreamed that up. Maybe I shouldn't have made you go, or just told you to keep your eyes shut when you paid your respects."

Hackett accepted his mother's explanation that there were no ghosts and dead people didn't move, but he never understood why she forced him to talk to his grandmother's corpse. That wasn't Grandma.

Hackett turned to Yu Lai, angered by his memories. "This near-death stuff is crap," he told her.

"Doctor Parnell is studying death experiences, not near-death experiences." Yu Lai responded. "These people have died and been resuscitated according to every measure of death we have."

"I don't care if you call it near-death experiences, death experiences or the Lord's resurrection. It's hallucination reinforced by bullshit."

Still, it was a lot like what he had been chasing for the last four years. Looking for Jean in every dream, wallowing in her memories, constantly dwelling on her absence in the hope of somehow recapturing her life. He was chasing Alice down the rabbit hole.

"There is not and could not be proof that these experiences represent anything beyond life, whatever you might call them." His voice hardened again.

Yu Lai fought on. "It will be the first reputable large-scale study of death experiences. Doctor Parnell already has commitments from Cornell, Southampton in England, Wishard Memorial and three other hospitals to participate in the study. He plans to kick it off in January. We should be a part of it."

Hackett looked away from the young doctor's deep black eyes and back down at the papers in front of him. He had read

Parnell's proposal and despite his dismissal, he knew that it was an attempt at serious science, not the New Age garbage he had originally worried about. Parnell's methodology would track patients who underwent full cardiac arrest, whose blood flow to the brain had halted and thus were clinically dead before resuscitation. It would include monitors to measure oxygen levels in the brain and interviews with patients who were resuscitated. By comparing the oxygen levels of survivors to that of non-survivors, doctors could conceivably discover better techniques for resuscitation. But it was the other part of the study that he knew would draw the most attention — the part of the study that tried to document out-of-body experiences. Parnell proposed placing pictures on platforms high above patients in cardiac care units. The pictures would be set up in such a way so as to not be visible to the patient or anyone else in the room and thus test the theory that consciousness was present outside the body after brain death.

"We have a reputation to maintain," he told Yu Lai. "By looking for a paranormal outcome, Parnell is already going beyond the bounds of science. Regardless of what we believe about death, the hypothesis that the human mind can see without eyes, hear without ears and think without a brain defies every law of physics."

Yu Lai stood her ground. "Einstein thought that the theory of quantum mechanics defied reason and every law of physics. 'God does not roll dice,' he famously said. Now quantum theory is regarded as fact. Parnell is not saying there is life beyond death. He is just saying that all of the anecdotal accounts of death experiences that defy our current understanding can't be dismissed without scientific investigation."

She continued to argue. It wasn't just a choice between science and the paranormal. Experiments had proven that time was relative to the observer. Two atomic clocks, one on a plane that flies around the world, and another stationary on land, will record time at a slightly different rate. When they once again meet, now would not be now. If three people stood at three different points spread across the universe, one's past would be another's present and yet another's future. If you could fall into a black hole, your trip would take an infinite amount of time, yet from the vantage point of earth, the same journey is infinitesimally short.

"If time is so malleable," Yu Lai argued, "why shouldn't it be observed differently at the point of death?"

Hackett liked the mental exercise of pondering the vagaries of time, but as for a theory of life after death, he knew it was nothing but abstract speculation.

~

Later that evening at home in Hackett's living room with the *Washington Post* dropped in front of him, images of letters lit up the nerves in Hackett's retinas, yet the words hardly registered within his wandering mind. Back and forth he flitted between newsprint and his internal babble of worry and stress. His mind slid away, conjuring images of death. It was Tuesday. He stared at the wedding picture of himself and Jean that sat on the mantle above the fireplace. It was too many feet away to see the detail, but he knew it grain by grain without really looking. He saw Jean's face, tried to picture its detail beyond the photographic image, to remember it in life, animated with happiness.

It was Tuesday, just like the day she had died. She would have been serving meals to the homeless at church tonight. He had accompanied her on occasion and marveled at the joy she took in such a simple task. He wanted to see her there, in her element, serving others.

It was Tuesday. He looked at the clock. It was six. He raised himself to his feet, his legs tired, not from exercise, just exhausted by existence. She would be at the church right now. Hackett walked to the door, telling himself that he had to stop wallowing in his loneliness. He stepped out into the hot humid bath of a Washington, DC August evening. Their house was a modest old Bethesda cottage, nestled on a treed lot. They had lived there since 1988, raised their daughter in it and made it their home. Over the last ten years, many of the homes around them had changed owners and been remodeled. The neighborhood had somehow grown without adding new homes. Instead, many of the existing houses had doubled in size, crowding their small lots and thinning the tree cover. The newness of it felt alien. Hackett preferred the old neighborhood with its quiet charm over the new neighborhood with its inflated real estate prices. He walked down Overhill Road, thinking once again of Jean and the day of the week. Memories fluttered through his head until he settled on one in particular. They had been a good couple, not a perfect one, and, of course, they had had their fights. Hackett remembered how she harped about his driving, nagging him until he could stand it no more. He remembered one day, driving down River Road by Great Falls. It was a beautiful day, but Hackett's thoughts were dark with argument. A car suddenly pulled out in front of him. Before he could react, Jean yelled.

"I saw it," he said after he jammed on the brakes.

"Could have fooled me," she replied. "You get more absent-minded by the day."

"Fuck you," he screamed at the only woman he ever loved. "If you don't like the way I drive, you can get out of the car and walk." He could not now remember one single other time in their life together where he had directed the words "fuck you" at her.

When Jean looked at him that day, he saw a river of deep anger in her eyes. They drove a few more seconds in silence, before he pulled to a stop at a red light. Anger pulsing in his veins, Hackett turned his head away, heard the door open, felt the car rock and then heard the door shut. He knew she had gotten out, but he still didn't look.

"Fuck you," he said again to the empty car, and he pressed his foot to the gas pedal.

He had only driven a matter of yards, before he stopped and begged her to get back in, but the memory opened such a raw chasm of pain in him that he almost cried just thinking about it. How could he have been so mean? He loved her more than anything, yet at times he had treated her with such cruelty.

It was Tuesday. He walked on, sulking, made a left on York Lane, eventually making his way to Old Georgetown Road and Flanagan's Harp and Fiddle on Cordell Ave. He gathered his emotions while he walked under the yellow awning, through the wrought iron bars and into the courtyard. He passed through the glass doors and into the pub where he had become a regular Tuesday dinner customer.

"Hello, Liam, it's a hot one out there." Hackett shook the collar of his shirt in an attempt to fan himself and evaporate the sweat from his chest, neck and back. He took a seat at the heavy oak bar right next to the line of beer taps. Dozens of sparkling wine glasses hung in rows above the bartender's head.

Liam acknowledged Hackett with a warm smile, a hello and a Guinness. "Did you sign up for that dating service that your daughter recommended?" Liam asked.

"No, didn't have the nerve."

"It doesn't take any nerve to sign up. It might take nerve to meet the first person, but signing up is like ordering a book from Amazon. You're talking to a computer, for Christ's sake."

Liam had a way of brightening Hackett's spirit. "I think I'll just try to meet someone the old-fashioned way."

"Well then." Liam rested his arm on the bar and leaned toward Hackett conspiratorially as Hackett raised the silky Guinness to his lips and took a small sip. "Then you are going to have to ask that pretty young doctor on a date, aren't you?"

Hackett spit Guinness foam out onto the bar as Liam roared appreciatively.

"I should have never told you about her. It is just a silly fantasy. She is half my age and ten times out of my league as far as dating is concerned."

"Tell me again, Doc. What's her name?"

Hackett shook his head back and forth, instead of responding.

"Was it Doctor You Lay Wang? Or did you just say you want to lay Doctor Wang?"

"It's Yu Lai," Hackett replied, "with an I sound, not an A." Hackett wiped the foam from his face and the tears from his eyes. "She would die of embarrassment if she heard you say that, as would I. Can you please forget that I ever mentioned her name? Otherwise, I am going to have to find a new place to have dinner."

"Okay, Doc. But you have to admit You Lay Wang is about the funniest name you've ever heard. Plus, some ladies are attracted to older gents, especially rich doctors."

A voice out of nowhere interrupted their conversation. "Yes, some women are attracted to rich doctors. There is nothing wrong with that, but only if the doctor is nice."

Hackett jumped with a start and turned toward the woman's voice behind his left shoulder. He looked at her in confusion for a second. "Hello Sarah," he finally said, his face flushed.

Aaron's mother had a wide smile on her face. "Good evening, Doctor Metzger. I thought it was you sitting there, but I could only see the back of your head."

"Not my best feature," Hackett responded, then laughed self consciously. "I was going to call you tomorrow. Aaron's test results don't make a lot of sense. I would like him to come back in as soon as possible so that we can draw more blood."

Hackett fumbled with his words as he explained that the lab must have screwed up. Sarah listened to him with apparent patience.

"Okay," she said when he finished. "I'll call your office for an appointment. Do you mind if I join you for dinner? I'd rather not eat alone." When Hackett turned to leave the bar with her, Liam winked at him.

"What brings you over to Bethesda? Don't you live by Catholic University?" Hackett asked as he settled into the chair across from Sarah.

"Just driving through after a bike ride at Great Falls, thought I'd stop for dinner and I remembered this Irish pub."

She talked on and on about her bike ride, the weather, and even baseball, a subject which bored Hackett to death, but he said nothing about that. "I'm so glad I stopped here," she continued. "What a pleasant surprise it is to see you outside of your office. Can I confide a secret?" Her eyes quickly darted to either side as if she was checking to see if anyone in the almost empty bar was eavesdropping.

"Sure, you can trust me." A flush of nervous energy lit up his face again.

"I've been wanting to talk to you without it always being about Aaron and epilepsy. I know it is an unmotherly thing to say, but I'm so sick of everything being about epilepsy, and you seem like such a nice, interesting man."

"You're too kind." Hackett wanted to say more, but the words didn't come out of his mouth. In the hospital and in the office, he was never at a loss for words. He always tried to stay two steps in front of the conversation, mixing small talk with clinical information, explaining the complex in easy to understand terms, offering compassion, humor or seriousness as the situation warranted, but that was all practiced and routine. He had never been good at real conversations.

She talked about books, music, Pilates, her hometown, her late husband. She talked of Hackett's work as a doctor, how amazed she was by what he did. When she asked him a question about his work, he talked for a few minutes before his heart fluttered and his tongue tied. "What was I saying?" he offered helplessly.

"You were talking about the man who got shot in the head with a nail gun and couldn't recognize his family members."

"Umm... uhhh," Hackett stumbled before he found the words and returned to his story. Sarah listened to him as if he was the most alluring man in the world. Slowly, he started to believe that she might really be interested in him. His excitement for her dredged up another pretty girl from his memory, though she was nothing like Sarah. It was a young woman he had met a few months before Jean's death. The girl had approached him on the Strip when he was in Las Vegas for a conference. Solicited him was not too strong a term. He knew that her interest in him had been feigned to tease out the real object of her desire, his money, but that only heightened his excitement. She had been barely more than a teenager, dressed in a provocative, brightly-colored low-cut shirt and form-fitting short shorts. How could he have been such a fool?

He looked at Sarah again, wondering if this could be different. For the first time in a long time, his fantasy for a pretty woman wasn't just about sex. He thought about companionship.

He imagined a relationship, fantasized that she wanted to be with him, to love him. Sarah was talking now, but Hackett was hardly listening. The beauty of her face held his attention like no words could. Reality settled in. He felt the old guilt swarming over him. Jean had been the only woman who had truly loved him, and he had betrayed her. He didn't have a chance with this woman. He didn't even deserve a chance.

# Chapter 5

A t six thirty, the sun was already beginning to drop in the September sky. The air glowed in hues of amber and gold around Ella Mae as she walked out of her Silver Spring apartment. Her miracle had happened. George had called. She felt young again despite her dowdy loose-fitting dress and the grey-haired man at her side.

"The weather is perfect. We'll sit on the deck and watch the boats come and go," he had told her on the phone. "Plus, I've got a little surprise for you on the ride. Bring a scarf."

Ella Mae hadn't thought much about his statement, but now with a scarf stuffed in her purse, she felt a little worried.

"Are you taking me sailing?" She wasn't dressed for it.

"No, but I've always wanted to try that."

"Then why do I need a scarf?"

"For the ride," George said and he pointed to the left.

Ella Mae's eyes followed George's finger, until they alit on the shiny black rear fender of a beautiful old convertible. Above the chrome of the rear bumper six red lights looked like rocket tails.

"Wow, what kind of car is that?"

"1960 Ford Thunderbird. My father had one just like it. I finally got one for myself. Mid-life crisis as they say."

"More like senior citizen's crisis," she responded with a smile.

"Like a dagger to the heart." George lifted his hand dramatically and placed it on his chest. "Do you like the car at least?"

Ella Mae walked up to the car and ran her fingers down the long ridge of the fin that defined the end of an automotive era.

She took another step and inspected the interior with its low-backed plush seats. "I love it, but I always thought that Thunderbirds were those small sports cars with the little round windows."

"That's the earlier T-bird. This is a second generation bird. I like it because it is so over the top. It is huge and it is gorgeous."

As they drove, Ella Mae shouted into the open air. It reminded her of the long-lost days of her Wisconsin childhood riding in the old Buick, windows down, no need for air conditioning, having to yell to be heard. Nervous, she talked about this and that, in rapid-fire, struggling to turn her words into conversation. George smiled and nodded, his head angled back in the wind, his hands turning the wheel and guiding the car smoothly across lanes and around corners. They were sailing.

They drove through suburban Maryland onto the back roads from Davidsonville to Galesville, whizzing past horse farms under a rustling canopy of green leaves drenched in the golden evening sun. Ella Mae's hand wandered over the leather seats, the dashboard, the door panels, even the side mirror, caressing the car as if it were a man. She glanced at George driving, his gray hair highlighted by the crackled glaze of western light. It was as if she were watching a movie.

Once at the restaurant, Ella Mae and George followed the hostess through the simple lobby, past the bar and out onto the deck. About twenty small boats were tethered to the dock, rocking ever so gently. The slight sound of fluttering canvas and the ring of cleats striking aluminum masts settled around them like a sailor's symphony. Beyond the boats, light sparkled off the gently rippling water of a sheltered cove.

They ate dinner and split a bottle of inexpensive chardonnay, talking and smiling all the way. Her rockfish was prepared simply, with butter and topped with crab imperial. Her potato was served with more butter and sour cream. The broccoli was steamed, a dollop of butter melting on top.

"Tell me about your family, you said you had a daughter, right?" Ella Mae asked between bites.

"Two grown daughters that don't bother to stay in touch and an ex-wife."

"Why don't you see your daughters?"

George waved his hand past his face as if he were shooing away gnats. "Custody battle when they were younger. Really, I don't want to talk about it. How do you like the food?"

"Not enough butter," Ella Mae said with a smile.

George smiled back, making it clear that he got the irony of her joke. He lifted his wine glass in the air. "To good simple food, and dinner with a beautiful woman. What could be better?"

Ella Mae's glass was no more than a foot off the table when it came to a sudden halt. "Are you playing me, George?"

"What do you mean?"

"You don't have to lay it on that thick."

"I meant it."

The smile returned to Ella Mae's face. "Okay, handsome, whatever you say."

~

A light wind rustled the trees above Hackett and a lone yellow leaf floated to the ground, prematurely announcing the arrival of autumn. It was eight o'clock and the sun had already set, leaving the porch light of a neighbor's house to illuminate the plate of food in front of him. He half listened to the conversation bounce between a new play at the Round House Theater and a herd of raccoons that seemed to be taking over the neighborhood. He and Jean had been regulars at these neighborhood gatherings, but he went less often now, finding them lonely and boring, despite the company.

"Do you have a raccoon problem, too?" a woman's voice asked. Her name was Susan or maybe Suzanne. She was a friend of the hosts, Al and Eileen. Hackett suspected that Eileen was trying to set him up again. "Haven't noticed one," he answered, but then again he seldom sat on the back deck or watched the yard anymore, so how would he know? Instead, he told her about a squirrel that had once come down his chimney and marauded through his house, climbing the curtains, knocking over pictures and ceramics, screeching and hissing at him.

"I grabbed the fireplace poker to defend myself, knocked about ten holes in my living room wall, before it was over." Hackett remembered the odd dull thunk of the poker sinking into plaster. He laughed aloud at the memory of his poor aim.

"Oh my, did it have rabies?"

"I didn't wait to find out. It chased me right out of the front door and then escaped up a tree."

"Oh my," she said again, reminding him of his mother. When she said "you poor dear," the comparison was cemented.

Once again, Hackett felt the touch of a woman's hand, light against his skin. He looked into her face and she smiled. When he smiled back his face felt stiff and awkward. She was thin. Her too-dark hair was cut short and stiffened with spray, and her skin hung loosely from her cheekbones. He noticed all that first, but still he thought she wasn't unattractive.

Eileen, the hostess, appeared behind Hackett. "Are you two getting on?" she asked. Hackett slipped his hand away.

"Swimmingly," Susan or Suzanne replied. "Hackett was just telling me how he did battle with a deranged squirrel."

Their hostess hung around for a brief minute or two. When she moved on, Hackett felt a hand settle on his shoulder and the woman leaned close to his ear. "Don't mind Eileen, she means well."

Perspiration beaded up on Hackett's forehead.

~

The cool black sky blew through Ella Mae's hair on the drive home, making it flare out behind her. She didn't bother with the scarf. *Screw the tangles*, she thought, *it's worth it*. They drove back down Davidson Road and then he turned toward the city on Central Avenue.

His house was a small two-bedroom Cape Cod, just off Route 295. Its modesty and sparse furnishing surprised her. It looked like he hardly lived there. Inside, he asked if she wanted more wine or a beer, and they both settled on Miller Lite. George moved to the stereo and grabbed a CD from a small pile. He inserted the disk into the player, and Ella Mae watched the circle of plastic slip from view. Soft jazz filled the room, not loud, but still fully present. George placed his hand on her shoulder.

Ella Mae looked at her feet then scanned the room, seeking something, anything to occupy her trembling eyes. She looked at a small vase on the mantle, empty and plain. It could have been purchased at a dollar store. There was one picture on the wall, an old picture. She recognized the Thunderbird. A man stood next to the car, dressed in slacks, a white shirt and bow tie. A teenage boy sat at the wheel grinning.

"Is this you? she said.

"Me, my dad and the original bird," George answered as his hand rubbed her back ever so lightly. Ella Mae shivered and her neck swiveled further. His hand fell away. "I really enjoyed dinner," George continued. "This may sound a little corny, but I was nervous all day. That disappeared when I picked you up. It's like we've known each other for years."

"You're playing me again, George. Try making your compliments more believable."

George's smile melted into a puppy dog expression. "I am serious. You need to accept a compliment in the spirit it is given."

George excused himself and went to the bathroom. Ella Mae released her breath as if she had been holding it all night. She sat down on the couch, folded her hands in her lap, laid her head back against the cushion and tried to relax. The toilet flushed behind her. She straightened. Next to a stack of coasters on the coffee table she saw an open envelope and a letter. Without thinking she picked it up. A photo of a five or six-year-old boy slid out onto the table, cute as can be. She flipped it over and read the sloppy immature writing — "I lov Pop Pop." Underneath it the signature — "Joey."

Ella Mae knew she shouldn't look, but she opened the letter, and saw the salutation. "See you at the end of the month. Love, Charlene."

George's hand reached over her shoulder, and took the letter.

"I'm sorry, it was just sitting on the table. Your grandson is so cute."

George walked to a small desk in the corner of the room and slipped the letter in the drawer.

"I thought you said your daughters didn't keep in touch," Ella Mae said, but there was silence in return. When George walked back to the couch, he stood in front of her.

"Let's start again. I really enjoyed dinner and I do find you attractive." He held out his hand. When she took it, he guided her gently off the couch. Without asking her if she wanted to dance, he casually lifted her arm and spun her in a slow circle, which ended in an embrace. Ella Mae imagined herself on the cover of a romance novel. She thought that he would kiss her, but his feet moved to the music and they danced instead.

When the music stopped, they were standing in the center of the room. She felt George's hand touch the bottom of her chin and gently lift her face upwards to his own. Her excitement was mixed with raw terror. All she could do was close her eyes.

The next moments were awkward. She waited, expecting his kiss. She heard his breath, soft but labored. When the kiss did not come, she opened her eyes once more.

"That's better," George said and he leaned forward keeping his eyes on hers until their lips touched. It was a tender kiss without childish urgency. It felt so good. He kissed her again, this time wrapping his arms around her and pulling her close.

"You are beautiful," he told her.

"And you are better than a romance novel," she answered, feeling as if she would swoon just like the woman on his book cover.

In the bedroom, Ella Mae felt scared despite the tenderness of his touch. *Can this be real?* she asked herself as her clothes slipped to the floor.

~

Sarah wore her new gold lamé dress which held tight to the curves of her ass and provided the perfect combination of support and freedom to her braless breasts. She walked into the club at Twentieth and L, next to her equally provocative friend. One man, then another rotated their heads in her direction. She smiled without directly looking at any of them. There was one empty stool left at the bar. Sarah stepped up into it and her friend Trudy inched in between the chair and the wall.

"He's a pain in the ass," Sarah said, continuing their conversation from the car.

"He's a teenager; of course he's a pain in the ass, but he'll be off to college soon, and he'll come back a man."

"Gone, but costing more than ever. Doctors, medications, food and clothes, and now college. If he thinks I am paying tuition when he can go to Catholic for nothing, he's dumber than he looks. How's a girl supposed to get a husband, anyway?"

"If you ask me, we're better off without them," Trudy responded.

A middle-aged man in blue jeans and what looked like a 1970s disco shirt, blue with a wide white collar, approached the women. "Buy you a drink?" he said, sliding in close to Sarah.

"You have to be kidding me," Sarah responded and swiveled her chair toward Trudy. "Better off without that one," Sarah said to Trudy. They both laughed as the man slinked away. "Truthfully, that boy's an anchor. What man would want him as part of the package?"

~

Susan or Suzanne, Hackett still wasn't sure of her name, had returned to talk to Hackett periodically, and stood next to him now as he said goodnight to Eileen.

"I think I'll be going, too," she said and followed Hackett around the side of the house. When they reached the sidewalk, she took his hand.

"I hope you don't think I am too forward," she said, "but, at my age I have learned that it seldom helps to waste time. I thought you might want to invite me over for a nightcap."

Hackett paused, tried to formulate a response, but words escaped him.

"Don't be a spoilsport, just one drink. I won't bite."

"Sure. That would be nice." Hackett flushed red under the streetlight.

Inside the house, as Hackett poured her a glass of white wine, he felt her eyes on him. Uncomfortable, he looked away. When his eyes finally came back to her, she was still watching. He didn't want to, but his head jerked away again. The tenseness he had been feeling all night, had settled deep into his bones. His eyes sought comfort in the photo of Jean which rested on the mantel. His guest took a short sip, put the wine on the coffee table and stepped closer to him, resting her hand on his shoulder and looking at the photo with him.

"Do you still miss her?"

"Yes," he said as he continued to stare at Jean. Finally, he turned to face the woman in his living room. "I'm sorry. I'm not very good company."

She just smiled and picked up another photo. "Is this your daughter?"

They talked about Amy, and then about his work. She told him once again, how happy she was to be retired, to learn water colors and read at her leisure, but it was lonely being divorced. Still, she was happy, she explained.

Hackett told himself to move on with life. He stepped closer to her as she talked, told himself that she could be his if only he would kiss her, but each time he tried, his will withered.

"Perhaps I should go," she said after another long silence.

"I'm sorry, Susan. This is embarrassing. I'm just not sure that I am ready to date."

It did not help that her name was Suzanne.

# Chapter 6

A s he sat at Flanagan's bar half watching Liam wash glasses, Hackett's mind focused on the embarrassing apparition of the pretty young girl he had met in Vegas nearly five years earlier. He recalled the tight shorts that revealed her legs right up to the curve of her ass, her small breasts pushed up by her bra until the flesh popped out. On the street, she had made eye contact with him, and handed him one of her sexy business cards.

"Private dances," she had announced. Hackett saw the card even now, and the pretty girl pictured on it, in mid-gyration, naked breasts and all. It wasn't the first time on that trip he had been handed such a card, but having her give him her own had a way bigger impact than when the small poorly dressed Latino men had handed him similar cards with photographs of women who could have been from another state, maybe even another planet. Those had seemed like some sort of scam, hardly real at all. But this was different. He had been mesmerized by the girl proffering her own photo, her reality undeniable.

"Do you think I'm pretty?" she had asked.

"Yeah, I guess so, sure," Hackett stumbled his way through his reply.

She talked rapidly, eager to keep his attention and draw him in. She asked him why he was in Las Vegas, what his first name was, where he was staying, and, of course, whether he'd like her to dance for him. "Fifty for a dance, no funny business."

"No, I can't." Hackett still felt the nervousness of that day, but now it was mixed with a heavy dose of guilt and regret. He should have walked away.

The girl called herself Star. She kept talking, kept cajoling. "It's not cheating, just a dance. Your wife will never know."

And so Hackett gave in. He brought Star to his room. She danced naked for him. It was the most exciting thing he had ever done, especially when he reached out and touched her breasts; what a marvel. Star negotiated the price upward from there.

The guilt in him raged after she left. He had never cheated on Jean. He had always been sure that he never would. Three weeks later, he had a urine test — gonorrhea. Telling Jean was the hardest thing he had ever done. She never looked at him the same way after that.

Liam's voice brought Hackett back to the present. "Don't worry, old boy," Liam said in an Irish version of a proper English accent. "She's coming."

"Who's coming?"

"Who else? Your pretty woman. She's been here two weeks in a row. She likes you."

Hackett was sure that Sarah wasn't coming, positive that she had just been kind, wasn't really interested in him. "Why would she be interested in me?" he asked.

"Maybe it's her Tao."

Hackett tilted his head to one side. "Her what?"

"You know, the Buddhist Tao, her dharma, or perhaps her karma?"

Hackett drew out the word "Je-sus" into two slow syllables. "The Tao isn't Buddhist and karma is the opposite of dharma."

"Listen to who's getting all intellectual on me. I know the difference. The Tao is the path to enlightenment, very similar to what's called dharma, while your feckin' karma is your fate or what awaits you in this world while you search for enlightenment. So I humbly submit that she is following a natural path to seek out enlightenment and that path leads to you."

"That's a strange crock of shit to come from an Irishman."

Liam smiled and nodded. "Not buying it?"

Hackett shook his head from side to side. "Hardly."

"Okay, maybe it's just Tuesday. She knows you come in on Tuesday."

Hackett thought about it. It made some sense, but why would she come on Tuesdays in expectation of meeting him? He was sure that they had never talked about him being a regular Tuesday night patron, or the reason for it. Then he remembered that Sarah had been bike riding at Great Falls and he put two and two together — her biking schedule matched his mourning schedule. Maybe it was karma after all. He shouldn't underestimate Liam's bartender intuition.

His mouth formed an involuntary smile, which faded quickly in the aura of another embarrassing memory. Hackett saw himself in the elevator with Yu Lai, heard his words as he asked her out, saw her cringe. *I am so pitiful*, he told himself. *What woman would want me?*

Like a sign from heaven, Sarah appeared on the street, waving to him through the window. His chest pounded, and his guilt was replaced with excitement. She obviously hadn't been biking, as she sparkled in a silver sequin dress under the hot summer sun. He couldn't believe how beautiful she was. For a moment, he felt like he deserved her, deserved everything, even happiness.

Sarah walked in the door. Her face lit up in a radiant smile, and she bounded across the floor to Hackett, hugging him and giving him a peck on the cheek. "Why don't you take me out to a nice restaurant tonight? It's my birthday. I want to celebrate." She turned momentarily to Liam. "No offense, but I want French — champagne, escargots, crème brûlée." Her hand rose up and stirred the air with a flourish.

"None taken," Liam answered. "Even an Irishman can't eat the same good food every night."

She turned back to Hackett with a childish grin on her face. "S'il vous plait, mon ami. How about it? Will you treat me on my birthday?"

Hackett felt like he was being toyed with, but that didn't matter; it felt so good. "Sure, where should we go? Bistro Provence is pretty good."

"Nope."

"Mon Ami Gabi?"

"Nope again."

The expectant look on Sarah's face made Hackett guess again. "Brasserie Monte Carlo?"

"Nope."

"Where to then? Downtown? Your wish is my command."

"La Ferme," she answered. "J'aime La Ferme and I haven't been there in years."

"Bon, c'est bon," Hackett responded, knowing that his half-assed French must have sounded incredibly stupid.

The restaurant was a mile or so away in Chevy Chase. They left Flanagan's arm in arm and walked back to Hackett's house so that he could change into more suitable clothing. When they arrived, Sarah complimented his house in a back-handed manner — "it's so quaint and homey, really cute, but I imagined something much more grand for someone of your stature."

Hackett went up to the bedroom, changed and refreshed his cologne as quickly as he could. When he returned to the living room, he found Sarah staring at the picture of Jean on his mantle. "Your wife looks like a happy and gentle soul, just like you would deserve."

"She was." His conscious mind wanted to think of Sarah and the night which was just now beginning, but his subconscious took hold and he was transported back to the day of Jean's death. He felt the familiar sense of foreboding as if he were once again standing in his bedroom right before finding her. He felt his hands on her soft chest, his weight pushing down, the crack of ribs giving way.

Hackett's mind returned to the present, his blood pulsing through his head. He managed to get a few words out. "I forgot my keys," then he turned and walked back up the stairs to collect himself.

Hackett lay down on the bed and felt the rise and fall of his chest as he tried to concentrate on his breathing and gain a measure of calm. He concentrated harder, remembering his meditation lessons, breathing in deeply and slowly. He tried to imagine the beach, waves crashing softly. He thought of Jean. "Acknowledge your thoughts and then release them," he heard his old meditation instructor tell him. It never really worked. He felt the weight of his keys in his pocket, where they had been all along. He breathed again, counting silently to prolong his exhale. In and out he breathed for two minutes before he walked back down the stairs.

In the living room again, he found Sarah holding a piece of deep red pottery that Jean had purchased at the Waverly Street Gallery. "You have such pretty and interesting things," she said, then pointed across the room. "Is that real?"

"Yes, it is. Isn't it amazing?"

Sarah put the pottery back on the end table and walked across the room to a glassed-in frame that was about eighteen inches square. "I had no idea that butterflies could get so big."

"It's not a butterfly, it's a Hercules moth. The biggest moth species in the world."

Sarah held her right hand up in front of the frame and spread her fingers. The moth's gold and brown wings spanned well beyond her fingertips and long wing tails looped down below her palm. He watched as Sarah bent her head from side to side apparently inspecting the big fat bronze belly. "We travelled all the way to Papua New Guinea to find that one."

"It's Mothra," Sarah said with a laugh.

"Exactly. This is the species that inspired the old movies, though only the Japanese could turn a moth into a monster. Jean and I collected butterflies and moths, but we liked moths bests; hunting at night was so much more fun."

Hackett drifted back to the trip so many years ago. He saw Jean standing in front of a white sheet in the dark forest, a big flashlight behind her making her frizzy hair sparkle. He remembered the moment that the big moth swooped in and fluttered around Jean's head before alighting on the sheet.

"I don't need all of you," Jean had said a month earlier. "But I can't go on like this. I know that being a doctor demands a lot, still..." She paused before continuing. "You can't let it take everything we have."

At first, her words just made him mad. He thought she was being needy. How could she not understand how important his work was? It was a matter of life and death. It was her tears that finally made him understand.

"Do you love me anymore?" she asked as her body shook with sobs.

"Of course I do."

"There was a time when I knew that, a time when you held me, and it felt like you'd never let me go. Now we hardly talk. We hardly even touch each other."

So they had gone to New Guinea. Their trip was amazing: the bustling press of Asian life in the city; the native islanders in their jungle villages with their bodies painted to impress the tourists; the nights spent hunting exotic moths and camping in raised tents. On the last night in the jungle, they slipped under a single sheet on a simple mattress draped in mosquito netting. He kissed her and held her close.

"I love you," he told her. "And I swear, I will never ever let you go." Those words still buzzed in his head. He had kept his promise for a long time, but not long enough.

Hackett walked up behind Sarah, put his hand on her shoulder, felt Jean's presence once more, but this time, he told himself, it was not a burden. He walked Sarah into the study, anticipating her reaction when she saw the wall of specimens that Jean had loved to show off.

~

"Have you ever had Dom Perignon?" Sarah asked as soon as the waiter set the wine menu on the table.

Hackett looked across the table, into a wide smile. "Can't say that I have, but tonight is as good a time as any to try it."

"Really?" The word bubbled out of her mouth. "You would order it for me?" She leaned forward, bumped into the table and rose off her seat for a quick kiss on the lips. He stiffened.

"Waiter," she called in a high voice.

The waiter was only feet away, but responded with poise and courtesy, ignoring her loudness in the quiet room. "Yes, ma'am."

Sarah turned back to Hackett. "What about escargots? Have you ever had escargots?"

"Not me."

"Oh, you have to try them, too. They are divine here."

Without waiting for his response, Sarah ordered the Dom Perignon and escargots, hurrying the waiter off to push the order. Hackett tried to force thoughts of Jean out of his mind. There was no reason for guilt. The dead harbored no jealousy. He knew that, though he wasn't sure he believed it. The harder he tried to push her from his mind, the more she intruded. His thoughts bounded back and forth between the two women. He imagined Sarah naked.

"Have you ever been to the Keys? I went there a lot when I was living in Florida. I love Key West, Hemingway's house, the bar and all that, but I like a real beach better, white sand and lots of it."

Hackett pulled himself back into the conversation. "You'd love Saint Lucia," he replied, "but you'd really love the Grenadines, a string of emerald islands, aqua water and sand."

"You'll have to take me there someday," Sarah said and her lips curled into a mischievous smile.

Hackett's eyes strayed from her face, down to the v-line cut of her dress, and the soft flesh just hinted at within. He lifted his eyes quickly, not wanting to get caught. Sarah was talking rapidly, like the Energizer bunny, flitting from superlative to superlative — beaches were utterly fantastic, white sand was better than cocaine, she laughed and said she'd never really tried cocaine, but she knew sand, escargots made her delirious, she'd love to take a bath in champagne, DC is too humid in the summer, winter is too cold, time to go south for a vacation, always time to go on vacation, she thought Hackett was funny, Hackett was warm-hearted, Hackett was more interesting than any man she had ever met. She said the last thing though Hackett had hardly spoken. His face flushed and his heart raced.

When the champagne was poured, she lifted the glass close to her mouth and proclaimed, "Feel the tiny bubbles burst against your nose? Isn't that just the greatest feeling in the world?"

Hackett kept his eyes on Sarah as the waiter placed the escargots in the middle of their small table. It was like watching a child at an ice cream stand. Her face lit up and she fanned her hand over the plate, directing Hackett to smell the garlic. Sarah gabbed on, and Hackett knew that he would be annoyed if someone else spoke so much. He tested all sorts of words in his mind, imagining the conversation, trying to make sure that he would say the right thing, but very little made it beyond his restrictive filter.

After the escargots and champagne, he ordered a bottle of Château de Beaucastel Châteauneuf-du-Pape—1995, or rather he acceded to her suggestion, the price be damned. When he took a bite of their chateaubriand, he decided that French food and her company were both worth the price. He loved the silky texture and the succulent buttery flavor of both the meat and her voice. Most of all, he savored the sight of Sarah across the table. She was beautiful and she looked like she was enjoying the meal even more than he. Her brown eyes, little rounded nose and soft cheeks were enticing. The more he drank the less he noticed the contrast between her dark eyebrows and blonde hair, or the mascara that was too heavily applied.

He sipped his wine, his eyes glancing away occasionally, not wanting to stare. For the first time that evening, he thought of her son and the doctor in him stepped back to the forefront. He was speaking before he realized it. "I'm worried about Aaron," he said. "His blood tests still don't make much sense."

"Not tonight," she said sharply. Her words were followed by a loud and visible exhale. After drawing a new breath, she appeared to calm, and remained silent for a few more seconds. Hackett was about to speak, when she began talking again.

"He is going to put me in an early grave. I've told you before, he is out of control. He's doing drugs, and I don't think he's taking his meds."

"Well, not taking meds would explain the tests, but..."

"Not tonight, I will not have him wreck my birthday dinner. We can talk about it later, or maybe even never. I don't care."

They sat eating in silence for some time. Hackett's mind became consumed with Aaron. He had questioned Aaron about his medications, and had been convinced that Aaron was taking them. Sarah had also told him previously that she was sure of it, because she was double checking. Hackett couldn't visualize a sound explanation. He didn't believe that Aaron would deliberately risk seizures. Taking drugs could explain it, but because of Sarah's previous concerns, Hackett had ordered a tox screen. The kid was clean, except for modest readings of THC, and they were so low it could have been secondhand smoke. Perhaps Aaron was just forgetful, and was too embarrassed to admit it. But why would he suddenly become forgetful? He had been taking medication for years and it was part of his daily routine. There was another possibility, one that Hackett couldn't see as the answer. Aaron could be seeking attention. He could be missing his meds on purpose in order to bring back the seizures. No, that just wasn't possible. Everything he knew told him that Aaron was a pretty well-adjusted kid. Hackett returned to stress as a possible answer. He could think of no other explanation.

"Shall we have crème brûlée?"

Hackett looked up, startled by her voice. Sarah displayed a happy smile. The discomfort of the previous conversation no longer registered. "Sure," he replied.

After dessert, Sarah insisted on a glass of cognac, and then another. With alcohol coursing through his veins, Hackett saw the world in a whole new light. This beautiful woman was interested in him, and he in her, genuinely interested. It wasn't just the feeling of the growing erection in his pants. He enjoyed her company, wanted to see her again, to go on seeing her. He dreamed of falling in love, but what struck him most of all was that Jean had quietly slipped out of his thoughts. A window had opened and the fresh air had carried his preoccupation away.

~

Hackett pressed the button on his key, and the horn blasted out a quick response. "Whoops, wrong one," he said. He looked down at the keys in his hand and they blurred before his eyes. Concentrating, he pushed the unlock button and heard the familiar sound of the driver side latch popping. He pressed again and heard the remaining latches in unison. Hackett watched Sarah open the door and lower herself into the passenger seat. He did the same, lightly hitting his head in the process. Once inside the car, he fumbled with his keys, shoving his hand back and forth, awkwardly missing the ignition. It was as if his mind could not direct his hand to do the simplest of actions. Hackett seldom drank to excess, and though he knew he was drunk, he didn't want to admit that to Sarah and risk spoiling the evening, so he told himself that he could drive. Finally, he felt the key slip in and heard the motor come to life. The sound sobered him. He abruptly turned the engine back off.

"I'm drunk," he announced and felt better for saying it.

"Me, too," Sarah replied, "but your house is little more than a mile away. I'm sure you can safely drive that far."

Hackett was about to turn the ignition once more, but his hand didn't obey. He laughed out loud.

"What's so funny?" Sarah asked.

"I have apraxia, it's a message from God. We should walk."

"You have what?"

"Apraxia. I don't really have it, it is a neurological disorder indicated by the failure of your brain to direct your hand to complete simple everyday behaviors. I have alcohol-induced apraxia." The laughter shook his body.

"Do you really expect me to walk a mile back to your house?" Hackett could see annoyance in her expression, but then it was gone and she was smiling again. "Why not," she continued. "If you're too drunk to drive, we have no choice, and if you're too drunk, that means I'm too drunk, and I'll have to sleep over." A radiant smile arced across her lips.

When Sarah leaned over and kissed him, Hackett nearly fainted.

~

Hackett awoke to a whole flock of birds chirping so loudly outside his window that he thought he might be in an Alfred Hitchcock movie. He lifted his right hand and cradled his head, checking to make sure it was still there. Slowly, he rolled over and looked at Sarah, asleep next to him. The sight of her was almost enough to wipe the cobwebs of his hangover out of his head. He moved slowly and quietly so that he would not disturb her. Once standing, he looked down at her again, staring at the breast that peeked out from under his sheet. He stood still for a moment, unable to move. He could not believe that she was there, so beautiful, so unlike anyone he'd ever dreamed would be interested in him.

He made his way to the bathroom, self-consciously shutting the door, something he never would have done while Jean slept. He sat down on the toilet so as to avoid noise, and even then, aimed his pee so that it wouldn't splatter in the water of the bowl. There in the almost quiet, he thought of Jean, and wondered if she would mind. He told himself that it was a stupid question, she would not, she could not mind. It was just him once more allowing himself to be consumed by the past.

He tried to quiet his thoughts and enjoy the moment. He stood and flushed the toilet without hesitation, as if to prove to himself that he was unafraid and in control. He washed his hands, dried them and opened the door.

That's when he saw them. He stood in the bathroom door, frozen once more, but this time it wasn't Sarah's beauty. This time, he saw his own two shoes lying on the floor by his bed. One shoe in particular drew and fixed his attention, its laces loose and free. Every day for four years, he had been careful to put his shoes away in the closet. Last night, in drunken anticipation, he had flung them off carelessly and focused not on Jean, but on Sarah.

He stepped backward, as if he were backing away from a coiled rattlesnake, and closed the bathroom door. He choked with emotion. He didn't want to think about it, especially after last night. He wanted to focus on the touch of Sarah's hand, his mouth on her breast, the ecstasy of entering her, but he could not. The memories flooded in.

It had been a Tuesday in August, typically hot and sweaty. He had come home from work, unlocked the door and called Jean's name. Hackett fell into it, the memory surrounding him as it so often did.

Jean didn't respond. The silence surprised him. It was Tuesday. She should have been home preparing the weekly meal for the homeless at her church. He walked upstairs to change out of his work clothes, anticipating a cold beer and a quiet evening. He didn't mind eating alone. It was Tuesday. Jean would eat at the church.

He called her name once more at the top of the stairs, but again she did not answer. An unsettled feeling crept into his mind. Something was wrong. Hackett opened the door, tried to release the feeling of horrible portent. He could not. He stood in their bedroom, time slowing. He saw Jean's tennis shoes on the floor. His eyes focused on one shoe which was tipped over, the laces loose and running across the floor all by themselves. That little out of place picture set his emotions into freefall. Fear gripped him. He turned and was compelled forward. When he opened the bathroom door, he found her sprawled on the floor.

His training kicked in first, his emotions followed. Little warmth was left in her body. He tried to bring her back. Chest compression after chest compression, he frantically worked on her through the sounds of breaking ribs. Tears flooded from his eyes and drowned her face. He knew that his efforts would not help, but he could not stop. And then he heard her voice, soft and whispering within his own mind, *I am still here*, she told him. *Don't let me die, please don't let me die.*

He pushed his hands deep into her chest, his rhythm quickening involuntarily. He bent and put his lips to hers, trying to breathe life into her lungs, blowing until his face was blue, willing to give her every atom of his own oxygen. No response was evident in her body, but he heard her voice again. *Help me.*

Now, sitting in his bathroom, with a lovely woman in his bed, her words taunted him. He had felt death in her cold skin, but her voice had been so real. He fell back into his memories once again. He was there, hands pushing through the soft flesh of her breasts, no longer feeling much resistance from her bones.

*Where's Amy?* his dead wife had asked.

"In California," he told her. "She loves you. Please don't die."

Hackett had kept talking to her as he worked. Time passed.

He had no idea how much. When EMTs finally arrived, he stood back exhausted and defeated. "Let her be. She's gone," was all that was left for him to say.

The sense of foreboding from those moments, enveloped his consciousness, smothering other thoughts, as he stood in the bathroom, another woman lying in Jean's place. There was no joy.

In the days and months that followed Jean's death, he heard her voice frequently, calling him, haunting him. His complicity in her death weighed on him. He should have prevented it. He felt a deep need, a compulsion to connect the dots and discover what he had missed. Perhaps there had been a change in her that morning as she rose from bed. Perhaps it had been there in her voice over the phone when she called him at work. How could he have saved her? He had so many unanswered questions. He had failed her, just as he had failed her with the dancer in Las Vegas, but this time there was no way to make amends, no way to prove that he was better than the sum of his weaknesses.

In those first months, he tortured himself with the notion that Jean's voice had been real. He was sure that she had been present while he tried to save her. He prayed that she lived on in death, hoped that even as he failed, she had a soft landing on the other side. Her voice became his torture.

And so he understood death as he never had before. He understood grieving and pain. He understood what it meant to miss someone and to know that he would never see that person again. He understood loneliness. Most of all he understood the foolish and painful illusion that life might somehow continue. There was no voice. Jean had not talked to him from beyond. He had tortured himself from within. She was dead. He had learned to accept that cold hard reality. Anger had settled into the dark hole that was his memory of that day, poisoning his spirit. For weeks he stayed home from work, for months the blackness held him captive, until slowly he emerged into the world once more. His sanity hinged on his acceptance that Jean's voice had been an illusion. Death was just death.

"I love you," he said aloud to the empty bathroom, no longer caring that Sarah was there. *I love you*, he imagined Jean's reply, once again so real, so present.

Hackett stood at the sink, flushing his face with cold water, trying to collect himself enough to go back out to Jean's bed and to the new woman sleeping upon it. Guilt lashed him. He didn't really know this woman. He had no idea why she had slept with him, doubted that there was any real possibility that she could be attracted to him when she wasn't drunk.

~

That first morning Sarah had excused herself, telling him she wanted to go home and change. She pleasantly kissed him good-bye and when she was gone, the dense haze of depression settled around him like an autumn fog. He tried to concentrate on her naked body and the feel of her underneath him as they made love, but his mind would not cooperate. He flitted back and forth between the guilt of betraying Jean and worry that it would never happen again. Later that day, the phone rang and he heard Sarah's cheerful voice. She told him she had fun and wanted to see him again. He felt his burden begin to lift.

Hackett proceeded cautiously at first. They went for walks in Georgetown, and on the C&O Canal. They went out together for dinner. They watched movies. They had brunch and sipped champagne. She invited him over for dinner with Aaron. And of course, she slept over again. Within weeks, Hackett asked her to go on vacation. Through it all, he told no one, except Liam.

# Chapter 7

H ackett sat in Jean's red leather chair as his fingers punched out the digits of his daughter's phone number. For years, he had tried calling Amy from the office or the hospital. Invariably, they would get cut off, usually in mid-sentence. It was Amy who finally told him to stop. And so Hackett had developed a practice of only calling her from home.

On the third ring, Amy's bright voice greeted him. "Hey, Pops."

"How's my girl today?" Hackett asked.

"I'm fine, Dad. No need to grill me on symptoms."

Two years earlier, Hackett himself had diagnosed Amy's MS. It was one more shock that had nearly unraveled him. At least it was the garden variety that relapsed occasionally, but was not yet progressing. With any luck she would live a long and productive life. Still, it was another burden sitting heavy atop his grief. MS could turn progressive with little notice, and could become a debilitating disease. He worried all the time.

"You sure?" It was a ritual he couldn't stop. "Any numbness in your extremities? Trouble walking? Fatigue?"

"Please, Dad, I'm fine. There's just one thing bothering me."

"What's that?"

"My father is annoying me, again."

"Can't help it. Fatherhood and medicine is an overwhelming combo."

They settled into small talk, until it was Amy's turn to trot out a well-worn question. "Any new love prospects?"

Hackett had meant to tell Amy about Sarah, but each time he

tried, something held him back. Objectively, he knew Amy wouldn't mind, but it still felt like he was cheating on Jean. Who would tell their daughter that?

Once again, he said "No."

Amy told him about a young man she had met at a party, nothing serious, but he was nice, and according to her, quite handsome, too. "And such a firm ass."

Hackett winced, and Amy's laughter rolled out. Hackett felt lucky that she confided in him.

"Cuter than that hairy guy?" Hackett asked.

"Much cuter and much less hairy." They both laughed. A few months before, Amy had broken up with a guy. His name had actually been Harry. When Hackett asked Amy why, she said the guy reminded her of Hackett.

"I thought girls were supposed to like guys who reminded them of their father."

"But, Dad," Amy laughed, "we went to the beach and he took off his shirt." Her laugh turned to a cackle. "There was hair everywhere. I couldn't help it, my words just slipped out. 'You have quite a pelt,' I said, and then I heard Mom's voice in my head. 'My God, Hackett, let me shave your back, it looks like a beaver pelt.' I laughed so hard that he wouldn't even talk to me again."

Eventually, the conversation turned to the wedding Amy was coming home for.

"Can't wait," Hackett said. In the split second that followed, he imagined telling her about Sarah.

"I gotta go, Dad," Amy said, cutting him off.

"Okay, honey. I love you, see you soon."

"Love you too, Dad," and she was gone.

~

The week before Hackett and Sarah were supposed to leave for Hawaii, Amy flew home. Before she arrived, Hackett combed the house, trying to eliminate any trace of Sarah. In the short-term parking lot at Dulles Airport, he waited nervously.

"I'm working night shifts at the hospital this weekend," he

had told Sarah, which was true for Saturday and Sunday, but not Friday when Amy arrived.

Amy walked out of the airport doors and stepped into the crosswalk. Hackett squirmed in his seat. His lunch churned in his stomach. *I have met someone.* He rehearsed the words in his mind. *She's really nice. I think you'll like her.* He saw Sarah as he thought Amy might — her heavy makeup, and her none too subtle sexuality. He felt an overwhelming urge to run away. Hackett opened the door and adjusted his belt, trying to relieve the discomfort, then walked to meet his daughter.

Amy talked through most of the ride home, telling him little things that happened over the last week — she had done really well on a project at work, her friend Shelly was pregnant with twins, her friend Mary had invited an ex-boyfriend to the wedding, even though the boy was still in love with her, worse, Mary had lied and told her fiancé that the boy was just an old high school friend, another friend couldn't come to the wedding because she had been in a car accident and broken her pelvis. Hackett listened, nodding, smiling and saying yes every once in a while. Amy talked and talked, covering Hackett's silence. The Dulles access road gave way to the beltway, which in turn gave way to River Road.

"What's the matter, Dad? You're awful quiet."

"Just thinking about work."

"Well don't. Your wonderful daughter is home for the weekend. I insist that I occupy your every thought."

My God, Hackett loved this girl. He knew other men had daughters that they loved and were close to, but his heart told him that their relationship couldn't compare to what he had with Amy. She, more than anything else, had kept him alive after Jean died. If only she would move back east.

Hackett opened the door and Amy walked into Flanagan's, squeezing past the people who waited for the music to begin on Friday nights. "Hello, Liam," she announced, waving over the heads in front of her.

Liam lifted the hinged counter and stepped from behind the

bar to greet her with a hug. Then he shook Hackett's hand, before turning back to Amy. "What brings you back home?"

"A wedding, and the old man, of course. You know how much he misses me."

"Yes, he has told me that a time or two, but he sure is acting a little less lonely lately."

Hackett raised his eyebrows at Liam, then quickly added, "Yes, I am trying not to be such a sad sack anymore. Used to be a time when I just sat at the bar and stared into my glass. Lately, I have even been seen talking to the other customers." He smiled at Amy, trying to convey humor, but he saw a question percolating up into her eyes. He talked quickly to change the subject, addressing Liam.

"Amy's friend is getting married. They've known each other since they were four. They went to pre-school together at Jean's church."

The mention of Jean's name hung in the air alongside Sarah's invisible presence until Liam directed the conversation elsewhere.

Alone at their table, Hackett stared into his beer. Both of his hands were wrapped around the near-empty pint glass. He slowly twisted it in one direction, tilted it, looked at the last remnants of foam clinging to the inside and then twisted it back in the other direction.

"Dad," Amy said.

He looked up as her worried face morphed into a funny grin. "Are you dating someone?"

"I'm sorry. I should have told you."

Amy peppered Hackett with questions. Even the easy ones made him squirm.

"How did you meet?"

"Her son is my patient." Hackett thought he saw an eyebrow arch up.

"How long have you been dating?"

"A few months." Another eyebrow.

"Why didn't you tell me? I must have asked you about women five times in the last couple of months." Amy smiled.

"I was embarrassed."

"Oh, Dad." Her smile broadened. "That's silly."

Then the questions got harder.

"How old is she?"

"Forty-two."

"Forty-two?" The pitch of Amy's voice lifted higher.

"Yes, forty-two."

"Wow! I guess that's okay; at least she's not younger than me. That would be seriously weird. Do you have a picture?"

Hackett pulled out his wallet and handed Amy the photo that Sarah had given him two weeks earlier. He had been so excited by it, even proud. She looked like a model. But it was hard to hand it across the table. He cringed when she studied the photo.

"She's absolutely beautiful." Hackett noticed that Amy had lost her smile.

"You think she is too pretty for your old man?"

"I didn't say that."

"You didn't need to."

Amy congratulated Hackett and wished him happiness, but the conversation slowed. Hackett found himself staring into his beer glass once again. He wondered what Amy was thinking, wondered if she would say anything if she disapproved. He knew she wouldn't.

"I know she's a little out of my range, but we get along really well."

"That's good, Dad."

Silence.

"We're going on vacation together to Hawaii next week." Hackett's words were greeted by another awkward pause.

"You are?" Amy said, then he could see her holding something back. "That should be nice."

Sarah's name wasn't mentioned again.

# Chapter 8

Hackett walked hand in hand with Sarah in the sheltered shallow water by the mouth of the Lumaha'i River on the north shore of the island of Kauai. Just to his east, Puff the Magic Dragon had played in Hanalei Bay. To his west, civilization faded into the rugged terrain of the Nepali Coast where Spielberg's T-Rex walked the earth. Over the tall white sand bank in front of him lay the steep beach that native Hawaiians had long ago called Lumaha'i — "beach that crushes bone." The scene around him evoked none of that violent echo of the past. Clear water stretched in a shallow, expansive pool, narrowing ahead of him where the dunes advanced to within yards of a rocky peninsula and waves rushed forward, mingling with river water. He felt Sarah's hand slowly slip from his, their fingers lingering upon each other for one last second before they fell apart — a wonderful, tender feeling that he could not have imagined a few short months before.

Sarah bent down and examined a shell, but Hackett's eyes were transfixed by the mouth of the river where waves rhythmically rolled in and out, one after the other marking the passage of time like a mammoth natural clock. He felt the soothing hand of nature, thought of meditation, and understood why the ocean was so often the picture that people would conjure to relax and clear the troubles from their mind. He thought of Sarah and looked back. She was now a few yards behind him, kneeling at the edge of the water, sifting sand and shells between her fingers, her breasts exposed and slightly red from the bright Pacific sun. She, too, was like a meditative image. She calmed his anxieties, made him feel secure in his future.

Hackett walked toward the mouth, the distance between him and Sarah growing slowly wider. He looked over his shoulder, saw her watching him, and waved. Her lips turned up into a joyous smile as her hand lifted in the air, returning his salute as a gentle breeze toyed with her hair. The closer he got to the mouth of the river, the louder the sound of ocean crashing against earth, like the gods were slamming trees against giant cymbals. This was heaven, he thought, at least his vision of heaven on earth, not the fantasy of an afterlife where your troubles magically vanished in God's comforting light. This was something he could believe in, a heaven where the natural beauty of the universe combined with the great fortune of meeting a beautiful woman in a bar and falling in love. He prayed that it would last forever. Once again his eyes drifted back to her, now ambling leisurely toward him. She waved again. He could see her breasts moving with the motion of her arm, remembered her underneath him. Yes, heaven.

At the mouth of the river, the rush of sea water and the spray of foam bubbled. Waves rolled on in their infinite cycle. He looked across the narrow channel at the beautiful shore line on the other side. It felt so close he wanted to touch it, and he felt an irresistible urge to go there and stand under the trees. Hackett stepped forward into the shallow water, once, twice and a third time. The sand gave way to a rocky bottom. He stepped from rock to rock, enjoying their cold hard strength beneath his toes. He set both feet upon the next rock, a rounded behemoth that lifted him higher in the water. He perched like a long-legged crane in the surf, water and foam caressing his legs. Behind him he heard a voice among the crashing waves, faint but urgent. He turned his head and saw Sarah waving at him. She looked frantic.

"What?" he yelled.

A moment before, the world around him had felt soft and tranquil, now the cymbals of the gods were again crashing, the sound of surf rumbling in his ears so hard that it was drowning out his voice.

"It's dangerous! Come back," he heard Sarah's high-pitched voice fighting with the din of the ocean. Hackett smiled and waved, then took a step off the big rock. As he did, his foot slipped and a wave hit him, knocking him off balance and into the froth. He felt foolish as he struggled for footing, finally rising out of the water and wiping the salty ocean from his face. He looked up to see Sarah laughing. He could not make out her words, but she was motioning at him to come back.

He took a step toward her and felt a change in the world. The water was suddenly rushing past Hackett's legs, dragging the entire river into the sea. Hackett struggled to maintain balance. His heart jumped. He turned to the ocean, saw it rising in front of him, just as a gigantic wave crashed over his shoulders, driving him upriver into the water and the rocks. His knuckles jammed against stone, pain shot through his knee, his head felt like it was being cracked open. The water slowed and he tried to stand, but the surf now pulled him backward, sending him tumbling again over the same rocks. He fought, but there was no way to gain control. He could not tell how far he was being dragged, but he knew where he was going, out into the sea, into the powerful currents that natives had told stories about over the millennia to keep children out of danger. Soon his tumbling and rolling stopped. He was in deep water. He could still feel Poseidon's pull. He flailed and clutched at the water until his head bobbed to the surface. Though not far from the place he had fallen, he was still slipping quickly backward. Hackett frantically dug his hands into the water, tried to claw his way back to shore, but it was no use.

In front of him, he saw the river from where he had come. To his left the steep white sand of Lumaha'i Beach looked peaceful, nearly empty. A couple of women sunbathed, oblivious to his plight. A man walked down the sand in the opposite direction, not knowing Hackett was being sucked away. Hackett yelled. Only the waves answered. He trod water and gulped for breath, felt the current continue to pull him away from land. His eyes scanned the beach. *Swim parallel to the shore,* his own words shouted within his head, as if he were afraid he would not hear them. He swam, already felt exhaustion with his first strokes. Panic gripped him. He gulped at the air, coughed as water splashed into his throat. Hackett told himself to calm down. The water swelled up and down around him, but no longer tossed and pulled at him. He floated, his excess weight providing welcome buoyancy so that he could catch his breath and look back at shore. The mouth of the river was receding, but the beach was still tantalizingly close. In the calm he heard a human commotion. He saw Sarah on the beach screaming and waving, a few people around her doing the same. They were telling him to swim down the beach to the east. Sarah began to run in that direction. He watched her feet slap on the wet sand, her legs flying through the air. When she got about a hundred feet ahead of him, she left the sand and plunged into the surf. Hackett thought of Pamela Anderson and Baywatch.

Once again Hackett began to move in the water. This time, telling himself not to struggle, to be patient and determined. He picked an angle that he hoped would bring him to Sarah. Stroke after stroke Hackett pushed forward. The water around him felt like Jell-O, thick and heavy, each splash of his hand a struggle against Poseidon. And with each stroke, he felt his chest tighten.

Seconds felt like minutes, minutes eternity. Hackett's breathing became difficult. He again gulped air, wondered if he would make it, thought about death, and the brutal reality of his lungs filling with water.

When he finally reached Sarah, he was drained, body and soul. He wanted to sink into the water, the only way he could imagine finding peace.

"Go back," he said. "I can't make it."

"Shut up," she replied and grabbed his arm roughly, rolling him over on his back.

"What are you doing?" he asked as she threw her arm around his neck and under his chin.

"Will you shut up," she howled, spitting salt water against the back of his head.

"You'll drown with me." Hackett's voice was soft, strained, without hope, pitiful. "Save yourself," he told her.

"If you don't shut the fuck up, I'll drown you myself."

Hackett felt their slow progress inch by inch, listened to Sarah's labored breath as she towed him toward the beach. He didn't struggle, said no more, just waited for the water to claim them both. All the while, he felt her breasts against his back and saw the sorrow of his own fading future.

It felt like an eternity.

~

Three days later, Hackett and Yu Lai walked back to Neurology after a consultation with a maternity patient. He reached up and scratched his fingernails against a thin line of scabs at the top of his forehead. He looked at Yu Lai, saw a student, nothing more. His infatuation with her felt distant, as if it were a childhood embarrassment. His behavior could have ruined their relationship, but she had never treated him differently. There had never been an ounce of accusation in her tone. He knew that she was a better person than he. For that he was thankful.

"Aren't you going to say anything about your vacation?" Yu Lai asked. Hackett blushed. "You obviously got some sun," she continued.

"It was beautiful. I had never been to Hawaii before. The Na Pali Coast was incredible, looked just like Jurassic Park."

"Who'd you go with?"

The red in Hackett's cheeks turned to cranberry. "Just a friend." He paused. "What about our patient? What is your diagnosis?"

"I haven't got a clue," Yu Lai answered.

"Think," Hackett demanded, but there was no bossiness in his tone. He shifted to full teaching mode. "Imagine these symptoms on someone else." Yu Lai walked on, as she tried to puzzle it out, but it was obvious that she was stuck. He teased her with a hint: "Make believe the patient was a young boy for a second."

"A young boy that just delivered a child?" she sputtered.

"Very funny, Doctor." Hackett swung his elbow out and bumped her, causing her to stumble just a little. "You can leave the pregnancy aside for one moment, but it is also important."

Yu Lai stopped walking, reached her hand up and scratched her head. He knew that she would figure this out. In her, Hackett saw a long line of students stretching back through the years. They were his legacy, and Yu Lai was one of the best.

"Muscular dystrophy?" Yu Lai asked obviously unsure of herself.

"Now you're on the right track."

"I am? I never would have guessed if you didn't say young boy, and I still don't see it."

"Well, that's because it isn't muscular dystrophy, or at least we don't call it that anymore."

"CMT?" Yu Lai's voice rose an octave on the M. "How the fuck did you guess that?"

Hackett laughed at her profanity and the loss of inhibition that it represented. In his day, residents, even chief residents like Yu Lai, would never let down their guard around senior docs. At times, he resented these young doctors their relative freedom. He felt like he had been trained on another planet.

The tiny touch of resentment dissolved. "I told you, think atypical. When can late onset CMT begin?" he asked. CMT stood for Charcot-Marie-Tooth disease, a degenerative nerve and muscle condition. They talked through the symptoms once again, allowing Yu Lai to see what Hackett saw.

"Bingo," Hackett said when Yu Lai put the final piece of the puzzle together. "Immobility and pregnancy as well can have a negative impact. I think our unfortunate patient hit the trifecta of CMT, heredity, pregnancy and immobility, even if she is a little old."

"Jesus, I don't know how you do it sometimes. You make me feel like I will never be truly competent in this field." The young doctor pushed Hackett playfully.

Hackett let the compliment wash over him, the discomfort between them long gone. When they made it back to neurology,

Hackett saw Ella Mae crouched at the nurses' station searching through drawers for something.

"What's the good word, Nurse Ratched?" Hackett said with a happy grin stretching across his face.

"Doctophelia," she replied with a smile that looked slightly condescending.

"What in heaven's name is that?" Hackett asked.

"That's when an aging doctor falls for a younger woman and starts smiling all the time. And I hear she's a patient on top of everything else."

Wrinkles furrowed Ella Mae's brow, but she said no more.

"So my love life is the talk of the town, I take it. By the way, Nurse Pulaski, she isn't a patient; her son is."

"Is that so?" Ella Mae answered. "You think that makes a big difference?"

"Yes, it does, and there is no reason to be spreading rumors."

"What do you expect when you take a girl to Hawaii?" Ella Mae stressed the word "girl," almost gagging on it.

The red hue of embarrassment returned to Hackett's face. "How did you know that?" He sounded more defensive than he meant to.

"We have our sources," Yu Lai chimed in. In contrast to Ella Mae's voice, Yu Lai gave off the impression of nothing more than playful teasing.

Hackett stood in puzzlement. He couldn't figure out how they knew. Then he thought of Amy. Amy loved good gossip and Ella Mae was kind of like an informal aunt to her.

"So," Yu Lai said when her laughter subsided. "When do we get to meet this woman who has cast her spell over the great doctor?"

"As a matter of fact," Hackett replied. "I was going to invite both of you over next Saturday for a barbeque to celebrate the winter solstice."

"Who has a barbeque in the winter?" Ella Mae asked.

"I got the idea from an old college friend who lives in Fair-banks. I figured if he could manage it with temperatures of thirty below and an hour of sunlight, we could manage it here in DC."

"Sounds pretty damn stupid to me, like a grown man trying to impress a girl." The anger in Ella Mae's voice was obvious.

"She's really nice; you'll like her. Plus she's already saved my life."

Hackett told them about Lumaha'i, told them how he hadn't known that Sarah had been a lifeguard in high school and again when she had lived in Florida. He described it all second by second, leaving out the fact that she had been topless, but stressing the comparison to Baywatch, which broke Yu Lai down with laughter.

"She sounds like quite a woman," Yu Lai said when Hackett finished.

"Sounds like a girl young enough to be your daughter," Ella Mae added.

~

Tupac Shakur's tremulous voice vibrated through Sarah's ear drums and shook the rag top on her BMW as the dead rapper told a story of people getting shot and no one caring. It was Aaron's CD. Ordinarily she would not have played it, but it felt right today. She absorbed its staccato rhythms, dystopian violence and most of all its anger as she drove her shiny BMW past the run-down, half-deserted businesses on New York Avenue then made a right on Bladensburg Road, following it past the cemetery and into the sullen, garbage-strewn open air drug market of the Trinidad neighborhood.

She felt so alive with the anticipation of a bright future that she tilted her sunglasses down over her eyes. Their week in Hawaii couldn't have been better, and the fact that she had saved Hackett from drowning felt like she had been living inside a movie. Things were moving fast. She could feel him falling in love.

She let up on the gas as she approached a small liquor store. Familiar faces crowded together, brown-bagging their bottles. In the alley, a man slumped against a dumpster, urine forming a puddle at his feet. She slowed the car to a crawl, watching the young men on the sidewalk just a few feet ahead as they in turn watched her. The first time she had driven into this neighborhood it had scared her, but it had made her feel alive, too. She had watched other cars pull over, saw drivers wave and kids approach. But driving by had not been exciting enough. She had returned on foot, dressing down in blue jeans and t-shirt, a handgun tucked in her purse. That first time on foot, she just strolled by, ignoring the occasional catcall. On her next visit she talked to some of the drunks, gave them a few coins, asked them about the dealers, the words they used, their unspoken rules. Eventually, she learned the system and no longer looked strikingly out of place.

Now that she was ready to make a buy, Sarah boiled with nervous energy. She made eye contact with one boy in particular, choosing a young one on purpose, rolled the window down about two inches and nodded. He was next to her car in seconds. She judged him to be no more than thirteen.

Sarah looked serious and determined. "Heroin?" she asked him.

"My man hook you up. Back this Beemer into the alley."

"I don't think so," Sarah replied and slid her hand to the open space under her CD player, then tapped her fingers on the nine millimeter, making sure the boy saw it. "I'm not stupid. I'll be back around. If he has it, get him to the curb."

Sarah pressed the button to raise her window and pulled back into traffic. Other kids waved and yelled at her as she rolled by. She paid them no mind. Eagerness implied desperation; desperation made you easy. Sarah did not want to look easy.

She drove two more blocks before cutting back on Sixteenth Street and returning to Bladensburg Road a couple of blocks above the liquor store. This time an older boy stepped forward. He looked nineteen, maybe twenty.

"What do you have?" Sarah asked.

"Brown rock, two fifty a gram."

"I have two hundred. Do we have a deal or not?" She flashed the cash with her right hand, far enough away that he couldn't grab it. The rest of the deal was done in thirty seconds.

# Chapter 9

Hackett's backyard was blanketed in snow. Everything was ready for his winter solstice barbeque. It was even better than he had dared to hope. The deck was swept clean. Tables and chairs were surrounded by an array of six tall kerosene heaters that he had rented. Their brilliant heat was so effective that he almost felt like he was inside the house.

"Do it again," he said in a voice loud enough to be heard over the small four horsepower engine. He couldn't believe that it was cold enough for the machine to work.

Alejandro, the young man from the rental company, waved his hand in acknowledgement and snow sprayed up into the air, beautiful against the blue sky. Within seconds fine white icy crystals showered over the deck. Hackett raised his arms over his head as if accepting a gift from God. "They are going to love this," he said aloud.

The excitement in Hackett had been building for days. It was another example of how Sarah was bringing him back to life. He could hardly remember getting this kind of pleasure from such a simple thing as throwing a party. It reminded him of the first time Jean had taken him on a moth hunt, trudging up a small hill at night, setting up the backdrop, turning on the light, each act small and boring under other circumstances, yet filled with excitement because a young Jean was by his side. Hackett conjured a vision from his memory — the wings of a beautiful pale green luna moth fluttered then went still as it alighted on the illuminated white sheet. He remembered its beauty, the haunting eyes that were printed on its wings. It had been the first big moth he had seen. The sight of it, and the fact that he was with Jean, had hooked him on the hunt.

The engine cut out and the snow ended, but Hackett stared upward. He wanted to dive into his memories, recapture the sparkling beacons that had dazzled him so, but the illusion was fleeting and dissolved, leaving a crisp blue sky in its place. A few minutes later Sarah walked onto the deck and shrieked in delight, before wrapping her arms around Hackett.

Aaron stepped through the door behind her. "This is fucking awesome."

"Watch your mouth," Sarah said, and Hackett could see that the boy had triggered the trip line of her anger.

Hackett motioned to Alejandro, the little engine roared back into life and soon it was snowing again.

"Look at that." Aaron beamed. "You have snow and the neighbors don't have squat." The boy paused, winked at his mother and said, "Absolutely friggin' awesome, huh, Ma?"

Hackett led Sarah down the steps onto the small brick patio and up to the brand new outdoor fireplace he had purchased at Home Depot. Firewood was stacked in a crisscross pattern in the metal base over the top of two starter logs which he had bought to make sure that the fire would catch on the first try. He handed Sarah a six-inch long butane lighter and held her hand, guiding her to the base where the end of a starter log was exposed. Hackett's eyes wandered over her, taking her in, but he realized that he saw something more in her than beauty and felt something more than lust. It was hope. The sorrow that had dwelt within for years had lifted in the last weeks. He thought about work, realized the days were passing more easily, death was a lesser weight dragging him down. He fantasized about being his younger self, happy and confident, without guilt in failure. Yes, he could be happy with her. She was not Jean, but with her there was new light.

By three-thirty, more than twenty people stood together in two groups, some under the warmth of the gas heaters on the deck, others around the fire on the patio. Hackett and Aaron stood alone next to the open grill as Hackett flipped burgers and sausage.

"She's a doctor?" Aaron asked Hackett, his eyes fixed on Yu Lai who stood with Ella Mae and her date at the fire. "I thought she was a college student. She even looks like she could still be in high school. She's hot."

"Yes, she is," Hackett answered before realizing how he sounded. "A doctor, I mean, she's a doctor."

Aaron laughed. "Don't worry, Doc, I won't tell Mom that you think the cute little doctor is hot. Mom would just start acting weird anyway. You know she's seriously psycho, Doc, don't you?"

Hackett returned Aaron's smile. "I think she is wonderful."

"Yeah, you'll learn."

Hackett dismissed the tension between the boy and his mother as the typical teenage drama. He had switched Aaron's medication a month earlier, having never figured out why it wasn't working. Although Aaron hadn't had another seizure, the last blood tests were still off. In more than twenty years of practice, he'd never seen anything like it.

"Have you made up your mind about college?" he asked.

"I can't very well make up my mind until I get accepted, but I don't think I want to go to Georgetown anymore, even if I'm lucky enough to get in. It's too expensive. You should hear Mom whine about money. Plus, it's too close to home. I'm kinda leaning toward the University of Colorado. That might be far enough away."

"What about Catholic University? Your mother talks a lot about that."

"No fucking way. Go to college where she works. Ain't happenin', even if I have to pay every cent myself."

Hackett felt bad about the tension between them. Sarah badgered Aaron too much for Hackett's taste, and Hackett didn't think Aaron deserved it. He was just another teenager trying to stretch his wings.

"I had a friend who went to school in Boulder. He loved it. It's a great town. The mountains are great. Denver is great. You could do a lot worse than that, but don't tell your mother I said that."

As they talked, Yu Lai and Ella Mae turned and walked in their direction, Ella Mae's date trailing behind, looking out of place. Hackett wondered who this guy was.

~

"I want to talk to you about Parnell's study again, and I brought reinforcements this time," Yu Lai said as she stepped up beside the grill.

She had continued to push for Hackett's support in joining the "death experience" study as she called it, and apparently was making one last push before following through with her threat to present the proposal on her own. In actuality, it wasn't much of a threat. Hackett knew that it didn't stand a chance without his support.

"Tell Doctor Metzger what you told me, Ella Mae."

"You need to support that study," Ella Mae said in the same forceful tone Hackett was used to hearing when she addressed the nursing staff.

"I do?" he responded, the words rising to a high pitch.

"Yes, you do!"

"And, why is that?"

"Because your stupid objections are narrow-minded and insulting."

The words were like a slap. Hackett had felt an uncomfortable distance between himself and Ella Mae since he returned from Hawaii, but he wasn't prepared for this frontal assault. He said nothing.

"Doctor Wang tells me that you think experiencers are either hallucinating idiots or frauds," Ella Mae continued.

The word "experiencers" jolted Hackett again, another warning to back off. It was what some of those who had near-death experiences called themselves. He always thought of that particular brand of people as 'the near-death cult'.

"I never used those words," he answered.

"Well, Doctor Wang says that you made it quite clear how you felt," Ella Mae shot back. "And I object to that kind of narrow-minded garbage — people who haven't died, questioning the veracity of those of us who have."

"You had a near-death experience?" He looked at Ella Mae, but felt Jean's presence instead, her skin pale in death, the sound of her cracking ribs, the taste of her lifeless mouth. Hackett recalled the words he had conjured from Jean's lifeless body as he tried to resuscitate her. *Save me. I'm still here.* He experienced a shadow of the frantic fear that had assaulted him, emotion so charged that his body had felt like it was in freefall.

"Death experience," Ella Mae corrected. "That's right, Hackett. I'm one of them. Are you going to tell me that I made it all up, that I am a naïve fool?"

"When I said that people made things up, I was referring to the imbecile who said that he died and relived the history of the world, all the way back to the beginning and then forward four hundred years into the future. I was in no way saying that everyone who has a near-death experience is a fraud."

Hackett tried to listen, but alongside Ella Mae's words, memories continued to play out in his mind. Jean had not forgiven him for the girl in Las Vegas, and she had not forgiven him for letting her die. He wanted to run away from this conversation.

"It's a death experience, nothing near about it." Ella Mae's voice was challenging him, taunting him. "So you think I was hallucinating?" she said.

He broke, his outburst erupting like a volcano, showering fire across the yard, singeing the unfortunate onlookers. "Yes, it was a goddamn hallucination. People die. They don't talk to you. They don't come back. If you had really died, you'd be dead, just like Jean."

There was only a momentary silence before Ella Mae continued. "I'm sorry, Hackett, but this is not about Jean and it's not about you. It's about me. I was the one who drowned in that river. It was my heart that stopped."

Hackett and Ella Mae stared silently across the chasm that separated them, so unlike the space that normally stood between them. Finally, Yu Lai spoke and apologized for bringing up the subject. Hackett seemed to calm, but Ella Mae's eyes still smoldered.

"Tell me, he who knows everything, what is consciousness?"

Yu Lai tried to intercede again, but Hackett smothered her words with his response. "We don't really know."

"That's right. You doubt things, simply because they are outside your experience. You know that there is absolutely nothing about the biology, chemistry or physics of the human brain that can explain consciousness, and you believe as a matter of faith, not science, that the human brain creates it. Blood provides oxygen, neurons transmit electricity, muscles contract and cause movement, but no one knows what creates thought. Your beliefs about what consciousness is and how it exists are no less a fantasy than mine. You're just making it up; at least I'm basing it on experience."

"That's not true; we can feel, touch and see. We can use our senses to test our theories. If you dismiss the facts of the real world, you might as well believe in elves and fairies."

"If you constrict the world to what you personally observe, you are condemned to ignorance. I remember you telling me about a savant that you had met. Tell me why a boy who is barely able to converse but can calculate pi to the twentieth decimal is more believable than what happened to me when I died?"

This time, it wasn't Yu Lai, it was George who interrupted, smiling widely but looking like someone had placed an ice cube up his butt. "Why don't we get a drink, Ella Mae? I think this conversation is going to melt all of this beautiful snow."

"Shut up, George." She kept her eyes on Hackett. "The fact is you cannot possibly know what happens in the moment between life and death. Your pronouncements are no more scientific than anyone else's, yet you act like you know more than God himself. Jean believed me. If you were a real friend, you would believe me, too."

The words stopped Hackett cold.

He wondered why he was arguing, what good it would do. Did it matter what Jean believed? Did it matter what he thought he had heard when Jean died? He knew that wasn't real, so why argue with Ella Mae? Why should her belief in some fairytale matter to him? He had no answers.

"You're right, Ella Mae. I don't know what happened to you. I shouldn't be so critical." He felt better for saying it, even if he wasn't sure he believed it.

~

Hackett stood silent for some time, letting the conversation unfold without him. For a while, he didn't even listen, but Aaron's excited voice pulled him back.

"I believe it," Hackett heard Aaron say. "When you have epilepsy, you need to believe in immortality, you just have to. And right before you have a seizure, when you feel the power of an aura, the overwhelming comfort in it, you know that death isn't the end. There's more than life, it's there just over the horizon, you can tell it exists even if you have no idea what it is." Aaron paused. All eyes had turned to him. He continued a little more slowly, collecting himself. "Auras pass so quickly. You want to hold onto them so bad, but you can't. As soon as you wake up from the seizure, the real world slaps you in the face, tells you that you are mortal and that the seizures will last till the day you die. In the cold light of day, after a seizure has passed, death is mighty real. It is waiting there for you, ready to drag you away at any moment."

Hackett took a small step backward, shrinking away, and the circle of people closed ever so slightly around Aaron.

"I read about a woman named Pam Reynolds, or something like that. She had a near-death experience and it changed her life. She was no longer scared of death. I'd give anything for that."

"Her name is Pam Reynolds Lowery. I've met her. She's an amazing person," Ella Mae answered.

"How wonderful it would be to be free of seizures, to be so certain that death was a myth."

When he talked about auras, Aaron's face had been bright, shining with nervous energy, but sadness now had hold of him. Ella Mae and Aaron discussed Pam Reynolds Lowery and other people who had died and lived to tell the tale. They talked about

Lowery's uncanny knack for understanding other people's emotions and reading their thoughts. They talked about a man who became a musical genius after being resuscitated, even though he had never played an instrument before. They talked about a doctor whose brain had literally been destroyed by meningitis, yet he awoke from a coma and thrived to spread the word that there was life after death. They talked until contentment filled Aaron's eyes. He compared the auras he experienced before seizures to near-death experiences — how the bright light enveloped him and washed his fear away. He talked about Joan of Arc's seizures, Aaron laughing, saying that he would have been a saint as well if he had lived 500 years ago.

Hackett listened to the conversation, relieved that he no longer felt a need to talk and defend himself. When Ella Mae related her own story, Hackett found himself surprisingly captivated. He also felt a little jealous. Ella Mae was so sure, and took such comfort from her experience. He realized that this was why she always talked about Jean in the present tense, and always told Hackett that he would see Jean again. The voices around Hackett drifted away again. He fell into an internal debate of his own. He analyzed their argument anew, told himself that Ella Mae was oversimplifying. Still, she was right in many ways. Consciousness was indeed the great mystery, every bit as unknowable as the source of the cosmos itself, maybe more so. He was a neurologist, trained to study the mind, but he hadn't thought about the mystery of consciousness in years, long ago accepting the miracle of life as a mundane fact without bothering to search for a deeper understanding. Instead, he hid behind science, as if scientific theory was always clear and enlightened. In truth, he knew that science was simply man's fallible attempt to describe nature. It wasn't immutable, it was ever changing, never perfected and very often wrong. There had always been three holy grails that man chased after in his quest to understand the world around him: the nature of God, the nature of the universe and the nature of man's own mind. Despite our long struggle to understand life through religion and science, Descartes still offered the closest thing to proof of existence — cogito ergo sum. I think, therefore, I am.

Modern physicists took Descartes a step further. Only through observation do subatomic particles take on the properties of matter. In many ways, solid matter is simply an illusion. *I observe, therefore, it is.* Some physicists even speculated that the theory of quantum mechanics could only be fully realized through a direct link to consciousness. The human brain itself being comprised of nothing but energy and space, ipso facto, all that truly exists is our consciousness.

*Is there really anything more to our existence?* Hackett mused.

It hurt his mind thinking about it. Trying to truly fathom subatomic physics and consciousness was a slippery slope that led him to confusion instead of enlightenment. It was a universe in which reality was distorted, and the impossible was proven fact.

Hackett had to agree with Ella Mae. His steadfast knowledge was full of holes and assumptions. Still, these stories of the afterlife required the abandonment of logic and a leap of faith that he was not prepared to take. He preferred the illusion of knowledge, however imperfect.

Aaron turned to Yu Lai. "What's the study that you want Doc to do?"

Yu Lai described the study, and gave a detailed description of how they would test for patient cognition of out-of-body experiences. As she talked, Sarah walked up behind Hackett and put her hands on his waist, listening for only a few seconds before speaking. "You mean that doctors and hospitals are actually going to study that malarkey?"

"Well..." Yu Lai paused in surprise. "Yes, they are, and some very prestigious hospitals have joined the study. Hopefully ours will, too."

The last word had hardly left Yu Lai's lips before Ella Mae spoke in a low but clearly agitated voice. "And don't call it malarkey when you clearly know nothing at all about it."

Hackett felt Sarah's hands slip from his hips. He watched as she took a half step away from him and raised her arms in the air as she began talking. He was reminded of a great ape projecting its dominance.

"Oh, I know all about it. I dated this guy in high school. He called it astral projection. He said he could leave his body and travel through space anywhere he wanted to go. He used to tell me he would visit me when I was naked in the shower and he tried to impress me by telling me what kind of shampoo I used. What a nutcase. Plus the idea of the dead coming back to haunt us is revolting. The dead are dead. They don't belong in this world anymore."

"It's not a silly study, Sarah," Hackett piped in, putting his hand on Sarah's back. Turning to Ella Mae, he said, "I'm sorry if I gave the impression that I thought it was." Hackett then turned his attention back to Sarah. "Out-of-body experiences have been studied before; we know that many people give very credible reports that have nothing to do with visiting people in the shower. It's a real psycho/physiological response. In fact, a lot of fighter pilots experience OBEs and a number of medical conditions can trigger them, too. It is also linked to a disorder called sleep paralysis, where the patient wakes up, but can't move. About ten percent of the population reports having an OBE at some point in their life."

Sarah smiled at Hackett. "Yeah, that sounds about right. And what percentage of the population experiences mental illness? I bet it's about the same."

Hackett desperately wanted these two women to get along, but he could do nothing more to stop the train that was rolling his way.

"Death experiences are not a joke," Ella Mae spat the words out, "and neither is mental illness, and I'd say that bullheaded bullshit like yours is much more common than either of those."

"Zing," was all that Aaron added to the conversation before laughing and eliciting a muffled little giggle from Yu Lai. Hackett thought Sarah would explode.

~

An hour or so later, after Hackett had moved Sarah and Ella Mae to neutral corners, the party settled back into a pleasant, relaxing pace, and Hackett realized he was getting a little drunk. He didn't mind. He needed some relaxation, wanted to lean against the liquid crutch. Before Sarah, Hackett had never been much of a drinker. At first, drinking had been a way to calm his nerves around her. He had felt like he needed a drink to just be social and not feel like a stumbling idiot. Now he realized that he had grown easy in her presence and was no longer drinking to be comfortable. He was just comfortable drinking. He leaned into Sarah's shoulder and kissed her on the cheek.

"Having a good time?"

"Marvelous," she answered. "Better if that bitch wasn't here."

"She's really a good person, and she's one of my best friends."

Hackett watched as Sarah's face melted into a smile. "Message delivered; I'll keep my opinion to myself." She leaned over and kissed him on the lips. God, Hackett was falling for this woman.

Out in the yard, next to the fire, Hackett noticed Aaron talking to Ella Mae. At least they were getting along.

"Pardon me," Hackett said to Sarah. "I think it is time for some more snow."

He walked over to the table where Alejandro was finishing the last bite of a burger. When the snow came, it was just a light sprinkle in the air.

"More," Hackett yelled over the motor's din and more snow filled the Bethesda sky. "More," he yelled again. To his delight the crowd started chanting with him. "More, more, more."

At full throttle, a white tempest formed in his teapot of a yard. His guests roared in approval. Hands were raised upward, just as his hands had been earlier in the day.

"What a party!" he announced to the world.

When he looked out again, his eyes were drawn to Aaron. He noticed Aaron's hands dropping to his side as if in a slow motion picture, but his head remained tilted upward, his face absorbing the blizzard, flakes melting against his skin. He looked as if he was caught in rapture. Aaron slowly lowered himself to the ground, and Hackett jumped into action, grabbing a pair of cushions off of the chairs as he ran to Aaron's side. Slowly he lowered the boy backward until the cushion was under his head. He placed the other cushion along Aaron's side, before yelling to no one in particular. "Bring another couple of cushions." He looked at Aaron's face, it was calm. There was even a slight smile on his lips. A crowd formed. Hackett loosened the jacket around Aaron's neck.

"Are you okay?"

Aaron shook his head up and down to answer yes, and simply said, "but." He then pulled in a small breath as if it was a struggle, and exhaled in the same awkward way.

Hackett pushed a long chair cushion under Aaron's shoulder and the right side of his back so that he was leaning slightly away from him. He didn't want Aaron to choke on vomit if it came, and he also didn't want to be covered in it. The short, difficult breaths continued, before slowing and slightly abating. It looked as if the seizure might not happen. Then his breaths sped back up and his eyes opened wide, staring into oblivion. He started making a sound like he was hiccupping. The hiccups led to grunts and growls and his body went rigid in Hackett's arms. Hackett held him loosely, so as to not constrict his movements and fight the muscle spasms that were about to come. As the seizure got fully underway, Aaron's head, legs and arms began to jerk, like he was the subject of an exorcism. Hackett looked into the boy's eyes and drew his hand across Aaron's hair, but he knew that these gestures of comfort were lost on Aaron. He thought about his early days as a doctor and how he tried to talk to patients in mid-seizure. He found it impossible not to do so at first, but chiding by a senior doctor and experience eventually rid him of the habit. Hackett looked around him at the frightened crowd, and now talked to them instead.

"He'll be all right," he told his friends. "We just have to let the seizure run its course."

He looked to find Sarah in the crowd and was surprised to see her standing off to the side, watching but immobile. He had expected her to be by his side, not in a panic; he knew she had seen too many seizures for that. He thought about what she had gone through all these years, and he could understand her at this moment. He was there to help her son, she wasn't needed, and so she was waiting, as she must have done hundreds of times before, waiting for the seizure to pass and then waiting again for her son to recover from the aftereffects. What hell, but it could breed the kind of solemn patience that he now saw.

Hackett had often thought about the life parents were forced to live when they had children with chronic conditions. He always marveled at the happy campers, as he called them — the ones who were so consumed with love that they ignored the hardship. Sarah was not one of those parents; she soldiered through, putting up with the hardship, not really accepting it. For that reason, he was careful in his conversations with her. He tried his best to be positive and not dwell on Aaron's difficulties. Especially after the one time when he screwed up and said those insensitive words. He could tell he had touched a nerve. He was talking about a baby he had seen with microencephaly. Sarah asked him about the condition and the prognosis and Hackett launched into neurologist mode, describing the small sloping forehead, the under-developed brain within, the developmental difficulties, and especially in this case, his opinion that there was a fairly short life expectancy. Hackett had lost himself in it, and in his sympathy for the parents.

"I don't know how they do it, I couldn't."

After he had said those words, Hackett noticed a different look on Sarah's face.

"Yes, it's hard," she had responded.

Hackett tried to retract it, telling Sarah that epilepsy wasn't as bad, and assuring her that she was doing well for Aaron, but he could see he had hit some kind of chord. Now, watching Sarah watch Aaron, he felt the pain that he was sure lay hidden below her relaxed countenance. Aaron's seizure eventually passed, and he slowly returned to normal. He sat on the ground, a half vacant stare still filling his eyes.

Minutes passed before Hackett helped him to his feet and walked him into the house, Sarah joining them. Inside the kitchen, Hackett's arm was still on Aaron's shoulder and he used his hand to turn Aaron to face him.

"Listen, Aaron," Hackett said. "I don't know what's going on, but I think you're not being completely honest with me."

"Whatta ya mean, Doc?"

"The blood results. The only way they make sense is if you're skipping pills."

"Christ, you sound like Mom. Why would I skip my meds? Does everyone think I am a fucking idiot?"

Sarah's arm raised and the sound of her slap rang out in the room. "Watch your language when you talk to Doctor Metzger."

Hackett's head nearly swiveled off his neck. "Sarah!"

"What? I keep telling you, it's probably the drugs."

Aaron roughly pushed past Hackett. "I don't take fuckin' drugs."

The door slammed behind him.

Hackett stood facing Sarah. "He needs to take his meds, and you have to make sure he does."

"I have to make sure?" The question hung heavy in the air. "He is seventeen years old. If he can't remember to take his own medicine, he deserves to have seizures."

"Come on, Sarah, you don't mean that. I don't know what is going on with Aaron, but he needs help. We both need to help him."

The anger that had radiated from Sarah seconds earlier seemed to fade into self pity.

"I don't know what to do with him. He used to be my little baby. He loved me. It didn't matter who I was underneath everything else. I was still his Mommy and he loved me."

Tears formed and began to roll down her check. Sarah wiped them away. She looked directly into Hackett's eyes, letting her silence speak for a few seconds. Hackett felt as if she were measuring him.

"A mother needs that from a child. It's the only love you can really count on. Then they grow up, and they become goddamned men," Sarah said, as she turned and walked away.

He watched her back recede as she walked into the living room, unsure who he should follow, mother or son, both in need.

# Chapter 10

Anger cannot always be controlled. It builds little by little, or it is stoked by a single volcanic eruption, but once it is lit, like gunpowder within a waxed fuse, it sparks along. The bomb will go off. That's how Sarah thought about the way she acted at Hackett's winter barbeque as she lay in bed later that night. It wasn't her fault; others had dragged her down the path, egged her on until she exploded.

Her fire had been stoked even before she arrived, as Aaron sat beside her in the car wearing headphones and singing to that godawful heavy metal music. One day it was rap, the next heavy metal and the next who knew what. And his voice! He couldn't sing worth a damn. Shut up, she had told him, softly at first, too quietly for him to hear, and so he had forced her to raise her voice. He still didn't stop. So, she slapped him, and he had done the one thing that proved to her once and for all that he was more his father's child than her own. He raised his hand to her. He did not strike her, but she knew that was just a matter of time.

To make matters worse, his bad manners and foul mouth embarrassed her in front of Hackett. Then that bitch Ella Mae called her out. Sarah had wanted to slap her so hard it would tear the ugly right off of her face. But the worst thing, the match that really made her explode was when Hackett took the boy's side. Hackett was hers, and hers alone. How could he care more about Aaron's feelings? She could not stop thinking about it as she lay in bed, sleep eluding her. Sarah remembered another conversation with Hackett. On one of their first dates at Flanagan's, she had asked about his wife. Hackett had talked sweetly, but then seemed to sink as his words rolled on. The words haunted her now. "Jean was the only woman I ever loved, the only woman I will ever love."

Sarah would make him love her more. She needed him to need her, but to do so, she had to do better. She needed to control herself.

The next morning she awoke at six, dialed Hackett's number immediately, knew that he'd be awake and getting ready for work, knew with certainty that he would hear her apology, look at the clock, and the time of day alone would convince him of her sincerity.

During the phone call, Hackett asked her to dinner, to make up for their argument. He sounded sad enough to cry at the thought that he had been insensitive to her needs. Then later in the day, he called from the hospital to cancel. One of his patients needed surgery. He said it could not be postponed. She told Hackett that she understood, but when she hung up the phone, other thoughts gathered like dark clouds in her mind. She wondered if he really needed to work. Perhaps, he was mad at her, had feigned his sympathy on the phone. Perhaps, he was taking that little Chinese doctor to dinner. She knew that these thoughts were her own demons taunting her, but she let them continue.

It was almost dinner time. She poured herself a glass of Kendall Jackson Chardonnay, thought about making dinner, thought about Aaron walking through the door and guzzling milk from the carton, thought about sitting silently at their kitchen table while he listened to his earphones. She had already told Aaron she would be going out to dinner with Hackett, told him she'd be late, even intimated that she might not come home until morning.

Sarah envisioned herself and Aaron sitting at the table in angry silence. She drained her glass and stood up. She didn't have a date, but dinner alone at the Colonel Brooks Tavern was better than dinner with a deaf and dumb boy.

~

At about eight-thirty, Sarah finished her Asian chicken salad and downed her fourth glass of chardonnay. Her anger was drowning in the alcohol, sadness bobbing to the surface in its place. She paid her bill and left a modest tip, not because the service had been bad; her tip was small because leaving a bigger one might bring someone the happiness that she herself deserved. Sarah walked out the door and headed slowly east on Monroe Street. A group of perhaps ten Catholic University students stumbled forward on the sidewalk in front of her. Words ricocheted between them like bullets. Sarah could tell they were drunk, or high, and it irritated her, reminding her of Aaron, deaf and blind to the people around him, living his own self-centered existence. Her pace quickened with her irritation. She was soon within feet of them. They did not seem to notice.

"Excuse me." Her words fell on deaf ears. "Excuse me," she said louder. When no one moved, Sarah grabbed a girl's shirt and yanked her to the left. "Get out of my way," she yelled.

She had their attention now. "Jesus Christ, lady." The sea of students didn't so much part as it separated into little drops, like a bottle of mercury had fallen to the ground and spilled its contents on the sidewalk. Sarah threaded her way through them, muttering as she went.

In a couple of blocks, she approached her townhouse and heard music coming from within. She stomped up the four steps of her little porch, opened the door, strode in and slammed it behind her. The forty-watt bulb glowed above her head in the foyer, casting a pale light across the living room and illuminating a dozen startled eyes. Music blasted and reverb gave Rhianna's voice a trembling electronic edge. Sarah flipped the switch for the main living room light and raised her voice to compete with the stereo.

"Get out of my house."

The kids scrambled like rats in a fire, grabbing beer bottles and coats.

"Get out," Sarah yelled again, "and turn that damn music off."

The music came to an abrupt end. Aaron stood next to the

stereo. "Come on, Mom, they're leaving. Lighten up a little," he calmly told his mother. She started shoving people out the door.

"Chill out, Mom. You said you were going out to dinner."

Sarah pushed another girl out the door and turned back to face Aaron. "And that gives you the right to invite these juvenile delinquents into my house?"

"I live here, too."

The last of Aaron's friends squeezed between Sarah and the wall, and then through the open door. Aaron grabbed his coat and followed them out, as the door slammed behind him.

After midnight, Sarah lay in her bed unable to sleep. She had turned the television on to watch Jay Leno, then cracked a book to read, but that hadn't helped either. As she stared at the street light outside her window, she heard the back door open, and knew Aaron had returned. She listened involuntarily to his every footstep, heard the refrigerator door open and close, imagined the sounds of him gulping and chewing.

~

Morning light streamed through the small, rusted casement windows of Sarah's living room. She heard Aaron stirring in his bedroom, tried to push it from her mind. It was ten o'clock and he was just rising. His closet door banged shut, then his bedroom door swung open, hitting the wall in the hallway. In her mind, she could see the round dent in the plaster, the one that grew bigger month by month, the only one like it in the house, another element in her long line of grievances. Next, the bathroom door slammed shut. In a matter of time, the toilet flushed and water cascaded through the pipes. She imagined his piss stains on the floor.

Sarah, put aside her book, unable to concentrate, and walked into the kitchen as Aaron took his seat and opened the prescription bottle that sat among the vitamins in the middle of the table. He upended the bottle and two pills rolled out into his hand. Aaron stared down as if something had caught his attention. He lifted one pill up and inspected it. She walked over to the table, and could see the small "a" imprinted on the pill. He dropped it back into his hand and picked up the other pill, turning it over. A capital "A" stared up at him. After a couple of seconds, he shrugged, popped one pill in his mouth and dropped the other back in the bottle.

Sarah turned from the table quickly and walked back into the living room. As soon as she sat down, she picked up her book and buried her head in it. She listened as Aaron shuffled around the kitchen, occasionally catching glimpses of him as he toasted and then ate three or four frozen waffles. Her eyes darted back and forth from the book to her son.

"Clean up after yourself," she yelled when she saw he had finished.

She heard him do as he was told. Then he left the kitchen and returned to his bedroom. Sarah tried to concentrate on her book, but the nervous energy in her stomach was too much. She stood and walked to the window, staring out at the street, wishing she were free of this dismal little house. She thought of Hackett, constructed her dream house on a bluff above one of the rivers in Annapolis. She saw the large entryway and expansive great room with a huge fireplace. She saw the green grass sloping toward the river and the pool with a white fence around it. It was beautiful, but she felt the unreality of it all and wondered if it was within her will to make it happen.

Then her dream was shattered by something familiar rustling in the other room. She had heard it plenty of times before. This disease had haunted her for too long. She had nursed this boy, cared for him, done everything for him and he had turned on her. Sarah walked through the living room, down the hall and knelt next to her son's quaking body, watching as the tremors slowed and he entered the familiar twilight of recovery. She felt his animosity running cold and deep. He hated her. She was his mother. She had given him everything, sacrificed everything for him.

Why were men so ungrateful? Her fingers felt the waxy touch of plastic. She looked at the syringe, slipped the needle beneath his skin, found the hot flowing blood within his vein.

She told herself he would feel nothing but release. He would no longer interfere with her plans.

Aaron's drifting eyes stopped and seemed to focus on his mother's hand, then floated away until they came to rest once again on her eyes. The seizure still had hold of Aaron. Sarah knew from experience that his mind remained clouded, but his eyes looked into hers nonetheless.

~

Hackett stood next to the bed in the emergency room. The patient, a woman of about forty, held her hand up against the right side of her neck and turned her head in his direction. "It hurts right here." She told Hackett that she thought she had pulled a muscle, but her neck pain hadn't gone away in over a week. A few days ago, she also had what she described as the "most godawful headache she'd ever had," so bad that she had thrown up, but that went away in a matter of a few hours.

"I wouldn't have bothered coming in, but this ma ma. This ma." Hackett watched her carefully as she tried to speak. "Earlier ta ta," she struggled to continue. "I got another headache and it hurt so bad that I kaa." She paused, tongue tied. "I couldn't see."

"Have you always had a problem stuttering or garbling your speech like that?"

"No, I don't know where that came from; maybe I'm nervous."

Hackett felt the telltale vibration of his cell phone in his pants pocket. He reached down, lifted his phone slightly out of his pocket and tilted it up. He saw Sarah's number and returned it from where it had come. Once again he looked at the MRI of his patient's brain that the ER had ordered. He saw no sign of strokes, tumors or lesions. He felt an additional solitary vibration from his pocket and knew that Sarah had left a message.

"How did you pull a muscle?"

"I'm not sure, I don't remember pulling it, but I am fairly active, so I just assume that's what happened."

"Have you been in any kind of car accident recently?"

"No."

"Some other neck injury? Do you ride a bike?"

"I do ride, but…" She halted again. "No neck." She paused. "No neck, ah, no."

"Have you been to a chiropractor and had your neck manipulated?"

"Yes, I go for regular adjustments because of lower back pain."

Once again, Hackett's phone began to vibrate. When he looked, he saw Sarah's number and felt a touch of annoyance. She had to know he was working.

"We need to get another MRI of your neck," Hackett told his patient, and then he explained his suspicion that she had a vertebral artery tear that most likely happened as a result of neck manipulation.

Hackett explained the condition and the treatment, before stepping out into the hall to call Sarah back. She picked up on the first ring, and breathlessly spoke before he could get a word in.

"I'm in an ambulance. They're hurting Aaron." Hackett could hear the commotion in the background.

"What? Who's hurting Aaron?"

"The medics, make them stop."

"Is he having a seizure?

"No, he was unconscious. He wasn't breathing."

"What happened?"

"Talk to him," Hackett heard her scream, and he could tell she had taken the phone away from her mouth. "He's my son's doctor, talk to him."

A voice came onto the phone. "Hello."

"Who are you?" Hackett asked.

"Jackson Reed, D.C. Fire and Emergency Medical Services. Who am I speaking to?"

Hackett quickly introduced himself. "Was the patient having a seizure?"

"No, he was in full cardiac arrest when we arrived. My partner is attempting to resuscitate."

~

Hackett had listened to the EMT for a few more seconds, satisfied himself that there was nothing else he could do, tried to calm Sarah and left work as quickly as he could. On the way to Washington Hospital Center he went over the possibilities in his mind. He didn't know if Aaron would make it, but it didn't sound good. Apparently Aaron had been alone, and Sarah couldn't say how long he had been unconscious. SUDEP — Sudden Unexpected Death in Epilepsy is what Hackett assumed. SUDEP was kind of like Sudden Infant Death Syndrome. The medical community didn't really understand what was behind it. It was rare, but more common in cases where the epilepsy was difficult to treat. Two years ago, Hackett wouldn't have characterized Aaron's epilepsy as refractory, but in the last few months, it had obviously become so. He mentally reviewed Aaron's condition and treatment, wondering once again why he had suddenly been so difficult to treat. He didn't get it. Maybe he'd missed something, could have done something more. A familiar nagging doubt haunted him.

~

Sarah sat stoically by herself in the corner of the Washington Hospital Center waiting room. It looked like the other people had evacuated the immediate area around her, afraid that whatever she had might be communicable. She stared across the room at nothing in particular, like she was in some kind of trance.

Hackett rushed toward her, feet slapping hard against the floor, expecting her to react to the noise, but she didn't look up. His stomach sank. Before he reached her, he slowed down and carefully lowered himself into the chair next to her, extended his arm around her and then pulled her towards him.

"This is his father's fault. He was his father's son. Why couldn't he have been different?" Hackett didn't know what to say. He just held her as she sat quietly. Hackett could feel her sobs.

"What happened to my baby? He was a good child. I should have been a better mother. I shouldn't have..." Her voice trailed off.

~

"The righteous perish, and no one takes it to heart; the devout are taken away, and no one understands that the righteous are taken away to be spared from evil." The pastor's words cut deep into Hackett. He could not understand how this so-called man of God thought these words were comforting. They echoed in his head: "the righteous perish, and no one takes it to heart."

"Death was peace," the sermon continued.

*Death is the end*, Hackett told himself

Hackett tried not to listen. He sat with Sarah in the front row, her friend Trudy on the other side. Ella Mae, George and Yu Lai were two rows back. A smattering of others were distributed in the pews. His mind drifted from Aaron to Jean, and back. The specter of death surrounded him, a black void with no bottom or top, no heaven or hell.

*Why are we here?* he wondered. He had hardly been able to get Sarah to accept any sort of funeral at all. She told him that she hated them, and everything about them, especially caskets. He hadn't realized, or maybe had forgotten, that he felt the same way. One of the few things she had done in the first days after Aaron's death was to order his remains be cremated. "I don't want to remember his dead body. I don't want to think of it buried in a casket," she had said to Hackett. After that, Aaron joined Jean's corpse in Hackett's dreams.

At the hospital, Sarah's body had quivered in Hackett's arms. She seemed to have been comforted by his presence, but when they left, she insisted that he drop her off at her house and leave her to grieve alone. She kissed him on the cheek, wiped her eyes and stepped out of the car. Walking away, she looked like a zombie, a live body with nothing left inside. Hackett wanted to be with her, to help, to comfort her. In truth, he needed Sarah as much as he thought she needed him.

The visions started on the drive home, his demons uncontrollable. He felt Aaron's body shake in his arms. He felt Jean's cold skin under his palms. He saw the exposed matter of Doris Carrollton's brain stem. An image came to him, one that he hadn't thought about for years. It seemed to wrap all the other images in a single blanket of guilt. Hackett had been ten years old. He remembered his mother lecturing him not to let the dog out the front door. He had done it so many times, he could not understand why she worried so. He saw himself running through the house, his hand grasping the door handle, the door opening a matter of inches, the dog brushing by his leg, squeezing through the opening, the high pitch of her bark ringing in his ears, the dog darting across the front yard in an instant, chasing a squirrel, the squeal of tires on pavement, the dull thud, and finally the blood pooling, the tongue hanging limp, and the eyes fixed.

Hackett's own car wheels eventually came to a rest in his garage. He sat aimlessly in the front seat for ten minutes before he finally went inside. Once within, he turned on the television, then stared at his hands instead of the screen. Voices disturbed the airwaves around him, but only random static registered. Still, his inner video tapes rolled on. He wallowed in alternating images of death, testaments to his guilt. Through it all were Aaron's lab tests, clear and consistent results that made no sense.

The next day he called Sarah, but she didn't answer. Concerned, he drove to her house after work and brought Chinese carryout for dinner. When she opened the door, she looked at him blankly. "Someone from the hospital has been calling. They want me to pick up Aaron's personal belongings. I don't want to deal with it. Can you?" She thanked him for the meal and his help, then sent him on his way.

The next morning, Hackett went to the hospital, picked up Aaron's things, collected some paperwork for Sarah, and as Aaron's doctor, asked for his records. He called Sarah, told her he would stop by that evening, asked if he could join her for dinner. To his relief she agreed.

Between patients at his office, Hackett opened Aaron's file. Words jumped off of the page: *Cause of death — Heroin Overdose.* He looked at the top of the document to make sure Aaron's name was indeed there.

At dinner later that evening, Sarah's reaction cut him to the core. "I told you. I knew he would kill himself with that crap. It's your fault. You wouldn't listen." Her voice had turned crisp and commanding. "I don't want anyone knowing that he died of an overdose. No one! You had no right to look at his file and I don't want you spreading rumors." Then she broke into a flood of tears.

Hackett watched Sarah cry. With each convulsion of her body, he felt his own pain. He recalled the deepest darkest days of his mourning for Jean which now felt so distant in comparison. He tried to comfort her. When the tears finally slowed, they both sat in front of their plates playing with their food. The phone rang. Sarah looked at it as if she wanted to banish it from her life. She let it ring six times before she huffed in exasperation, stood and walked to the back door where the phone hung on the wall.

"Yes."

Hackett heard a young voice from the handset and assumed it was one of Aaron's friends.

"No," Sarah replied sharply.

Hackett heard the distant voice again, but not the words.

"No, I don't want to talk about it," Sarah said and hung up the phone.

Sarah seemed to pull herself together that evening and in the subsequent days leading up to the funeral. She began to exhibit a kind of stony will. She only notified a few people and told Hackett that she had long ago cut off communication with her own parents. "They never cared for me and never even met Aaron," she said.

She also refused to publish any notices of Aaron's death. "I don't want any of his damn friends coming to the funeral. Fucking druggies, it's their fault my baby is dead." Hackett stayed silent, gave her grief room, hoping that its flow would eventually come to a trickle and stop.

Hackett's mind returned to the funeral. He looked around the church, and it made him even more sad. He counted just twenty-two people and most were his own friends from work. Not a single one of Aaron's friends were there. His eyes returned to Sarah. Her arms hugged her own chest tightly, as her dry red eyes stared forward. *She is a strong woman*, Hackett thought. *Maybe too strong.* He imagined Aaron's friends, also absorbed by grief, and wondered how they were dealing with being shut out of the funeral. He felt disappointed in himself for not being able to convince her to notify Aaron's school of the funeral arrangements, or call any of his friends, but he knew that if he had the opportunity to relive those moments, he would have done nothing differently. How could he interfere in her suffering? It was all too familiar to him. He put his arm around her stiff body.

The service ended. Hackett eased Sarah to her feet. She walked forward into the aisle.

"What is he doing here?" she whispered. "I don't want to talk to him."

Hackett quickly scanned the church and saw Aaron's best friend Alec in one of the back pews slowly lifting himself from the seat, a girl crying by his side. Hackett remembered Aaron introducing Alec for the very first time. Hackett had eaten dinner over at Sarah's house. He thought that Alec was a funny kid, always smiling and joking about something. Now, he looked like hell. As they approached the pew where Alec stood, Sarah's fingernails dug into Hackett's arm.

Alec's voice quavered. "I'm sorry, Mrs. Filicidees, I can't believe..."

Hackett reached out for the boy's shoulder, a simple gesture to comfort him, but Sarah jerked Hackett away, leaving Alec's words hanging in the air.

Outside the church, Hackett tried to talk to Sarah. "I know you're grieving, but the boy must be in terrible pain as well."

"He can go to hell for all I care," Sarah said and marched Hackett straight to the car, not bothering to greet any of the people coming out of the church.

# Chapter 11

When office hours came to an end, Hackett walked into the elevator and punched the button for the lobby instead of the parking garage. Over the last two weeks, Aaron's death had buzzed in his head like a swarm of angry bees. *What did you miss?* The bees batted their wings. *You failed him, just like you failed Jean.* The bees danced, their abdomens vibrating. The agitation held him tight within its disquieting embrace, making his teeth grind and his left eyebrow twitch. Eventually the chatter slowed and settled in his heart, becoming an ache that was just a little easier to bear. But as he walked out onto the street, the bees began to buzz once more. The cold empty blackness of death closed in.

The day itself had been long, comprised of dull patients with maladies that did not challenge his mind and personalities that did not engage his heart. His only reprieve, if it could be called that, was another reminder that life was cruel and death was always just around the corner. Late in the afternoon, a tall, athletic-looking black man with the slightest touch of gray highlighting his hair limped into the examining room. Probably an ex-basketball player, Hackett assumed, as the man talked of old, tired muscles. Hackett had half-listened to his nonchalant recitation of symptoms. What had been back pain and an assumed pinched nerve had eventually gone away over many months, but his muscles never seemed to recover. He had trouble playing sports, and even running was difficult. He was always tired and it didn't seem like his muscles were obeying his brain.

Hackett half-consciously examined the man, glad to at least

not focus on Aaron. It turned out that what Hackett had at first assumed was a bad knee wasn't that at all. Instead the man had nerve damage resulting in drop foot on his left side. Hackett puzzled over the other symptoms without much concern, until he noticed a tremor in the soft flesh between the man's thumb and index finger. It made Hackett's heart skip a beat: a tell-tale sign of ALS, Lou Gehrig's disease. He couldn't be sure, but it was enough to make Hackett schedule a battery of tests.

On the sidewalk, an unseasonably warm wind blew dark clouds across the skyline, their gloomy portent not going unnoticed by Hackett. He needed to walk and clear his head, and so he moved forward with no clear destination. He had cared for ALS patients before, prepared them for the inevitability of helplessness and death. He knew all the things to say, how to be frank yet comforting. Hackett imagined his patient's slow decline, saw the latent vitality that still existed in him, hoped for strength of spirit. Perhaps he would be one of those rare patients who faced the unthinkable with dignity, a patient who moved forward, savoring what was left of life no matter how difficult it might be. The man had told Hackett about his daughter who had just turned twenty. Would he live to see her give birth? Would his granddaughter play in the wilted lap of a man in a wheelchair, squirming and giggling as the man sat immobile and silent. *I don't know it's ALS for sure,* Hackett told himself, but his intuition told him differently. He had seen the symptoms and knew what the future would bring. At that moment, he hated himself for his surety, and he wondered how this profession that he had found so rewarding for so many years had to a large extent become tiring and depressing.

He walked, feet to concrete, eyes down, arms limp at his side, block after block, lost in thought. Lightning flashed in the distance and thunder followed. Hackett finally looked up, realizing that he was in front of the hospital, as the first fat raindrops of the coming storm slapped his face like wet bullets. He turned, seeking shelter behind the familiar concrete and glass walls.

When the double doors opened on the third floor, he heard

the roar of Ella Mae's voice, and felt the roll of thunder once more. It brought a smile to his face, and finally drove ALS from his mind. Hackett snuck up behind her and whispered his favorite nickname into her ear. "Hey Nurse Ratched, you're going to scare that poor girl to death." Ella Mae jumped and let out a hoot-like scream before turning and slapping Hackett with the adult diaper she had been holding.

"Too bad it wasn't full," she said loudly before smiling. And then without lowering her voice, "First year nurses, I wish they had never been born."

"You're all bluster, Ella Mae. You know that, don't you?"

Ella Mae smiled at Hackett. "What are you doing here? You're not on the schedule."

"I don't know." He smiled back. "I was out for a walk and it started raining, and here I was, nowhere else to go."

They talked about the weather and the newest patients before Ella Mae brought up the near-death study. "I really appreciate the fact that you went to bat for the study," Ella Mae said. "Especially after I attacked you like that at your party. I heard that Cardiac Care was not very supportive, and I know that there's no way it would have been approved if you hadn't argued for it."

Hackett waved Ella Mae off and talked instead about his ALS patient, which led him into a depressing monologue about death and medicine. Ella Mae listened thoughtfully, telling him that it would pass. He had borne a lot of pain. It was natural to get down about it every once in a while. The weight on Hackett's shoulders lightened, though ever so modestly.

"What's really bothering you, Hack?"

The question, as logical as it was, caught Hackett off guard. "Nothing," he said and then felt an uncomfortable reverberation rising within. The bees were buzzing again. "Well, not nothing. I can't believe Aaron is dead, and I can't stop thinking about him. It's like when Jean died. There are things I should have seen, things I should have done."

"Oh, Hackett, don't beat yourself up. There was absolutely nothing you could have done to save Jean. I thought you finally

THE MOMENT BETWEEN ~ 125

understood that. And Aaron? What in the world do you think you could have done? He had epilepsy. That was not in your control."

Ella Mae was looking directly into Hackett's eyes as if she was begging him to go easy on himself, but his heart would not let her in. He looked away. Silence held for a few seconds, and then he talked in a low nervous voice. "I promised I wouldn't tell anyone."

"Tell anyone what?"

The words flooded out of him. He told her about seeing Aaron's death certificate and the cause of death, about Sarah's outburst that day in the office, accusing Aaron of taking drugs, about the tox screen, about his failure to order another, about how he had struggled with Aaron's medications, never solving the problem, and through it all about his own denial that Aaron was taking drugs. "I should have believed her. She was his mother, and she told me he had a problem."

When he was done, Ella Mae looked stunned. "Aaron couldn't have overdosed. That makes no sense. Maybe someone mixed up the death certificate, Hackett. You work in a hospital. You see all the mistakes people make. Did you double check? Talk to the doctor in the ER? Check the lab results?"

"No. I don't need to. It is pretty goddamn clear."

"Something's not right, Hackett. Something's definitely not right."

# Chapter 12

Fresh leaves of spring rustled above like a giant green flag rippling across the sky over the C&O Canal towpath north of Great Falls. Ahead, Hackett could no longer see Sarah's small yellow and blue clad figure. The April air was cool, perfect for riding, but it didn't help him much. He was out of shape. Actually, saying he was out of shape was poor use of the English language. It implied that there had been a decent shape to him at some point.

He pedaled on alone. His leg was scraped up from a fall; thank God she hadn't seen him tumbling head over heel. His wrists were a little numb. His calves and thighs ached, and his ass hurt. He wondered how far ahead Sarah was and whether she would stop to wait for him. Sarah often bragged about pushing herself to exhaustion and leaving other cyclists in her dust on her long rides out to White's Ferry. He breathed in deeply, feeling the dust in the air, suddenly glad for all of it.

Ten minutes later, he saw the familiar colors of Sarah's biking shirt and shorts coming in his direction. She rode up to him, looking fit, and breathing normally, although her face was red and a sheen of sweat covered her forehead.

"Are you doing okay?" she asked brightly. "Sorry I left you behind, but it is such a nice day for a workout."

"No problem," Hackett answered, and he watched as her eyes tracked down to his leg. Involuntarily, he rubbed his hand over the abrasion and felt the sticky, drying blood. "Took a little spill," he added.

From her bike pack, a small first aid kit appeared. It wasn't much of a scrape, but over his protests she insisted on cleaning it with sanitary wipes, applying a gauze bandage and then wrapping it in white medical tape. He smiled when she finished, loving the attention.

"You are quite the nurse. We'll have to get you a job at the hospital."

"Not for me." She beamed back at him. "Too many sick and dying people. Who needs that? God bless you, though. I don't know how you do it."

Hackett saw a momentary saddening in Sarah's expression, and she fell silent as she had been doing from time to time since Aaron's death. Just as quickly, her expression changed. Her eyebrows lifted and her lips curled down into a clownish frown.

"Speaking of the hospital, what's going on with that stupid study, the one your rude friends wanted you to do?"

"The near-death study?"

Sarah nodded.

"It was approved two weeks ago. Doctor Wang just did a walkthrough on the final setup in Cardiology and the ER."

"I can't believe you let that little Chinese imp wrap you around her finger. People are going to think you have lost your marbles."

"Hold on. Yu Lai is a good doctor, and I don't care what others think."

"Well, I for one am surprised that you didn't stand up to her and that fat bully of a nurse. I can't believe that story she told. She's in la la land."

"I try to concentrate on the real-world applications of the study. There is so much we don't know about why we can resuscitate and save some patients while others die, why some brains seem to retain enough oxygen and a bare minimum of electrical activity. If we understood it better, more people would survive."

"That's not what your friends are trying to prove. They believe in ghosts and zombies. They think that the dead are alive and watching us."

"I don't think they would put it that way."

Sarah leaned forward and lightly kissed him on the lips. "Don't be naive."

He watched as Sarah put the first aid kit back into her pack. Once again a silent shroud seemed to fall over her.

"Are you thinking of Aaron?" he asked.

"Yeah," she said simply.

"It would be nice to believe that Aaron was still here somehow, or that Jean was watching over me, but I don't believe in life after death either." He paused, feeling Sarah's silence hovering between them once again. "I envy them that. I wish I could believe."

"Let's not talk about it anymore. What do you want to do about dinner? It's Tuesday; do you want to go to Flanagan's?"

Hackett ignored the question. "God knows that I wasn't very good at grieving when Jean died."

A flash of anger widened Sarah's eyes, but now that Hackett had started talking he couldn't stop. "I was a real mess, but you can't ignore what happened. I know you must miss Aaron desperately, and it must really hurt. You shouldn't bottle it up, especially if you feel guilty about being angry at him."

"Angry? I wasn't angry," Sarah exploded. "And don't you dare tell me how to feel about my own son. You have no goddamned idea how I feel, and this has nothing to do with your fucking wife."

Her anger left him speechless. A long silence followed them as they slowly pedaled toward home. Occasionally, one or the other would utter a word or two. Hackett retreating shyly after each one. Sarah maintaining a steely gaze. After they showered and changed at Hackett's house, a semblance of conversation finally returned. On their walk to Flanagan's, Hackett pushed the last of it back down into the darkness and tried to focus on lightening Sarah's mood. On the towpath, Hackett had explained his bicycle crash in a perfunctory manner too embarrassed to go into many details, but now as it faded into the past, he retold the story with gusto, exaggerating his clumsiness, using his humiliation to break down the wall of tension between them.

"I curled up on the ground like a little baby, wailing to the man on his bicycle, 'please don't hit me, I'm old and fragile.'" Hackett's voice took on a pitiful tone, like a little boy pleading with a bully.

Sarah was laughing lightly. "What did he do?"

"His eyes drilled into mine with the kind of malice you might see in one of those professional wrestling matches on TV. I could see his lips mouthing, 'screw you, old man,' and I knew that he meant to kill me."

Sarah stopped walking, put her hands on her hips in protest and tried to stifle her laugh. "So I'm supposed to believe that he ran you over on purpose?"

"He wanted to, but I was saved by divine intervention. The sky above us parted, a beam of heavenly light glowed around me like a deflector shield on *Star Trek*, and much to his disappointment, the man's bike steered clear of me."

They were still laughing when they walked into Flanagan's.

"Well, look who's all happy out, aren't ya," Liam said in his thick Irish brogue. "Cover me for a second, won't ye, Doc? I must use the jacks."

"All right, now, but don't ye be takin' feckin' donkey's years or I'll help myself and the colleen here to a pint or two of gat, now won't I," Hackett responded in a poorly articulated imitation of Liam's accent.

Sarah looked at Hackett as if he was crazy. "What the hell are you saying? I have trouble enough understanding the foreigner, without you talking like that, too."

Hackett sported a wide grin, obviously enjoying himself, and continued in his Irish accent. "Liam is using the jacks, which in English means he is taking a piss, and me and my pretty colleen, which is you, are going to have a pint or two of Guinness, even if he doesn't take donkey's years to get back, which is a long time." As Hackett finished talking, he reached over the bar, grabbed two pint glasses and began to fill one up with the chocolaty beverage.

"My God," Sarah replied. "You have spent far too much time in this bar."

When Liam returned, Hackett and Sarah moved to their now regular table by the front window. They talked and watched the passers-by through burgers, fries and another round of Guinness. After Sarah took the last bite of her burger, she pushed her plate towards Hackett.

"You can finish the fries if you want, I'm quite full."

Hackett demurred, even though they tempted him. "You know what today is?"

"April twenty-second," Sarah responded.

"Quite true, but it also happens to be exactly eight months since we first had dinner together at this very table."

"I knew that," she said with a wink.

Hackett pulled out a small oblong jewelry box and passed it across the table. "I'm so glad we met. I was a pretty sad and lonely guy before that."

Hackett watched as she opened the box, drinking in the excitement of her smile as her eyes alit on the one-carat ruby necklace within. "So you like it?"

"Oh, Hackett, it's incredible, so elegant. You do know how charming you are, don't you?"

He simply smiled, sensing that it was enough of an answer in itself. Sarah reached across the table, took Hackett's hand, and leaned forward. He thought she was going to kiss him, but her head held steady a few inches away. Her eyes glistened with moisture, and then a tear rolled down her cheek. He could sense that she wanted to talk, but was fighting emotion.

"You're such a good man. I don't deserve you."

"Yes, you..." Hackett managed to speak just the two words before she waved her hand in front of his face.

"Sometimes I say things in anger that I have no business saying, and I never even have the good sense to apologize." Hackett again opened his mouth to speak. This time, Sarah put her finger against his lips. "I had no right to say that about your wife or your friends. I guess I'm not too good at grieving. I look for others to blame, and you happen to be convenient. The truth is I blamed you after Aaron died, because you never believed me about the drugs. It was such a stupid thing to do. You did everything you could to help him. If anyone deserves the blame, it's me. I really owe you an apology. It's long overdue."

"Don't blame yourself. You tried to tell me. You tried to get him help."

Sarah wiped her eyes and forced a smile onto her lips. "A girl could fall in love with a man like you," she said and leaned forward to kiss him.

He wanted to say it right then and there — I love you, too, but the words "could" and "man like you" resonated in his mind. Her statement wasn't a confession of love. So he held his words out of caution, though he couldn't have explained why caution was either needed or wanted.

# Chapter 13

S arah walked up the escalator stairs, stepping around people who strolled through the Metro system, past eyes blinded to the world by mobile phones. She moved in and out of the sea of humanity, pushing forward, focused on the life ahead, dismissing the life at hand. She reached up to her chest and lightly fondled the ruby necklace Hackett had given her. She imagined her future. She would sell her house, and he his. They would build a mansion on the water in Annapolis. She'd quit her job. After all she had been through, she deserved it. But she knew that there were still hurdles to overcome.

She would erase the memories of her dead husband that now snuck into her thoughts. Even with the future so close, the past hung heavily in her thoughts, and a low thrum of anger rumbled over her. James would never have bought her such a thing. She remembered the relief she felt when she poured his ashes into the Anacostia River, creating a small cloud in the air and a dusty film that floated downriver, mixing with the sun-faded plastic bottles and tattered Safeway bags that choked its weedy banks. She had been more nervous on that riverbank than she had been when the EMTs arrived at her front door and James lay dead inside. As the ashes had been swept away, she exhaled, finally feeling safety's comfortable embrace. No one suspected a thing, and even if they did, they had no proof, not one gray speck of it. She smiled, remembering the empty Popov vodka bottle that accompanied his ashes downriver. Now he was cheap swill himself. It was the ignominious end he deserved. She was rid of him for all time. Even Aaron was no longer there to remind her of

James. She told herself that she loved her boy, but he, too, had betrayed her trust, forsaken her love. She would not take responsibility for what had happened.

The light changed from red to green. Sarah stepped off the curb quickly, not seeing the car coming at her until its screaming tires burned on asphalt and the front fender nose-dived toward her thigh. She jumped back a step, then slammed her purse down on the hood of the car. The surprised driver lifted his hands from the wheel and shrugged off his negligence. Sarah stared back with an icy scowl and a rigid middle finger.

One half block later, the heavy glass door of the small jewelry store opened reluctantly. She stepped in, walked up to the counter and stood in front of an aging woman with stiffly-formed blue-gray hair and a formerly fashionable if conservative dress. Sarah noticed silvery hairs growing from the mole on the woman's chin. That brought back her smile. Some people were so ugly, they were funny.

"Good afternoon, madam. Can I help you?"

Sarah reached her hands behind her neck, unfastened the necklace and laid it on the glass case. "I am interested in selling the stone in this necklace and replacing it with a faux stone that is similar in appearance. My husband and I need the money, but he is too proud to let me sell any of my jewelry."

"Harvey," the woman behind the counter called. "Can you help this woman with an appraisal?"

A man, every bit as old, just as immaculately dressed and out of style as the woman, walked slowly down the ten-foot length of the counter. Sarah repeated her query to him. First he held the stone up very close to his eye and looked into the light. She wondered how his ancient eyes could see anything useful, then he peered at the gem through his jeweler's glass.

"Very nice," he said.

"How much?" Sarah asked in reply.

"I'll need to take it out of the setting to weigh it before I give you a definitive price. But it does seem to be a high-quality stone. Are you sure you want to part with it?"

Behind Sarah, a bell rang and the store door opened. "Good

afternoon," the salesman's voice rang out. "Someone will be with you in just a minute."

Sarah picked up the necklace and looked at the stone once again. It made her smile. In truth, she would be sad to see it go, and knew that she wouldn't enjoy wearing the necklace as much after the stone was replaced. The new customer stepped to the counter, and Sarah heard Ella Mae's voice.

"Hi, Sarah, what a coincidence seeing you here." Sarah masked her emotions, and tracked Ella Mae's eyes as they shifted to her hands and the necklace hanging from her fingers. "Isn't that the necklace Hackett bought you?"

Sarah answered without skipping a beat, explaining that the chain had broken, hoping that the jeweler wouldn't say anything stupid and give her away. She turned to the old man, thanked him, reclasped the necklace around her neck and said her good-byes. It was only when she was out on the street that she replayed the exchange in her mind and wondered if Ella Mae had noticed that she had never paid.

*Would she tell Hackett?* Sarah tossed the thought around in her head. *What was there to tell?* she decided. Then she thought about her credit card bills once again. She needed to start cutting them down. She didn't want Hackett to find out she was in debt, either before or after they got married. She remembered a friend, more than ten years ago, a friend who hid her credit card balances from her fiancé until after her wedding day, a friend who was divorced within months of letting the cat out of the bag.

~

Step by step, Sarah walked with pain growing in her feet. She had dressed well that morning, including black leather pumps. Her clothes and her finely applied makeup gave her the confidence she needed to sell the necklace, but the pumps weren't the best choice for walking. Her feet nagged at her, and the leftover discomfort from the confrontation with Ella Mae weighed her down. She crossed Connecticut Avenue at N Street and decided that she needed a bite to eat. She passed the Luna Grill; *too expensive,* she told herself. When she saw the faded signs for The

Big Hunt and its run-down bar décor, she opened the door and entered, then sidled up to the mostly empty counter.

"What'll ya have?" the bartender asked.

"Glass of chardonnay and an order of fries." Sarah stared on as the young man poured her a glass from a one-and-a-half liter bottle. It reminded her of the Dom Perignon and the dinner at La Ferme. The contrast was amusing — cheap bar wine versus expensive champagne, her cheap swill of a life with James and the promise of a bubbly future to come. *He really does love me.* She felt sure that it was more than just an infatuation. She looked into the mirror behind the bar and stared at her own face, watching a smile break. She had led a loveless life, but Hackett was changing that. She wasn't sure that her husband had ever really loved her, even when they were young. The thought of his confession of adultery two months after they had married made her stomach turn even now.

The only true love that she could remember was the love of motherhood — the love of her own mother who had protected her from an angry father, but had died before her tenth birthday, and the love of her young son, whose devotion had melted into smoldering antagonism over the years. She wondered why that love had faded. "Aaron," she said softly, his name barely a whisper on her tongue.

Sarah let her guard down and thought about him. She imagined a life with Hackett made possible by Aaron's absence. She allowed herself to wonder if marriage would have been possible if he had still been alive, his seizures still a burden. *No, it wouldn't have worked*, she decided. Sarah felt her own overwhelming guilt in such thoughts. *I will not think of him. I have a new future now. Hackett loves me.*

She concentrated on the problem at hand, thought about the necklace. She imagined herself stepping into another jewelry store, selling it, stuffing two thousand dollars back in her purse. It would pay down about a third of her smallest credit card bill. That wasn't enough. She wanted to be debt free. She didn't want Hackett to see her as a burden. She needed him to believe in her. As she had done so many times before, she imagined telling him that she couldn't pay off her credit cards. She had no doubt that he would offer her cash, but then the questions would come. What happened to the insurance settlement? She couldn't tell him that she had spent $500,000 in three and a half years. She thought about all the clothes she had purchased, all the champagne she had consumed, all the trips she had taken. Had she really wasted that much money? At least she had the townhouse to show for it, but that had cost less than two hundred thousand.

*I could lose him.* The thought chilled her. Sarah took a dainty sip from her wine glass and caught another glimpse of her reflection above the whiskey bottles. She saw her own sad countenance. *I deserve to live alone. He couldn't love me, if he really knew me, if he knew my secrets.*

The bartender placed a paper napkin, a knife, a fork and a bottle of catsup on the bar. Sarah forced a weak smile. In a minute he came back with a plate of fries. He smiled at her. Once again she forced herself to focus on the problem at hand. She had to get rid of her debt. She was sure that Hackett was going to ask her to marry him, and she needed to take care of it now.

The bartender returned. "Are you from out of town?" he asked.

"No." Sarah could feel her smile broaden reflexively in response to his athletic good looks and the friendly tone of his voice. She figured he was in his early thirties.

"I just asked because we don't get much local traffic on Saturdays other than the regulars."

"Just doing a little shopping. I live in DC."

"You're a little classy for our clientele. We usually get old drinkers or young partiers."

Sarah put on a false injured look. "So you're saying I'm not young."

The bartender's smile widened. "I just meant that you are pretty and well dressed, a refreshing change in this dark and dreary place."

"Well, thank you then. It's nice to be noticed."

A patron at the end of the bar raised his glass and the bartender took his leave, but Sarah still saw his head turn in her direction periodically. It was a tonic for her worries. For a moment, she lost herself in a fantasy with the naked bartender at its center, then the proverbial light bulb went off in her head. Hackett didn't know she had bought the townhouse for cash. He'd expect her to have a mortgage. Most people didn't think of a mortgage like it was debt. She could get a home equity loan and even have some extra cash that would tide her over until the marriage. Her hand involuntarily slapped down on the bar. "Yes," she said aloud.

Within seconds, the bartender was in front of her. "Do you need something else?"

"A bottle of Dom Perignon and some big fat juicy snails."

"Sorry, we just ran out of both." He flashed a self-satisfied grin at her.

"Another chardonnay then." Sarah raised her glass in the air. "My mood has just improved decidedly."

The glass was on the house. The bartender's name turned out to be Hoover. It had made her laugh out loud. Hoover hovered over Sarah leaving only when other patrons managed to get his attention. At about three, Sarah turned down her fifth glass, and told him it was time for her to leave.

"How about I take you out dancing tonight?" Hoover offered. "I know a great place for salsa."

Sarah looked at him and thought once more about her fantasy.

"How flattering," she said and winked at him. Then she announced in a louder voice, "But I'm in love and that just wouldn't do."

# Chapter 14

A storm of happy voices blew around Hackett's cramped living room. Outside, a light rain washed the July smog out of the Bethesda sky. As he entered from the kitchen holding a magnum of Dom Perignon, a hush fell and all eyes turned in his direction.

"What's the occasion?" Yu Lai's voice conveyed a sparkle of excitement.

Ten people stood before Hackett, all of them from his office or the hospital with the exception of Amy, Ella Mae's new boyfriend, and Sarah's friend Trudy.

"We asked you all to come over under the pretext of a dinner party, but we do have an announcement. Sarah and I are getting married."

Even before Hackett uttered the final word, Sarah raised her left hand in front of her, level with her chin and displayed a glittering engagement ring with an oversized diamond at its center.

Amy looked as if she was hiding behind Ella Mae. She had arrived the night before, and Hackett had told her about his plans to marry Sarah. Amy had looked visibly shaken. "If you really love her," Amy said. "Then you have my blessing, but isn't this a little fast?"

Hackett thought she was about to cry. "It won't change our relationship," he said.

Hackett looked away from Sarah and the big diamond he had bought her. He wanted Amy to smile, but he saw the same apprehensive look in her eyes. It turned to a startled expression when Sarah's friend Trudy screeched, "It must be three carats."

Ella Mae stood next to George and rolled her eyes. Thankfully, Yu Lai stepped next to Sarah and Hackett's attention was drawn to her.

"Congratulations. I'm so happy for you." Yu Lai leaned in and gave Sarah a hug. Sarah squeezed her back lightly, and continued to talk to Trudy.

"Isn't Hackett amazing?" Sarah said. "My old ring looked like it was purchased at a dollar store. In fact, I think it just might have been." The two girls giggled.

"Did you set a date?" Yu Lai asked.

Hackett fumbled for words. "Next month." Sarah beamed. "Why wait?"

Hackett turned his attention to the bottle in his hand and pulled back the foil covering the cork. "We've decided to get married in St. Lucia." His voice trembled. "There is this wonderful little hotel called the East Winds Inn."

Hackett had readily agreed to a quick, exotic wedding, but now he felt like he was excluding everyone. He made a nervous display of untwisting the wire and releasing the cage from the cork. He grabbed the cork with his right hand and pulled, but it wouldn't budge, so he wrapped both hands around the neck of the bottle and pushed upward with his thumbs. The cork popped like a toy gun and bounced off the ceiling, ricocheting across the room. Bubbles chased the cork out of the bottle and down the rim, until they dripped on the floor at Hackett's feet. Hackett stood dumbfounded until Sarah grabbed two glasses and tried to capture the wayward bubbly.

Trudy shrieked and giggled. Hackett poured. Champagne glasses were passed from hand to hand, until the room was filled with the light spray of tiny popping bubbles. "A toast and a confession, not necessarily in that order," he said. "I never thought I would marry again and more importantly, I never even hoped to fall in love again, even though Amy always said that I would and that it would be good for me." Hackett raised his glass in her direction before continuing. "One great love is as much as any man deserves. And, when I met Sarah, marriage was the last thing on my mind, even though I confess to a large measure of stifled lust."

Sarah beamed and slapped Hackett on the ass. "I should hope so," she said.

"Yes, she is, as you have all no doubt noticed, quite a beautiful lady, which makes my shock all the more pronounced, but her beauty isn't what ensnared me. I had forgotten what it was like to enjoy life." He paused. "To Sarah," Hackett cocked his glass upward another notch. "Her smile, her laughter, her energy, my love. The woman who has taught me how to live again."

Hackett turned to Sarah and gave her a soft slow kiss, then he turned back to the room. One by one he engaged each person around the table with a smile and sometimes a simple nod, conveying his sincerity without further words. When he looked at Amy, she tipped her glass and smiled, then mouthed, "I love you, Dad." When he looked at Yu Lai, he was surprised to see her wipe a tear from her eye. Then amidst a beaming smile, she announced, "How beautifully poetic."

Ella Mae's eyes were the last in his tour. She looked down at the carpet, her face betraying sad emotion. After the toast, people settled into conversation and Hackett went into the kitchen to get the party platter he had ordered from Safeway. He stood alone at the kitchen counter and peeled back the plastic wrap. Footsteps aroused him from quiet thoughts. He turned to find Ella Mae standing near him.

"How are things with George?" he asked.

"Really good. Maybe a little too good. It scares me."

"Just jump in, my friend, the water is warm. It's easy to be pessimistic about happiness, but don't let that wreck your life. When you get the chance, grab the golden key and run."

"I would," she said. "He's really nice, but sometimes, I still feel like I don't really know him." Hackett waited for her to continue. "He never talks about his family, except for his dad, who died when he was in high school. He has two daughters, and at least one grandchild, but that is about all I know. Well that and the fact that he hates his ex-wife because she left him and took the children."

"Maybe his family memories are too painful. It's funny, I still think of Jean all the time, but I don't talk to Sarah much about her."

The conversation slowed. Eventually, Ella Mae took Hackett's hands and looked into his eyes. "Hackett," she said his name and no more. Her words fell away and concern was etched into her face. Hackett waited once again.

"Are you sure?" she finally asked.

"Yes," he said. "I am sure."

"It's only been a year."

"Did Amy talk to you? I know she is a little upset."

"She's concerned."

"What about you?"

"I'm way past concerned. I think you're making a mistake. Please take some time. Draw out this engagement a little more. Make sure she really loves you."

"Don't insult us." Hackett's words came out soft and sad as opposed to hard and angry. "I know that everyone probably thinks that she is out for my money, that she's too young and too pretty for me, but it's not like that."

"Listen, Hackett, I didn't want to tell you this, especially with Aaron's death and all, but he and I talked a lot at your party. He was pretty open about his mother."

Hackett felt his heart skip a beat. "I know," he said. "They didn't get along very well, but that happens when kids turn into teenagers."

Ella Mae had a pained look on her face, like she didn't want to say any more, but the words still came. "It was more than that, Hackett. He talked about you, too. He liked you a lot. He told me that his mother didn't deserve you. Then he said something really odd. He said that you didn't know her yet. He said that she was still hiding her dark side."

"Jesus Christ," Hackett said, shaking his head in disbelief. "That's a terrible thing to say about your mother, and it is just plain wrong. I know her, she is a good and decent person." Hackett's voice began to rise. "If you are worried about the money, don't be. We've talked about it. She has told me to do whatever I want to with my money and to draw up a prenuptial agreement to settle it."

"Really?" Hackett could hear Ella Mae's surprise.

"Really! You are one of my best friends and I love you dearly, but I am an adult and I can make my own decisions."

He watched as Ella Mae's eyes turned downward once again. "I'm sorry, Hackett. I just thought I owed it to you to speak my mind. Forget it, okay?"

# Chapter 15

Sarah grabbed her helmet and pushed the button to open the garage door. She rolled her bike out onto the driveway, hit the remote again and was on her way before the door shut. Yesterday, the temperature had hit ninety-five. She rode through today's eighty-eight degree air with ease.

She loved riding right out of their garage, no need to drive her car for thirty or forty minutes out of the city to have a decent ride. All that she had to do was make a right on Wilson Lane, ride three miles to McArthur Boulevard, and then another half mile and she'd be on the towpath. It didn't matter that Wilson Lane was a little cramped with traffic. Sarah was glad to be out of her old house, it was such a dump. She would have been even happier if she could sell the thing, but the housing crash meant that she would have to practically give it away. Like Hackett said, it's better to hang on to it for a couple of years while the market sorts things out. In the meantime, Hackett insisted on paying off her mortgage. Hackett also told her to go ahead and quit work if she didn't like it.

She was still giddy about being married. The honeymoon was incredible, even if Amy had been a little bit of a damper at the wedding. At least she didn't stay around long.

Sarah had wanted to do everything, and Hackett indulged her, even if he had been a little scared at times. They took scuba lessons, and went on a reef dive, rented Sea-Doos and zip-lined, but the best adventure of all was the trip to the Grenadines.

They awoke early one morning, were picked up by a shuttle bus and taken to the airport where they climbed into a twelve-seat prop plane. It was so different from being in a big jetliner. As they raced down the runway, the plane vibrated so hard she thought it might shake apart. Her heart throbbed with excitement. Then the plane lifted off the ground and for the first time in her life, she felt like she was really flying.

"Shit," Hackett had said under his breath.

Sarah looked at him. He was trying to meditate as she had seen him do a few times before. To her it was a stupid waste of time, and she could tell that it wasn't helping him in the least. The propellers beat the air right outside her windows, the pressure thumping through her ear drums and squeezing her heart. She saw the wings bend slightly in the wind. It was exhilarating. They flew up over the spine of the island, the pilot taking them close enough to see blue bags of green fruit hanging from the banana trees.

They went south for about an hour, soaring above the watery expanse until a group of small islands came into view. They looked to Sarah like emeralds amidst a patchwork quilt of deep dark sea and iridescent light blue shallows.

When the pilot announced that they were about to land on the tiny island ahead, Sarah couldn't see an airport, couldn't even see room for one. The plane made a small circle offshore, flying so close to patches of crystal clear baby blue ocean that Sarah could see fish, even a shark, its long tail fin bending with the refracted light. The plane banked, then straightened, coming in low over a village. There was still no sign of an airport. Hackett gripped her arm, nails digging into her flesh. Lower and lower they went until they were nearly skimming the rooftops. Her heart skipped a beat when the plane banked once again. At the last second, a sliver of asphalt split the center of the island, seemingly reaching up to save them. As soon as the tires screeched and she felt safe, Sarah realized that they were running out of pavement. The ocean was once again racing towards them. The pilot hit the brakes, the nose dipped, the tail reared up, and with one last flourish of exhilaration, they stopped before the pavement ran out and the sea reclaimed them. Sarah felt goosebumps running down her arms.

"Wasn't that great?" she shouted to Hackett over the drone of the engines. Hackett looked so scared, she thought he would have a heart attack. She gave him a big kiss. "Thank you so much for marrying me, Hackett. You've changed my life." She threw her arms around him.

As she rode her bike down Wilson Lane, she thought about that flight and the sailing trip that followed. It had been one of the best days of her life. She knew that the honeymoon was just the beginning. They got home, and she moved into his house. She still thought about a big new house, but that idea faded just a little more each day. She enjoyed Bethesda. It was within walking and biking distance of everything they needed.

"Do you like it here yet?" Hackett asked her nearly every day. She was finding it easier and easier to say yes.

She turned left off of McArthur Boulevard and followed the road to a little dark tunnel under the Clara Barton Parkway which led to Lock 9 of the canal. Once on the towpath, she got into a rhythm, riding fast, but balancing her speed to adjust to the foot traffic, occasionally yelling out "coming on your left" to warn pedestrians of her approach. When she was almost to Great Falls, the traffic ground to a near standstill, but on the other side, it opened up and was clear sailing. Sarah used the time to think. She was already busy planning their next trip. She pedaled and dreamed of biking through Italy.

Sarah locked her bike outside the store at White's Ferry. Her legs ached and her chest heaved, but it felt good. After buying a sandwich and a bottle of water, she walked down to one of the picnic tables by the river.

She watched cars roll onto the cable ferry headed for Virginia and others roll off coming into Maryland. She watched the river gurgle, swirl and slowly slip past. She got lost in her thoughts and imagined Hackett at work, saving people's lives. He was an amazing person, and he made her believe that she really could love a man after all that she had been through and all that she had done. She leaned her head backward. Heavy eyelids slid over her corneas and she fell into that peculiar bright version of darkness where sunlight shines through translucent skin. She hovered in the moment. *Yes — I am happy and in love.*

"Look who I found." The voice shocked her. She knew who it was even before she opened her eyes.

"What are you doing here?" She looked behind him, scanning the ferry, the store and the road, but she didn't know what else she was looking for.

"I came back."

"Why?"

"Ran out of money?"

Sarah felt sick. "Well don't look at me."

"How can I take my eyes off of you?"

"Get lost, Victor."

"Why be so rude? I've been back for six months. It was really hard to find you. I thought maybe you moved to another city. I was about to give up, then I remembered how many times we rode our bikes out here. So I gave it a shot and bingo. It's a holiday after all."

Sarah had changed back to her maiden name when her husband died so as to erase her past and start again. She had cut herself off from everyone but Aaron. A new name, a new house, a new job, but here was Victor standing before her, reminding her of all the bad memories, putting her in danger.

"How about I take you home? You can get cleaned up and we'll go out on the town."

"That's not happening."

"OK, how about we find a bar around here?"

"No!"

"Well then let's just get a bottle and a motel room and catch up."

Sarah stood up, but before she could take a step, Victor grabbed her arm. "Don't be rude."

"Let me go, Victor."

"Or what."

"I'm leaving, Victor, and if you try to stop me you'll regret it."

Sarah pedaled her bike down the towpath, kicking up dust in her wake. She remembered her affair with Victor, an affair she had initiated and she had ended. She had used Victor, but he hadn't minded.

*Why was he showing up now?* she asked herself. *Just when my life is getting on track.*

She rode on, thinking about discipline. Victor thought he was smart and tough, but in reality he was as stupid and weak as most men. He was no match for her. She remembered her stepmother's words through the closet door. "You will know discipline and you will learn respect," the voice taunted her still. *The bitch was right,* Sarah told herself. *I did learn discipline. I sat in that dark closet for hours. I learned how to bury my fear. It made me stronger.* She was not worried about Victor. If he found her again, if he tried to interfere, she would know what to do.

~

Hackett sat by himself in the hospital cafeteria. A large manila envelope sat on the table beside him. Inside was an MRI. He could still see the image, even though the picture was now wrapped in manila. Both lateral ventricles were swollen. It made him think of medical school and the professor who first taught him about the brain. "The ventricles are natural shock absorbers. Imagine a car accident. You're not wearing a seatbelt, because you are a moron, and so your head rams into the windshield. The four ventricles are cavities in your brain filled with spinal fluid that help cushion your less than brilliant gray matter as it is slammed around inside of your skull. If on the other hand, you are smart enough to wear a seatbelt, but unlucky enough to have hydrocephalus, your ventricles expand, intracranial pressure rises and squeezes your brain like someone is blowing up a balloon in your head and reducing your brain to mush." Hackett had always loved the way that professor had a knack for descriptions that stuck in his head forever.

Hackett would have to drill a hole in the man's skull and plunge a catheter through his brain. Still, his mind drifted. He thought about Sarah, the honeymoon, and how perfect it had all been. She wanted to travel again. God, how he'd love to pack it all in and travel the world with her.

He pushed that out of his mind. Right now, he had to concentrate. Hackett hadn't touched the hamburger in front of him, though he knew it was getting cold. Instead, he sat still and reviewed the procedure in his mind. He had a reserve of mental videos that he played over and over again before all but the simplest procedures. It played once. He rewound and started it again, losing himself in the silent details. He became so fully absorbed that he could smell the blood slowly oozing from the scalp. Second by second, step by step, he practiced each cut, each turn of the drill, each millimeter that he would measure twice to ensure accuracy, until his conjured vision ended in success. The old feeling of self confidence filled him. Happy and without self doubt, he let the vision evaporate. He looked down at his burger, no longer hungry. He thought of Sarah, smiled, but another face stared at him from his subconscious. Jean smiled. He heard her say that it was good to see that he was so happy. *I am*, he answered, *but I still miss you*. He saw her laugh, listened to her tease him and tell him that he had no choice; after all, nothing else was possible. They sat together in silent memory, holding hands, Jean kissing him softly on the neck.

As he sat, deep in thought, two cold, thin, delicate hands clamped over his eyes.

"Guess who and guess what?" Yu Lai said into his ear.

Contented, he let Jean slip away.

"That's easy — it's Doctor Wang and we're back in kinder-garten."

"Don't be a smart ass," she said and released her hands. "Really, guess who I just talked to and guess what happened."

"I give up."

"Okay, I'll tell you then. I just talked to Doctor Spanger about a new interview. They have someone who was in cardio last week and describes a full-blown death experience in great detail. Her story is fantastic."

"Yeah, I'll bet that she didn't describe what was on the elevated pictures."

"Well no, she didn't, but it is still great to get some positive results."

"Come on now, Doctor," Hackett answered. "The study has been going on for eight months, and by my count, there have been over one hundred cardiac arrests in the hospital and this is only the first clearly reported near-death experience." Hackett couldn't resist using the words "near-death" and throwing a little cold water on her joy.

"Listen to you, manipulating statistics to serve your own skepticism. First of all, you can't count the people who were not revived. We can't very well get answers from dead people."

"You seem to be trying." Hackett enjoyed making her squirm just a little.

"Don't be silly. Plus, you know damn well that most of those cardiac arrests occurred outside of Cardiac Care and the ER, and thus don't fully meet the study criteria."

"What I know is that this study is guaranteed not to have a sufficient completion rate to be statistically significant. It's going to go from scientific study to anecdotal evidence before it's even published."

"You are incorrigible. You just want to poke holes in the study any chance you get. Why did you agree to sponsor it anyway?"

"If you recall, I was being squeezed by my favorite doctor and my favorite nurse. I didn't stand a chance. Anyway, we've got more important things to deal with. Are you assisting me with this ventricular drain or not?"

~

Hackett folded and draped a blue sheet over the shaved skull. He double checked the placement and spacing of the lines he had drawn on the slack skin before making one final "X" on the spot known as Kocher's Point.

He pressed the scalpel into flesh, felt the customary resistance and remembered the words he had heard as a student so many years ago as he cut into his first cadaver. "It isn't Jell-O. You have to apply a little force." He drew the scalpel back, made a neat one-inch incision on the scalp four inches above the right eye and withdrew his hand to watch the first neat bubble of blood rise out of the wound. There were no large veins or arteries in this area, so it was a slow trickle, no need for suction. He used a dull instrument shaped like a tongue depressor to scrape the periosteum away from the outer skull.

He then grabbed the Midas drill, turned it on and slowly pushed his way down through the bone. The drill buzzed, and he could feel the vibrations in his fingertips. At precisely the right depth, he used his fingers to back the drill bit up and out of the bone. He wasn't quite down to the brain. Next, he used a thin wire-like blade to cut through the dura matter.

"Insert the catheter tunnel," Hackett directed Yu Lai as he stepped back.

He watched her hands, steady and sure as she took the bent metal tube, slid it under the scalp at the incision and pushed it along the outside of the skull.

While she worked, Hackett relaxed, confident in her abilities. He thought again of Sarah and of Jean. He felt a new comfort in their mutual presence. It was like he had awakened to a new world. He did not have to forget Jean to love Sarah. He did not have to compare one to the other and decide which woman he would commit his life to. They simply existed side-by-side, neither needing supremacy in his thoughts.

Hackett refocused on his work, realizing that this, too, had become less of an effort, more like it had been before Jean's death. He watched Yu Lai as the tip of the catheter approached its mark, thought about her, wondering how well he truly knew her. Of course, he knew her skills, her intelligence, her temperament, but he didn't know her inner motivations. He wondered why she was so obsessed with the near-death study. What did that reveal about who she really was? He had asked her if she had known about Ella Mae's episode when she had first brought up the study, but she had said no. Apparently that had been just as big of a surprise for her as it had been for him. He had also asked if she knew someone else who had gone through it, but again she said no.

With one final push of Yu Lai's fingers, the sharp stainless steel cut through skin. It occurred to Hackett that perhaps her interest in death was more basic, a crisis of faith or a need to deal with her own mortality. He had never thought of her as the type to be overly afraid of death. Years ago, in his own residency, he remembered being dismissive of it. Although he had been seeing death up close for the first time in his life, it was still like some distant star in his own universe. It was coming, but it was light years away.

Was Yu Lai so different from the way he had been? He felt sadness for her. He thought of a lifetime spent as a doctor sensing the Grim Reaper hovering around you at every turn. He wouldn't have made it, and perhaps the long, decorated career that he imagined for Yu Lai would not unfold.

He looked back at the small, dark hole and the cleaved flesh of his patient's scalp. Ever so slowly Hackett pushed the needle-like catheter into the frontal lobe at a precise angle. Through the folds of the cortex it went on its slow journey into the brain, down deeper through gray matter and into the frontal horn of the lateral ventricle.

"We're in," Hackett said and held up the tail end of the catheter so that both he and Yu Lai could see drops of spinal fluid fall and darken the blue sheet.

At that moment, he felt success and believed in his patient's survival, but it wasn't what really held his attention. The thing that he wanted most at that instant was Yu Lai's success. More than any other student in his last twenty years, she was a reflection of his own skill, a way for his work to continue. His daughter was his connection to the future in so many ways, she would have his grandchildren, but Amy was not a doctor. Yu Lai was his connection to the future of medicine. Without his daughter, his genes would die. Without Yu Lai, his skills would fade away and leave nothing for posterity.

# Chapter 16

Exhaustion battled anticipation within Ella Mae. The night shift from Thursday had dragged into a day shift on Friday, the day had given way to evening and still George had not rung her bell or knocked on her door. His flight was supposed to have landed two hours ago. She dialed his cell phone once more, the keypad blurring as she slowly pecked out ten digits. It rolled over to voicemail once more.

George had been traveling, and when he was on the road, they hardly spoke. He worked for a chain of discount furniture stores, and crisscrossed the country working hours that made her nursing sound like part-time. Ella Mae tried not to mind, but she had become dependent on George's company, especially now that Hackett was married to *that bimbo*. She had to set new sights, and she felt that she was lucky to have a man, any man. And George was good to her. He showered her with attention, at least when he was in town. Unfortunately, he never really opened up about himself. He had told her in vague terms about an unhappy marriage and children who he saw only occasionally. She knew his daughters' names — Rose and Charlotte, and the grandson Alec she had seen a photo of, but George remained closed, even about the boy. For all she knew, his ex-wife's name was simply "the bitch."

When Ella Mae tried to get him to open up, he would say it was too painful. He had lost his marriage and his children, and so, he had to focus on his new life. "I want to think about you," he would say. It all made her feel exceedingly uncomfortable.

Her mind wondered from speculation about his family, to

the reality of his smile. For someone who suffered from what he described as a deep and abiding pain in his heart, she was amazed at how happy he appeared with his never-ending smile. She saw him in her mind's eye, his smile beaming, his white teeth shining. She liked teasing him about it. "Will you wipe that shit-eating grin off your face," she had said to him as they lay on the couch on the last night he had been home. "You'd think we just watched *Mrs. Doubtfire* instead of *Schindler's List*."

"The movie's over, and I'm thinking about you," he answered and then nuzzled his face between her boobs, sputtering raspberries as if he was a toddler.

Ella Mae had shrieked with laughter, while she wiped away the last holocaust tears from her eyes. Those thoughts played across her mind like a dream, weaving reality and fantasy together into a wonderful delirious mush, until she wavered on the cliff's edge of sleep. Ella Mae's eyes fluttered one last time, reality dissolved into darkness, thoughts lost cohesion, and she fell asleep.

When she awoke, the room was dark. Half dazed, she tried to get her bearings, wondering whether she had slept through the night. She picked up her cell phone and looked at the time — eleven p.m. Only then did she remember that she was waiting for George. Her first reaction was worry that she had missed him, but she knew that even if he had forgotten his spare key, she would have heard him at the door. With that realization came anger.

He was now six hours late. She checked voice mail on both her cell and home phone, even though she knew that either call would have woken her up. There was nothing. She called his cell phone again — no answer. She sat on her couch stewing and thinking. After a few minutes, she called United Airlines. His flight had arrived on time. They would not tell her if he was on board.

Worry encircled her. She emailed him, not expecting an answer. By three a.m., she went to bed. The next morning, she once again woke up to an empty apartment. It was a feeling she was well used to. Until recently it was just about the only feeling she knew in the morning, but now it seemed exceptionally sad and depressing. Again, she wondered what could have happened and why he hadn't called. What if he had had an accident in a rental car in Seattle? She would have no way to contact him. She couldn't even call his office. He had gotten so angry the one time she had called him at work. "Just call my cell. I don't like people at work knowing about my personal life," he had lectured her.

Ella Mae again imagined a car accident, pictured him lying dead in the smashed-up vehicle, wondered if anyone at his office even knew to contact her. She might wait for weeks or months. She might never find out.

She paused with her hand on the phone, wondering if she was acting like a fool. He probably just got hung up at work. What did she expect? They weren't married. Her hand lifted off the receiver. She didn't want to drive him away. Ella Mae sat staring at the phone, imagining the worst, which wasn't that he was dead in a morgue, but that he was alive and well — done with her. She thought of her long years of loneliness and the few boyfriends who had come and gone. She thought of Hackett and Sarah, now married. It still saddened her. Her mind drifted back to the time after Jean's death, when she had spent so much time with Hackett, bringing him meals, helping him clean out Jean's closet, taking care of funeral details. She remembered one day in particular. They stood together in Hackett's house talking about Jean, when tears came to Hackett's eyes. Ella Mae put her arms around him to comfort him and he buried his head between her shoulders and neck. She could still feel how his body shook and the warmth of his tears on her skin. It was then that she realized how much she wanted him and always had. She had coveted her best friend's husband and then her best friend had died. She held on to him, savoring the bittersweet moment, but she did not act on it.

She looked out her window at the cloud-covered sky and windblown trees. She had lost Hackett to a thinner, prettier, younger woman. Wasn't that the way the world worked? Women grow old, the men around them who don't die are either still married or divorced and chasing women half their age. Being a middle-aged woman was a lonely burden. At least she had found George. Would she lose him, too?

~

George didn't call until Sunday. When she picked up the phone, she heard his cheerful voice, "Hi, Pookey."

"Where have you been? Why didn't you call?"

"I know. Sorry, I should have called, but we had an emergency. On Friday morning, I got a call just before I was supposed to board the plane. Both the manager and the assistant manager of our San Jose store quit without giving notice. I had to fly to California instead of DC I was up to my neck in alligators the whole weekend. I won't be back in DC until next Friday."

The tension that had tied her in knots all weekend exploded from her mouth. "Goddamn it. You could have at least called."

"I know," he said, and Ella Mae heard a hardening in his voice, "but I told you how it gets at work. I didn't have time to breathe. I still don't. You wouldn't have wanted to talk to me before now. It wouldn't have been pleasant."

Ella Mae backed off. The rest of the conversation was cordial but strained. When she hung up the phone, she felt uneasy, blamed herself for not understanding. If he hadn't always been so unfailingly nice, so perfect, and if she had more experience with men, she would not have backed him into a corner like that.

# Chapter 17

Hackett rode doggedly ahead, chasing a horizon of blue sky and white clouds, in turn being chased by a wall of grey. His legs ached, his ass bone was worse and his wrists were starting to get numb. The last thing he needed was rain. He pedaled over the crest, coasted to a stop where the road ran aground, blocked by vineyards. A woman's voice behind him yelled "left." He did as she directed, turning away from the blue sky, his hope fading with the horizon. Even in his worn-out state, the Italian countryside looked beautiful. He concentrated on the vineyards which carved lush green stripes into the slope on his right, backlit by the sun. Each row of immature grapes ended with a rose bush that formed an arc of vibrant color alongside the black pavement. The tour guide had told Hackett that the rose bushes served as sentries posting watch for disease. "The roses, they are the more fragile plant. They will succumb to the attack before the grapes, leaving the farmer time to do treatment." He loved the light Italian accent in the guide's clear English. Hackett pedaled. He thought of Sarah, let her beauty and that of the Italian countryside wash away his exhaustion.

When Jean had been alive, Hackett would have never left work so soon after his last vacation. He felt the weight of that guilt as his legs slowly pumped and his heart pounded. They had been married twenty-seven years, but he had not spent nearly enough time with her. First his studies, then his residency, then his work had been the real focus of his life. He would not make the same mistake with Sarah. Work never should have been that important.

Just behind him, a few women pedaled bikes identical to his and wore the same blue shirts. He had been slowing down to catch them for the last half hour. He imagined Sarah somewhere ahead, between him and the medieval Tuscan hill town of San Gimignano, riding with the faster lead group, pedaling hard up a steep winding road that he, himself, would walk.

The idea of a bicycle tour and the specific destination had been Sarah's idea. He had been immediately worried that he would not be able to keep up. The travel guide billed this trip as "moderate/difficult," but the company had assured him it could be as easy as he wanted. Back in the U.S, he had expected to stay on the easy side. However, when he arrived, he couldn't stand the idea of embarrassing himself and riding in the van while Sarah forged ahead, so each day he struggled to complete the circuit. He felt like he was a senior citizen trying to compete in the Tour de France.

Hackett lost himself in the long slow torture of exercise. He barely noticed when one woman and then another passed him. He did not bother to respond to their cheerful greetings, which were barely audible above his heartbeat. In time the world around him went silent, and the silence became strangely soothing. He pedaled, unaware that the gray clouds had overtaken him until he felt a fat raindrop slap his face. Within a few seconds the rain splattered uniformly on the pavement and eventually soaked his shirt. He pedaled. Sometime later, he realized that the rain had stopped. He was in a trance of dull ache when finally he rounded a corner and saw the tour company's familiar Renault chase van on the side of the road, surrounded by his fellow travelers. Hackett laid his bike against a tree and walked slowly toward the van and Sarah's smiling welcome. She was talking to a fit and attractive young couple with whom she had been riding since they arrived. He forced a brave smile.

"You look a little ragged," Sarah told him as he guzzled water. "Perhaps you should take the van the rest of the way to San Jimmy."

Hackett's lips curled half-heartedly. "I can make it if I take my time." He spoke slowly, his hand on his chest. She put her hand on the wet fabric of Hackett's t-shirt and patted him, as a father might comfort his child. "You're such a good sport. If you're game, I'll ride with you the rest of the way."

The fifteen-minute break wasn't enough to erase the pain in Hackett's chest or awaken his tired legs, but it did restore the sun, which gave Hackett a slight mental reprieve. The two of them let all but a few riders go before climbing on their bikes and heading out. They rode slowly, Sarah talking about the beauty around them, reclaiming it for Hackett, pulling the veil back from the hardship he had felt minutes earlier. They coasted down a long hill, punctuated with little uphill breaks that were hardly cause for effort. Little by little, he felt better.

The sun above now sparkled, and the landscape looked like jewels. Hackett's eyes focused on a single rose bush. "Stop," he yelled, braked, dropped his bike by the side of the road, and stared, mesmerized. Each flower petal and each leaf was covered with beads of water suspended as if by magic. Hackett felt like he dare not breathe or he would disturb the equilibrium and the beads would roll away, plunge to the ground and burst. He imagined the scene in time-lapse photography. The images faded, his pupils refocused on the droplets still hanging steadfast to the plant. Each droplet shimmered with reflected light, mirroring the blue sky and trees above him. In one especially large bulbous drop he could even see his reflection with Sarah by his side. Life was like that, Hackett thought, happiness suspended in time, until you blink and fate changes everything. He vowed to hang onto the moment, to make his time with Sarah count. He put his arm around her, content with his bride and his life.

"Maybe we could retire here?" Hackett said.

"Retire? You're so young."

Hackett smiled at the absurdity of her words. "You're kind, but I'm not young. Think how wonderful it would be to spend our time traveling the world."

"What about money? How would we live without money?"

"Who needs money, it can't buy love." He smiled at her.

"Don't be so stupid." Her voice grew harsh. "If you had lived without money for as long as I had, you'd never say that." Hackett didn't push, he was only musing, but her stridency took him aback. He hadn't really thought of Sarah as ever having to struggle, though he knew that to some extent she had. He thought about his life of privilege. It embarrassed him. He told himself not to be insensitive.

"I'll be happy as long as we're together," Sarah added, and Hackett dropped the subject.

That night the van left the hotel and dropped the riders off at the walls of the old city to find dinner for themselves. Hackett, Sarah and Sarah's young biking companions walked up the short steep hill past tiny shops with pottery, clothes and linens spilling from doorways out onto the narrow stone street. In one store, two stuffed wild hogs guarded artisanal cheeses and cured meats. The group stopped in the central square at the top of town, next to a small gelato shop proudly proclaiming in English: "Gelato World Champion." Hackett stared up at the town's distinctive stone towers looming above him. The square teemed with open air restaurants and tourists. While most of the group planned on eating at one of the restaurants before them, Hackett had his sights set on Cum Quibis, a place one of the tour guides had called the best restaurant in the area, so Hackett looked at his sightseeing map and pointed across the square.

They walked through the human mass into another road full of shops. Down the backside of the hill, they made one more turn before they finally came to a small doorway and stepped into a candlelit space with arches of brick and stone holding up centuries-old rafters. The hostess greeted them at a small table in the center of the room and walked them barely fifteen feet further through another archway and into a tiny courtyard surrounded by high walls. The town, the restaurant, the courtyard, and even the tables were the definition of romance.

"Would you like cocktails?" the waiter asked in accented but perfect English.

"I think we'll start with a refreshing bottle of white wine, maybe something local, but later, we just have to have a Brunello di Montalcino." Hackett had studied the wines of Tuscany before he left, determined to impress Sarah and treat her to the best.

"Excellent! If you are looking for a nice light white, may I suggest our Vernaccia di San Gimignano? You can't get any more local than that and it is beautifully refreshing, perfect for a warm evening such as this."

They sipped their white wine while eating crostini with salami, buratta cheese and fresh fig, moved on to an exquisite bottle of the 1997 Biondi Santi Brunello di Montalcino and some black truffle risotto, sipping, eating and gabbing pleasantly.

"Tell me more about this study your hospital did. It sounds fascinating," their young dinner guest asked.

Hackett had gotten an email earlier in the day from Yu Lai and had mentioned it on their walk. She had left the hospital just after the study concluded, her residency also complete. The hospital had offered her a position, but in spite of his sorrow at seeing her go, Hackett had encouraged her to accept another offer from New York Presbyterian. It was, after all, consistently ranked as one of the best neurology hospitals in the country.

"As I was saying, joining the study was my colleague's idea. About the best that I can say for it is that there were some intriguing if indefinitive results — about what I expected."

"So you didn't prove the existence of life after death?" The young man named Ted smiled and arched his eyebrows.

"As I feared when we started, the subject matter doesn't lend itself to statistical verification, and that's not just because it seeks to elucidate the seemingly unknowable, it's also based on sporadically-observed phenomena."

Ted's smile turned into a grin. "Say what?"

"While it is clear that some people do report what is commonly called near-death experiences, most of the people who have a full cardiac arrest don't cooperate by living or by having it in a room where we are waiting to study them. As a result, few make it through the study and interview process. Of those who do, about half have some memories of the events with about ten percent matching the definition of a near-death experience and only one or two percent having explicit recall of seeing or hearing events related to their resuscitation. So while we will likely end up with interesting anecdotal stories that will continue to stoke the debate, it is hard to imagine ever getting a sample size large enough to statistically prove that there is consciousness after cardiac arrest and to really know what that consciousness involves."

"But the way you described the study, the patients couldn't possibly guess what images were hidden above them in the operating room. Therefore, if anybody at all got it right that would be proof positive to me."

"That's not the way science works. We have to eliminate the likelihood that chance, inadvertent error or fraud were involved. We do that through statistics."

"Did any of the patients get it right? You know, was anyone able to recall what was on the hidden images?"

"Just one. Twenty-three hospitals, over two thousand cardiac arrests and one person met all the necessary tests."

"He saw what was on the card?"

"That's what I'm told."

"Wow, that's amazing. I'm not a scientist, but that really makes me wonder."

It was exactly the kind of reaction that annoyed Hackett. It was the antithesis of science. Unless they proved beyond a shadow of a doubt that consciousness after death did not exist, the anecdotal results would be taken as confirmation that it did.

He remembered his conversation with Ella Mae just before he left for Italy, after he had first reviewed the preliminary data. "Not significant?" she had yelled at him. "Ten percent of the people reported experiences very similar to what happened to me. Another forty percent had memories that weren't clear, but could have been evidence of a death experience. I'd say that is pretty damn significant."

He argued back, stating that it didn't prove anything.

"It proves you're stubborn and the study should continue."

"It proves that we are wasting our time, that it will take years and years to get a sample size that even comes close to being sufficient."

"So what? That just means it is hard. Those physicists that built the hadron collider in Switzerland have spent billions of dollars and millions of man-hours to prove that a quark exists. They don't hide behind such bullshit."

He didn't want to argue with Ella Mae. For her it was personal, so he backed down. Now he found that his patience was also too thin to argue. He didn't need the aggravation.

~

Back at the hotel after dinner, Sarah and their two new friends stared up at the stars and the sliver of a crescent moon hanging high in the night sky while Hackett unfolded a white sheet and hung it from a big bracket that linked together like a tent frame. They were standing in a flower garden at the far reaches of the property. Hackett explained that most moth hunters used bucket traps, but he preferred the old-fashioned approach. With a bucket trap, you just set the trap and went to bed; with a bed sheet, you could watch the moths approach, see their full beauty in flight as well as when they landed on the cotton fabric. Hackett set his beacon up on a tripod and flipped the switch. The sheet glowed like the moon had broken orbit and landed on earth. All around it, garden flowers basked in light.

"This is perfect," Hackett exclaimed. "Hawk moths love the light and they love the flowers." It was the first time in his life that he had gone moth hunting without Jean. That fact wasn't lost on him, but he didn't dwell on it either.

Next to him, Sarah opened a folding wooden chair, pulled a bottle of wine into her lap, and attacked it with a cork screw. When the bottle was opened, she offered her three companions a glass, but Hackett turned her down. He felt exhausted. If it weren't for his own anticipation of how Sarah would react to the sight of a hawk moth, he would have been in bed already.

They formed a semi-circle of chairs about ten feet away from the sheet and waited. "Do we have to be quiet?" the young woman asked.

"Well, for the sake of the hotel guests, we probably shouldn't scream, but I don't think the moths are going to mind our conversation."

For the first few minutes, they carefully inspected each moth that arrived, but nothing special appeared on the sheet. Soon, all but Hackett lost interest. The others sat, talked and sipped as Hackett investigated the creatures that came to visit. After about an hour, Sarah no longer seemed to care what was in the air. "I don't mind sitting out here and drinking wine," she told Hackett. "But I hope you're not going to make us stay out here all night."

"Just a while longer," Hackett told her, feeling the need for sleep in his own weary body. He sat down next to Sarah, and let his old bones settle. In a matter of minutes he lost hold of the conversation and heard his pillow calling. His eyelids fluttered and slipped down over his pupils. A momentary sleep arrived, but his tranquility was shattered by Sarah's shriek and the soft flapping of wings. Sarah jumped to her feet and flailed her arms.

Now awake, Hackett stood brimming with a wide smile. "That, my dear, is a hawk moth."

"Jesus Christ," Sarah said, her voice calming. "It looks like a fat little mouse with wings."

Hackett looked at the furry body, quite rotund and oversized for the creature. "In the light of dusk, many people mistake them for hummingbirds, as they feed on pollen and nectar, but I like your mouse description better."

Hackett stepped forward. With a large clear plastic bowl he trapped the giant just as it landed on his sheet. He directed Sarah and the couple to come close to inspect his quarry. It looked incredible up close; its big furry-looking brown body was actually covered in a kind of scales instead of feathers or hair. Hackett guessed that the body alone was four inches in length and an inch and a half in width. If you spread the wings out, they probably spanned six or seven inches. The skinny proboscis stretched another three inches in front.

"They're gross," Sarah announced. "Not nearly as pretty or big as that Hercules moth you have at home. Stick a pin in it like your other moths."

Hackett explained that he hadn't pinned moths for years, he just took their pictures now. He demonstrated by slipping his hand under the bowl and taking a picture of it next to the moth.

The young couple was eager to do the same, but Sarah refused. The moth disgusted her and it showed.

~

Sarah turned the bathroom light out and walked across the moon-lit floor towards the bed where Hackett lay. He still marveled at her nude body, lean from exercise, but curved in all the right places. How could she love him? he wondered. But she had married him. She was here now. She showered him with kisses that landed up and down his neck, face and finally lips. His disappointment over her reaction to the moth disappeared immediately.

"You make me feel like a queen, and I want you to feel like a king." She kissed him again, this time with what seemed like a touch more seriousness. "Or maybe a sultan, and I am one of your harem girls."

Sarah moved her lips from his mouth to his chest and roughly grabbed a handful of his ass. Hackett felt a surge of excitement. She nibbled and bit at his chest laughing as she went lower and lower. "I guess you're not that tired," she said as she grabbed hold of him, but Hackett struggled through sex. The aches and pains in his body, along with his lethargic limbs left little room for pleasure.

~

Hackett opened his eyes to an overcast sky and a hazy sickness in his head, chest and stomach. At first he assumed it was a hangover, but when he sat up in bed he felt dizzy in a way that didn't feel at all related to alcohol. Sarah walked out of the bathroom, already dressed in her green, red and white Italia bicycle shirt and shorts.

"Hurry up," she urged him in a voice that sounded dull and distant. "I'm hungry and we are already running a little late."

"You go ahead. I don't feel a hundred percent. Maybe if I take a shower I'll feel a little better."

Hackett assured Sarah he was okay, and she agreed to go down to breakfast without him. In the bathroom, he turned the hot up and the cold down until a cloud of warm vapor filled the room. He stepped into the stream of water, felt hot pin pricks assault his skin, and hung his head down into the onslaught. Soon, his hands were braced against the wall to hold him up. Exhaustion settled deep into Hackett's bones as he waited for relief, but the shower didn't help. He stumbled back from the bathroom and crawled under the covers. When Sarah came back, he told her to ride on without him. "If I get some sleep, at least I'll feel better for dinner," he said, but he wouldn't feel better.

At about ten in the morning, Hackett was roused from sleep by a sharp pain in his chest, and then his shoulder. Even in his continuing haze, he knew what it was. He rolled over with difficulty, picked up the phone and dialed zero. "I need an ambulance," he spoke into the phone and was alarmed at the effort it took. *Thank God everybody speaks English*, he thought as the girl at the desk questioned him about how he felt.

He explained that he was a doctor and that he was having a heart attack. "Dio mio," she said, her voice rising in alarm.

"I'll be alright, it isn't that serious." He said the words to calm her, but he knew they were bullshit. He could no more predict how serious it was then she could. He hung up the phone and lifted himself out of bed. Step by step he eased himself into the bathroom, where he found the jar of aspirin in his travel bag. Hackett thought about death, not the temporary death in his bullshit study, the real death, permanent, black and empty. He would never again touch Sarah's skin or see her smile as she sipped wine. He would never again see droplets of rain cling to rose petals, and he felt certain that he would not see Jean's face waiting on the other side. Emotional pain seared into him just as another sharp jab sliced into his shoulder. He broke a single pill in half by jamming it against the side of the sink, then popped it into his mouth and chewed. The spittle of nausea pooled around his tongue. He swallowed hard.

Back in bed, surrounded by white sheets and soft pillows, he felt no comfort. Instead, death haunted him. Two or three years ago, he would have gone willingly. Now, he thought about all he would miss as opposed to all he had lost. The years ahead loomed over him, creating a powerful dread in anticipation of his own absence. He wanted to stay with Sarah, to experience their life together. He felt the touch of her hand on his shoulder, heard the sound of her voice as she whispered in his ear, and felt the fullness of her breasts under his palms. He thought about work. It had kept him going in the years after Jean's death, but now it felt like nothing more than a sideshow — something to span time when he and Sarah were apart.

"Please, not yet," he said aloud to the empty room, and he heard a voice respond — *What about me? Have you forgotten about me already?* Hackett hadn't realized how little Jean's voice had danced in his head in recent months. He missed it, even though he knew it was a symptom of his depression and loneliness. He heard her tease him again. *This pretty young woman has really gotten into your brain.* The memory of her voice brought a measure of happiness back to him. He told himself that he would gladly die to see her again, if only that were possible. That thought passed quickly and another replaced it.

*Is it alright if I want to stay?* he asked Jean, but she did not answer.

Hackett slipped down into conversation with his dead wife, asked her to tell him about the moments of her own death, and heard her reassure him that it had been easy. He asked her if he had comforted her, and was assured that he had. In a conversation within a conversation, he warned himself to maintain focus, fearing that if he drifted too far into his daydream that he would simply drift away and die. As he conversed, the rap of knuckles on his door rattled his consciousness. He did not move. His eyes did not open. The knock came again, louder.

"Yes," he answered and felt his conscious thoughts return.

"It's Amelia from the front desk, are you okay?" The young woman's voice trembled with nervousness.

"Yes."

A girl of perhaps twenty entered the room and pulled up a chair by his bedside. She looked scared and lost. Now wide awake, the doctor in Hackett returned. She wasn't a nurse or a doctor, but she would have to do. He asked her if she knew CPR.

She had taken a course, but she never had to use it. Hackett led her through a quick review, then went over it again and again, watching as she practiced on a pillow. The repetition reassured him and took his mind off the situation.

After his lesson, they waited for the ambulance in awkward silence. He thought of Jean and Sarah. He pleaded with God, or at least with the universe, to let him live.

~

Sarah could not let him go. She had been chasing him for what felt like an eternity. She would not let him escape now. Every muscle in her body ached, not with screaming pain, but with a tiresome unforgiving exhaustion. An hour earlier, the three of them had been riding side by side. It had been a quick but comfortable pace. Then the hills came and they slowed. They all knew that the next ten miles would be tough, they had talked about it, decided to attack it together. For a few more minutes they pedaled in unison, contented. Then Ted broke the pact and broke from the pack.

"I'm gonna push it a little," he said. The meaning of the words didn't register in Sarah's mind until twenty seconds passed and he had separated from the two women. She still didn't quite comprehend that he meant to go it alone. Within another minute, his intent was unmistakable. Sarah gave chase.

The pavement wound upward toward the sky. Every once in a while, the grade would decline and she would work harder, knowing that he would gain distance if she did not. Slowly, she reeled him in. Quickly, he would slip away again.

The road now stretched out in front of her, a long steep uphill. In the distance, she could see Ted's legs pumping in methodical rhythm. She put her head down, pushed the fatigue back down into the hole where it belonged and willed herself to endure. In the distance, Ted slipped around another curve. Harder. Harder. She attacked the hill. Finally, she reached the curve around which Ted had vanished, hoping to see that the distance between them had disappeared as well. Instead, the road dropped dramatically and the pavement snaked around yet

another corner. Again, she attacked. Her legs and gravity propelled her down the steep hill until pedaling became irrelevant.
The game changed from grinding work into a desperate gamble
to maintain speed and control. She barreled headlong, her
pursuit transformed from determination to mania. She came
into the curve quickly, braking just enough, slowing down as
little as centrifugal force would possibly allow. As soon as she
was through the fulcrum, she again pedaled hard and hurtled
out of the curve like a rock from a sling shot. The trees parted,
the countryside opened up and a new hill stood up before her,
with Ted ahead. She had closed the distance, but not by much.

They battled like that for thirty minutes. Gradually, the small
town in the distance drew closer, a lightly sloping hill down and
a slightly larger climb up to its stone wall. He was within reach
now, his bicycle rocking slightly from side to side, no longer in
perfect balance. He saw her. She knew it. She pushed herself
down the slope, knew that she would catch him. At the bottom of
the grade, the road bent slightly to the right. She didn't see the
splash of gray gravel on black macadam until her wheels were
in it. Her arms and legs stiffened, the bike lost traction, first in
dribs and drabs, then—

There is nothing quite like losing control of a bicycle at
thirty-five miles per hour. You feel the moment that slip turns to
all-out slide. Your muscles go from tense to locked. You tell
yourself that you can recover. You believe it until that last
millisecond when the front wheel grabs pavement and turns
sideways. At that moment, you transition from preparation to
freefall. All you can do is pray for a soft landing.

Sarah saw the blacktop that lay before her. She watched it
approach in slow motion as she hurtled through the air. She saw
the grass just beyond, told herself to roll, tucked her shoulder
and prayed for green. She felt the hard pavement, heard her
helmet crack against the black. She tucked. Grass and dirt
attacked the skin of her face.

Sarah pushed herself slowly into a sitting position careful to
test her limbs as she did. Her biggest worry was the pain in her
shoulder, a broken collarbone, perhaps. She sat up rubbed it, and

reassured herself that it was uninjured. Reflexively, her hand rubbed across her face. She felt dirt and grass caked on her skin. There was a trickle of blood, too.

Reassured that she had broken no bones and sustained no serious injuries, Sarah turned to the bike. The wheel was in a lot worse shape than she was. She tried to pull it back to round, hoping that she could make it rideable. When that didn't work, she stomped on it, to no good effect.

Sarah had just picked up her bike, and begun walking it up to the village, when she heard a car approaching from the rear. She stopped and turned to see the chase van coming toward her with Luca the tour guide waving out of the window frantically.

*At least I don't have to walk,* Sarah thought.

"Sarah, Sarah," Luca yelled. Sarah heard the emotion in his voice and wondered how bad she and the bike looked.

"I'm alright," she yelled back. "Just took a spill."

The wheels of the van screeched to a halt next to her, and Luca jumped out, almost even before it stopped. She thought he was overreacting, and a big smile formed on her face.

"Your husband. They took him to the hospital. It was a heart attack."

The smile was still stuck on Sarah's face. It felt awkward and out of place. "What?" she asked.

"The ambulance took him to Firenze."

"Why?"

"He say to the woman at the hotel he had a heart attack."

The smile that had been pasted to Sarah's face finally cracked under the weight of his words. "Is he okay?"

"They said he was conscious when the ambulance arrived, is all I know." He shrugged.

The emotion that welled up inside Sarah surprised her. Without meaning to, she let go of her bicycle. It hit the ground with a dull thud that she hardly heard. She felt a constriction in both her stomach and her throat, then felt tears rising in her eyes.

"No, it can't be. We just got married," she said. Her own voice sounded muffled.

# Chapter 18

Hackett stayed in the hospital in Florence for a week. They spent another week in a small apartment before flying back to America. At home Sarah finally felt like she could relax, her mind no longer tortured with worry.

On the day of the heart attack, Luca drove her all the way to the hospital. When he pulled up to the emergency room doors, she jumped from the car without saying goodbye. Inside she ran to the reception desk, panting.

"What have you done with my husband?" she yelled.

"Scusi," the young woman standing before her replied.

"Where's my husband?" Sarah said in an even louder voice.

"I not speak English," the woman said, raising her hands in the air.

"You just did," Sarah screamed back.

Before she could say anything else, a man's voice came from behind her. "Can I help you, signora?"

They brought Sarah upstairs. Hackett had already come out of surgery and lay in the recovery room with wires and tubes coming out of his nose, chest and arm. Sarah carefully sat down next to him as if he were so fragile that the slightest bump would kill him.

"He is okay," the nurse told Sarah, but that was apparently all the English she knew.

Sarah stared at Hackett. He didn't look okay. His skin had turned from blotchy white to a cold gray. His chest seemed to rise and fall so slowly that she didn't dare look away for fear that his breath might not continue. She stayed with him until his eyes fluttered open.

"There you are," she said, and she felt the flood of warm tears building once more. "You're going to be okay," she told him without benefit of knowledge.

When the doctor finally came in, Sarah immediately pulled him back out of the room. "Is he going to be alright?" she asked once the door was closed. The doctor did his best to reassure her, but her mind focused on the words "serious" and "another attack is possible." She returned to Hackett's side, red and puffy. That night and the next, she slept in the chair next to him. On the third night, she felt confident enough to get a hotel room. In the long hours of the fourth day, she worked with needle and floss on a pattern she had found in a store by the hotel. It soothed her, kept her from asking Hackett how he felt every few minutes.

That afternoon, he awoke from one of his many naps and restarted a conversation they had been having about the future. "Recovery is slow," he said, even before she had seen that he was awake. "But I'll be fine. You'll see. I'll exercise, and pretty soon I'll be sailing past you on our bike rides."

Sarah laughed. "That will never happen, my dear."

"I'm sorry I ruined your vacation. I'll make it up to you."

Seconds passed. Her hands returned to the needlework in her lap. Minutes passed. Silence regained its primacy in the room. Sarah's thoughts drifted. She thought about the time they had spent together. She thought about the plans she had made. Everything had fallen into place, just as she had hoped — everything except the pre-nuptial agreement. Why had she agreed to that? It had made so much sense at the time. She had thought that she could eventually do away with it. Now time had shown her that she was not in control.

"Hackett." His name popped out of her mouth, and other words followed without thought. "When we get back home, we should talk about finances, and our wills. We should talk about the future."

Hackett's eyes fluttered. "Yes dear, we'll talk at home."

~

Sarah gradually fell back into her own schedule. Hackett slowly recovered. Unfortunately, the specter of losing him still hovered in her mind, a dark cloud in an otherwise clearing sky.

"You gotta stop worrying. It ain't doin' shit for you," Trudy told Sarah as a plump young Asian girl with doll-like hands filed her finger nails.

Sarah sat in the next seat, her own nails in the care of another girl — Vietnamese, Korean, or Chinese, Sarah couldn't tell. "We just got married. What am I going to do if he dies?"

"He ain't gonna die, and if he did, you'd survive. Besides, he's a doctor. If anyone knows how to care for himself it ought to be a doctor. He sure acts like he knows everything."

The plump girl in front of Trudy grabbed hold of a pair of cuticle scissors and clipped off white slivers of soft dead skin. Sarah thought of all the dreary, meaningless jobs she had worked. She thought about James. She had married him without understanding the real world. She had been a child chasing cotton candy dreams.

She was that girl no more.

*You have to plan for the future,* Sarah had drilled that mantra into her own head. This time, she thought she had. She had found a man who could give her everything she wanted, wealth, happiness and perhaps even love, but she hadn't planned as well as she should have.

"Watch out, you cow," Trudy screeched at the girl who held her hand. Sarah saw her yank away. "You cut me. Jesus, now I'm bleeding."

The girl grabbed a tissue and squeezed Trudy's finger. The tiniest drop of blood colored the soft white fibers.

"Sorry, very sorry," the girl said in some sort of Asian accent.

Trudy's head turned to Sarah. "Did you see what this twit did?"

Sarah laughed barely audibly. "You'll live."

"Listen to you, all full of sympathy. I listen to you moan

about your husband and I comfort you. Some woman nearly cuts my finger off and you could care less."

"Nearly cuts your finger off?" Sarah's inflection rose. "How can you compare that drop of blood to Hackett having a heart attack?"

"Jesus Christ, will you just stop. Your precious Hackett isn't going to die. You are letting this heart attack run away with your mind. Now you're even going back to work. I can't believe that."

"I have to! You don't know how cruel this world can be. One day you have a loving mother. The next day she's dead, and your father marries a crazy bitch. One day you fall for a handsome boy with a fast car, the next day he's an unemployed drunk. Life tends to fuck with the person who isn't prepared. I should know."

Sarah saw Trudy staring at her, the surprise on her face evident. Her worry over Hackett was making her careless. Trudy was her only friend, but even with Trudy, Sarah generally guarded herself, didn't talk about the past. "I just need to take care of myself. I am not the kind of person who likes relying on others."

"But you hated working. All you talked about was getting married and quitting. Now you're going to work again? I don't get it."

"It won't be that bad. I'll be working with Hackett. It won't be full time. Plus, we can always go on more vacations."

"Don't bullshit me. I'm the one who sat at the desk next to you. I'm the one that listened to you whine about needing a man like Hackett to deliver you from the daily grind."

"Yeah," Sarah acknowledged. "But I signed that goddamned pre-nup. I have to be prepared."

# Chapter 19

On his first day back in the office, Hackett sat at his desk drawing a heart on his blotter. Not the simple cartoon depiction with lovers' names and an arrow, he drew the heart as he remembered it from anatomy class: the left ventricle, the right ventricle, the left atrium, the right atrium and, of course, the arteries which had been rerouted within his own chest. He had returned to the office, scheduling a few patients per day, but he had not yet returned to the hospital. As he sketched, he wondered if this gradual return to his practice was the best approach. He was finding it pretty damn stressful to spend his time waiting.

A knock on the door interrupted him. It made him think about the hotel clerk in San Gimignano. He sensed her nervousness once again, shivered at how close he had been to death. Before he could speak, the door opened and Sarah walked in. She looked like a girl, skipping up to his desk and slyly slipping behind it to give him a kiss. It seemed odd having her there, but there were benefits. He grabbed hold of her ass and squeezed the firm flesh.

"Watch it, buster. Gotta be professional in the office." She kissed him again. "Did you take those bills off the reception desk?" she asked.

"Yeah, I was going to go through them just now."

"Give 'em back." She smiled again. "That's my job."

Hackett knew that Sarah was trying to be helpful, but he was a little worried. The idea of Sarah working for his practice had seemingly appeared out of thin air. She had been so eager to quit her job at Catholic University and seemed so happy with the freedom of unemployment. But when they had returned from Italy, she badgered him about working in the office until he gave in. He guessed that it had something to do with his heart attack, but she denied that. "I just want to be helpful, and it will save money at your practice," was all that she said.

As if she was reading his mind, Sarah said, "Now don't you worry, I got that book on medical bookkeeping, and I have been on the phone with the insurance companies for a week straight making sure that I know the procedures. Plus we still have Beth and she has been very helpful breaking me in. I told you, I'm good at this kind of thing."

Hackett relaxed just a little. "At least let me grab your ass again," he said and reached for her, but she jumped out of his way, blowing him a kiss as she did. Hackett wanted to follow her, to stand over her shoulder as she worked and make sure that she did it right. He had been carrying on this argument with himself since she first raised the idea of working at the practice. With employees, he could make decisions as he saw fit. That wasn't the way it worked with a wife. He would have to consider her needs and desires. There was another reason he was uncomfortable. Sarah had an innate intelligence, but she had not gone to college. She was not a professional. He loved her, but he really didn't trust her to work for him.

~

A royal blue fish hovered in the aquarium water, so bright that it looked as if someone had implanted a tiny flashlight in its belly. Its long shredded fins rippled and shimmered like magical feathers. In the opposite corner, a blue and orange fish with a frog-like face stared out through the glass as it gulped. Other fish skulked at the bottom in search of algae. Aside from the gurgle of the aquarium pump and the occasional tinkle of silverware, the restaurant was silent. There was only one other couple eating. It was the kind of place Hackett hated, a suburban storefront with Formica tables and cheap art, not a beer or wine bottle in sight.

The fish in the tank looked more appetizing to him than the tofu and green beans on his plate.

On the drive home from the office, he had suggested going to Flanagan's for dinner, even promised to have a salad and skip the Guinness, but Sarah said no, exclaiming that the salads at Flanagan's held as many calories and as much fat as the hamburgers. Hackett wondered why he had given in.

The other couple sitting in the restaurant hadn't said a word since they arrived. Hackett imagined their thoughts, guessed that their children and grandchildren visited them no more than once a year, assumed they would soon be in a nursing home. He looked up at Sarah, saw the same bored look on her face.

"How's your food?" he asked.

"Pretty good," she replied.

"Mine tastes like wet cardboard and canned beans." Hackett readied a smile, in the hope she would laugh. She had been quiet and sullen since their argument that afternoon when Hackett had chastised Sarah for being rude to Beth. He had apologized, but she seemed to simmer still.

"You're the one with a heart condition. I'd rather be at La Ferme." Anger bubbled behind her words.

Hackett chewed on, while Sarah moved her food around her plate. "Did you like work today?" he asked her.

"It was fun, and I learned a lot, but it would be better if we were a little busier. How long can you go without seeing more patients?"

"There is no need to worry about that."

"Really? We went on vacation, then you were in the hospital, then you were recuperating, now you are hardly working. You pay a fortune in rent, probably too much in payroll. We need the income."

"There are always plenty of sick people in the world." Hackett smiled at her again, hopeful.

"It's not a joke. You're getting better. You'll lose patients if you keep referring them to other doctors."

The man at the other table looked over at Hackett, then turned away when their eyes met. Hackett felt embarrassed. He bent forward and talked a little more softly. "It'll be alright, and if you are going to work for me, you're going to have to let me take care of the business decisions."

The food at the end of Sarah's fork hovered by the opening of her mouth, then retreated. She looked directly into Hackett's eyes, made sure that she had his attention, then laid the fork back on her plate. "This is a marriage, not an employment relationship."

"I know, but I'm the doctor. It is my practice."

"This is our future, goddamnit. Don't I count?"

Hackett shrunk in his chair. "Of course you do. You know that's not what I meant."

"Then what did you mean?"

"Never mind. I just meant there is nothing for you to worry about."

Sarah's lips parted, but no words came out. Hackett continued, "I was going to look into scheduling more patients anyway. I can't stand sitting there playing with my pencils." The tension in Sarah face slackened just a little, but still she did not talk. "And I promise that I won't treat you like an employee."

Sarah allowed a small smile to crack through her frown. She looked like she was about to talk, but a sound startled her just before the restaurant's plate glass windows exploded. It felt like the whole room moved. Glass flew toward Hackett, showering their table with sparkling shards. The front fender of a red car pushed into the dining room, upending a table which slid into Sarah's back and nudged her forward a few inches. Hackett saw the car plow past her, upending tables and smashing chairs. He watched the bumper strike the man's chair and push him hard forward, bending him in half, face first into his dinner. There the car stopped, pinning the man to the table, as his wife fell backward and somersaulted across the floor. The crash of glass, chairs, tables and silverware continued for a few milliseconds more.

Sarah stood up. Looked at her hands, moved her arms, felt her legs. "Am I hurt?" she asked Hackett.

He stepped towards her. "I don't think so."

On the floor, the old woman crawled toward her husband. "Henry," she called. Then louder — "Henry!"

The scene was jarring. The distraught woman was spellbound, her husband in front of her pinned between a table and a car bumper, a stunned middle-aged woman still at the wheel.

"Put the car in park and lift the emergency brake. Do not let that car move," Hackett yelled at the driver, who did as instructed. Hackett moved calmly but quickly. The man lay motionless, his head flat on the cockeyed table. Hackett grabbed his wrist first — no pulse. Touched his neck — nothing. He knew that no more than seconds had passed, so he quickly surveyed the man's body for signs of trauma — again saw nothing. He had no choice, regardless of what the injuries might be.

"You," he said, pointing to the waitress. "Do you have an AED?"

"A what?"

"A defibrillator."

"I don't think so. What's that?"

"Call 9-1-1."

When he saw her dial he turned to Sarah and called her by name. "Help me with this table."

Hackett held the man's shoulders and told Sarah to slide the table backward. When the car door opened, Hackett glanced over his shoulder and his eyes met the driver's. "Don't move," he said, his command stern and authoritative. The driver froze. He lowered the man gently to the ground and rolled him to his back, put both hands on his collar and ripped his shirt open. Buttons scattered among the broken glass. He ran his hands across the skin of the old man's chest.

"Pacemaker?" he asked the wife.

"No," she answered.

Hackett opened the man's mouth and checked his airway — clear. He placed one hand within the other, palm down on the man's chest and began compressions.

~

On the drive home, Sarah sat at the wheel, occasionally turning her head in Hackett's direction and offering an awkward smile.

"Fate can be fickle. He was having dinner one second and gone the next. I can't stop thinking about your heart attack. It could have been like that."

"I guess it could have been, but it wasn't. You'll have to put up with me at least for a little while longer."

"I'm sorry I got mad earlier. I'm just worried and I'm trying to maintain control of things."

Hackett looked at her, understood her fears. "I'm not going anywhere," he assured her.

"Stop it. Don't treat me like a child. We both have to deal with the fact that you had a heart attack. I'm not going to make believe it didn't happen."

Hackett looked at Sarah, making an effort to convey his understanding with his eyes. "I don't mean to be patronizing, but we have to live our lives. What comes will come."

"We can be prepared. That's why I'm helping at the office. I need to be prepared."

Once again, silence filled the space between them. It had never been there before his heart attack, but now it hung like a shroud whenever their conversations got difficult. Hackett settled into it. He turned inward. He wanted to be understanding, but he was the one who almost died; he was the one who deserved understanding.

Eventually Sarah's voice interrupted his thoughts. "Jesus Christ." Her exasperation was clear.

"What?" Hackett asked.

"Death is trailing behind you like a hungry puppy."

Her words shocked him. Quite honestly, the man's death in the restaurant weighed less on his mind than their discussion about the office. It made him realize just how common death was for him.

"Have you changed your will?" Sarah asked. That question knocked him backward a little as well. He felt like a pinball within her conversation. "I asked you in the hospital, and you still haven't even acknowledged my question."

"I'll look into it." He said the words to placate her, not really wanting to talk about it.

"What does that mean?"

"It means I'll look into it."

"You better do more than look into it. I signed that damn pre-nuptial agreement. The least you can do is take care of me if you die."

Hackett felt the tofu sour in his gut. A vision of Jean at home in her red leather chair appeared in his mind. He wanted to yell "no." After Hackett and Sarah had married, he talked to his lawyer about the will. His emotions had gotten all wrapped up in it. The idea of removing Jean's name felt like a betrayal, like he was casting her off. He and Jean had shared in everything. It was their money.

Sarah couldn't understand what she was asking. Changing his will was another step in erasing Jean from his life, plus there was Amy's health. Who knew when she might decline. His money, the money he had saved with Jean was his daughter's insurance policy. Sarah had no right to ask him to change it.

Hackett had never told Sarah about his conversation with the lawyer, or about his decision not to change the will. In fact, he didn't remember discussing the will with her at all, not in the hospital, not before, not after.

"I have taken care of you already." Hackett's voice turned hard. "When we were married, I set up a life insurance policy in your name, and under Maryland law, you get thirty percent of my estate regardless of what my will says."

Hackett looked at Sarah, expecting to see some sort of understanding, perhaps relief. He had thought about her, taken care of her. Her eyes remained steely hard.

"What's in the life insurance policy?" she asked.

"A half million dollars."

Her eyes rolled. "And then just a third of the estate?"

The tofu boiled.

# Chapter 20

Hackett sat outside the office of Jeff Hovanian, the hospital's CEO, drumming his fingers on the arm of his chair, wondering why Hovanian had called him in, half hoping, half fearing that Hovanian was going to ask him to step down. By the time the door opened and the square jawed, immaculately coiffed Hovanian stepped out to greet him, Hackett was a bundle of nervous energy.

"You look great," Hovanian said as he clasped Hackett's hand, the grip strong but not crushing. Hovanian's shirt sleeves were turned up precisely, tie loosened ever so slightly. Both appeared calculated to give off the perfectly mixed signals of authority and casual comfort that oozed from his pores.

"Feeling great," Hackett replied. Hackett had known the man for just three years, but it felt like much longer. To Hackett, Hovanian represented the new breed of hospital administrator, the kind that was absorbed in finances and disconnected from medical care. Hovanian's first year had been exactly what Hackett had feared when he was hired, a whirlwind of cost-cutting and new policies. Every new administrator seemed to need to throw out their predecessor's practices, as if they were exorcising a demon. Thank God that crap had slowed down, but it left a bad taste in Hackett's mouth nonetheless.

Hackett took a seat, and watched Hovanian settle into his plush leather chair behind his big walnut desk. Not for the first time, Hackett looked at the ostentatious elegance around him. His feet rested on a beautiful oriental carpet, the weave so tight and pattern so intricate it would not have been out of place on a museum wall. Behind the CEO hung a signed Picasso print. Hackett knew from previous visits that it was number eleven of four hundred. Next to the Picasso was a bevy of photographs of Hovanian standing with presidents and dignitaries. Bill Clinton and both Bushes were among the famous. He was even paired with Bono from U2 in one photo. There was no cost-cutting evident here, nor in Hovanian's multi-million dollar salary.

The next words out of Hovanian's mouth took Hackett by surprise. "I understand that you are moving forward with an extension of that near-death study. Are you absolutely sure it's on solid ground scientifically?"

Hackett couldn't have guessed that this was why Hovanian had wanted to meet. He had submitted the paperwork for the next round of the study, but he hadn't even made a final decision. He was just going through the motions for Ella Mae and Yu Lai, even though the latter was now in New York. Sitting in front of Hovanian, Hackett found himself aligning with his friends and resenting the interference.

"That's a medical decision," he said firmly.

"Well, yes it is, and I don't want to interfere, but last year's study didn't seem to produce much in the way of results, and Senator Hardish has approached me about it."

Hardish, a recently retired senator from Oklahoma, was also a newly appointed member of the hospital's board of directors. The few hairs remaining on Hackett's head stood straight up.

"What does he care?"

"He's concerned about wasting money and he's concerned about the hospital's image."

Without really meaning to, Hackett dug himself into position. "It's a good study. The lack of results so far is attributable to sample size, and I don't need approval to authorize this."

"Don't misunderstand me, Doctor Metzger. I am not taking a position myself. I am just inquiring. If you think this study is worth it, I'm inclined to back you. That is, unless a majority of the Board are in opposition. In fact, I fear that the senator's position is at least partially influenced by his feelings that the study does not adequately reflect his Christian beliefs. That motivation does not sit well with me."

Just as quickly as Hackett's hackles had risen, they laid back down. He realized that he had pre-judged Hovanian's intentions, and was now just a little impressed to see that Hovanian had principles.

"Sorry for my presumption," he said, and then he found himself launching into a rather impassioned defense of the study. He talked about the sample size, going into detail about the number of cardiac arrests that fell within the parameters of the study and how the results reflected the fact that Doctor Parnell was being careful to maintain its integrity and validity. Hackett even fell back on the dreaded anecdotal evidence to arm Hovanian with a Christian tale for the senator.

After he finished the story, he said, "Many Christians who undergo these experiences believe that their religious beliefs are validated." He neglected to say that the same was true with people of other religions.

~

As Hackett talked to Hovanian, Sarah pored over a stack of insurance forms at her desk in the office on 19th Street. She had always known that a doctor's practice was a gold mine, but now that she understood the details more, she realized she had underestimated the potential, especially if she worked the angles. The only sticking point was that Hackett's heart attack had seriously dented his income. That wouldn't do. He would have to go back to the hospital and increase his patient load, but there were also things she could do. It would be easy. All she had to do was change a form here and there, increase the billing, and the money would flow in.

She looked at her files on the computer, studying the charges, figuring out which ones she could increase that would generate the most money and not look out of place. She looked at each insurance company, trying to understand which charges got questioned and which didn't. The more she dug, the clearer it became that the insurance companies would be a risky target in comparison to Medicare, but a neurologist's office wasn't nearly as good a location for Medicare fraud as a nursing home. She would have to take her opportunities where they arose.

Her first effort would be to comb through all of the records and find similar cases that resulted in different kinds of billings. She would then see if she could add the additional services that were missing. When she had all of that in hand, she would figure out how to divert the extra money to a separate account.

When Hackett got back to the office, she was buried so deep she didn't even notice him sneaking up behind her, until she felt his hand on her rear end.

"What you doing, girl?" he asked.

"Just making sure things are in order. You know, I think that Robin may not have submitted all of your charges to insurance companies over the last few months. Maybe she was distracted by her pregnancy." Sarah planted the seed, not knowing if she would need to use it later.

She let Hackett ask a few questions before changing the subject. "How was your meeting?"

"Oh, that," Hackett answered. "It was nothing. He just wanted to talk about the near-death study, but I did tell him that I was resuming my full duties."

He saw the smile light up Sarah's face.

"You did? That's great! I thought you were going to ease back into your schedule." She stretched the word "ease" into a long, mocking tease.

Hackett looked at the self-satisfied smile on her face and once again felt his anger bubbling. "I don't see why it should make a bit of difference." Now he saw her smugness turn to something else.

"You don't see why it makes a difference? Perhaps I don't count. Perhaps I should just keep my opinion to myself. I thought we were married for Christ's sake."

"Never mind," he said. "You're right. I'm just irritable."

"Irritable? I'd say you were being a self-centered ass. I'm not supposed to comment on our future, my future. It's all up to you.

Just like your will. It's like we were never married. I'm supposed to be happy with the leftovers."

~

Ella Mae's eyelids hung heavy. She heard voices from the television talking to her as if they were ghosts from another realm. Her mind drifted, random thoughts grabbing what was left of her consciousness and riding away with it. She was in that wonderful semiconscious state where reality and fantasy merge into blessed delirium. Thank God, it was saving her from another lonely night at home. She had suffered through so many such nights, more than any human deserved. Her life before George seemed to be a long narrowing path leading to a singular existence. She now saw George in her imagination. She talked to him, told him that she loved him. She wasn't quite asleep enough for the dream to take complete hold of her, but in the twilight, she felt his warmth and wanted him to talk back.

Ella Mae had often wondered whether the time would arrive when she existed in total solitude, an island surrounded by humanity, a person having no meaningful contact with other sentient beings. For so long her road to loneliness seemed inevitable. She was an only child who was loved and coddled by her parents, especially her father, who doted and showered her with limitless affection. He died when she was just eleven, leaving her shattered. After his funeral, her mother took her to live with her grandparents in Green Bay and she lost her childhood friends as well. Ella Mae held close to her mother out of fear of losing her, too. She didn't make a lot of friends in Green Bay, didn't even try. She felt unattractive and unwanted. By the time she was in her early twenties, her mother had begun a long battle with cancer. For Ella Mae, nursing became more than a profession. It became a twenty-four-hour reality.

On the day of her twenty-sixth birthday, after she had gotten a job in DC and was now caring for her mother, Ella Mae sat in the airport, feeling guilty while she waited for a plane to take her to Fort Lauderdale and a much-needed vacation.

The plane took off and she ended up in the frozen river, unexpectedly chasing her own death instead of her mother's. By any measure, it was a terrible experience, but she came to view it as a gift. It helped her deal with death, and it helped her deal with her own perceived inadequacies. On that day, as Ella Mae slipped beneath the surface, she stopped breathing and her heartbeats ceased. She felt at peace and she received the most wonderful of gifts. A light appeared to her, like a glowing ball. Without hearing the words, she knew that this wonderfully beautiful thing was her father. He told her not to fear her mother's death and not to regret his own. She comprehended the truth in his thoughts. Life and death were simply part of a greater journey. She did not hear. She simply understood. And what she understood was that it was not her time. *Go back!* She felt her father's words, and then she was once again alive, at peace for the first time in many years.

Ella Mae's mother died within six months. Ella Mae mourned but did not obsess. She learned to live her life, and the hand she had been dealt. She covered her loneliness with humor, her rejections with outward bravado. Within a few years, she had met Hackett and through him Jean, her one true friend in the world. When Jean died, she tried to focus on what she knew. Death was not the end, but perhaps because of the passage of time, or perhaps because she had already suffered too much loss, knowing what death brought no longer felt like enough. She missed Jean and felt her loneliness all the more keenly. It was her feelings for Hackett that filled the void of her missing friendship. Because of Hackett, she was not alone.

Her floating thoughts did indeed bring sleep, peaceful, beautiful sleep, until a ringing phone jarred her back into semi-consciousness. New and unfamiliar voices from the television confused her. For a moment, she wasn't sure where she was. The phone rang again. She searched for it, found it and raised it to her ear.

"Hell...o." Her voice sounded a little garbled. "Hello," she said once more struggling for normalcy in her vocal chords and clarity in her mind.

"Ella Pulaski?"

"Ella Mae," she corrected out of habit.

"My name is Allison Townsend."

Ella Mae recognized the name as George's ex-wife. She wasn't sure how to respond. "Yes," was the only word that came out of her mouth.

"I got your number from George's cell phone. I take it that you are screwing him."

"What?" Ella Mae was stunned.

"You heard me." The words shot back at her.

"I don't see how that is any of your business."

"You don't?" The woman's anger flowed hot across the fiber optic cables. "You're fucking my husband and you don't think that's any of my business?"

It all fell into place. George was still married. That explained the radio silence when he travelled. That explained the extra cell phone she had seen in his car and at his house. She felt sick. Ella Mae let her vent, figuring that it was her right. Eventually, Ella Mae told her everything: how they had met; the lies George had told; and how stupid she must have been.

She was exhausted when she hung up the phone. She realized that she had been breathing so deeply and rapidly that she felt light-headed. She closed her eyes and tried to relax, and that was when the full weight of what had happened finally got past her surprise.

The tears came in an avalanche, each heave of her body reinforced by her pounding fists and kicking feet. She screamed and wept and screamed and wept and screamed and wept some more.

A knock came at her door. She answered it with an outburst of pain, and a shout. "What?"

"Are you alright?" a woman's voice asked from the other side.

Ella Mae wiped her tears and tried to compose herself. She cracked the door open.

"Should I call the police?" a young woman asked.

"No," Ella Mae managed to say in a calmer voice. She pulled herself together. "I'm sorry. I got some bad news." Ella Mae knew that she must have looked terrible. She continued to wipe at her face as the woman stretched her head to look around Ella Mae and into the apartment.

"Is anyone else with you?" the woman asked softly. "Are you in danger?"

"It's nothing like that. I'm totally alone."

The women leaned closer and her voice dropped to an almost inaudible whisper. "Just wink if you want me to call the police."

"No really," Ella Mae said, realizing just how frightening her screams must have sounded through the thin apartment walls. "Please come in and see for yourself. There's nobody here but me. I was just distraught."

The woman came in and Ella Mae showed her the empty apartment. She asked if there was anyone she could call. Ella Mae said no. Finally, she left. Ella Mae sat back down on her couch and contemplated what she had just been asked. The words sounded dreadful as she played them back in her mind. "Is there anyone I can call to come be with you?" She was once again alone. Ella Mae thought about George and knew she would miss him, even though she never wanted to see or talk to him again. As she had feared, her miracle romance was nothing more than a fleeting dream. She sat in her apartment for another fifteen minutes staring at her hands before she picked up the phone and called Hackett, the last person left on her short list.

# Chapter 21

The glare of the bright hospital lights sliced through Hackett's eyes, and the clopping, rhythmless slapping of his own feet striking the floor made his head throb. Hackett wondered how he had let himself be dragged back into this mayhem. His first weeks back had been one crisis after another. Months before, he had picked Yu Lai's replacement from what he considered his least promising class of residents in years. He had known before he left on vacation that the new chief wasn't working out. The best thing he could say about Sally Drexall was that she was average and tended not to totally screw things up. When he finally returned to work, he realized that she was becoming proficient at something, and that thing was messing up. The added responsibility of being chief had turned her into a nervous wreck, and Hackett's increased scrutiny sent her over the edge. Within two weeks of his return, she quit, resigning her position and leaving the hospital, telling him she was not cut out to be a doctor. Hackett then promoted his second choice, another unexceptional student. Hackett hoped that John Wilkes' ample ego would at least be better than Sally Drexall's thimble full of self-confidence. Once again, Hackett was being proven wrong.

He was running down the hall, feeling his chest pound, thinking of the text that Ella Mae had just sent — "Where r u? Get back b4 JW kills patient in 408."

Pain stabbed at him like a long thick needle was being plunged into his brain. Hackett couldn't even have lunch in peace anymore. He made a mental note to take some Advil after the crisis was over. *Four*, he told himself. *Maybe six.* His mind was overloaded to the point that his brain was bursting. He was worried about the patient, about whether his new Chief Resident could handle the job, about his wife's increasing emotional insecurity, his own health and of course, he was still worried about Ella Mae.

When he arrived at Ella Mae's apartment after the call from George's wife, she had been a mess, crying inconsolably about George's betrayal and beating herself up because she wasn't worthy of happiness. Hackett had never seen her so vulnerable. He knew how much George had meant to her and how lonely for men she had always been, but she seemed like one of the strongest people on earth. He had always admired that about her.

That night, as he sat on her couch holding her and feeling incredibly uncomfortable, she just kept crying. Eventually, with no conscious thought, he realized that he was rocking her back and forth like he had done for his daughter as a crying baby. The recognition of what he was doing made him feel even more odd. He would have giggled out loud if it all hadn't been so distressing.

They never really talked that night. It turned out that Ella Mae had nothing much to say. In response to her sobs, Hackett found himself muttering meaningless words to her and not expecting an answer. After an eternity, her cries faded, her eyes got heavy and she fell asleep. He comforted her still, unable to free himself. It felt intimate in a creepy way.

He let her sleep like that for about an hour, then he gently lifted her head and tried to slide out from under her without waking her. He didn't think it would work and sure enough, her eyes opened. Ella Mae wiped back the tears that no longer wet her cheeks.

"What time is it?"

"Almost eleven."

"I'm sorry I kept you here so long. Sarah must be worried you got into an accident or something."

They walked to the door of the apartment and Ella Mae paused, grabbing hold of Hackett's hand. Her sad eyes looked into his as if she were about to talk, but then the tears came again. She buried her face in his neck. The salty rain poured.

"Oh, Hackett, I am so stupid, so incredibly fucking stupid."

After a long minute, Hackett told her that he should get going. "Okay," she replied, her head still muffled in his neck, and then he felt her lips against his skin. It was a kiss, a kiss on his neck, not a friendly kiss, he thought, more like a hungry kiss. Hackett imagined her exposed breasts once more. Thankfully, Ella Mae pushed herself out of his embrace. Neither made eye contact, and Hackett quietly slipped out the door.

Since that night, Ella Mae had refused to talk about George, except to say that it was over and she had wiped him from her life. To Hackett, she was putting on a brave front, but that's all it was. Her jokes were flat and her smile had lost its brightness.

When Hackett walked into room 408, the patient was being wheeled out. Hackett felt an overwhelming sense of relief when he saw the seventy-three-year-old man breathing on his own. He passed the patient and entered the room. Ella Mae looked like she was about to explode.

"What happened?" Hackett asked.

Doctor Wilkes' voice had an air of triumph. "We saved him; cardiac arrest. It was a little touch and go for a while, but we did our job."

"See to your other patients," Ella Mae said to the nurse who stood next to her, and waited like a stone statue until the nurse left the room.

"You better follow procedure next time, or I'll physically throw you out the door." Ella Mae's eyes burned with the fires of hell.

Even for Ella Mae, it was a direct and nasty way to start a conversation with a doctor, resident or not.

"I followed appropriate procedure, used the appropriate discretion. It probably saved the patient's life."

"We are not in Mexico. We do not experiment on patients in this hospital." Ella Mae's words shot out of her mouth and assaulted Wilkes.

"Hold on," Hackett interrupted. "That's enough. Calm down and tell me what happened."

192 ~ Gareth Frank

"The patient—" Wilkes began to say, but Ella Mae's words walked all over him.

"The patient was in cardiac arrest. Nurse Jackson began CPR, and then this idiot orders four milligrams of epinephrine. Not one, not one point five. He orders four. I thought he had made a stupid mistake, and so I corrected him and told Nurse Jackson to administer one milligram. Einstein here goes ballistic and starts screaming at me not to contradict him."

"Damn right," Wilkes responded when Ella Mae was finished. "You act like you're the damn doctor around here instead of the nurse."

"Okay. That's enough arguing," Hackett said. "Doctor Wilkes, what is the appropriate dosage?"

"The standard is one milligram, but new evidence suggests that higher doses might be more effective."

Before Hackett could answer, Ella Mae jumped back in. "Nurses can read as well as doctors. That article was in the *Washington Post*. Does that pass for a fucking medical journal to you? It was pure speculation by a couple of doctors. There hasn't been a single study confirming it."

Hackett put his hand up in the universal gesture to get Ella Mae to stop talking. "Please give us a moment," he said to her. When she left the room, he read Wilkes the riot act.

Later in the afternoon, Hackett returned to the nurses' station and asked Ella Mae to take a walk down the hall. "You were absolutely right, but—"

Before he could finish, Ella Mae was lecturing him. "But nothing, you need to fire that son of a bitch."

"Jesus Christ, Nurse Pulaski, calm down. Just because you are usually right doesn't mean you can fly off the handle and publicly attack a doctor, or tell me how to do my job."

"Fine," Ella Mae retorted before Hackett could say anymore. "It'll be on your conscience when he kills somebody."

Hackett found himself looking at the back of Ella Mae's head as she walked to the nurses' station, wondering what had gone wrong with the world around him. For a year, he had been flying on the wings of life. It had taken a long time after Jean's death for him to once again be comfortable with the world, then he had met Sarah and he had soared. Since his heart attack, it was all falling apart. If he still had Yu Lai behind him, or if Ella Mae were still the rock of the neurology ward, or if Sarah would just be rational, maybe he could hold it together, but he couldn't handle all three problems when he himself was not even one hundred percent. He turned and walked down the hall alone, his chest cramping with anxiety.

~

Hackett lay on the couch in his living room, hyperactive thoughts cracking together like billiard balls. One problem after another bombarded his consciousness without hope of solution. After a half hour the billiard balls still rolled and occasionally collided, but his problems became as abstract as the blurry numbers that slid by on the rolling orbs. In the background, he heard a car drive by and then fade away, and noticed how utterly quiet the house was. It reminded him of the days after Jean's death, when he had sat in shock on this very couch, waiting for a noise, any noise to distract him. Back then the silence of the house had been oppressive. It seemed to have its own peculiar properties. It was not just the absence of sound. It was as if someone had turned up the volume on emptiness to the maximum bearable level, until that emptiness was pure pressure crushing his skull.

He lay still, listening to the house once more, reflected on how different this silence was than the silence of his grief. There was a quiet whir, almost below the range of his hearing. He heard a bird. He heard a board creak, the product of some slow expansion within the house itself. He found himself falling deeper and deeper into these sounds of silence, sliding into relaxation. And then, louder than the crack of a cue ball breaking the rack, the garage door opener kicked in. Hackett quieted his jumping heart, looking for the path to peace that had just been yanked from his reach. After the garage door shut, he heard the soft clicking of Sarah's bicycle gears. He heard her bump the plastic trash can with a light thud. And he heard her quiet rhythmic footsteps once more, then the door slammed.

"Hello," Sarah yelled.

"In the living room." Hackett closed his eyes again. Sarah's footsteps came closer, until he sensed her standing above.

"Taking a nap?"

He opened his eyes. "Trying. Tough day."

"What happened?"

Hackett's mind shot back to the hospital, and he saw the back of Ella Mae's head as she receded down the hallway. Though he had previously decided not to bother Sarah with his aggravations, he found himself reciting back the facts in a whiney voice. He ended the story by talking about Ella Mae, knowing that his words sounded much harsher than they should.

"I don't know why you put up with that woman. She lost a boyfriend, and now she's mad at the world. Fuck her."

"No, no, it wasn't that bad. I was in a bad mood, so I made it sound worse than it was."

"Cut me a break. She's a bitch, always has been, always will be."

Hackett felt the tension in his chest rise again. Anger lifted Hackett to his feet, and poured from his eyes. "She is my friend." His words were loud, an unmistakable challenge.

"You always defend that bitch," Sarah yelled and raised her bicycle helmet into the air. Hackett flinched, but the helmet crashed to the floor instead of smashing into his head. In slow motion, he saw it bounce up onto the end table where it struck a small ceramic figurine, knocking it to pieces. Hackett shattered with it.

"Jesus Christ, Jean bought that."

"Oh, your precious fucking Jean bought a tacky Hummel. All you care about is that blowhard friend and this ugly gaudy little statue. I'm your wife now. What about me?"

He wanted to hit her, thought that he could actually do it, but she was gone before his mind and body resolved their intentions. Hackett felt his blood pressure rise. *Calm down*, Jean's gentle voice whispered to him like a distant, ghostly train whistle. How he craved her company, needed her steady, reassuring presence. He thought about Ella Mae and blamed George for her anger. He thought about Wilkes and blamed his youthful arrogance. When he thought about Sarah, he just blamed her. An ugly and increasingly frequent thought came to him. She wanted him to change his will, and cut what remained of Jean out of his life.

Hackett sat back down on the couch listening to the non-silence all around him — Sarah's angry footsteps on the floor above him, the metal clips from her bicycle shoes assaulting the wood, the clothes hamper slamming shut, the whine of plumbing pipes as she turned the shower faucet, the screech as shower curtain hooks dragged along the pole, and then the long pitter patter of the shower beating against the tub, each sound amplified within his ears.

*I miss you*, he silently told Jean.

# Chapter 22

The white mesh fabric of Sarah's cross stitch sat on the table. Just one small flower in the center was complete. Sheets of paper with intricate patterns lay next to the fabric along with about twenty skeins of embroidery floss and her needles. She heard a small click as the electric space heater turned itself on once again. Sarah could have worked upstairs where it was warmer, but the basement was far better for her purposes.

Six months had passed since Hackett's heart attack. The panic that Sarah had felt in those early days had grown to anger over the realization that Hackett was not the caring and giving man she had believed in. She had thought that he was different, that he loved her and would take care of her, but all men eventually showed their true colors. As she worked, she felt a coldness in her spine, a memory that she preferred to bury, but still raised its ugly head. It was the night that James drank a bottle of vodka and told her that he was going to kill her. For most of his adult life, James had been like a wet blanket, weighing her down, but not oppressing her. He would go to the bar, or drink at home, sullen and silent until he fell asleep. Not that night; on that night they had fought about Aaron at dinner. James had been drinking beer, and was already half drunk. She remembered arguing in front of their son, telling James that he was a useless father. He was a failure in parenthood just as he was in everything else. He accepted her insults as he had numerous times before, but Sarah saw something different in his eyes, something raw and hurt. It made her feel good. She dissected him with words.

As if James sat in front of her now, she watched his face as she peeled back the skin of his emotion. It was so satisfying. He stared back at her, his soul beaten and bloodied. Slowly, he wrapped his fingers around his beer bottle and turned his gaze to it for a second or two, before tilting it back and gulping down the last ounces. He returned the bottle to the table and stood, glaring at Sarah, then he walked to the sink, kneeled down and removed a bottle of Popov vodka from behind the garbage can. He returned to his seat, paused again, unscrewed the cap and took a hard drag without looking away. Sarah stared back with cold determination. When he still didn't turn away, she pushed her chair back from the table and stood.

"You're a loser, a total fucking loser." As if for the first time, she saw Aaron, a boy of ten, a bystander gawking at a car accident. She didn't care. "Look at your father. He's a loser. For heaven's sake, don't grow up to be like him."

She left the table, and went to her bedroom, closing the door behind her. For the next hour, she worked on her cross stitch. It took the first thirty minutes for her inner dialogue to calm, another thirty minutes to close out the world around her.

Aside from the television, the apartment was silent. She no longer cared if James was within. She counted squares, strained her eyes to read the tiny pattern. She relaxed a little, but her serenity did not last. There was a jarring crash. Sarah saw the wood splinter around the door handle, and the door fly open. James stood before her, his hand on the vodka bottle, a few ounces splashing in the bottom.

"What the fuck do you think you're doing?" she yelled.

He said nothing. She looked into his bloodshot eyes and saw his fury. "I asked you a question."

He stepped forward without a word, grabbed her by the arm and lifted her from her chair. She swung hard, slapping him in the face. "Get out!" she yelled.

Aaron ran into the room and rammed his father with his shoulder. James stumbled, before slowly righting himself, his eyes remaining fixed on Sarah. She watched as he pushed Aaron away with one hand and stepped forward again. "I'm gonna beat you til you're fucking dead."

"You don't scare me. You are pitiful and you are weak." Sarah watched with satisfaction as his anger burned. Then he did something that she never would have imagined. He threw the almost empty vodka bottle across the room. It smashed against the wall, glass flying everywhere. She raised her hand again, but he was already on her, pushing her backward into the wall with such force that she thought it would give way and envelop her. She saw his fist coming, and slid her head away from it as it smashed into the wall next to her. Aaron was screaming, pulling on his father's leg, begging him to stop.

That was it. James slumped to the ground and cried.

The next morning, Sarah woke up, walked past the couch where James slept and calmly went to the kitchen. She returned with an eight-inch vegetable knife, stood over the couch and debated slitting his throat. She watched him as he slept. It would be so easy. She measured her hate and found no limit to it. Slowly, she knelt in front of him, held the blade up to his skin. She could do it. She knew she could. It would be easy. Sarah imagined his blood flowing, the pool stretching across the carpet. It felt good.

"Wake up," she said. "Wake up," louder this time.

His eyes fluttered, his arms stretched. She could tell that he saw nothing.

"Wake up, you son of a bitch."

He had a puzzled look in his eyes. Then, she saw that he saw. She moved the knife closer.

"You ever touch me again, I'll kill you."

She hoped that he would piss his pants. He said nothing.

"Do you understand?"

He gulped air. "Yeah." She could barely hear him.

"Do you believe me, bitch?" Her voice was soft and serious.

"Yeah."

She saw the fright in him and it made her feel better. She wanted to do it then, to cut him open and watch him die, but she did not. It had been the first time in her life that she had known with certainty that she could kill someone. She had occasionally dreamed of killing her father, and far more often had lurid fantasies of killing her stepmother, but she had often wondered whether she could follow through with it. At that moment, when she held the knife up to James' throat, she felt the power of her resolve and knew that if she needed to, she would kill.

James never took another drink, never again raised his hand against her, but Sarah nursed her hatred just the same. She also faithfully made the payments on his life insurance policy.

Hackett wasn't James, and he wasn't her father. He would never physically hurt her, but he was a man just the same. Driven by selfishness. She thought of the day that she found Hackett nursing his headache on the living room couch. He didn't love her, not really. She had been blind. She had let a fantasy make her weak, let anger get the best of her, but anger would not help. It would not bend him to her will, and it would not make her safe.

It had been Trudy who stopped Sarah's destructive behavior. "Don't be an idiot," Trudy had said, after Sarah had ranted and raved about Hackett yet another time. "You have everything with that man, a nice house, great vacations, a bottomless bank account, plus he's head over heels for you. You're gonna drive him away."

The fact that Trudy had said something intelligent took time to sink in. Sarah seldom listened to Trudy's opinion, but over the following weeks, Trudy's words came back to her again and again until she adopted them as her own. She resolved to treat Hackett with tenderness, to let him touch her, enjoy her. She needed time for her plan and she needed Hackett to be happy with her. As for her future, that was in her own hands, as it always had been. She would do what was necessary.

And so Sarah had begun to work on her plan. She smiled now, remembering the conversation she had with Hackett about working in the office. She remembered his surprise, saw the doubt in his eyes. He was a child, so easy to convince.

Sarah looked away from her cross stitch and down at the papers in front of her, one set of copies, one set of originals. One by one she flipped through the copies, looking at the barely legible, but nonetheless distinctive initials at the bottom of each page. As she had before, she wondered why a doctor who had to write his name and initials so many times was able to remain so consistent. The H started with a downstroke, reversed direction moving upward on a slight angle to the left, cut horizontally and then looped up before coming back down on a curve which led directly into the next letter. The M began and ended below the H, two sharp peaks followed with a final flourish. She looked back at her copies, column after column. They just didn't look right.

Sarah gathered all the papers together. She would not rush this. She placed the papers back inside a manila envelope and stood up. She stepped across the room, reached out and pulled a framed painting off the wall. She held it in her arms and looked at the familiar field of bluebells on a Texas prairie. It was pleasing to look at, but rather primitive in style. Her mother had painted it; not that bitch of a stepmother, her real mother. She had taken it with her when she ran away from home. Over the years, they had changed apartments countless times, abandoned households, left their clothes and furniture in piles on street corners, but she had kept the painting close.

Sarah laid it upside down on the floor, twisted some old nails that held it within the frame and lifted up the backing, inserting the envelope behind the painting before closing it again. Everything was falling into place, and she was once again in control of her own destiny. Hackett had been acting like a man-child, throwing his temper tantrums and driving her to distraction. She had let it get to her. Not any longer; she would not let him distract her from her goals.

Once the painting was back on the wall, Sarah grabbed her winter coat and headed for the garage. Her first stop was the bank in Bethesda. She carried a stack of checks already endorsed and ready for deposit in her new account.

# Chapter 23

A wall of wine stood next to their table, and an open bottle of sauvignon blanc sat in front of them. Both Sarah and Ella Mae sipped the liquid which the waiter had said contained hints of citrus, melon and grass. Hackett tasted nothing but the faint minerals of his bubbly San Pellegrino water.

"He didn't just have a double chin, he looked like The Pouch from Dick Tracy," Ella Mae was laughing as she spoke. "And, talk about stupid, when I asked him what books he'd read recently, he told me that he read a book about how to be comfortable talking to other people, then proceeded to talk about his goldfish — not fancy tropical fish, goldfish. Seriously, he told me about each one by name — Goldie, Bubbles, and the big one was Charlie, like from Starkist Tuna. The book had advised him to talk about subjects that he cared about, so he talked about his goldfish. If this is the rest of my life, please God, kill me now."

Ella Mae loved her own stories, and her laughter was contagious, even though, to Hackett, the man she ridiculed sounded a little like him.

"Did you walk out of the coffee shop right then and there?" Sarah asked as she wiped her own tears away.

"Nah." Ella Mae paused and Hackett watched her eyes focus on Sarah, who lifted her glass of wine to her lips and took a sip. Hackett knew that Ella Mae was timing the punchline.

"I just told him to shut up and take me home. I hadn't had sex since George."

Sarah spat her wine across the table and all three laughed even harder. Hackett could tell that the whole restaurant was watching. He didn't care. Life was great. He marveled at how much Sarah had changed over the last two months. Her storm of anxiety had lifted. She had put her worry about money and her anger at Hackett behind her.

Sarah dabbed at the splattered wine with her napkin, still chuckling. "No, you didn't," she said, then she turned to Hackett. "She's so nasty, but don't you love it."

"Oh, Hackett." Ella Mae's voice interrupted his thoughts. "I forgot to tell you, Cecilia wanted you to call her about Mr. Wyman. She had a question about your medication order." Cecilia was the third chief resident since Yu Lai had left.

"Three's a charm," Hackett had said to Ella Mae, just two weeks after he had fired "dick brain," as Ella Mae called Wilkes.

"What did she say?"

"Nothing, but I'm guessing that she thinks you screwed up."

Hackett saw what he recognized as an affectionate smile on Ella Mae's face. He knew that she liked the new chief resident. Hackett had overlooked Cecilia when he promoted Drexall and Wilkes. He hadn't thought she was very smart and he had questioned her patient skills. It turned out that what he mistook for a slow intellect had simply been a tendency to listen and learn before she talked. He had always been proud of his ability to see talent, and he looked at his mistake with Cecilia as one more piece of evidence that he had not been the doctor he should have been. Finally, he felt like he was regaining his footing, both putting his work life in order and settling into a more balanced relationship with his wife. When the conversation slowed, Sarah stood and excused herself to go to the bathroom. Hackett watched her backside proudly as she walked away, knowing that other men in the restaurant were staring at her as well.

Ella Mae leaned forward stealing his attention. "What's going on, Hackett?"

"What do you mean?"

"You know what I mean. Why the dinner? Why is Sarah being so nice to me?"

"Perhaps she realizes that she has been unkind and is trying to make it up to you?"

Ella Mae's skepticism contorted her face, pulling her lips down at the corners and raising her eyebrows up towards her hairline. "Ya think?"

"Well, maybe she is being nice for my benefit. Maybe she figures being nice to you is a way of being nice to me."

Ella Mae's head slowly bobbed back and forth. She looked like a parent unhappy with her child's obvious lie. "Come on, Hackett, I know her well enough to know that's not the way she works. I don't know what it is, but she wants something — something from me, or you or both of us."

"Stop it. Sarah can be tough, but she is not manipulative. She is just being nice and you should just accept it."

Ella Mae's head tilted away from Hackett, as if he had slapped her. "I wish I could believe that."

~

The next day Sarah left the office at lunch, telling Hackett that she had some errands to run. Instead, she walked over to Farragut Square, bought falafel from a food truck and sat on a park bench. Bite after bite, she savored the stuffed pita sandwich, loving the little flavorful chickpea balls, yogurt sauce and diced cucumbers. It didn't last long enough.

Sarah used the napkin to wipe her lips then pulled a packaged hand wipe from her purse to finish the job before reapplying her lipstick. When she was satisfied, she grabbed her cell phone and dialed. She had debated calling Victor, told herself that she could do what she needed to do without him, but the vision of James confronting her in bed on the morning of his death haunted her. It would be better to have help and Victor was the only person she could turn to.

Victor's phone flipped to voicemail. Sarah hung up, not wanting to leave a message. Instead, she pulled a piece of paper out of her purse on which she had written down the phone numbers for hospitals in the Gaithersburg area. She dialed the first one and asked for Victor Kliskov in the pharmacy. She found him on the second try.

"Hi, Victor, it's Sarah," she had said, trying to sound matter-of-fact.

"Hey, baby doll," he answered, mimicking her casual tone.

"I've been thinking about you since you surprised me on the trail. I hope you understand. I was caught off-guard."

"You need some shit? Oxy? Something else?" he asked, and then his voice softened. "Or maybe you just want to make it up to me, huh, baby?"

Sarah walked back to 19th Street, feeling excited and in control, but when she walked into the office, she found Hackett at her desk shuffling through medical files.

"You'll mess up all my hard work," she told him. "What in God's name are you looking for?"

"Mrs. Webster called. She said that the statement from her insurance company is all wrong and that she was overcharged. I'm looking at her file, and I think we must have made a mistake."

"I doubt it. She's the one who probably made the mistake. Who looks at insurance statements, and since when does a patient know what charges have been incurred on their behalf?"

"No, it isn't her. Look here," Hackett said pointing to a line on a form. "I didn't do that."

Sarah looked, then quickly grabbed the file. "I'll check into it and make a refund if it's necessary. Don't worry about the books; that's my job. The last thing I need is you screwing it up."

~

Sarah took Friday off and met Trudy for coffee at Catholic U. From there, it was a short walk to the Colonel Brooks Tavern. She opened the door and spied Victor in a booth on the far wall, his smile bright and alive when he turned to see her walking toward him.

"I knew you'd get in touch," he told her. "We're made for each other, and oh my God, has anyone told you how sexy you look today?"

The compliment tickled Sarah's ears and fluttered across her ego. She kissed him on the cheek and then sat down, staring at his familiar sharp angular features and muscular frame. When she looked into his eyes, her mind drifted back in time. He had pallid doe-like eyes that had once captivated her. They made him look strangely boyish and exuded a non-threatening comfort. Years ago, when they had just met, she had the feeling she was falling into a pool of soft blue water. His peculiar mix of softness and strength had been irresistible. Later, she came to understand that his strength was a physical mirage. He was among the easiest men to manipulate that she had ever met. Sarah looked into those eyes now, felt that doughy center of gravity.

"It's nice to see you again," she said and watched his pupils soften even more.

Victor talked with the confidence of a high school quarter-back who had never thrown an interception or been turned down by a girl. His eyes focused on her and her alone, reducing the rest of the world to abstraction. Then, as he complimented her on how good she looked and how fit she was, he brushed his hand against her leg. The touch was light. It did not linger, more effective that way, a subtle tease that could be disowned if need be, even as it flamed desire. It was a dance. Sarah understood. She reached across the table, rested her hand on his, and traced her finger across his palm.

"You don't look so bad yourself."

Sarah sipped chardonnay. Victor chugged beer. They talked of old times, each in a sanitized way, avoiding any mention of James, acting as if she had been single when they had last met. Finally, Victor asked what she had been expecting him to ask since she walked into the tavern. "How's your son? Is he still having those fits?"

Sarah had prepared for the question, planned her response, but her anger flared anyway. "Jesus Christ, Victor, he had a name. His name was Aaron and they were seizures, not fits, and he died."

Victor told her he was sorry. In response, Sarah told him that he didn't even know Aaron and that Victor was the last person that she wanted to talk to about it. As she knew he would, he moved on, uninterested in her son or what had happened to him.

"Tell me about your travels," she said to change the subject.

He told her that going to Thailand had been stupid and naive. It was a third world country where people didn't speak English. He hated everything but the women. She told him about Saint Lucia. He had tried Australia and New Zealand as well, but he couldn't make a buck. He confessed that he left New Zealand to avoid being arrested for fraud. She told him about Italy without once mentioning Hackett. Victor never said anything about her wedding ring or asked if she was married, though she guessed that he understood.

"Let's blow this joint," he finally said.

He suggested her place, but she said no. She wouldn't risk that. He suggested his apartment, but she didn't want to go all the way to Gaithersburg.

"Let's get a hotel," she countered.

So, they took a cab to Union Station and she paid for a room at the Phoenix Park Hotel with cash.

"I see you're flush," Victor said as they walked away from the front desk.

"Saved a little for a special day. Don't go jumping to conclusions."

As they walked to the elevator, she looped her hand through his arm and felt his familiar taut muscles. When the hotel door closed behind them, he grabbed her and pulled her to him. His hands were everywhere. He clutched her dress, slipped his fingers beneath her bra, tore at his shirt, fumbled with her zipper, yanked at his own, pulled her dress up, pulled her underwear down, all the while laughing and kissing her. They fell on the bed.

She felt his weight upon her, recoiled under his athletic thrust. He pounded her to the verge of orgasm then roughly rolled her over and entered her from behind. She wanted to scream, but she lost herself and laughed instead. The comparison to Hackett was just too funny. Hackett was like a little boy in bed, timid and fast. The sound of her laugh seemed to heighten Victor's urges. He moved in violent bursts. The bed rattled and banged. She heard a couple laugh in the next room, knew that they were listening. She came once and then again.

Sex with Victor had always been hungry, hard and satisfying. He was the type of man that attracted her, tall and strong, a dick with simple urges and a brain without the complexity of regret. He took her breath away that afternoon in the hotel, but she was playing him just like before. He could be counted on to do what was needed.

# Chapter 24

The blotter in front of Hackett was brand new. A new brass lamp sat to his right. Instead of the cheap Bic pen he was accustomed to he held an expensive metal pen with a delicate moth etched on one side and his name on the other. Hackett glanced around again, and felt as if he sat in a foreign land. He looked up on the wall in front of him and stared at the painting that had not been there the day before. It was the Palio horse race in Siena, Italy. He recognized the big tall clock tower on the main square of the old city, saw the people corralled behind barriers on the square, as if they were a million sardines swimming in a barrel, remembered Sarah saying how exciting it would be to go to the horse race on the old town streets and watch the thoroughbreds gallop and crash into the Renaissance-era walls. The idea had unnerved him. He looked at the people in the painting again, marveled how the painter had managed to dab and smear paint, and yet convey the perfect sense of a trapped mob, heads struggling for air, eyes paining to see the race. Above them, people hung out of windows, drank on crowded balconies. The horses ran like Dante-inspired beasts, one crashing against a wall next to a cafe, pinning the rider's leg against the stone, another slipping and sliding through the sand and dirt which had been trucked into town to cover the stone streets, still another horse, this one sans rider, running free, the jockey's head hitting the ground as his legs and arms still flailed in the atmosphere above.

It was an orgy of bloodlust. Hackett thought about the painter, imagined him as a god toying with the subjects in his creation, manipulating their desires and fears, bringing out the worst in them. He didn't understand why he was so drawn to it, or why Sarah was so fascinated by the race itself. Sarah had told him that she would also love to see the bulls run through the streets of Pamplona. How odd it was those kinds of things excited her.

It was Sarah who had, of course, transformed his office. He appreciated her thoughtfulness, but sometimes he felt like it wasn't even his anymore. He didn't need this type of perfection. He didn't want his patients to focus on excess. It was even more than that. She was too damn good at cleaning up. On a Saturday, like today, when she wasn't in the office, he could find nothing he needed. He had left his current files in his inbox. Robin, his old office manager, would have known not to take them, but Sarah with all of her efficiency had snatched them away. He stood, slid his chair back, walked around his desk and out into the hallway. He had already discovered through experience that she had rearranged the patient files. He opened and shut drawers. When he found the right one, he leafed through files in search of the name Mecklington. He saw nothing. His hands returned to the left side of the drawer. Again he searched, and again he came up empty-handed.

Hackett scratched his head then walked to Sarah's desk. The sight of it made him laugh. She managed to keep his office spotless, like he hardly used it, but hers was a mess, files piled upon files. He wondered what that said of her, only neat on behalf of other people. He sat down and started his search. He quickly found the cases from yesterday, but Mecklington wasn't there. He searched through everything on the desk and came up empty. He slammed his hand on the pile of files. Then he noticed a brown cardboard file box on the floor, opened it, saw patient files within and hoisted it up to the desk.

The very first file was Jeff Mecklington's. He opened it and flipped pages back to the beginning. The man had been a patient for three years. Hackett had diagnosed him with Lewy Body Dementia and had treated him with both donepezil and rivastigmine. He wanted to check his notes. After he got what he was looking for, he closed the file, but in doing so he caught a glimpse of something that looked out of place. He opened it back up. There in front of him sat a billing for an MRI. He hadn't ordered that. He looked more closely. The date of service was four months old, but the billing was recent. He also did not recognize the provider. There was neither a report or a CD from the MRI. It made no sense. Hackett picked up the phone and dialed Sarah's cell.

"Hello," he heard her breathless response.

"I'm looking at the Mecklington file. There's a charge for an MRI. I didn't order it."

The phone went silent for a few seconds. Hackett could hear heavy breathing and assumed she was out riding again.

"Are you screwing around with my files? I told you to leave them alone. Where did you get that?"

"It was in a box under your desk."

"Jesus Christ, Hackett, are you snooping on me? Leave my shit alone. Those are the files that I am investigating. Remember, you told me that Robin must have made some mistakes. I'm working on that."

"Sorry, Sarah, but you need to ask me when you think something's wrong. This is a recent MRI billing. You're the one that must have screwed up, not Robin."

"Okay, fine. Blame me. I am halfway to Mount Vernon. I'll look at it on Monday."

"Please do."

"Just put it back, Hackett, and stay out of my stuff."

Hackett hung up the phone, a little angry at being chastised about his own practice, especially when she was clearly wrong. He wondered why he had let her take over the practice to such an extent. His thoughts turned away from the office and he saw the interior of his own house. He inventoried all the changes in furnishings and artwork — the new couch, the remodeled kitchen, Jean's missing knick knacks, his den walls no longer covered in specimens, and once again, there was Sarah's discerning, but disturbing taste in art. He thought of the strange painting in the hallway. She called it "self portrait of a blind man," a haggard depressed face floating in a pool of vibrant colors. Sarah said that the artist had killed himself shortly after completing his masterpiece, and so the painting's value had to climb. Hackett was surprised how all these gradual changes had seemed like a normal progression. He had even liked each new purchase, but as a whole they added up to an assault on his old lifestyle.

# Chapter 25

Sarah sat with the phone cradled between her shoulder and ear, a brown file open in front of her. "Yes, that's correct," she said. "The charge was made on November 31st, the date of the patient's appointment."

The woman at the other end of the phone sounded annoyed. "Well, honey, that beats all. I think you can see why we're not paying."

"No, I do not. Everything is in order."

"Listen, honey, doctors don't usually have office hours on weekends let alone days that don't even exist. Check your calendar. There are thirty days in November."

Sarah hung up the phone, chastising herself for her sloppiness. Now was no time to leave a trail or cause Hackett to ask questions. She took the file and stuffed it into the very back of the cabinet, totally out of order. It would be safe there until she could get back to it. After that, she walked back to Hackett's office and told him she was taking the rest of the day off for a bike ride.

~

With her bike steadied against her hip, Sarah punched in a phone number. It rang four times and then rolled over. "Wasssup, baby cakes? Hit my phone with a message."

Victor's childish recording grated on Sarah. She hung up, refusing to create any record of their conversations. She swallowed the last of her Vita Water, dropped the empty bottle in the trash and walked toward her bike. The sun was bright, the sky was blue, but the ground was still wet enough that the brown leaves made a squishy sound under her feet. The wind also chilled her despite the layers of clothing protecting her body. Sarah loved to push her bike riding as far into the fall as she could, even into December. As long as it was above freezing and wasn't raining, she was game for a ride.

She swung her leg up and over the seat, settled in and was pedaling hard within a matter of yards. After a couple of minutes she was in a groove, pumping rhythmically and singing along with the voice of Celine Dion, the singer slapping her chest in Sarah's imagination. A few minutes later, the sound of her cell phone disrupted her rhythm and pissed her off, but she braked to a stop anyway and fumbled with her pack to get the phone.

"Hey Victor."

"Hey baby cakes. I just got out of the shower. Laying naked on my bed. Want to join me?"

"Listen Victor, I'm not going to wait much longer."

"Well then," Victor said, his voice rising and dropping on a sing song rollercoaster. "Come on over."

"Not that, stupid, the other thing."

"Do you have enough money?"

"No, but I'll get it. In the meantime, you need to get some of that stuff."

"I got a better idea. Why don't you just empty out one of the doc's bank accounts and we can fuck our way from Belize to Patagonia. It won't last forever, but what does?"

"Grow up, Victor," Sarah said and hung up the phone.

# Chapter 26

S now had been falling for hours, covering the streets around the hospital with a downy late-night blanket. Hackett stepped out into it, leaving the hospital behind, marveling at the beautiful empty streets, concrete, asphalt and everything else buried under the soft white crystals. It was after midnight. Hackett had been in the hospital for ten hours, but now felt curiously awake among the blustery, swirling flakes.

His feet danced through the deep unshoveled snow on the sidewalk and when he came to the corner, he bounded up and over the snow bank which had just been deposited by a passing plow, for once feeling like the heart attack was a distant memory. Hackett held his palms skyward and looked up into the streetlights to get a better view of the dancing flakes. Then he turned and saw two men exit the hospital behind him. *Well, almost deserted.* A block further, he bent down and picked up snow to make a ball. He packed it tight, wound up like a baseball pitcher in a cartoon, and threw it at the street sign in front of him.

Bang!

Hackett never really expected to hit it. He had no talent for sports, and so a kernel of pride grew within him. He formed another ball and hurled it at a sign in a shop window advertising men's suits, two for $399. The ball smashed against the glass and stuck in place, another direct hit. "Damn right!" he shouted.

Hackett heard a noise behind him and looked back. The two men who had exited the hospital, at least that's who he assumed they were, stood just a few feet away, their faces covered with ski masks.

"Hello," Hackett said.

"Give us your money," one of the men replied in a deep voice.

"What?" Hackett asked, stunned and confused. He had thought the ski masks were for the weather.

"Give us your fucking money," the other man yelled. His accent was thick, maybe Russian, but Hackett understood this time. As he reached toward his back pocket to comply, a fist came at him like a blurred missile shooting through the snowy night. It knocked him right off his feet. The sounds around him suddenly seemed dull. He made no attempt to get up. Hackett felt a hand on the back of his own head, recognized that it was covered in a thick leather glove, felt the man's strength as his head was forced forward into the snow. Despite the discomfort, he focused his mind, as he would in the operating room, thinking about the scene of the two men walking out of the hospital like it was the incision he would make on a patient's scalp. He imagined them by the door, before either had put on their ski mask. He ran through it second by second, trying to imprint it on his mind. Both men were white, one shorter than the other, younger than Hackett, but not kids. He doubted that he would be able to recognize them. He saw them as they stood behind him just a few seconds before. One wore a leather coat and jeans, the other a puffy down jacket and sweat pants. Had they been waiting for him in particular? He saw no other details, but recalled the smell of menthol cigarettes right before the punch. There was another aroma as well, perfume, a light flowery perfume. How odd, he thought.

His ability to lie still slipped away as he struggled for breath. He tried to pull his head out of the snow, but the hand pushed harder, and the shock of a boot being driven into his kidney sent a wave of pain and fear through him. Finally, he felt the weight lift from his head, and he raised himself slightly, gulping the icy wet air. Hands rifled through his coat pockets. First, they pulled his cell phone out, then one of the men pulled on his coat with wrenching force. Pain seared through Hackett's shoulder, his buttons gave way and the coat slipped partially from his torso. He felt his wallet disembark from his pants, his keys scraped hard against his leg before they, too, disappeared, and finally, his watch was yanked free of his wrist. He lifted his head a little further out of the snow to breathe, trying hard not to move too much and cause a reaction.

"Get rid of keys," he heard the accented voice say. "You ready?"

The words gave Hackett hope it would soon be over.

"Hold him down," the other man answered.

Hackett felt a knee high on his back by the nape of his neck, and a hand on his head once again. A huge weight pushed down on him. He felt a sharp pain and worried that his spinal column would snap under the pressure. His face was now at least six inches deep. Icy cold stung his skin and the snow sealed his mouth making it impossible to breathe.

He struggled to be free. "Hold still for a second, old man, it'll all be over." There was no accent.

Enormous pressure bore down on him. He thought his neck would snap. He had to breathe, had to break free. His panicked struggle was met with more force, the pressure unbearable. He lost consciousness.

~

When he awoke, all he felt was a cold numbness. His face was still buried in the snow and there was a frozen ache from his scalp to his toes. He could not move.

One by one, he tried to move his arms, legs, fingers and toes. Nothing. He analyzed the situation as if he were his own patient, and he concluded that his spinal column had been severed. He tried to roll his head over and out of the snow. Nothing.

*Paralyzed!*

The word hung in the air around him and cloaked him in fear. That was his initial diagnosis, but he was not without feeling in his extremities. They ached with cold pain. Perhaps his neck was broken, and the spinal cord not severed. Perhaps his vertebrae pinched the nerves. It didn't seem much better, but it gave him hope.

It was then that he first registered another feeling, one that he had ignored in his panic. He felt oddly faint, tired but not sleepy, conscious, but not fully alert.

*What is going on?* he asked himself.

He told himself to assess his condition once more. He tried to move his head.

Nothing.

He tried to move his eyebrow and blink.

Nothing.

He tried to move his tongue.

Nothing.

He realized he wasn't breathing. He wasn't gasping for breath, he simply wasn't breathing. How long had he been there? He wasn't sure. All he knew was that it had been no more than a minute since he had regained consciousness. He concentrated his mind, tried to focus all of his diagnostic skills, but it didn't add up.

He assembled the facts once again. He had been attacked. He had been kicked in the side. He had been held face down in the snow. He had felt pressure and pain from the knee and the weight of a man on his back. He had passed out. He couldn't move. It all added up to a spinal cord injury, but he couldn't open his eyes, couldn't move his tongue. That didn't make sense. He wasn't even breathing. The reality of that last fact settled in.

*Am I dying?* he asked himself.

He concentrated, listening to the world around him. It had an eerie, muffled quality. Even though he was face down, he could make out the glow of a streetlight above him. He turned his concentration inward. He felt and heard the slow rhythm of his own heartbeat. He had no way to time it, but he had listened to the rhythm of countless hearts, knew the cadence. He could tell that his was very slow. Thirty beats per minute, he guessed.

*I am dying.*

Hackett lay motionless in the snow, listening to the solitary drumbeat of his own heart as it continued to decelerate. The feeling was oddly reminiscent of meditation. Only once or twice in his entire life had he been able to reach such deep concentration that the world around him seemed to fade until only his internal awareness was left. Those moments had been fleeting, but beautiful. This moment was more than that. He no longer felt panic. He accepted his fate, willed himself to remember his daughter Amy, her voice, laughter and smile. He thought of Jean, and felt her warmth despite the cold all around him. Finally he saw Sarah, naked before him. His heart stopped, as it had nearly done the first time he had seen her nude, except this time, it stopped for real. Hackett focused every ounce of his attention in an effort to feel and hear his heart, but there was nothing.

The cold night around him disappeared. He felt as if he were bathed in a warm light. The thought that he was dying was present, but seemed to be of little consequence. He told himself to get up, and to his surprise, he felt movement, not the slow movement of lethargic limbs, but a light ease of movement, like being set free from the invisible chains of gravity itself. He no longer looked through his eyelids into the dull glow of snow. Instead, he saw snowflakes all around him, hanging motionless in the air, engulfing him in a beautiful radiant cloak, ignoring the wind and the ever-present tug of Mother Earth. He took in the beauty of a world that shimmered with stunning elegance. It seemed that he could see in all directions at once. He was kneeling, but felt as if all physical sensation had disappeared, replaced by simple thought and recognition. He saw his own head below him, still face down. A dusting of snow covered him from head to toe. He lifted higher, leaving his body prone and helpless. The snow around him resumed its fall, flakes gracefully drifting to the ground, gently piling on the other him, covering him. He saw each and every flake, their fluffy edges and the crystalline structure within. They sparkled with delicate color. He was Neo, living in *The Matrix*, minus the violence. He was Robin Williams in *What Dreams May Come*. He was Bruce Willis in the *The Sixth Sense*. He was all those things, but this was real.

The snow bewitched him, falling, spiraling, swirling. The flakes formed together in groups, first twos, then threes and fours, mesmerizing him. He effortlessly counted. Snowflakes huddled together like a colorful bubble bath. He counted and summed instantaneously, seeing thousands and thousands of flakes. Beautiful numbers flew by into infinity. He saw another vision as well, there within the snow, but separate. He was again a small child standing alone in the woods behind his house, the trees looming above, his mind lost in them. He had counted leaves as he now counted snowflakes. He had almost totally forgotten that feeling, the comfort in it, the reassurance of numbers and solitude, the times when he could wash away his childish fears.

He noticed something else, a marvelous web or grid shining through everything. It was almost as if everything was supported on multi-dimensional translucent graph paper. Each snow flake, each atom, in its rightful place.

*I am dead.*

Hackett's thoughts were effortless and without time. Snowflakes fell, and simultaneously hung motionless. He was drawn to memories of Ella Mae. He felt her smile, heard her voice. Her death experience was with him, a comforting light. He felt the truth within the words she had spoken at his winter barbecue.

*Forgive me. I was wrong.*

Without the benefit of eyes, he saw Yu Lai.

*I couldn't have known,* he told her.

Hackett was being drawn up and away from his body. The snowflakes around him were swept up in a marvelous breeze and formed beautiful patterns that resembled an impressionist winter landscape. The wind changed and he watched the snowflakes swirl and coalesce into a horde of beautiful moths, wings fluttering softly. And then they, too, were gone. He was swept up with purpose, a need to move back down the street, to go to the hospital. It was just one thought in an endless stream, but it guided him. He wanted to observe everything. He wanted to understand what was happening. He was a neurologist; his training gave him a unique perspective to evaluate this beautiful experience, to observe and question it. He was flooded with the memories of more than thirty years of medical training and practice, everything he had studied and read was all there as he floated without movement. The street passed under him, and he himself passed through the walls of the hospital. This was not fantasy. There was no confusion, no flight from reality that accompanied dreams or drugs. If anything, the clarity of his experience exceeded anything he had felt in life. He realized that time and place were no longer boundaries. The universe around him was hyper real. He had been so wrong; this was no hallucination.

He thought of the Tao and dharma, the oneness of the universe at the core of both. He wanted to understand this strange consciousness of death. Hackett focused his mind and directed his flight. *No, not flight, the term is insufficient*, he thought. Words and language could not adequately describe what he felt as he drifted through space.

He entered the cardiac unit and saw the familiar faces of nurses and doctors as they worked. He had but one goal. He floated up towards the ceiling. A small bracket holding an eight and a half by eleven sheet of card stock passed through him until he was staring down at a dollar sign and an ink drawing of a puppy.

*Here is your proof*, he told his friends, though they were not there to hear him.

Hackett drifted up through concrete, air conditioning vents, and plumbing pipes. He passed through hospital beds and felt the wondrous energy of human thought as he passed through bodies. He was again out in the dark night among the beautiful geometry and colors of snow. A light appeared to him and communicated without talking. There were no voices or words, yet he understood everything. Hackett absorbed it all, yearning for more.

"I am here." Her thought filled him with warmth. He didn't have to hear her voice to know it was Jean.

"Where are we?" he asked. His question and her answer passed without movement of time. He recognized the truth of it, even though it was inexplicable. "I was so weak, so stupid. How could I have ever hurt you?" He wanted to say everything he had not said in life. His heart ached for her understanding. Hackett felt the weight of his mourning. There had been a facade of relief since he had met Sarah, but the shroud of grief had never really lifted. He had only been distracted from it. Now, in her presence, he felt the infinite sadness of loss, and with it, the beauty of reunion — a joy so deep that he could drown in it.

There was no need for forgiveness, she told him. She knew his love, always knew the truth of it. That was all that was important now, not his human mistakes. He was good. He had lived the life given him to the best of his ability. He had made her happy. She loved him without regret.

Hackett looked at the snow around him, and it was no longer snow but other points of light, other souls, he presumed. No, he knew. Individual beacons populated space until the infinite grid shimmered through everything and was everything. Hackett heard their ethereal call, understood that this grid was the universe itself, conscious thought its backbone. Within that same instant, a moment which was not past, present or future, he experienced a fullness beyond his earthly comprehension. He stared out at the grid, saw its infinite beauty not just as a lustrous pattern, but also as a mathematical truth. Equations that he had never seen materialized before him, made perfect sense, though his mind would have never comprehended them during life.

At that moment, Hackett knew no fear. Worries melted away, and he realized that they had never been important. Again he thought of dharma and the oneness at the center of all things. He thought of the baffling contradictions of theoretical physics and was no longer confused. His consciousness spanned everything, transcended everything. It was beautiful and powerful.

A deep resonant hum inhabited space, like the low drone of chanting monks. He understood that it was the sound of thought itself. His new reality was so much fuller than the reality he was accustomed to. Everything was so different — seeing, hearing and touching were all contained within a single new sense of shear understanding. He saw from the inside out, 360 degrees and more. A great consciousness flooded over him. Meaning did

222 ~ GARETH FRANK

not come to him slowly, encumbered by words pronounced in linear time. It came fully formed, questions asked and answered slowly, clearly, completely, yet somehow instantaneously.

"There is a greater purpose." The words which he did not hear, but were nonetheless clear, were from Jean. Hackett's mind opened to a billion memories. They did not flash before his eyes, for he no longer had eyes to observe and time no longer flowed in sequence. It was as if each moment of his life played out before him simultaneously, not just in memory, but in substance. It reminded him of that sense of déjà vu that he sometimes got when he heard an old song that had defined a certain era of his younger life. He would hear the song, and momentarily, be transported back in time. With the help of those songs, he had somehow felt the intangible emotion of something that he thought had been forever lost.

In death, every memory was like that, but magnified a millionfold. He didn't recall memories, he relived them, feeling every emotion keenly, seeing every detail, hearing voices, cars passing, hearts beating, even sensing touch in his absent fingertips.

The memories bombarded him without haste. His mother held him in her arms, her voice singing a lullaby he had not previously remembered, every note now clear. He made love to Jean, feeling the soft moistness of her lips as he watched Amy graduate from high school. His first real friend from junior high greeted him. He lay under his grandmother's piano, his body shivering with sound as she played a ragtime tune, the strings ringing above and vibrating within, the perfect notes of a song he hadn't heard since he was five. Love washed over him, and he felt for the first time how his love felt to others. He understood that he had brought people joy in abundance and it surprised him, but he also saw the searing emotional pain he had sometimes inflicted. He felt everything: joy, sadness, hope and fear, each holding equal beauty. He worried that the pain he had caused, *his* hurtful pain, had overwhelmed the good in his life, but through it all Jean's love burned brightly. She gave him understanding that he was good and had done the best he could, no need for regret. He was loved.

Hackett felt the familiarity of Jean's love, singular in his life, a love that was unconditional. In turn, he felt an even greater love, a love that he had not felt before and could not have even understood. It was a universal love of brilliant intensity.

In his journey, he saw Sarah as well, and he realized for the first time how he had wronged her, how his love for her was propelled by a love of beauty, a vain and lustful need to possess. In this and other painful memories, he felt the assurance and forgiveness of the greater love that was all around him. He had wronged, but he had done no wrong, for he had lived the only way he knew. He had done his best.

His life review lasted forever, and it was over before it started. Hackett understood time as an illusion that his consciousness now transcended.

Even as his memories played out, he felt drawn forward toward a distant light. The feeling of peace and oneness with all things was overwhelming. His life had not been perfect, but perfection had still been found. It lay before him in death.

"You cannot come. It is not your time. Amy needs you. Our friend needs you. There are things that you must still do." He felt Jean's presence within those words. The thoughts came to him unlike anything else in death. They held him tightly and pulled him back, a thick knot in his brainless existence, unavoidable, but clear. In response, he felt anger. He did not want to go back, could not leave such beauty. He could not leave Jean, not again.

He would fight God if necessary. His anger burned, but Jean's thoughts calmed and reassured him. Memories of her flooded in — their first kiss, their last, the birth of their daughter, their wedding, their fights, even their lovemaking. Hackett felt her arms clenched tightly around him, her hands trying to pull him to her with such force that their bodies might melt together. He was inside of her once again, surrounded by her flesh. He felt peace and ecstasy at once, but more than that, he felt their souls united. He told her that she was perfect, his only true love, he would not leave her again.

*We all live lives of illusion.* Unlike an instant before, her words were slow, her voice heard as well as felt. It filled him with questions instead of answers. *I was not perfect,* she continued. *You just made me so. Sometimes we create the people we want, other times we let them create us. Perfection is not love, desire is not love. Go back. Open your eyes. Live your life. Love uncondition-ally.*

Hackett recognized that her words were not chastisement. He understood that he had so desperately sought happiness that he had turned Jean's death into his own living grave. Still, even in his own death, he could not let go of his mourning for her. Sadness came for him. *There is nothing left for me in life,* he pleaded.

There was no place for such dissent, no free will. What was, simply was. Karma.

Hackett felt himself being pulled backward, drawn into a vortex. Unlike his earlier effortless flight, he struggled, his arms flailed and legs kicked. He wrestled with thoughts as well, screamed questions at Jean. He wanted to know why he had to return, and what he had to do. There were no answers.

In reverse, he saw the points of light fade, the snowflakes regain their place and then a fluttering of matter flying through him as he descended back into the hospital. Down he went flailing through people, blankets, beds and concrete, until he saw his own body lying on a bed in the emergency room. Doctors and nurses worked frantically.

The shock of re-entering his body felt as if he had jumped off a high dive into eight feet of mud. He felt his body jerk and he saw a doctor he knew, Doctor Bellog. Pain shot through him, and the world went black. In his last conscious thought he marveled at how empty and lifeless the living world could be.

~

Hackett awoke in the ICU. Beeps and other electronic noises surrounding him. His chest felt as if the entire population of China was standing upon it.

He opened his eyes and looked directly into two more eyes staring back at him.

"Good morning, Doctor Metzger. I'm Nurse Ocampo. You're in ICU."

Hackett looked up into the round, aging face of a Filipino nurse. "A dollar sign and a puppy." His words came out in a whisper. The nurse smiled at him, and he felt her warmth. She was a good nurse. He was sure of that even if he had never seen her before. She had children and grand-children, he thought, imagining them surrounding her, but he didn't know why that came to mind. He stared at her, drawn in by her image, and felt a touch of sadness in her. It made him think of Jean, and he wondered if she, too, had lost a spouse. Hackett thought of death. He wanted to assure the nurse that death could be peaceful, even wonderful. He felt Jean's presence once more, understood that he carried her with him in life as well as death.

Back in the world of the living, Hackett felt unmoored. Perhaps it was the medication, perhaps it was exhaustion. Whatever it was, consciousness and sleep were interchangeable, thoughts were uncontrollable. Aaron now occupied his mind. Why had he not been there in death? Hackett wondered. He had seen so much in death, so much that he had believed his whole life had played out, but that had not been true. It had been a selective vision. Aaron had not been there. Many memories had been omitted. Hackett sought out Aaron now. He tried to recreate his death vision, to see Aaron to reassure himself that Aaron was content. He couldn't. There was no going back.

The next time Hackett awoke, Sarah was standing beside his bed. He looked up into her smiling face, but it looked disconcertingly empty. "Look who's back from the dead," she said.

He tried to smile. It hurt. He wanted to tell her that he would be better, that death had changed him, but he could not find the strength. Instead, he just looked at her, all of her, body and soul. She looked different to him. He stared, seeking to understand what had changed. He studied her face, saw the distinctiveness of an awkward, self-conscious smile, imagined what it had to be like for her staring down at his messed-up, paralyzed body, trying to smile at him. He opened his mouth, but his words did not form.

"Does it hurt?" she asked. "Don't try to talk just yet if it hurts."

He felt a deep confusion and resignation about being alive. He also felt a solitary loneliness. He thought of Jean's voice, and he remembered the odd sensation of knowing her thoughts without hearing words. *Live your life*, she told him again.

Hackett turned to Sarah, struggled to speak, felt the warmth of her hand on his cheek, but Jean's memory still held sway. *Desire is not love.*

"I'm sorry." The words slowly tumbled off of his tangled tongue. "I'll be a better husband."

He could see her confusion, wanted to explain that she deserved all of his love, not just his cravings, but the effort was too much. He closed his eyes.

When he awoke, Sarah was still by his side. "What time..." Again, his words came out slowly, barely audible. "...is it?"

"It is almost noon. You've been asleep for about thirty hours."

For the first time, he realized that someone was standing behind Sarah. He tilted his head and his eyes made contact with Ella Mae. He saw a tear form in her eye and slowly roll down her cheek. Warmth radiated from her.

"You really scared us," she said.

A slight rush of air escaped Hackett's lips. He stared into Ella Mae's eyes and tried to force out the words. In desperation, he lifted his hand and curled his fingers, beckoning her closer. It was then that he realized what he had done. He curled his fingers again, marveling at the sensation. He concentrated his effort on his toes and felt his feet move as well. Hackett felt tears of joy in his own eyes. He was not paralyzed. A slight but clear smile lit up his face.

Sarah leaned down. "What is it, dear?"

Hackett shook his head, looked and pointed at Ella Mae. When he turned back to Sarah, he saw her step back and felt her anger. The sensation was so clear that it spooked him. He felt like he could almost hear her thoughts. He thought again about his death vision, compared how he felt now to how his thoughts had been in death. It was a faint echo, reminiscent, but not real.

Ella Mae leaned down, nearly putting her ear on Hackett's cheek. "What is it, Hack?"

"Dollar sign and puppy," he whispered.

Ella Mae's head jerked. Her eyes stared into his.

"Dollar sign and puppy," he repeated.

Ella Mae looked hard into Hackett's eyes. She said not a word, but Hackett felt her understanding. Then he watched as tears poured from her cheeks.

"Are you sure?" she said as her hand wiped the tracks on her face.

Hackett nodded affirmation.

As Ella Mae walked from the room, her head turned back to Hackett one last time. "I'll check," was all that she said.

~

Ella Mae typed out a quick text message. "Can you meet me in ER, stat?" She started to run again, but her heaving chest slowed her back to a walk. She had never been thin. Even as a high school student, Ella Mae had been a little stocky and athletic. Oh, how she missed those days. She now got out of breath just thinking of exercise. As soon as she told herself that there was nothing to run for, she felt the urge to take off again.

Hackett had experienced death just like she had. Ella Mae knew it, but she wanted proof. She wanted a flag that she could wave high. This time she would not hide from it. She was approaching fifty years old, and she would finally tell the world. A headline under the *Washington Post*'s banner flashed through her mind, "Local neurologist reveals the truth behind death."

When she reached the emergency room, she paced the hallway back and forth outside the treatment rooms, looking nervously at the clock every few seconds, pleading to heaven for Cecilia to show up. Suddenly she felt a vibration in her breast pocket and leapt a foot in the air.

Cecilia's text message jumped out at her. "With patient. Emergency?"

"Sort of. Come when done," Ella Mae typed.

Ella Mae paced back and forth, up and down the hall. She recognized a nurse coming out of one of the treatment rooms, blood spots soiling her shirt. "Were you here night before last when Doctor Metzger was admitted?"

"No," the nurse said and hurried down the hall.

Another nurse and another passed. Ella Mae asked them as well, but neither one had been there. She resigned herself to checking each and every room, staring into the empty space in front of her, yearning to lay her eyes on the paper sitting on the raised platform by the ceiling, but she couldn't let herself spoil it. She needed a witness, and not just any witness. She needed Cecilia.

Eventually, Ella Mae sat down to wait. She only lasted about five minutes before her nervous energy lifted her out of her chair and back onto her feet. She walked to the open door of the empty treatment room, stepped right up to an invisible line on the floor that separated her from validation. She looked into the room and tried to imagine if Hackett had been there. It was impossible to tell. Her eyes wandered up to the platform. She looked right through it, as if she could see what was printed on the other side. Her desire told her it was a dollar sign and a puppy. She was sure.

Her heart and her mind battled for her will. She shook her head and took two steps backward before turning and walking away. Her restlessness led Ella Mae to the vending machines in the waiting room. She pulled two dollar bills out of her pocket and fed one of the machines, before pushing E-14. The corkscrew turned and a king-size Snickers bar fell into the tray at her knees, along with her change. She opened it immediately. It was gone before she reached her chair. The candy rebelled in her stomach. She texted Cecelia two more times. Finally, the doors down the hall opened and Cecilia emerged.

"What is so damn important?"

Ella Mae could see the annoyance in Cecilia's face, but didn't care. "I need a witness."

"A witness for what?"

"I need to check the elevated pictures."

"Why? Nobody is supposed to touch them."

"Hackett died. He told me what he saw. I'm gonna tell you, and then we are both going to check together."

"We can't, it will pollute the results."

"We can and it won't, as long as we document it."

They argued, but Cecilia conceded. Together they walked into the treatment room.

"A dollar sign plus a puppy. That's what Hackett said."

Ella Mae grabbed a chair and dragged it across the room. She stepped up onto it and reached her hand up for the card. She waved the hand vigorously in the air, trying to force the nervous trembling to stop, and then she grabbed the card and jumped off the chair without looking at it. Standing in front of Cecilia, she flipped it over.

Triangle + eye.

"Shit," Ella Mae yelled. "Let's try another room."

"You don't know which room he was in?" The exclamation in Cecilia's voice was clear.

"No."

"We can't go tearing up every room."

"Yes we can."

They both tried to enter the next room at the same time, but Ella Mae threw her arm in front of Cecilia as if to bar her way. Again, she grabbed a chair. This time there was no hesitation. She jumped on the chair, grabbed the card and flipped it over.

99 + a red fish.

In the third room, a nurse was bandaging the head of a patient. Ella Mae scanned the room for a chair and saw none. She turned in a circle trying to figure out what to do before grabbing an intravenous stand and pulling the pole out of the socket.

"What are you doing?" The nurse asked her, as the bandage flopped in front of the patient's eye.

"Nothing, do your job and shut up."

Ella Mae proceeded to swat at the card, missing it twice before connecting and sending it sailing across the room. Her eyes followed the paper as it cartwheeled through the air and came to a rest on the floor with its purple baseball hat and handshake visible to the world.

They went into four other rooms, but found no dollar sign and puppy. At the threshold of the last room, Ella Mae paused and breathed deeply. Inside, a teenage girl lay on the examining table, unattended. Ella Mae ignored her. "It has to be here," she said to Cecilia. "Hackett wasn't dreaming. I know it."

"You have too much invested in this emotionally. I should have never gone along with it."

"Too late. I wouldn't stop now even if you left."

Ella Mae's previous excitement had been deflated by lack of success. She walked up to the bed saying nothing to the girl. Once again she dragged a chair into place and grabbed the card. Her hopes saw a dollar sign and a puppy, but her eyes saw only white. She flipped the card over once more — white emptiness.

"Shit!" Her profanity echoed down the hall. "Who in the hell put this up here?"

~

Hackett's struggle to keep his eyes open was a losing battle. He drifted in and out of sleep no matter how hard he tried to stay awake. Sarah sat silently beside the bed, reading a book whose title was visible to Hackett, but held no interest. As consciousness came and went, Hackett fluttered between a dreamy remembrance of his death experience and a desperate impatience for Ella Mae's return. As soon as his eyes flickered open, he turned his head to the door and watched for her approach. As he stared, his eyelids again grew heavy and visions of snowflakes captured him. In slow motion they formed groups of twos, threes and fours. He counted them again and again. He wasn't able to get very far, and he did not follow the numbers to infinity as he had in death, but it was still beautiful and comforting. The flakes formed into bubbles, the bubbles coalesced into larger forms, each and every one distinct. Their appearance somehow translated into a familiar number which was the sum of its parts. Over and over he counted and summed.

He awoke once again, this time with a start, as if someone had clapped their hands next to his head. He looked toward the door and saw the empty hallway beyond. He looked at Sarah in her chair, and was startled to see Jean in her place. Emotion overwhelmed him, but it wasn't Jean. It was Ella Mae sleeping. He looked at her closely. He wanted to reach out and touch her cheek, but he dared not.

Ella Mae's head jerked, and a loud snort popped from her throat. She wasn't simply snoring. Hackett recognized it as apnea and wondered if she was being treated for it. He watched as another snort awakened her. She rubbed her eyes and finally opened them, looking directly into his. A smile formed on her face. Once again, Hackett thought of Jean. He remembered one particular night awaking to Jean's moonlit face and her dark sparkling eyes looking back at him.

He smiled. "Hello, Pumpkin," he said using the name he sometimes called Jean.

"Hello, Dumpling," Ella Mae said back with a laugh.

Hackett felt a laugh rise up in his chest. Pain rose with it. "Dollar sign and a puppy?" he asked holding his chest.

She shook her head to tell him no, and a sadness emanated from her.

*How could that be?* Hackett wondered. He remembered the beauty of his experience. He relived the journey through the hospital and once again floated through the card seeing the dollar sign and puppy shimmering on the paper. It was not a dream, not a hallucination. He knew that. He fell down into it, once again happy and secure beyond what words could describe.

When he looked back at Ella Mae, he saw only sadness. "Can you feel it even now? Is it still real for you?" he asked.

Ella Mae nodded her head, yes. He watched her frown switch into a smile, knew that she understood him.

"What happened downstairs?" he asked, his words still labored.

"We looked at every picture in every room. Nothing matched what you saw."

"It had to. You made a mistake."

"We didn't. We checked every platform in the ER. I have the pictures here."

Hackett followed her eyes to a stack of cards in her lap.

"It wasn't the ER," he said. "It was Cardiac Care."

# Chapter 27

Hackett raised himself out of his chair and shuffled into the kitchen, his mind still lost in the physics book he had been reading. Two weeks after the attack, his feet slid along underneath him in the same drop-foot manner as had his tall, athletic ALS patient. Peripheral neuropathy caused by hypothermia was Hackett's self-diagnosis. The emergency room doctor had come up to visit Hackett when he was still in the ICU, explained that there was no sign of a heart attack and surmised that Hackett had been knocked unconscious, suffered a concussion and then cardiac arrest as a result of hypothermia. "You were lucky the snow plow driver saw your legs and ass sticking out of the snow before he buried you. Your core temp was eighty-four when you arrived in the ER. Much lower and you wouldn't have survived."

The realization that Hackett had been dead for a couple of hours had set his body and mind humming with excitement. The police arrived sometime after that. Hackett responded to their questions and filled them in on the details of the attack. "Is that everything?" one of the officers asked. "Not much to go on."

Hackett found the statement to be absurd on its face. He remembered every millisecond, played it back and forth in his mind studying it. Each movement, every sound, all of the pain, were like textures in his mind. It was a rich mosaic. One man's voice, the accented one, had the quality of a snow plow grinding against the street, hopping, popping and banging its way along. Hackett remembered the other man's voice: "Hold still for a second, old man, and we'll let you go." It had an oddly reassuring tone considering what had happened. It was the taller man in the leather jacket.

His memory of the attack was clear and surreal. His pain was accompanied by various hues of red flashing like lightning in the night sky. The snow around his face slipped and crunched as his head was pushed down into it. He could not escape the fascination of it all. How could the police say it wasn't much? The voices were so clear that he was sure he could pick them out in a crowded train station. The aroma of cigarette smoke and perfume so distinct that he might have been a bloodhound. It was all more realistic than the present itself, but it paled in comparison to what had happened after death. "You haven't really lived until you have died," he had told Sarah in those early hours of his second life.

Hackett had spent many of his waking moments in the first days after the attack observing his surroundings and trying to make sense of how different the world and he himself seemed. Everything looked and felt different. Part of it was this blurring of the line between his senses. Synesthesia, a word from his neurological studies kept popping into his mind. It was a mental process wherein one sense is accompanied by the stimulation of an unrelated sense — colors associated with feelings, numbers with shapes, sight with touch, and so on. Colors, shapes, figures and even smells flooded his mind imbuing everything with distinct and easily recognizable cues. The police officer had asked what his assailants were wearing. Without effort, Hackett could see them standing outside the hospital. The picture was finely textured and vibrant despite the night sky and the snow storm, but it was more than a photo or movie. As he looked at one of the men in his memory, he could feel the leather of his coat and smell the aroma of freshly tanned cow hide from the small factory in his hometown that had been long shuttered. He smelled menthol cigarettes and perfume as he lifted his head from the snow and saw smoke trails within a beautiful image of wild flowers on a spring day. Everything seemed linked to something else. Sights triggered sounds. Sounds triggered smells.

Smells triggered emotions. It was a big smorgasbord of memory whose patterns fit easily into a whole and needed no translation.

And, there were the numbers, too, beautiful comforting numbers in everything. He could not escape them, had no desire to. Leaving the hospital, he stared at the cars in the parking lot. Like the snowflakes after the attack, they formed into pairs and groups. He counted and summed — 363 cars within sight. He was sure of it. Unlike the rest of this new, more vibrant world, the numbers had a somewhat familiar feeling. His childhood memories came back to him, the days of isolation when he sought comfort in the library or among the trees. He had all but forgotten how consoling it was to count books in long neat rows, shelf upon shelf. Or to see the trees in the woods and imagine them towering in all directions until they stretched to infinity. He thought of Daniel Tammet, a young man in London who had grown up with high functioning autism and savant capabilities. The way Hackett now saw numbers was just as Tammet had described, and although he had never connected it before, memories of his own early childhood also reminded him of Tammet's book.

Finally, and perhaps most surprisingly, Hackett now felt like he could read people's emotions just from looking at their faces. He had long been a student of body language, but this was so much stronger. Faces lit up before him with emotion.

He played his mental videos of both the attack and his death experience over and over in his head, for the sheer wonder of reliving them. He also hoped that if he concentrated hard enough, he could perhaps divine some ultimate truth, but there were a couple of things that he couldn't quite recapture, no matter how hard he tried. One was the overwhelming sense of knowledge. In death, he had seen the universe and understood it, not in a mystical sense, but as scientific and mathematical truth. His memory of that feeling was now elusive. It was like trying to read Einstein's original *Theory of Relativity* manuscript, with no notes of explanation in the margins. The other thing that lay just beyond his grasp, were the memories of his life review. The only way he could explain them was that they had been more than memories. He had seen the past unfold anew. In comparison, his existing memories were incomplete and often just plain false. He could not now recreate life as he had lived it in death, but he recalled its raw truth, the deep river of its emotion.

His life review taught Hackett that the past was not static, it became a reflection of the present. Time was malleable. Our brains changed the past as each day rolled by, and now his life review was another memory, fading and changing along with the rest.

He knew without a doubt that his entire death experience was real. The idea that it was hallucination was laughable. It was as real as anything on this earth, all the changes that he now felt proved that. But it didn't explain what it meant, it didn't give him the answer to the big questions that had haunted man since the beginning, but somehow had seldom worried Hackett — was there a God and was there a life hereafter?

After all he had been through, he didn't understand why he equivocated about those questions, but he did. In the hospital, he had asked Ella Mae if she thought her death experience was proof of God and the afterlife. She looked at him like it was the stupidest question in the world. "Of course it was," she told him. "Proof for me and everyone else in the world who has died and come back to talk about it."

"Why?" he asked. "What was it that made you sure that you had stepped off the cliff of life and God had been revealed? Why isn't it possible that everything we saw happened in an instant of hyperconsciousness, the key unlocked and our brains reaching their full potential?"

Ella Mae's shock was so obvious that her thoughts, if not her exact words were clear before she spoke. "I passed through death, so did you. I saw God, so did you. Are you nuts, Hackett? There is no other explanation."

"Think about it," Hackett had demanded. "I am not saying what we experienced was a hallucination. It was obviously so much more than that. I wasn't in some dreamy nonsensical state. If anything, my conscious mind was clearer and more alive than it had ever been. I know that the things I saw existed, and are not understandable in the normal state of being. But did I really die, or did I stand on the cliff and peer over? Was it Jean of the present that I talked to, or was it the Jean of my past? Was it the all-knowing God who created what I observed, or was I just observing the natural universe?"

He and Ella Mae argued and argued, neither one being moved.

~

One leg after the other, Hackett dragged himself into the kitchen. He knew that there was a good chance that he would recover most of the function in his feet, but that would take time. He walked slowly, staring at everything around him. He re-membered standing in this same spot shortly after his release from the hospital, counting the cans and jars in the pantry — StarKist tuna stacked three high, mayonnaise, coarse brown mustard, chipotle in adobo sauce, applesauce and the distinctive shape of the can of smoked mackerel he had bought at Trader Joe's: one glance and he knew, one hundred and sixty-three cans and bottles, a beautiful prime number.

He looked at Sarah as she scraped the inside of a spaghetti squash with a fork, creating yellow translucent strings. She dropped them, first onto his plate and then her own, before topping them with puttanesca sauce. The aroma was beautiful, especially the sharp briny quality of the olives. He listened to the soft sound as she grated parmesan onto her own plate, and gently laid the grater on the table, denying him even that modest pleasure, a sacrifice on the altar of good health. Before Italy, he wouldn't have even eaten it, but now he had to admit that it was pretty good for a heart-healthy meal.

Sarah smiled brightly as she served him, but her loving concern seemed hollow. He couldn't get over the way he felt, and how wrong it was to feel that way. As he had so often since he woke up in the hospital, he thought of Jean's words. *Live your life. Love unconditionally.* Sarah had been incredibly sweet and caring since the attack. She cooked, cleaned and nursed him without a hint of complaint. Still, Hackett couldn't escape the feeling that she was hiding her anger. He hated himself for doubting her. After all, it was he who bore the guilt, he who had lusted more than loved.

He tried to dismiss his unwanted intuition, but couldn't. It seemed like people wore their feelings like loud brightly-colored clothes. A number of his students had visited him before he was discharged. Hackett noticed that one student's face radiated contempt. Previously, the kid had simply seemed reserved and distant. Now, distaste leapt from his features.

Hackett, who had always been so grounded in the observable, was now being overrun by intuition. People seemed to glow with emotion. He struggled to analyze what was happening, slowing down his thoughts, and studying people's faces and movements in search of an explanation. Body language and facial expressions explained some of it, but everything was heightened. It was as if his best diagnostic skills were turned on and wouldn't turn off. He observed people in a way that he had consciously never done before his death. A person's face, body language and vocal timbre appeared like colors in his mind. He recognized subtle shading around the eyes. Different hues became different emotions. False smiles radiated in red, like a firetruck. A grimace of pain appeared tinged with yellow. Anger was purple. Happiness was blue. The colors became maps.

Sometimes, there was more. He would look at an individual and feel as if he were falling, not truly falling, perhaps drifting was a better term, and he would feel a deep connection to them. At times, words or sentences appeared in his head, leaving him with a certainty that the person in front of him wanted him to know a particular thought. He was convinced that one woman waiting at a red light had lost a child. Another man glowed with happiness and nodded at Hackett when their carts passed at Safeway. *Me too*, he felt without hearing, and knew that like himself, the man had experienced death.

When Hackett turned his newly-trained eye on Sarah, she baffled him. He could sense that she was forcing herself to project a pleasant countenance. That false assurance was really all that he objectively saw, but anger was what he felt, and he worried that the anger was being generated by his own imagination. He settled into his chair, picked up his fork, stared at his spaghetti squash, and his mind drifted.

"How would you like to go for a trip down to Charlottesville tomorrow? We could go to Monticello." Sarah's question swam into his brain, a twig floating down the swollen river of his own thoughts.

Hackett had been dreaming of numbers again. At that very moment, he was following a trail of prime numbers transformed into a beautiful array of shapes and shades of blue — *71, 73, 79*. His obsession with primes had stolen his ability to concentrate on other things for the last three days. They held a natural and simple beauty, divisible by nothing but themselves and one. He was swept up in them, and along with them came associations of childhood. It was an odd, but intensely pleasant experience.

Through the numbers, he felt Sarah's irritation tugging at his thoughts. *She'd rather go to Monticello with Trudy*, he thought before he heard himself answer, "That would be wonderful." *127, 131, 137,* his numbers marched on.

Why was he doubting her? He hated this inner dialogue. She had given him no reason to feel this way, yet he couldn't shake it. Sarah was still talking, but Hackett's prime numbers floated on, leaving her in their wake. He remembered the feeling of death's total freedom and the love that he had felt all around him. That was the truth he needed to remember.

Hackett pulled himself back into the conversation at hand. He wasn't sure what Sarah was saying and so he just took up where he had drifted off. "We could even go wine tasting. I'll swirl and spit, all the pleasure, none of the harm."

"Have you been listening to a word of what I have been saying?" Hackett saw anger flash purple around her eyes.

He once again lost himself in thought. This time the literature he had been reading about death experiences caught his attention, especially the case studies. Like him, Pam Reynolds Lowry had become sensitive to people's thoughts and emotions. Other experiencers had developed previously undiscovered talent for music, but Hackett had heard of no one who had suddenly become a mathematical savant. He felt like he was turning into Rain Man.

There was another difference between his experience and the literature. It could be summed up in one word — certitude. In every other case study he read, the person who experienced death developed a firm and unshakable faith in the afterlife. Hackett's mind had changed about so many things, and he no longer was so dismissive of life after death, but he wasn't "dead" sure. He thought back to the conversation he had with Yu Lai after Doris Carrollton's death. She had argued that death was gradual. No one understood when someone was totally and fully gone. That doubt nagged at him. Had he walked up to the edge? Had he jumped off? Had he hit bottom? Was there a soft landing for him that kept him alive?

He picked up the book lying on the table, didn't realize that Sarah was still talking until she slammed her plate down and rose from her chair. He looked at her back as she walked away. The book was another fascination drawn from his experience. *The Lightness of Being*, by Frank Wilczek, was about finding the grand unifying theory of the cosmos. Wilczek described it as turning $E=MC^2$ back to front and hypothesizing that matter is simply another form of energy, $M=E/C^2$. Hackett thought about the inverted equation, ignored his wife once again. Simple algebra told him that the value of M did not change with its position in the equation, but there was more to it than that. By flipping the equation, Hackett's perspective flipped as well. $E=MC^2$ evoked a theory of mass as fuel, a plain and simple concept like what happened when you burned a log. $M=E/C^2$ made him think of something entirely different. It exposed mass as naked energy. Mass equaled energy divided by a mere constant number. It was a simple fraction of energy. Quite literally, mass did not really exist. Everything in the universe was an illusion. Mass was a figment of energy, a figment of imagination, a figment of consciousness.

Another thing about the book struck Hackett. Wilczek theorized that the universe was unified by a grid of energy on the subatomic level. The grid either represented the interaction of subatomic particles or was the interaction. It flowed through everything and was everything. Hackett couldn't escape the notion that this theory was connected to the grid he had observed in death and that cosmic energy was the ultimate consciousness. A few of Wilczek's words lit Hackett up inside with a burst of color. "Through the patchy clouds, off in the distance, we seem to glimpse a mathematical paradise."

Had Wilczek seen what Hackett had seen?

This book, this intuition, this fascination with numbers made Hackett feel like he had a new mind which inhabited an insignificant shell. His death, which was now the most significant moment of his life, had been transformative in other ways as well. Mortality, which had consumed him after Jean had died, now seemed wondrous. There was less of a reason to fear death, and so his interest in saving lives and his career in neurology were less compelling. He felt no pressing need to return to the office or the hospital. He longed to read physics and literally play with numbers.

In between his thoughts, like background music in an elevator, a vision of Sarah's purple hued face visited him. *Her smile is a lie*, he told himself. It nagged him. He wanted desperately to wipe it away. To do so, he concentrated on prime numbers and felt the rhythm merge with his breath. *Breathe in... Two, three, five, seven... Breathe out... eleven, thirteen, seventeen, nineteen.* Hackett felt his heart settle into it. He concentrated, slowed its beats. He had always struggled with meditation, but it now felt easy and natural. A calm ecstasy that reminded him of his death experience came over him. He allowed himself to sink down into it.

~

Sarah walked down the basement stairs, sat in her upholstered glider and picked up her new cross stitch pattern. She had to calm down and clear her mind. Over the years, hiding her emotions had become second nature. She remembered the darkness inside of her bedroom closet, the initial panic she had felt when her stepmother locked her in. She shivered at the thought of her own childish screams and tears, but she had learned to control all of that.

Since Hackett had woken up after the attack, her thoughts had been ugly and bothersome, and Hackett seemed to see right through her. She felt like she was losing control. She counted the cross stitch grid methodically and stitched carefully. Visions of dead bodies floated in her imagination and populated the finely spaced fabric — James, dead in their bed, Aaron lying on the floor, foam dripping from his mouth. Sarah counted stitches trying to ward off the visions. She could see both of them clearly, but she could only imagine Hackett face down in the snow. *He should be dead, but here he is babbling this bullshit about life after death and making believe he is a human calculator.*

"Pick two numbers, any two numbers," she heard him say. It had been a day after he woke up, four days after the attack. She had no idea why he was asking. "Go ahead," he said, obviously seeing her confusion. "You pick two numbers and I'll tell you their product."

He was such a flaming idiot. "Two and eight," she said.

"Too easy," but Hackett gave her the answer anyway—"Sixteen. Bigger numbers."

"Thirteen and seventeen."

"Two hundred and twenty-one. Bigger."

"Thirty-eight and sixty-three."

"Two-thousand, three-hundred and ninety-four," he replied an instant later, and insisted that she check it on her Blackberry. When she read him back the same number, his grin stretched from ear to ear. He looked like the Cheshire Cat minus the purple and red stripes.

Sarah felt her world falling apart. Her anger bubbled over. *Stupid fucking parlor tricks*, she said to herself, and jabbed a needle through the fabric and into her own finger. "Fuck!"

"Are you alright?" Hackett's voice drifted down the stairs.

"Stabbed myself with a goddamned fucking needle," she yelled back. Then in a calmer voice, "It's nothing."

She stitched a row of white next to an existing row of cream. There was no printed pattern on this cross stitch. It was all in the counting and the grid. It took painstaking concentration. Stitch after stitch she lost herself in it. Slowly Hackett evaporated until all that existed was fabric, needle and floss. It was as if she was a child once again, sitting in the darkness, holding the afghan blanket that her real mom had knitted for her, feeling the pattern she knew so well, the colors that to this day remained bright in her mind. She counted now as she had counted then. Around she had gone, one stitch at a time from the outer rim of the blanket to its core, and then she would start over.

~

Small flames licked the faux logs of the gas fireplace in the bed and breakfast as Hackett lay still watching Sarah in the bathroom, naked before the mirror. Hackett had been trying hard not to let his numbers and memories of death distract him from the life in front of him. It had been a struggle, but it was easier now that her clothes were off. He stared at the perfect curve of her breast, her nipple saluting him. They hadn't had sex since the attack. Each time Hackett had gotten too close or suggested it, she seemed to recoil. "I'm scared of what might happen to you," she had said over and over.

Finally, she had agreed to resume their sex life. Hackett thought back on their day, waking early for the drive to Charlottesville, lunch at a small place on Main Street, a tour of Monticello and then wine tasting at Horton Vineyards. It had been a wonderful day in spite of the cold weather. Then they had the perfect romantic dinner, lit by nothing but candles and fire in the huge, old stone fireplace of the farmhouse. For the most part, Hackett had been able to remain in the present. Sarah hadn't seemed so happy in a long time. It was as if they were back in Tuscany before his heart attack.

Hackett's mind drifted to the hotel outside San Gimignano and Cum Quibis, the beautiful little restaurant. He told himself that life was wonderful, that there was a reason he had been sent back. He had no time for negative thoughts, but still something hovered under the surface of his consciousness, nagging him. Those unformed doubts followed him like the numbers in his head.

The light clicked off in the bathroom and Sarah emerged from the darkness into the shifting and flickering light of the fireplace's gas flame. The smell of her new perfume filled the air, and a bouquet of aromas filled his head: vanilla, anise, citrus, spice, a number of flowers, all subtle, yet nonetheless strikingly unique. The sight and the scent filled him with joy. Hackett told himself that he would remember the aroma forever.

She came to him and lay beside him, touching him softly. "I'm sorry for making you wait so long," she whispered, "but absence makes the heart grow fonder."

Hackett searched for the features of her face in the darkness, trying to divine her thoughts and emotions, then he chastised himself for it. This was his marriage; how could they have a normal loving relationship if his suspicious mind kept up this mistrust? He knew it would destroy them if he didn't let it go. He imagined her smile in the darkness, remembered Tuscany and her happiness, remembered Jean telling him to live his life. He kissed her and searched for her love.

Hackett caressed his wife, took his time listening carefully for sounds of her enjoyment and focusing his attention on what gave her pleasure. He thought of how perfect her body was. He thought of his high school and college fantasies, how he always dreamed of touching such a beautiful girl. It was over quickly. He rolled off her and sighed, feeling pleasantly exhausted. "I love you," he told her, but his own thoughts argued back. *Beauty is not love. Am I that shallow?*

"Love you, too," Sarah answered.

He watched as she rose from bed, walked back to the bathroom, turned the light on and disappeared behind the wall to use the toilet. Hackett rolled over, feeling his own fatigue. He grabbed one of the extra pillows and pulled it close, feeling the clean cool fabric against his skin. He exhaled and felt like he was sinking into the bed. Slowly, his mind let go of Sarah's naked image. In its place, he saw Jean, naked, young and beautiful in her own way. He stared at her, remembered their lovemaking. He felt

Jean under him rocking and expressing her excitement with an almost silent murmuring moan. He felt her back arch and heard the little giggle that invariably escaped her lips just before she had an orgasm. *I love you*, she said to him, and that was the only truth he felt sure of.

When Sarah appeared once again in front of the mirror, she washed her face and hands, then appeared to investigate a zit on her chin. She stood back and smiled at herself. A chill ran through Hackett. He saw her smile. It could have meant anything, and most likely was a sign of her happiness, but he felt belittled by it. It seemed smug and dismissive. She turned off the light and walked back into the room, now wearing a nightgown. He tried to remember his happiness, to push the unwanted thoughts from his mind. Sarah lay down beside him, silently rolled over and simply said goodnight.

As Hackett lay on his back, sadness washed over him. He looked back on his own life. All of the accomplishments seemed insignificant. He had gone from addled child, to odd adolescent, to smart young man, to confident and respected doctor with a loving wife. With Sarah's help, he had overcome the depths of grief and despair. He even survived that damn attack, only to fall off a metaphorical cliff and land once again as the addled child. He had heard so often about old age being a return to childhood, but he wasn't elderly yet. This was something else, a crisis of spirit, or maybe just his true soul bubbling back to the surface.

Life was like that. Hackett had seen far too many people cruise along decade after decade, thinking they were gifted by God's grace. He'd seen them ride the mortal coil, but when it was their time, they didn't just shuffle off, it crumbled around them. Going gently into the night was pure fantasy for most. Rage against the dying, Dylan Thomas had said. *Rage?* Hackett asked. *Who rages?* He saw life as collapse — an ending that generally sputters.

He hardly slept that night. In the morning, Hackett opened his weary eyes. Though it was the dead of winter, he heard the sound of a solitary bird chirping. He took it as a good omen. In the light of a new day, he would end this pointless habit of trying to look into people's souls. It had seemed like a gift when he was recovering from the attack; now it was becoming a burden.

As if on cue, Sarah walked out of the bathroom, wearing tight black slacks, a pretty white sweater and a big smile. "Morning, lover boy." She walked to the bed, bent over and kissed him on the forehead. Hackett tried to smother his discomfort.

# Chapter 28

"I just wish it would all go away, the numbers, the inability to concentrate on what's in front of me, and especially this intuition," Hackett said to Ella Mae.

"I think it's amazing. I felt like a different person after I died," Ella Mae exclaimed, "but I didn't experience anything like what's happening to you."

"But I'm second guessing everything, questioning everyone's intentions, especially Sarah's."

"Maybe that's a good thing."

"No, it's not. She deserves better."

"If you say so, but I still think your sixth sense is wonderful. What does my face tell you right now?" Ella Mae smiled as she asked the question.

"Nothing really. You're simple." Hackett stopped abruptly and raised his hand. "I didn't mean that as an insult. When I see your face, I just see friendship. It is very reassuring. I never have to wonder what you're thinking or feeling."

His words were a lie, perhaps just a little white lie, but a lie just the same. The truth was that he could read her face right at that very moment. He saw her cheeks blush pink, and the creases around her eyes light up in a happy shade of blue. He remembered Ella Mae running back into his hospital room waving the card in the air, screaming "You were right! You were right!" She held the picture in front of him, dollar sign and a puppy. It was no surprise to him, but he felt such extreme happiness for Ella Mae in that moment. He knew it was the verification that she needed for herself, proof that she was right and the world was wrong.

Hackett also remembered Sarah's face at that same moment. It bore a look of utter shock. "You saw that?" she asked.

"Yes," Hackett answered with a smile.

Sarah's response was odd. He thought about it once again, puzzled over it. "No, you didn't. You couldn't have. Death is death. People don't fucking come back to haunt us." She must have been in shock. Since that day, Sarah had refused to talk about his experience. Hackett tried to dismiss it from his mind.

He changed the subject.

"Doctor Parnell has decided that my case can't be included in the study," he said to Ella Mae.

"Because I took down all the pictures?"

Hackett saw sadness creep into her eyes. "It wasn't that. The main reason is that I am involved in the study. He is totally right. My experience can't be used, it would put the entire study into question."

"We can still go public. We have to."

"I don't think that is a good idea either."

"Why not?"

"Either way, it tends to show bias. I have removed myself from the study, and advised Parnell to delete all of the cases from our hospital. That's the only way to avoid tainting the study. If the final results are convincing, I might be able to go public later, but not now."

Hackett saw the disappointment on Ella Mae's face.

"I have been meditating more lately. You really should give it a try, it will make you a happier person," he told her.

"Why, do I look that sad?" she asked as concern painted itself across her awkward smile.

"It's not that. I think everyone should meditate. I've always thought so. It's just that I was never very good at it. It's been easier since my experience, at times it even reminds me a little of how I felt."

The conversation drifted from meditation back to the Parnell study before getting sidetracked onto Ella Mae's inability to find a man. Hackett could see her slipping into melancholy. They sat silently for a minute, Ella Mae apparently lost in her own thoughts. Hackett's mind began to slip as well.

With the calm, he opened up. "I don't think I am coming back to the hospital." He should have told Sarah first, but he wanted Ella Mae to know.

"Not at all?"

"Well, not to work. It's not like I am banning myself from the grounds."

"Don't you think you should take more time to think about it? You're still adjusting to what happened. The hospital's been such an important part of your life."

"Yes, it has, but I have lost interest in it. Patients deserve a doctor who is consumed with medicine, not one whose mind is constantly adrift. Plus, there is so much more to the world."

"Can you really spend your days playing math games that only you understand?"

Hackett laughed. "No," he said. "I need more than that."

"Like what?"

"Like everything. I might go back to school and get a degree in physics, maybe even work at CERN, chase the Higgs boson. I want to go back to Italy and learn the language. I'd love to study eastern religion, it makes so much more sense now. My God, there is so much I want to do."

"Well, I guess you don't need the money. You'll always have your practice to fall back on."

The smile on Hackett's face grew brighter. "I'm gonna sell the practice."

"You can't."

"I can."

Hackett watched Ella Mae's face and read the deep concern written there. It took a little while, but slowly the serious lines of her expression cracked and a smile seeped out. "If that's what you want, then good for you," she said. He saw sincerity in her face.

"There is something else that is bothering me." The words popped from Hackett's lips. He had been worried about it, thought about talking to Ella Mae, but hadn't decided. He continued anyway. "When Jean sent me back, she told me there was something I needed to do. Something that might involve you and Amy." He paused, expecting Ella Mae to react, but she just waited for him to continue. "I don't know what it is and I don't have a clue about how to prepare."

"What did she tell you?"

"That was about it. She said I had to go back to life and that both you and Amy needed me." Hackett paused, drawn in by the expression of pure happiness that lit up Ella Mae's face. It embarrassed him, but he pushed it aside and continued. "I struggled to ask questions, but I was already being drawn back to my body."

Ella Mae's expression turned to a frown. "I still remember that feeling of coming back into my body. Death was beautiful, but that feeling was hideous, like jumping out of a plane without a parachute."

Ella Mae didn't have any answers for Hackett. The best she could do was tell him to live life, and the rest would take care of itself.

~

Sweat formed a glistening sheen on Sarah's breasts and shoulders. She was not sated. She lay on her back, angry, thinking not of the sex but of Hackett's crazy behavior. Victor rolled toward her and touched her nipple lightly with his finger. "You can't really have run out of money. You're married. It's communal property."

His needling pissed her off. Of course she hadn't run out of money. That was just what she told him. She needed to step back, to conserve and not be rushed. "It's a short-term problem. We have to be patient."

"I can be patient, but I worry about Misha. I need to give him more soon."

"Not now, no way, I need to do this right. If Hackett knows I'm taking money, I could lose everything."

Victor lifted his hand off of her breast and gripped her jaw firmly. He turned her face towards him. "We'll lose more than money if we don't pay up." They were staring into each other's eyes, trading hardened gazes. "We can't fuck with Misha. He's bratva," Victor added.

Sarah thought about the Russian word for mob or gangster. Victor had used it before. Just saying the word seemed to frighten him.

"Then get rid of him."

Victor's fingers clamped down on Sarah's face. He stared into her eyes like he was Dirty Harry, or perhaps Michael Corleone. "Stop talking bullshit. Just get more money."

Their eyes remained locked for a few moments longer, neither saying a word. Victor slowly shook her face from side to side and then released his grip. Even then, Sarah maintained her stare in stony silence. She could control Victor, she always had.

"I can get a little money, but I will not lose sight of the big picture. If you can't keep him happy, figure out what to do with him." Her lips curled into a smile, she reached over and grabbed hold of Victor's manhood. "I need more." She squeezed the limp appendage. "Or are you so worried about Misha that you can't get it up?"

Victor pushed her with a laugh. "I'm good to go, but you better get me five thousand as a down payment."

He entered Sarah, and she smiled. *Such a boy*, she said to herself. *Victor and this Misha, even if she didn't know him, she was sure — he was a boy, too. No more than two thousand.*

# Chapter 29

A warm breeze rustled Ella Mae's curly dark hair as she rambled down the street. She missed Hackett's presence at the hospital, but she was happy nonetheless. They had pledged to have lunch at least once every week. So far, they had been averaging twice a week instead. For Ella Mae, it felt like her old friendship with Jean. They chatted about nothing and everything. The change in Hackett amazed her. He had always talked incessantly about work. It was what they had in common. Now they had something to share that was much more personal, much more important, but she knew there were big differences, too.

Ella Mae turned on M Street and walked down to the small restaurant they had chosen for lunch. She walked up the narrow steps, opened the door and glanced around, looking for him.

"Can I help you?" the hostess asked.

"Meeting a friend, but I don't see him."

The hostess sat Ella Mae at a small table by the window, from where she vacantly stared out into the bright sunlight. Eventually, her eyes came to focus on a couple walking down the sidewalk hand in hand. The couple passed and another couple appeared further away, a hazy image with form, but no detail. She watched their commingled hands sway gently as they walked. Saw their happiness without seeing their faces. Her eyes drifted away, watched other couples walking by, the city seemingly alive with love. To her right the door opened, and the hostess welcomed someone. Ella Mae recognized the woman's dress. It was the couple who had been holding hands.

"Table for two." George's clear and distinctive voice shocked her. Ella Mae stared down at her own pudgy, pale hands, felt them begin to sweat. The hostess sat George a few tables away, his back to Ella Mae. A slight sigh escaped from her lips.

George talked about the Orioles and the upcoming season. Ella Mae listened. The woman named players and talked in RBIs and ERAs. *A better match than me*, Ella Mae thought, but then remembered that George was a chameleon who could blend in with any woman. Ella Mae looked away, covering the side of her face with her hand, feeling her broken heart.

The door of the restaurant clanged shut. "Hey there." Ella Mae heard Hackett's voice. She raised her finger to her lips to silence him, panic colored her face red. Hackett looked back at her quizzically. He silently strode over to the table and took a seat without talking.

"Why are you upset?" he whispered. "Why do we need to be silent?"

Ella Mae wanted to answer, but she choked up on the words. She averted her eyes and played with her napkin, all the while feeling the pressure of silence on her ear drums.

Hackett reached across the table and whispered once more. "You are loved, and you will find love."

His voice was soft and reassuring. Ella Mae felt the comfort in it, and she gained strength from it. Slowly she lifted her head and glanced toward George, raising her eyebrows for Hackett to follow. He looked. She saw his recognition.

"Do you want to go somewhere else?" he asked. Again, his voice was soft, compassionate and barely audible.

Ella Mae felt kindness in the touch of Hackett's hand. She nodded, held her tears back and felt Hackett's hand lift her own from the table. He pushed back his chair. Together, they walked to the door. It opened, though Ella Mae could not tell if it had done so by itself or at Hackett's urging.

Outside, the sunlight jolted her. She looked at Hackett. "Wait," she said and she summoned her will.

"Atta girl," Hackett told her. "Do you want me to come or wait here?"

"Come."

Ella Mae looked at Hackett for a few seconds, taking strength from his smile. "Ready?" he asked.

"Ready," she answered and they walked back into the restaurant. She went right to the table and stood directly behind George. "Has he told you he's married?" she said in a clear voice.

The woman looked up at Ella Mae, her face lit up in surprise.

"I'm divorced now," George answered.

Ella Mae maintained eye contact with the woman, refusing to look at George. "He told me he was divorced, all the while he lived two lives, one here and one in Seattle. He's a very good liar, a real professional."

The woman's eyes shifted from Ella Mae to George. Ella Mae could sense fear and shock. "Who is she?" the woman asked.

"An old girlfriend who I wronged. I was scared to tell her that I was just separated."

"Forgot to tell his wife, too. I'll give you some advice. Get up from this table and run. I've never met a more dishonest man in my life. Does he still travel all the time? Does he tell you it's just for work?"

The woman sitting in front of Ella Mae shoved her seat from the table and stood. Ella Mae hoped that she would grab the glass of water from the table and fling it at George, but she didn't cooperate.

"Don't leave, Barbara. We can work this out," George pleaded.

Ella Mae remembered George's wife on the phone, remembered him afterward trying to tell Ella Mae that everything would be okay. He'd get a divorce, they would be together. Stepping in for George's newest victim, Ella Mae reached down, felt the cold glass in her hand and threw ice water in his face.

~

Hackett followed Ella Mae to the sidewalk. He was proud of her, and he could tell by her expression that she was proud as well. They walked silently to the corner before she stopped. He saw her body shake, and he wrapped his arms around her. "You did good," he said. "Real good."

They found another restaurant and talked about what had happened. Ella Mae told Hackett how she couldn't help missing George, especially at night. "He was such a good liar. At times it still seems like his words were true and his actions were fabricated instead of vice versa. I think of his smile and his arms around me, and I believe in the fairytale once more."

"It's natural." Hackett smiled. "As they say, love is blind, but that's not always good. Sometimes our passion is so strong we can't see the truth that is staring us in the face."

Ella Mae stared at Hackett for a few seconds before responding. "Maybe I shouldn't say this—"

"No," Hackett said, and raised his hand in front of Ella Mae, cutting her off in mid-sentence. "Don't say it. Sarah's not like that."

But Ella Mae didn't stop. "I'm worried. I should know the warning signs, Hack. Be careful. She'll break your heart, too."

Hackett could see the concern on Ella Mae's face as if it was printed on a billboard. He saw something else in her eyes as well. He felt warmth from her and could see her love for him. He felt the closeness between them that he always took for granted. He didn't have that many close friends, and she was his closest. He owed it to her to listen and to be honest in return.

"I really don't think it is like that," he said. "I am worried about Sarah, but it is different. It is not about love, I feel that in her still, but she has had a hard life. I think she has always worried about money, and my death scared the crap out of her. Sometimes she acts so irrationally about it. I'm trying to be understanding."

"What has she said?" Ella Mae asked.

Hackett told her about the pre-nup, the insurance and the will.

"And that's not enough?" Ella Mae asked. "How much money does she need?"

~

Sarah waited in line for the teller as the man in front of her reached back and picked at his own butt. He was short, maybe five-six, and probably weighed over two hundred pounds. His jeans hung loosely on his hips, exposing his white fleshy crack. She wondered why people like him were even allowed to inhabit the planet. He moved ahead to the next open teller. In a couple of minutes, it was her turn. She handed the teller a check for two thousand dollars made out to cash and then watched as the woman handed over twenty crisp one hundred dollar bills.

~

Hackett was on the living room couch reading his physics book, but he couldn't concentrate. His thoughts didn't wander to numbers or death. It was his conversation with Ella Mae that haunted him. He was convinced that her suspicions of Sarah were exaggerated, but there was something there nonetheless. He kept returning to one inescapable reality — Sarah's anger. He saw it as a reflection of his failings. He hadn't put her first. He hadn't loved her as he had Jean. He hadn't changed his will. He argued back and forth about the will in particular, not knowing which point of view made him more uncomfortable. He convinced himself that he needed to talk to her and put everything on the table. The back door opened.

"Hello, honey," Sarah said from the kitchen. "What an annoying day. It's good to be home."

He waited for her footsteps to approach the living room before resting his book on the couch beside him. "What happened?"

"I spent the morning food shopping; you know how I hate that. Then when I came out of Safeway, I backed into some old lady in a beat up old car. It was totally my fault."

"Much damage?"

"Not much, just a little scratch on my bumper, but I smashed her fender pretty good. She was hysterical. I hope you don't mind, but I thought it was better to pay her off than deal with the insurance."

"That's fine. What did you give her?"

"Two thousand goddamn dollars. She can probably replace the old clunker for that. Do you think I was being stupid?"

*Fucking idiot.* Hackett felt Sarah's thought pass through his consciousness. She was angry at him again, but why? He looked at her, wanting to understand. She was smiling.

"Who cares? It's just money, and you're right, something that small isn't worth an insurance claim. Hell, we have a thousand-dollar deductible," he told her, hoping it would calm her down, praying that the anger he felt would disappear.

Sarah bent down and kissed him on the cheek. "You're such a darling."

He mustered his nerve. "Are you unhappy?"

Sarah looked at him quizzically, her surprise evident. "Unhappy about what?"

"Unhappy with me, with our marriage?"

"Are you?" she asked in return, and Hackett once again read surprise in her face, not anger, not unhappiness, just surprise.

Hackett's words poured out. He told her about his death experience, about how he lusted for her. He told her that he feared that she thought his feelings were trivial.

"Don't you love me?" she asked.

He assured her that he did, and he meant every word. He apologized if his actions hadn't always shown it.

"You've been wonderful to me," Sarah told him, then she paused.

Hackett felt her unspoken words. The silence drove him on. "I've decided to increase my insurance. I don't want you to feel insecure about my health and your future."

"Thank you," she said.

It looked like she was waiting for him to continue, and so Hackett barreled forward again. "I have some other news, too. I have decided to quit the hospital."

Sarah stood still. He could almost see her processing what he said. He began to wonder if she was upset. She finally talked.

"I guess that's good. Less stress, and you can focus on your practice full time. You might even make more money."

Hackett thought about how reluctant he had been to talk to Sarah. The burden of his guilt lifted. They could be happy. He talked in rapid fire.

"I'm going to give up the practice, too. We can relax, I'd like to go back to school, plus we can take the whole summer to travel. We can go back to Italy. We can't afford to travel everywhere, but we can still go a lotta where." Hackett ran out of breath.

"Are you crazy?" Sarah's voice rose. "What about the money?"

"I have plenty saved, more if I sell the practice. We'll have to watch what we spend, but we can get by. I've gone through the numbers."

"Gone through the numbers? All your pretty shapes and colors. That bullshit is making you lose your mind. I don't want to get by. I want to live."

A purple ugliness radiated from her face. This time, Hackett could not mistake her anger and the fact that it was directed at him.

"We can be happy," he argued. "We don't need millions of dollars. We don't need to drink Dom Perignon every night. We'll be together. We'll travel. We'll have a roof over our heads."

"Have a roof over our heads!" The purple surrounded her now.

*You fucking asshole.* Her unspoken words shouted within his head as Sarah stormed out of the room. Hackett brooded on the couch, slipped down into his anger, let it smother his soul like a heavy blanket. Sarah could be so tender and caring, but her ugly side was there as well. He had not wanted to believe it, had pushed it away, preferring to attribute it to stress brought on by concern for him. Now he could not avoid it.

Hackett sulked, nurturing ugly thoughts for some time, until he lost himself in the feelings. He wished that Sarah would walk back into the room. He would tell her that his decision was final. She would like it or lump it. The thoughts droned on until they sickened him. He heard Jean tell him that love was not perfection. He dismissed her as well.

The back door slammed and then the garage door opened. Familiar sounds told him Sarah was getting her bike, then it was quiet and he was alone.

Hackett closed his eyes and sought solace in numbers. He focused on pi, imagined a perfect circle. Inside the circle, he imagined an octagon, with the point of each corner lying directly on the circle. He imagined another octagon, just slightly larger, each side of the octagon lying flat against the outside arc of the circle. He could bisect each octagon creating squares and triangles to calculate the area. The difference between the area of the two octagons equaled the area of the circle. He imagined Archimedes calculating pi, and saw the first ten digits in his head— 3.1415926535. The digits floated as beautiful shapes and colors across his thoughts. He imagined them going on forever. Alongside the numbers, he pictured trees, ants, people, stars, grains of sand. It was the infinite universe, more comforting than his conscious thoughts could express. Between digits, he heard Jean's voice, again: *love is not perfection.*

Eventually, he opened his eyes, relaxed and refreshed. His anger at Sarah seemed silly and unimportant, her anger at him, no more significant. He told himself that she would understand in time. He didn't debate the point, or wonder what he would do if she remained steadfast. His surety was like a rock. Hackett lifted his book, lowered his eyes and read on, contented.

Two hours later, Sarah's bicycle chain rustled in the garage and echoed inside Hackett's sleeping brain. The back door opened, Hackett woke up and Sarah walked into the kitchen. The earlier argument now felt old and stale. He told himself not to let anger control him.

"Hello," he greeted her, projecting cheerfulness in the hope of getting it back in return.

"Hello, yourself," she replied, mirroring his gay demeanor. He heard her place her helmet and pannier on the kitchen table, and then followed the soft sounds of her approaching footsteps.

"I'm sorry, I overreacted," she said from the end of the coach. "I just freaked out. There have been so many shocks and so many changes. I couldn't handle one more."

"I'm sorry, too. Anger takes us captive and clouds our minds. It makes us say and do things that we don't mean."

"I am fine with whatever decision you make about work. I just have one request."

"What's that?"

"Take a little more time to think about it. Not just about the money, but about what you would be giving up and the cost your decision will have to others. You're an incredible doctor, you save lives. Don't think that you'll be easily replaced."

Hackett had thought about all of it, and he knew he would not change his mind. He had dissected her last point especially. She was wrong. He had changed. He could not be the doctor that he had once been. He had no desire for it, and, therefore, he would not and could not concentrate on it the way that he once had. If he remained at the hospital, patients would die because of him. He could feel that. He could also feel that Sarah would understand. Wasn't she demonstrating that now? Wasn't she proving her love and allowing her feelings for Hackett to out-weigh her own worries?

# Chapter 30

A bright April sun warmed Hackett's back through the window of his office on 19th Street. It was Saturday. He was again in the office on a weekend so that he could concentrate on the proposals he had received to buy the practice. On the desk in front of him sat a stack of papers with letters and resumes. He was slow-walking the process for Sarah's benefit, but he knew that the longer he waited, the more she would try to talk him out of it, and the more his practice would dwindle.

Another thing bothered him. In truth, he knew he would feel a loss if he gave up the practice. Neurology had been his life's work. He had left a mark, but felt that it was nothing permanent. It would soon evaporate into thin air. Hackett pulled a letter off the top of the stack. It was stapled to a sheaf of perhaps twenty pages. He read the doctor's name, vaguely remembering it and a face he had seen at medical conferences. He stared at the words. The paper blurred. Hackett shook his head and brought the words back into focus. The first paragraph was drivel of no consequence. "I am happy to present this proposal," blah, blah, blah. Hackett thought about the clarity of his death experience, the beauty of the grid, and how he had felt as if the universe lay open and understandable before him. He could no longer see the equations, but he still remembered that feeling of knowledge. "Enlightenment" was the word that came to mind. He drifted into a beautiful oblivion. His thoughts unmoored him from time. When he refocused on the paper in front of him, twenty minutes had passed. As he had recently done so many times, he reflected on this inability to concentrate on life. He

262 ~ GARETH FRANK

knew that it would interfere with resuming his practice. He couldn't focus on his patients if his mind was constantly in the clouds. He needed to sell his practice before he screwed it all up.

Hackett felt his mind slipping again. He enjoyed the feeling, the pure relaxation of it. He found himself staring at the black indentations in the drop ceiling, counting them, when a number just popped into his head—2123091413. It was a phone number, a beautiful radiant phone number.

Hackett dialed. It rang four times, before rolling over to voice mail.

"Hi, this is Hackett. Give me a call on my cell. I need to talk to you."

Hackett gathered up the folders in front of him and straightened his desk. He looked at the painting of the Palio with all its gory detail and felt certain that Sarah would forget about the practice and her worry about money as soon as they started to travel again.

When he stood up to leave, he felt his cell phone vibrate against his hip. Hackett grabbed the phone excitedly, fumbled it and nearly dropped it before answering.

A soft voice sailed over the airwaves, "How are you, Doctor Metzger?"

"Don't call me Doctor Metzger anymore, we're colleagues. It should be Hackett now."

"Hello, Hackett," Yu Lai answered. "I was going to call and see how you were doing. Are you back at work?"

"Gradually getting back into the practice. To tell the truth, I quit the hospital."

"I heard. It really made me sad."

"Listen, Yu Lai. I have something important to talk to you about. I want you to come back to DC and join my practice."

There was a marked pause.

"That's a surprise," she finally said.

"Don't say no yet."

"I'd really love to do it, but Presbyterian is working out really well."

"I'll make you an offer you can't refuse."

"Oh, and you're the Godfather now." He heard the levity in her voice.

"Fucking A," Hackett said and laughed. He heard a surprised giggle in return.

"Here's the deal, I have been thinking about selling the practice, but I can't do that. I want you to be my partner. You'll be the senior partner. I'll be window dressing. In a couple of years, you'll be in position to take over Neurology at the hospital. I'll get you a job there now and help make that happen when it is time. In the meantime, you get my entire client practice. It's worth a couple of million at least."

"How much would I need to buy in?"

"Nothing, zip, nada, zilch. I want you, money isn't the issue."

"Jesus, Hackett, that is quite an offer. Are you sure?"

"Yes, I am. If you don't take it, I'm not sure what I'll do. I might just let the whole practice evaporate by inertia. I don't want that."

"Let me think about it, okay?"

"Sure, but if you act soon, I'll throw my golf clubs into the deal."

"You don't even play golf."

When Hackett hung up the phone, he felt a wave of happiness and relief. She hadn't said yes, but he knew that she would. He thought about Sarah. She would be upset that he was practically giving the practice away, but this way there would still be a continuing income. He would make her see that this was the right path.

# Chapter 31

Water slipped, swirled and gurgled slowly down the Potomac River just twenty or so feet in front of Sarah. Across the river, cars loaded onto the little Jubal Early Ferry. *The Jew ball is early*, Sarah said to herself, remembering the stupid phrase that Victor had uttered years ago. *He's such a moron, but he's sexy and useful.* She had been waiting for about fifteen minutes. Promptness was not one of Victor's strengths. Sarah's eyes slipped back across the water, and her head swiveled further to scan the line of cars starting on the Maryland bank stretching back to the White's Ferry store. He was nowhere in sight. She would leave in five minutes if he didn't show. She tilted her bottle of Mega Water up and took a slow sip.

Minutes slogged by. These men were driving her crazy. Why had her whole life been populated by such idiots? Hackett's voice rippled through her memory like echoes in an empty hallway. "I've decided against selling the practice after all," she heard him say.

It had been a pleasant surprise, until he mentioned that little Chinese bitch. "I've asked Yu Lai to join. She'll be marvelous and she can carry most of the load immediately."

"Most of the load?" Sarah had asked. "What about you?"

"I'll give advice and keep my hands in it."

Sarah had smelled a rat as soon as that girl's pornographic name had been uttered. She spat out her next words. "She better be paying good money to buy in."

"It's not about the money," he said next. Her head could have exploded.

She had to deal with Hackett soon, before he gave away everything. This time, she would do it herself to make sure it was done right. Sarah drummed her fingers on the table, heard car engines turn in anticipation of the approaching ferry. She looked and saw Victor about a hundred feet beyond the last car. Even at that distance she could see a difference in him. He moved more slowly than was his custom, and he favored one leg. She trained her eyes on him. As he got closer, she could tell that he had been on the losing side of a fight.

"What happened to you?" Sarah asked when he got close enough for conversation.

"Fuckin' Misha is what fuckin' happened. I told you we can't fuck with him."

Victor held out a small paper bag. "You're sure?" he asked.

Sarah took the bag and looked inside — a syringe and two small vials. She looked up at Victor's swollen face and the splint on his fingers. "You let that little prick beat you up. You're twice his size."

"Misha is a tough little bastard and he'll cut ya as soon as look at ya. Plus he had a friend, a big fuckin' friend."

"What did he want?"

"Money, what the fuck you think he wanted? We still owe him twenty thousand. He said the two grand was interest."

"What did you say?"

"I promised we'd get him the money."

"We? If you told that psycho about me, I'll kill you myself."

"I didn't tell him, but he ain't stupid. Who else puts out a contract on a doctor, other than the doctor's wife?"

"Shit," was all that Sarah said.

She stared down at the picnic table and picked at the green, peeling paint trying to collect her thoughts. Hackett was driving her nuts. His idiocy about Yu Lai and the practice was as much as she could handle, and then a couple of days ago Hackett had asked her about the books. One minute he was willing to give away his whole practice and live like a monk, then the next minute, he's droning on about overbilling.

"I've been reviewing files and some of our charges. There are too many mistakes. I think we may need to bring in an auditor. Things are so much more comforting when they add up," she remembered Hackett saying.

She thought of his words, felt like hitting the stupid shit. "Things are so much more comforting when they add up." *What kind of idiot says such a thing?* Sarah looked up from the picnic table to find Victor staring at her and waiting for her to talk.

"I can't take any more money now," she said. "Especially not twenty thousand dollars. He'll have to wait."

"Wait," Victor growled. "He won't wait. He'll put a bullet through my head."

"Be quiet, you idiot." Sarah's eyes dug into him. "Stop panicking. We can handle that fool. How much time do we have?"

"One week."

Sarah picked at the green paint once again as if she might find an answer by peeling back its layers. She didn't want to pay Misha. She toyed with letting Victor deal with it. He had recruited Misha, so it really was his problem, but she also knew that Victor was right. Misha either already knew who she was, or would figure it out soon enough.

"Okay, I'll get the money," Sarah said as she looked down at the bag in her hand.

*Misha would have to wait*, she told herself. *One thing at a time.*

# Chapter 32

Hackett was just exiting the Beltway onto Wisconsin Avenue when his cell phone vibrated on his hip. He rolled to a stop at the light and glanced down at the phone to see Yu Lai's number. "Hey, Doc," he answered cheerfully. "Calling to tell me good news?"

"Hey, Doc," she said back. "Maybe."

"I'm all ears."

"How long can you wait?"

"Not very. I really need you."

"I'd like to give them six months' notice."

"They'll take one."

"Come on, Hackett, don't be unreasonable. That's not enough time."

"Sure it is. You could give them two weeks and they would figure it out. There is no reason to prolong your exit. Once you tell them, they will already be moving on. It's a big hospital." He knew that her reluctance was mostly about her own feelings of guilt. Presbyterian had chosen her over the best candidates in the country. She figured she owed them, but the way he saw it, they could replace her with any of a few dozen eager, highly skilled applicants. For him, she was the only choice. "I need you more than they do. Please."

He pleaded and begged for the rest of the drive down Wisconsin Avenue and into his neighborhood. He pulled into the driveway and cut off the engine.

"Although I would hold out for you even if it took a year, I have to tell you that I will probably ruin the practice by then. I can't keep my mind where it needs to be anymore."

"Two months is the best I can do," he heard her say.

"Deal. Give your notice immediately. You won't regret it."

Hackett jumped out of the car and practically ran to the house in spite of his loose, shuffling feet. He opened the door and shouted Sarah's name, excited to share his news with someone. Her faint voice replied from the basement and he heard her moving around.

Reality seeped back into his thoughts and curbed his enthusiasm. She would not be happy. He knew that. He decided not to tell her, at least not yet. He walked to the basement stairs and eased himself down using the handrail. There was more shuffling, and for a moment, he wondered what all the commotion was about. Halfway down the stairs, he looked past the railing and saw Sarah sitting in her glider, picking up her needlework.

"Aren't you done with that pillow?" he asked. It was the same one she had been working at on and off for months.

"Oh, I just do this for relaxation. I don't care how long it takes to finish." As she talked, Hackett saw her eyes move away from him and then back in his direction. She seemed nervous, and he was struck with a strong sense that she was hiding something. Her eyes darted back and forth again.

"Well, that's good," he said with a smile. "How about you get changed and I'll take you to La Ferme for dinner. I can break my diet this once."

Hackett expected the suggestion to brighten Sarah's face, but instead, he saw the purple hue of a false smile. *She's always mad about something these days. If it isn't quitting the hospital, it's selling the practice. If it isn't selling the practice, it's the way I have changed since the attack. I wish that she would just relax and enjoy life.* "Don't you want to go? Screw the diet for once. It's La Ferme, your favorite, escargots, champagne, maybe even Dom Perignon."

"Sure," she said and her face brightened, even though it was still highlighted in purple. "Let me take a shower and put a nice dress on."

He grinned back, feeling the tension in his own forced smile. *Why can't she be happy?* Sarah walked past him, kissed him on the cheek and disappeared up the stairs. He stood rock still, feeling the moisture from her lips. "Enough of this doubt," he told himself. He looked back at Sarah's chair, and at the cross stitch laying on the table next to it. He felt a strange lightness in his head. Unable to stop himself, he saw Sarah as if she was still sitting in the chair. He saw the awkward look on her face. He had startled her. He relived the moment in detail, watching her eyes as they self consciously glanced away from him. He saw her smile once more. This time, it screamed purple with deception. He imagined himself in her place. He looked where she was looking, but all he saw was the basement wall. He replayed the moment, followed her eyes again, and then again. The painting on the wall came into focus. He stared at it, wondering why her eyes would have been drawn there, and why that made her uncomfortable. It was an old painting by Sarah's mother. He knew that it held emotional significance for her. Perhaps she was just thinking of her mother and he was seeing sadness.

Hackett felt drawn to the painting. He walked to the wall and stood in front of it. He looked at the bluebells dotted across the prairie. They were mere splashes of paint, but they were effective, reminiscent of Monet or Degas. He could see why she liked it. Without thinking, his hands lifted the painting. He took it from the wall for a closer look, examined the strokes of paint, the prairie grass, the sky, and again those arresting bluebells. It made him feel better. He let his suspicions cede just a little.

He held the painting for a few moments longer, could see that there were precisely eighty-nine flowers painted on the landscape, a beautiful blue prime number. He let the flowers and the number soothe him. Slowly, he reached to place it back upon the hook. The painting hung awkwardly. He tried to straighten it, but the back side was uneven and it wouldn't lie flat.

Hackett adjusted it once more and stepped back to look. It was still crooked. This time, when he lifted it from the wall, he flipped it over and looked at the back. The old brown paper was puffed out and it looked like it had recently been repaired with

Scotch tape. He pressed on the back, noticing that it was unnaturally thick. He had no doubt that there was something more than a painting within. His mind drifted, and he imagined Sarah hiding love notes and such behind the painting, safe from prying eyes.

Involuntarily, his fingers were drawn to one corner, where the tape looked as if it had been pulled free. He felt an over-whelming urge to peel it back and peak at the hidden treasure. It made him feel like a naughty child, searching through his parents' drawers, looking for secrets. His fingers pinched the tape. It pulled free easily. He drew back the brown paper to find what appeared to be a legal document folded over and stapled to blue paper. He extracted it from the painting and opened it.

The letters on the front page dropped in and out of focus. He felt faint. The contents of his stomach rolled. He looked again. It was his own last will and testament.

~

All through dinner at La Ferme, Hackett's mind drifted from the conversation, and focused on the will. At first, it had appeared to be a simple copy of his will, but he had quickly opened it and leafed through the pages, knowing exactly where to turn. There was no reference to Jean. Her name had been replaced by Sarah's, his entire estate bequeathed to her. What was worse, Amy was only mentioned as a secondary beneficiary in the event that Sarah predeceased him. He thought of Amy and her illness, imagined her growing older, getting sicker, needing the money to take care of herself. *Greedy bitch.* The silent words that had reverberated inside his head as he stared at the will came back to him now.

Hackett had folded the will up, shoved it back inside the frame and re-hung the picture. All the while, his hands shook and his anger boiled. He had wanted to shout Sarah's name with all of the hateful volume he could muster, but something held him back. He smothered the words. *I need to think this through,* he had told himself.

In the basement, lost within his anger, he had kicked at the end table next to Sarah's chair, sending her cross stitch flying across the room. The pain that echoed in his foot sobered him momentarily. He wondered if Sarah had heard the crash. He listened to the house, water flowing from the shower drain and cascading through the pipes above his head.

It all played back in his mind as he chewed a large wad of New York strip. Alongside his anger, the meat tasted like an old shoe. His eyes drifted from his plate up to Sarah's face. She was stone silent, staring at her own food. Hackett once again fought the urge to confront her. He needed to protect his assets for Amy. Sarah looked up and smiled, a radiant purple smile of deception. It was so clear now. Hackett smiled back and felt an odd sense of accomplishment. He knew her now, but she did not know him. He thought back on all the time they had spent together, all of her pandering and false emotion. He realized that she had toyed with him, controlled him, that he had been a fool captivated by her beauty.

*Beauty is not love. Desire is not love.* Jean's words held a whole new meaning.

"How are the scallops?" he asked.

"Delicious," she answered.

*Choke on them*, he wished.

~

Sarah left the house early the next morning, shouting to Hackett that she was going for a long bike ride, "probably out to White's Ferry, maybe further, not sure when I'll be home."

When she arrived at the Ferry, she turned her bike off the towpath and coasted down to the picnic table.

"Holy cow! You're early. Somebody die?" she asked.

"Me, if we don't pay Misha and get him off my back. Where's the money?"

"I don't have it. He'll have to wait a little longer."

"Are you fucking crazy? I told you, today is it. If I don't give him the money, I'm dead."

"Calm down. I have a plan." Sarah looked at Victor and almost pitied him. He was such a big strong man, but he acted like a frightened boy.

"Jesus Christ, Sarah, don't you understand we have no time for your plans? We have to give him the money now!"

One word scared Sarah more than Victor's panic. "What do you mean now?"

"He told me today was the deadline. I told you he was serious. You said you'd get the money. You told me you had the fucking money!"

Sarah stared into Victor's eyes. They were the eyes of someone who had lost control. "What do you mean now?" she asked again.

"Jesus Christ!" he screamed and cupped his head in his hands.

Sarah felt his panic seep into her own bones. Her head darted back and forth. She scanned the parking lot, the woods, even the river. Everything about Victor told her that Misha was there watching them. She wasn't ready. She jumped up and grabbed her bike. At the same time, she saw a figure coming toward her. She swung her leg over the bike as an arm stretched out in front of her and grabbed the handlebars.

"Where you going?" Sarah knew it was Misha even before he pronounced the word "going" like he was saying "go-ink." Misha spoke past Sarah. "What is matter, Veector? You look seeck."

"If you don't let me go, I'll scream bloody murder," Sarah said, not waiting for Victor to answer Misha's question.

"If scream, I let go now, but catch you later and cut your pretty teets off."

Sarah looked at him, her hate and fear boiling together, but she needed to keep calm. He was right. Screaming would only be temporarily effective. She wanted to be permanently effective.

"You have money?"

"No, but I can get it. That's what I have been telling Victor."

Misha turned to Victor, and Sarah could see what Victor must have seen: a cold sociopathic evil emanated from the smaller man. *Yes, Victor was right. This is a dangerous man.*

"I told you, Veector, no games."

"She said she had the money. I swear to Jesus." Victor's voice broke and Sarah saw tears in his eyes.

"Come. We talk in more private. Too many ears here." Sarah felt Misha's hand squeezing her arm as if he was about to wring a cat's neck.

"Where are we going?"

"Just down the river a little. We're going to talk about how you get me money, and how you both not get dead."

"I swear, she told me she would bring it," Victor cried out.

"Shusssssh," Misha said softly.

Misha held Sarah's arm tight and wrapped the other arm around her shoulder as if they were lovers. Sarah planted her feet, but Misha drew her in close and she could feel his hot, humid breath on her ear. "You not get hurt if you do what I say." He turned his head away from her. "Come, Victor. I don't need new excuse to cut your balls off."

They walked down a narrow path along the river until they were secluded in thick woods. Misha grabbed Sarah by the shoulders and held her roughly in front of him, staring into her eyes for effect. "You understand one thing. The money is already gone. You still have life. You keep it that way. Okay?" His eyes expected an answer. She nodded. "Goot. Stand still. Don't run or speak." He turned to Victor. "What I do with you, Veector? What you think?"

"I'll do whatever you ask. I'll help get the money from her."

"Goot boy."

Victor and Misha stood looking at each other, Misha smiling, Victor quaking. Misha reached up and gently put a hand on Victor's shoulder. "I see it's not fault of you. This one is tough bitch. She needs to know that we are..."

As the word "serious" rolled off his tongue, Sarah saw Misha's fist strike forcefully into Victor's stomach. It was only when he withdrew that she saw the knife and the blood. She looked at Victor, shock pouring from his face.

"I need to show this bitch I'm serious," Misha said, and then he plunged the knife into Victor's chest. Victor fell to the ground. Air escaped Sarah's mouth and a tiny shriek escaped with it.

"Quiet, lady. I not kill you. I want the money, but if scream, I hurt you plenty. The only way you get home to your not-so-dead husband is to do what I say."

Sarah nodded her head to show that she understood and watched as Misha threw the bloody knife into the river. "Don't worry, lady. I have more knife."

Sarah couldn't take her eyes off Victor. She had seen death before, but not of the violent sort, and it shook her. Victor lay in a crumpled, wheezing mess. Blood was pooling on the ground around him. She promised herself that she would not die. If anyone else was going to die, it would be Misha.

~

Sarah drove and Misha talked. Occasionally, she nodded and gave one- or two-word answers when it became necessary. He told her that it would be simple and that she had no choice. They would go to her bank. "The one with the big money in account," he added.

He told her that his price had gone up to one hundred thousand, because she and Victor had screwed around with him. She protested, but gave up quickly. "Do you just expect to walk into a bank with me and walk out with one hundred thousand dollars?" she asked.

"No. You walk in alone. You not ask them to call the police or do anything so very stupid, because I will give police evidence that you try to murder husband."

"What about the ten thousand dollar limit on withdrawals that banks have to prevent money laundering?"

"No limit. You just need to fill out form like they tell you."

"How am I supposed to explain this to my husband?"

"You smart bitch. You explain, or maybe you find someone else to kill him."

She tossed it around in her mind. She needed to buy time, figure out a way to get rid of him.

"No, that won't work and it's an unnecessary risk," she added.

"Risk for you, not me," Misha cut in with a laugh.

"I have cash, but it's not a hundred thousand dollars."

"I tell you one hundred. You not in charge."

"Seriously, I can give you seventy, and it's less risky. If the police start questioning where I got the extra money, who knows where the investigation leads."

"Okay, seventy thousand and your jewelry?"

To make his point, Misha placed his left hand on her crotch and held his knife to her stomach with his right hand. He squeezed her roughly, and then lifted her shirt, exposing the flesh of her belly.

"Don't move," he said, and he dragged the blade slowly across her skin. It took all of Sarah's will power to remain steady and not flinch. Small beads of blood appeared in the knife's path. "You fuck with me, I go deeper. It would be a shame to wreck such beautiful skin."

Sarah had money in the safe deposit box, but she didn't have that much, not seventy grand. What she did have in that box was her Kahr nine millimeter. "The lady's killer," the gun store salesman had called it.

~

Hackett's hand hurt from all the signing and initialing he had just completed, and his chest ached from the stress. He tapped his jacket pocket, expecting to feel the nitroglycerin that he carried with him since his heart attack. Nothing was there. In his hurry to leave the house, he had forgotten it.

"Once again, I very strongly advise you to call the police immediately. Use our phone. Do it now," his lawyer told him.

Hackett didn't need any special psychic power to read the concern on his attorney's face. "That won't be necessary. I've heard your warning, but Sarah isn't violent. She is my wife. I don't want her to get arrested, and I owe it to her to tell her myself."

Hackett got into the car. He left the office satisfied that he had followed the only course available. He had written a new will, signed a motion to nullify the pre-nup and cancelled his life insurance policy. His heart had beaten in his chest and rang in his ears the whole time he talked to the lawyer, through every initial and every signature. Hackett rammed his elbow into the seat back beside him and swore. He sat still for a few seconds, waiting to put the key in the ignition, and listened to the drum beat inside, worried about what the stress was doing to his heart. *Damn her,* he thought. *Damn me. Why didn't I see? Why didn't I listen to Ella Mae?* His fingers strangled the steering wheel. Hackett forced himself to let go and sat back in his seat. He closed his eyes and tried to meditate, but his thoughts raced back to Sarah. Without directing it, his hand lashed out and his palm rammed into the steering wheel. He thought about her betrayal and his loss. It wasn't the sex that he thought about this time. It was the loneliness he had felt after Jean's death, the great gaping hole that had opened in his heart and in his life. With Sarah, Hackett had learned to live again, but that, too, was over. He felt the loneliness as it settled back in. The agony of it infected him. He didn't know if he could bear it again.

Hackett ordered himself to meditate, demanded inner peace, as if demanding was all it took. His eyes stared forward. His jumping heart controlled the rhythms of his chest. Impossible.

It was no better on the drive home. He was so lost in thought that he hardly saw the road in front of him. Finally, he made a right-hand turn into his neighborhood. As he rounded the corner, a car slowed in front of him. Hackett was way too close. He slammed on the brakes and his tires squealed. The old beat-up car in front of him was unfamiliar, but the driver's hair wasn't. It looked like Sarah. A man was sitting beside her, his hand resting on her shoulder.

Hackett was shocked by his own surprise. *This, too?* he asked himself.

~

Sarah heard the tires squeal, and jumped at the sound.

"Calm down, lady. You drive and don't cause trouble." Misha poked her gently with the knife to remind her.

~

Jealousy flowed in Hackett's blood. He wanted to step on the gas and ram them. He dreamed of jumping out of his car and dragging the man onto the pavement, beating him, and leaving him on the side of the road. The car in front of him moved slowly forward. He drifted with it, his mind at half speed. He stared at the rear window, looked at the back of her head. Was it really her? Maybe his eyes were playing tricks on him. He looked into the driver's side mirror and tried to catch a glimpse of her face. They moved forward. The car turned right onto the road on which he had lived for over twenty years. Hackett felt sick. He slowed and took the turn, falling back just a little so as not to be seen. Slowly, he drove down the street, saw the car turn into his driveway and roll right into his garage. He pulled over and watched, expecting Sarah to open her door, but instead, he saw the man get out first. It appeared that he was helping Sarah get out on the passenger's side. Hackett wondered if she was hurt, maybe a biking accident. He felt a little of his anxiety recede. When she stood, she looked fine. Hackett watched the man slip his arm around her and pull her close into his embrace — so much for the biking accident. His heart raced on. They opened the door at the back of the garage and walked into the kitchen. Slowly, carefully, Hackett got out of his own car and walked toward the garage, scanning the front windows as he went.

~

The kitchen door slammed shut behind Sarah. Misha pushed her roughly forward until she stumbled into the table. A vegetable knife lay a few feet in front of her. She reached for it, but Misha grabbed a handful of her hair and smashed her face into the wood. She lurched forward, struggling for the knife. He yanked her head up, pulled her back easily, and then knocked the knife to the floor.

~

Hackett crept softly into the garage past boxes, tools, and garbage cans, past his daughter Amy's old bike with the busted pink handlebar basket and the faded streamers. His heart beat like

Buddy Rich's bass drum. Just before he reached the door, he heard a crash and what sounded like a scuffle within. Carefully, he peeked through the glass in the door and saw the man holding Sarah by her hair, blood dripping from her nose.

The man pulled her head backward. "You are tough beetch." He held his knife up to her neck. "But you pretty beetch, too. I think maybe I fuck you before I take your money."

The gravelly voice scratched Hackett's memory, banging, scraping and popping just as it had that snowy night outside the hospital. Once again, he felt the force of the man's knee on his neck. His heart pounded. He looked around the garage, thought first of finding a hammer or wrench on the work bench, but his eyes registered nothing within easy reach. He briefly thought of taking the man down with a chainsaw, as if he were in a scene from a Quentin Tarantino movie. He felt the uncomfortable hiccup of a laugh bubble up inside of him. Without thinking, he grabbed and felt a cool, wooden handle among the garden tools. Careful not to make a noise he lifted the pitchfork up and stared at it. In that moment, Hackett thought about all the times he had cut into human flesh. He had seen blood, he had seen death, but as a doctor, he had always strived to save life, not take it. Now, holding the pitchfork, he tried to convince himself this would be no different. He watched his hand shake, like a ninety-year-old patient holding a coffee cup. Could he do this? He wasn't so sure.

Noise within the house drew Hackett's attention. He looked through the window again, saw Misha ripping Sarah's shirt open. Saw him pawing her beautiful breasts, the breasts that he himself would no longer hold.

Hackett snapped. He rammed through the door and stepped inside. Misha's whole body turned. His pants fell to the floor and his eyes registered surprise. Then he laughed.

"Look who's home," he said.

Hackett's blood boiled and his face turned cherry red.

"Don't be stupid, old man," Misha continued, and raised the knife momentarily in Hackett's direction. Slowly he pointed it back at Sarah. "I kill your pretty wife anytime I want."

Pain burned in Hackett's chest as if Misha's knife had already dispatched Sarah and found its mark in him, but anger, not pain, controlled Hackett. He charged forward. Like his death experience, this headlong attack defied time. It seemed to end before it began. Hackett put all his weight behind the pitchfork, setting it deeply into Misha's rib cage. Sarah's scream pierced the air, loud and chilling, the reality of it sinking into Hackett just as the tines pierced the man's vital organs. The small Russian, who had moved with such evil confidence, lay mortally wounded on the kitchen floor, Hackett atop him, staring directly into the Russian's eyes.

What Hackett observed was an expression of bewilderment, red and clear. Hackett's voiced quivered.

"You killed me, and now I think I have killed you. It's not so bad. You may even enjoy it." His own words surprised him; they were more Tarantino than Metzger.

~

Next to Hackett, Sarah slumped to the floor, sobbing. She hardly watched as Hackett rolled off of Misha and crouched next to her, holding his own chest.

"Sarah, I need you to get yourself together. I think I am having another heart attack." She heard the words as if she were buried in the ground beneath him.

"Sarah, please help me." She pushed herself onto her hands and knees, looked at him, no longer sure if any of this nightmare was real. "I need my heart pills," she heard him say.

Sarah looked at Misha, blood pooling around him into a big crimson ocean. She remembered his knife, ran her hands over her neck, her chest, her stomach. She could find no wound and felt no pain. She turned back to Misha, met his blank stare. She bent closer, sensed no danger, only her own anger. She spat. Saliva and blood dripped from his forehead. She stood, stepped back and kicked his dead face.

~

Hackett wobbled but managed to stay on his feet before collapsing on the red leather chair in the living room. His face was flushed and his breath rapid. "Sarah," his voice sounded weak. "I'll call 9-1-1. I need you to get me the nitroglycerin from upstairs. The bottle is on my nightstand."

As Sarah walked toward the stairs, he dialed. He explained that they had an intruder, whom he thought was now dead, and that he feared he was having a heart attack. The pressure in Hackett's chest grew stronger as he talked. "I have to put the phone down," he said, feeling an acute need to calm himself.

"I need you to stay on the line, sir. Keep talking to me." The woman's voice was forceful and commanding.

"You talk, I won't hang up," he answered.

"Sir, I need you to stay on the phone."

Hackett heard her, but he knew that the thing he needed most was to steady his nerves and his heart. He breathed in and out slowly, talked to himself instead of the phone. Without thinking he laid the phone back in its cradle. Breath by breath, he fought to calm himself. He focused all of his concentration on it, tried to remember everything from his meditation classes. His desire to cleanse his mind and drift away battled with the panic which still gripped him. *Let it go*, he told himself. *I can't*, he argued in return. *Breathe in... breathe out... in, two three four... out, two three four... in, two three four... out, two three four...*

Other numbers came to him, little by little they filled him until there were clouds of beautiful numbers. He focused on them. *In...* His breathing slowed. *Out...* He felt peace, just beyond his grasp.

~

Sarah's eyes lit upon the prescription bottle on Hackett's nightstand, but she turned away and stepped toward the chair that sat before the bedroom window. Her hand pushed against the back, until the chair leaned up against the wall, then she bent over and peeled back the fabric by the right front leg. She extracted the paper bag Victor had handed her one week earlier, poured the contents into her hand. Carefully, she unwrapped the syringe, fixed the needle and plunged it into the vials one after another, drawing in every milliliter of the liquid within. "Enough to kill a horse this time," Victor had told her.

She moved slowly, cautiously, hoping that Hackett would die before she returned.

~

Pain shot through the muscles of Hackett's leg. *Concentrate*, he told himself. He felt his chest rise and fall in lethargic rhythm, saw the cloud of numbers once more. Breath by breath, he slowed the world. The cloud around him gained substance. Hackett's mind conjured the snowflakes of his death experience. He saw them. They were beautiful, just as they had been that night. He could almost hear the universe of voices he had heard then, chanting as one. It filled him with calm. With his vision came a longing to see Jean.

Hackett's breaths now maintained a perfect rhythm. He no longer felt the pressure in his chest, was no longer captive to the panic which had embraced him. He heard an inner voice tell him not to stop, to go deeper. Snowflakes hovered all around, blinking like lights. The grid that he had seen in death seemed to flicker on and off.

Hackett felt Jean's presence, vague and distant, but still he felt it. He also felt his heart beating. Clearly, strongly and methodically as it pushed blood through his body. He understood that he was not dying and it saddened him. He ached for Jean, wondered if he could stop his heart by force of will, and if that would bring Jean to him.

A light appeared.

*I love you*, Jean's soundless voice echoed around Hackett.

*I want to go with you this time.*

*But you are not dying.*

Hackett wanted to argue with her, but he knew that this vision of Jean was not the same as before. He had not died, and the light would not come for him. With that recognition, he relaxed and talked to Jean, content with what he had. *I told myself that it was love*, he explained.

*I know. You did your best.*

Hackett drank Jean's comfort as if it were the finest champagne, but soon he sensed a change in her. His own anxiousness returned as well. *What is it?* he asked.

*Wake up.* Jean's words were urgent. *Wake up now.* It was as if she screamed into his ear.

Hackett opened his eyes. Sarah stood above him, syringe in hand. Her anger was purple and raw, her intentions loud. The needle sank into the flesh of his thigh. In a single moment, Hackett's will to live battled his desire to see Jean once more. Time stopped and he debated. Time continued and he acted, striking her hand, knocking the syringe free before she could discharge its deadly serum. He saw Sarah's surprise, felt her determination as she grabbed hold of his arm, her strength seemingly much greater than his own. The needle came for him once more. It sunk deep into his shoulder. Hackett shielded himself with his left arm and reached behind him with his right, pulling the only thing he could from the wall, and smashing it against Sarah's head. He saw the picture frame shatter, points of glass impale themselves in her scalp, a wing of the largest moth in the world flutter to the ground.

A siren wailed in the distance. Hackett assumed it tolled for him, but knew that he could not wait for it. He grabbed her arm and tried to free himself. The needle ripped through muscle, broke against bone and eventually fell to the floor, but the fight was still not over.

Sarah's teeth sunk into his arm. Hackett released his grip and punched her in the back of the head, knuckles cracking against bone. She slipped, grabbed hold of his leg. He clawed at the ground, pulling himself forward, dragging her into the kitchen.

"It's over," Hackett told her through clenched teeth. "I found the will you forged. I filed for divorce. You will have nothing."

He could not tell if Sarah even heard him. She tried to stand. Her arms slipped and slid. She fell back to the floor, into the puddle of Misha's blood. It looked like she was swimming through red slime. Again he thought of movies, surreal and violent.

"Sarah, stop," he said. "Did you hear me? I have a new will, I revoked my life insurance, filed for divorce and I am nullifying the pre-nup. You'll have nothing."

Slowly Sarah stood, her back to him. He could not see her face, but her anger was still as plain as day. "It's over, Sarah," he said, believing that his logic would get through.

She turned to face him with a big kitchen knife in her hand. Her face was a bloody apparition. "Go to hell." She belted the words out, mixing them with sinuous spittle and blood.

Hackett moved with speed from some hidden reserve, grabbed the pitchfork and pulled it from Misha's body, stepping back as soon as it was free. They stared at each other, weapons raised, neither moving. Hackett said nothing. He did not know the creature before him, realized too late that he never had. Could he actually kill her? he wondered. He did not know the answer. The siren called again. This time it was close. Sarah stepped back. Car doors slammed. A hand banged loudly in the living room. "POLICE," they announced, and then they were inside.

"He tried to kill me," Sarah screamed. She dropped the knife and fell to her knees. Her hand pointed to Misha's dead body. "Hackett found us together. He stabbed Misha with a pitchfork. Oh my God, look at what he did, then he tried to inject me with something he must have stolen from the hospital."

Tears were pouring down Sarah's face in rivers. She fell into the policeman's arms. Hackett was so flabbergasted that he had trouble speaking. She deserved an Academy Award.

"It was her," he finally said, but by this time, guns were leveled at him. He was being ordered to drop his weapon. The world swam before him. His knees felt weak. Self control slipped away. He tried to do as the officer said, but his body would not obey.

"Drop it now." The order was shouted at him.

He felt the wooden handle slip from his grip, heard the clatter as the pitchfork hit the floor. A policeman seemed to fly across the floor, knocked Hackett backward, and he hit the floor with a thud. *Was that me?* he silently asked. The policeman rolled him over, cuffed him.

Sarah was wailing. Then she pointed her finger. "He tried to inject me with that thing." The syringe lay on the floor. On the other side of the room, a policeman crouched over Misha's body.

The man with his knee in Hackett's back recited familiar lines. "You have the right to remain silent…"

Hackett found his voice. "It wasn't me. It was her…" In mid-sentence, Hackett's eyes focused on the pitchfork once more. "I mean." He paused again. "I killed him. I had no choice, but it was my wife who tried to kill me."

"Shut up." The policeman's knee dug harder into Hackett's back. "You can talk after me," he said, before again launching into the memorized words. "You have the right to remain silent. Anything you say can and will be used against you in a court of law. You have the right to speak to an attorney, and to have an attorney present during any questioning. If you cannot afford a lawyer, one will be provided for you at government expense."

While that policeman talked, another wrapped his arms around Sarah protectively, and escorted her out the front door. Saliva flooded Hackett's mouth. The world swayed, then swirled. The policeman lifted his knee off of Hackett's back. Began to lift him to his feet. Hackett retched. The officer let go as vomit streamed to the floor. Hackett tried to step back but slipped, and fell face first into his own puke.

~

Still stinking of vomit, Hackett sat in a small interview room, looking at a detective on the other side of a small table. A camera stared at him from over the detective's shoulder. Slowly, Hackett told his story, starting with the will and his meeting with the lawyer, proceeding to the moment he saw Sarah driving in front of him. Second by second he described it, making sure to capture every detail. Periodically, he realized he had forgotten to mention something, so he paused to backtrack. *They have to believe me*, he thought. *If I give them all the facts, the truth will come out.*

"You had the pitchfork," the detective interrupted. "You expect be to believe that your wife was going to attack you with a syringe after you had just plunged that thing into a man's chest?"

"I didn't have the pitchfork anymore. It was still in his body."

"You were holding it when the police entered the house."

"That was later, after she attacked me."

"She attacked you with a syringe, but you fought her off with a pitchfork, even though that pitchfork was still in the chest of the man you admit you murdered."

"I didn't murder him. It was self defense. He was attacking my wife."

"The wife that was trying to murder you?"

Hackett took a deep breath, then rested his face in his own hands. "Sarah went upstairs to get my heart medicine. While I called 9-1-1." He lifted his head only slightly, looking through his fingers at the detective, who was shaking his head back and forth.

"Come on, Doctor Metzger, you can't expect me to believe that."

"Just talk to my lawyer. He can tell you about the will. She was trying to murder me for my money." This time, Hackett laid his forehead against the table, and stretched his fingers out flat against the surface.

"We will talk to your lawyer," the detective said in a softer voice. "But it sure would help if you told us a plausible story."

Hackett barely lifted his head. "I'm done talking to you. I am requesting my lawyer, and that is all I have to say."

The detective gathered his materials, picked up the camera and walked out the door. Eventually a uniformed officer entered, walked to Hackett's side, lifted him up by the arm without saying a word, and cuffed him once more. Hackett let himself be led out into a narrow hallway and down a flight of stairs. At the end of a row of cells, the officer opened the metal bars, pushed Hackett in and closed it with a heavy clink. Only then did he remove the handcuffs.

Once more Hackett bowed his head toward his own open hands, stopping before the two came together. Dried blood cracked around his knuckles and the edge of his palms. For the hundredth time that day, he relived plunging the pitchfork into the man he had learned was named Misha. He felt the tines strike rib and deflect into soft flesh. He saw Misha's surprise.

Though he remembered a moment of satisfaction, he now felt an overwhelming revulsion. He had consciously taken a human life. Did that make him a murderer? Hackett sat in the cell, waiting for what felt like an eternity. He imagined a life in prison. He dreamed of suicide instead.

His lawyer came eventually, told Hackett he'd be out soon. Not yet, there still had to be a bail hearing, probably tomorrow, but he'd be out.

"I promise." The lawyer's words had rung hollow, but the next morning, the door at the end of the hall opened, and Hackett's lawyer rushed in, a smile bursting forth. "You're going home," he said.

~

Two days later, they finally let Hackett back into his own house. He walked to the front door and pulled back the crime scene tape. The living room looked fairly normal, other than a few shards of glass on the far side of the carpet. Hackett's stomach tightened as he walked forward. At the edge of the carpet, he bent down and carefully lifted what was left of the picture frame, along with half of the moth. He placed it on the coffee table. Then with a piece of paper from his desk drawer, he returned and gently slid it under the remaining damaged wing, placing that, too, on the coffee table.

Hackett stepped forward once more. Glass crunched under his shoe. He stopped in the doorway, not sure if he could go further. He had asked his lawyer whether the police would clean up the house. The lawyer thought maybe a little, but probably not much. Hackett peeked his head through the doorway. The blood was now dark, almost black, but it was blood just the same. He stared at the odd patterns that Sarah had made as she struggled. He almost expected to see Misha's body, but thankfully that was gone. He turned and walked up the stairs.

In the shower, visions of blood and death haunted him. He let the hot water run over his shoulders, hoping that everything would wash away. Sarah came to him disjointed, like a fitful dream that did not need reason. He saw her naked, felt the heat of her breath on his neck. He saw purple lines of anger and deception on her face. He felt her love as she sat next to him in the hospital in Italy. And he saw her downstairs, about to plunge the needle into him. His emotion swelled. His words filled the shower.

"Oh, Jean, how could I make such a mess of things."

Jean's words in return were but a soft memory. *I love you,* she said. *I will always love you.*

# AFTER

The soft winter sun broke through Hackett's bedroom window and came to an easy rest on his eyelids. He lifted his arms above his head, stretched and let out a yawn. The clock on the nightstand registered seven-thirty. There was no place else he needed to be. Yu Lai would be on the way to the office in plenty of time for the first appointment. He would saunter in at noon, consult on a few cases for perhaps an hour and then be on his way back home. He rolled over and draped his arm around the soft shoulder lying next to him in bed. He loved the morning, and the way their two bodies felt together. He looked at her, saw her smile, her eyes still closed, her heart his. Hackett felt so much more comfortable with her than he had with Sarah. He talked to her with ease, didn't worry about her reaction, didn't care what others thought.

In the morning silence, the echo of Jean's voice came to him — *unconditional love*. He felt her presence, not the old shadow of grief that had haunted him for so long, and not the hyper-real death experience. Jean was just simply and comfortably there, a part of him.

Hackett kissed Ella Mae's cheek and floated back into dreamy comfort. He tried not to think of Sarah anymore, but she still invaded his mind. When the police had searched the house, they quickly found the pharmaceutical vials in the drawer of Hackett's nightstand. Later, the detective questioned Hackett, the evidence of the vials presented to him as the coup de grâce proving his guilt.

Hackett listened as the police told him that the vials contained succinylcholine. He knew it all too well. "Sux" was a depolarizing muscle relaxant used during the administration of anesthesia to relax muscles during surgery and make it easier to pass a breathing tube down a patient's airway. The world spun slowly around him as he was confronted with the "evidence of his guilt." Hackett hardly heard. Instead, his mind slipped backward in time. He saw the snow falling and the two men standing on the sidewalk. He felt the icy cold on his cheeks and the unbearable pressure of the man's knee on his back. He remembered the exact moment that he realized he was paralyzed.

**Succinylcholine**. The word flashed like the neon lights of Las Vegas. He breathed in deeply. Once more, the memory of smoke and perfume lit up his senses. It was not just any perfume; he had smelled it before. He had smelled it on Sarah.

**Succinylcholine**. He defined it, as if he was talking to his students — *Succinylcholine is a depolarizing muscle relaxant often used to facilitate the insertion of breathing tubes. It works by keeping muscles from contracting, and causes paralysis of the muscles in the face and those used to breathe and move. Malignant hyperthermia is a possibly fatal syndrome that can be caused by succinylcholine. Symptoms may include fast heartbeat, fast breathing, high body temperature, and spasm or stiffness of the jaw or other muscles. Overdose may result in cardiac arrest.*

**Succinylcholine**. It was the perfect poison, widely used in hospitals, but seldom tested for in toxicity screens or autopsies. Sarah had failed to kill him once and had apparently been about to make sure that it worked the second time. Oddly, he thought, it may have been the succinylcholine that also saved his life by raising his body temperature and slowing the effect of being buried in snow.

Sarah's lies had not held up. Hackett was free and she was behind bars. It had not helped her when police found her bicycle chained to a tree at White's Ferry, just one hundred yards from the body of a pharmacy technician.

In time, the police asked Hackett what he knew about her ex-husband. They speculated that she had killed him as well. "Is it possible that she killed her son, too?" The question had floored him. "No, never," he had said, but now the question haunted him. Could she have really killed Aaron? What could she possibly have gained by that? The answer chilled him. She had gained Hackett. He was responsible for Aaron's death.

He had been living with an evil that he could not fathom. Nothing comported with the person he had thought he knew. Hackett considered the mass murderers at Columbine and Red Lake High Schools, serial killers like Ted Bundy and Jeffrey Dahmer. What had their families thought? How did they reconcile the person they knew with the crimes they had committed?

Even now that the evidence was so clear, Hackett couldn't overcome his need to believe that the Sarah he knew was not the Sarah who murdered. He told himself that everything couldn't have been a lie. He thought of their early days together, looked for signs that her love was authentic, dismissed the hundred reasons why he knew it wasn't. He equated his lack of objectivism to the hysterical blindness cases he had treated. He had been blinded by her beauty, and he wished someone had been there to hold up a picture of a penis or a sign that said "asshole" to shock him out of his delusion.

Hackett tried to leave his memories of Sarah behind as he lay in bed. Once again, he looked at the woman next to him. Ella Mae made him feel comfortable and loved in a way that Sarah never had. With her, Hackett could be open about his continuing love for Jean. He missed Jean no more and no less than he had during his time with Sarah, but with Ella Mae, it was perfectly alright to acknowledge his feelings. She understood. She mourned as well.

Ella Mae's eyes were still shut, but Hackett knew she was awake. He leaned over and kissed her again. "Good morning."

She looked at him, and he saw a question mark in her expression. "What?" he asked.

"What do you mean, what? Are you trying to read my thoughts again, Carnac?" she teased.

"No, you just look like you want to ask me something, or perhaps tell me something."

Ella Mae rolled her body toward Hackett, leveraging her strength, and punched him in the arm.

"Jesus, that hurt," he said and rubbed the spot of her assault.

Ella Mae smiled. "Well, don't be so right all of the time. I was once again thinking about how stubborn you are. I don't see how anyone could experience what you have, and still be such a flaming skeptic."

"I wear that badge with honor. Look it up in the dictionary. A skeptic is someone who asks questions instead of accepting the seemingly obvious. Without skeptics there would be no progress."

Hackett knew what she was asking. Ella Mae could not understand why he was so questioning of the afterlife, even in the face of what she thought was final undeniable proof. Had not Hackett's experience proven that life after death existed, that God existed? Had not Jean come to him again, warned him about Sarah, saved his life?

But for Hackett, Jean's warning from the grave as he sat in the living room having a panic attack, thinking that it was a heart attack, was not proof. He knew that his ears would have picked up the sound of Sarah coming, even if he could not recall it. His subconscious had created Jean as a warning to himself.

"You can take the man out of the doctor, but you can't take the doctor out of the man," Ella Mae said in reply.

"What's that supposed to mean?"

"Doctors are always so damn sure of themselves. It doesn't matter how many times you guys are proven wrong, the one thing that never changes is your unfailing confidence in your own conclusions."

Hackett laughed; not even Jean had been able to put him in his place so quickly. "Yes, I am still a doctor. It is in my blood and my soul. It is hard for me not to be sure of myself, but still I can't simply force myself to believe something that is so patently unproven."

Ella Mae shook her head from side to side. "You believe so many other things that aren't proven. If you can concede the possibility that you flew through walls, why can't you concede the possibility of God?"

Hackett just smiled. He had heard all of her arguments before, and she his, but neither could resist the game. "I do concede the possibility of God. I don't concede the fact of it."

Hackett hated to be pigeonholed as an unbeliever. It wasn't that simple. Death had not provided certitude, but it had changed the way he viewed the world. Death had changed the very definition of the word "*reality*." He believed that his death experience opened a window into a deeper consciousness, one unfiltered by the limitation of normal human cognition. This deeper reality was the true reality, even if he did not completely understand it. Still, he had no proof that it was independent of and beyond life.

"More word games; you can't explain away everything," Ella Mae told him.

"How can we know?" he argued. "We came back, our death was temporary at best. We cannot know what would have happened next. We cannot know if consciousness would have continued after our body had been destroyed by fire or eaten by worms."

In death, remarkable as his experience had been, Hackett had not found the unassailable truth, or been given irreproachable evidence. He had only seen his own memories, and what he believed was the natural world, in a new light. He didn't understand why others jumped to conclusions about the nature of God.

Hackett had tried desperately to explain his new philosophy to Ella Mae, but she had no such misgivings. For her there was but one lesson to be learned from her death experience. There was life after death, and God was at the center of it. Hackett argued, and Ella Mae waved her hands in exasperation. Adequate words did not exist for him to convince her. The best he could do was to fall back on the word "reality" and define it as a physicist might.

"One of the things that quantum mechanics tells us is that observation is reality, not the other way around, and observation is a subjective perception. We do not observe a static world. Our observation creates the world we observe," he said to blank stares.

"Don't start that again. You create the most absurd explanations in order to avoid the obvious."

Now that Hackett had started, the words rolled out. "But I did not create all of this. There are proven theories, and they define the only truth we really know. There are no 'things' in the subatomic world. Subatomic particles are not really particles at all. They are an interaction between 'things,' which themselves do not exist unless they are observed. They are no more than patterns of probability."

He knew that his words meant nothing to her, but he plowed on. "If reality is dependent on our observation, we can't be sure that it continues after death, and since we continued to exist after our supposed death." Hackett used his fingers to form air quotes around the word "death," then continued, "We can't be sure we actually experienced that final irreversible moment. There is just no way to prove we crossed over." Again he formed air quotes around the last two words.

Hackett talked as if the subatomic world was the only physical reality. Daily life was the illusion. The hard wood of the night table to his right was a figment of his observation. On the atomic level, particles observed no such boundaries. There was no surface. There was also no clear line between his body and the bed — all matter was interchangeable. The universe was explained by beautiful theories populated by wondrous numbers. Only the mathematical proofs were rock solid. Humans made everything else up, including the idea that they know God.

"Your subatomic illusions sound like proof of God to me," Ella Mae said. "You describe the most marvelous miracle, and use it to deny the existence of the supernatural."

Hackett felt her annoyance but marched on. "I don't need to know God to believe in the beauty of the universe. What I experienced defied the constraints of time and space, but so does cosmic reality. Perhaps we will someday prove that consciousness is the missing variable in a universal theory of physics, and death opens up a window that allows us to understand it. That doesn't mean that I have figured it all out, and it definitely doesn't mean that reality fits into a nice little 'Man is God' egocentric package. I am still searching for the truth."

Hackett saw what he called Ella Mae's gotcha grin. "With your stubborn brain, the search is guaranteed to have no end and reach no conclusion. You just like to stare at the puzzle."

Hackett acknowledged the truth in her words. The puzzle fascinated him, always had. A smile passed his lips and he looked into Ella Mae's eyes, willing the argument to end. They sat in silence for a moment, neither needing to prevail, neither willing to give in.

Hackett lay his head back on the pillow and breathed the air of happiness. That too was a new reality he could not deny. In the stillness, Jean's voice whispered, echoing Ella Mae's argument — *Science cannot explain God. Can't you see that unconditional love is all the proof that you need?* He stared at the ceiling, waited for her to continue. For an instant he opened himself to the possibility he had just so vigorously denied.

Hackett felt Ella Mae's hair brush against his face. Then the weight of her head depressed his pillow. He settled into his own breath, the woman within his mind just as real as the one in his bed. His mind settled into beautiful, detailed memories of death. He heard Jean again, in that beautiful, soundless way of knowing. He felt the effortlessness of his experience, the joy that wasn't just happiness, but something pure and eternal. He thought about moments in life that had made indelible impressions, like the birth of his daughter, the first time he had made love to Jean, even Jean's death.

Hackett felt the flicker of new understanding. Every moment of life was fleeting, no matter how important. It came and went in an instant. Death, on the other hand, was a permanent moment, not in the way he had thought before — death being a permanent blackness, a void of experience. No, death was permanent because time became immaterial. All experiences lived side by side. In death, the moment lasted forever.

He wanted to hold onto that idea. No, he wanted to hold on to that certainty. It wasn't life after death, it was life and death coexisting within the timeless universe.

He hesitated a moment, lingering with his thoughts, before he turned his head and kissed Ella Mae on the lips.

"Let's make love," he said, and knew that her soft giggle and her warm lips meant yes.

Afterward, Hackett stepped from the shower, alive and happy. He looked out into the room, saw Ella Mae reading in bed, saw her tennis shoes lying on the floor, laces running free, and he smiled, assured that everything was as it should be. Standing there naked, he felt the absence of grief for the first time in many years. He realized that his death experience had given him so much more than he had first believed — more than the calming effect of numbers, more than the clarity of his intuition, more than his realization of Sarah's true nature and even more than the simple joyful love he had found with Ella Mae. Death had finally liberated him from the pain of Jean's absence and given him the certainty of her presence. She was part of him. They were part of each other.

**THE END**

# Acknowledgements

It takes a lot of work and even more support to write a novel. I have been fortunate enough to benefit from many kind and giving people along the way. Thanks to my writing teacher Amin Ahmad, as well as the staff and fellow students at the Writer's Center in Bethesda, Maryland. If you live in the DC area and you want to learn about writing, there is no better place to start. Thanks to editors, John Paine and John Rickards, who are incredibly insightful teachers, as well as Jack Buckley who provided his editorial insights over many pints of Guinness in County Donegal. Thanks to Three Women Press and especially my fellow author Maryann McFadden, who took me under her wings and adopted my book as if it were a needy child. Thanks to Emily Wenstrom, Michael Adams, Jennifer Dillow Rothenberg, Adam Brown, Andrew McGuire and Chris Peot, who as members of my writing group have given me their valuable time and advice. Thanks to Denise Tola, CRNA, PhD, for her medical insights. Thanks to the love of my life Roxanne, and our children Julia and Joseph, who bring me so much happiness and inspiration. A special acknowledgement to my union, AFSCME. There are few places on this earth that could have provided me with such an enriching and rewarding career.

And finally, thanks to my father and mother, who raised me with love, care and much needed guidance, especially when I tested the limits of their patience.

# About the Author

Gareth Frank is a former union organizer and administrator. He received a Master's Degree at the University of Wisconsin and later studied at the Writer's Center in Bethesda, Maryland. **The Moment Between** is his first published novel. His shorts stories have been published in various journals and have been nominated for the *Pushcart Prize* as well as the *Silver Pen Write Well Award*.

9 781732 294202